VAMPYRE LAW

Elizabeth Ramsey, MD
Series Book 3

Tammy Battaglia

ISBN: 979-8-9925641-6-7 - hardcover

ISBN: 979-8-9925641-5-0 - paperback

ISBN: 979-8-9925641-4-3 - ebook

CONTENTS

BEFORE YOU BEGIN...

I would like to thank you for joining me on this journey by offering a free eBook copy of *The Master Rises*, a novelette prequel to the Elizabeth Ramsey, MD Series. Just follow the QR code link and tell me where to send it.

CHAPTER ONE

KATE

KATE HEARD FOOTSTEPS CLOSING in behind her as she ran toward the lab.

Her adrenaline spiked, and she willed her legs to go faster as she pleaded with herself not to trip.

She wove between the trees, the lights from the tall buildings of New Orleans' central business district glinting between the branches and acting as a compass as she ran.

Kate!

She was so startled by the voice in her head that she locked her legs, heels making furrows in the soil beneath her feet as she skidded. Her momentum carried her toward a large tree, and she only had time to raise both arms in front of her before she plowed into it.

Jon was immediately beside her.

"I heard you inside my head," Kate said, rubbing her shoulder, wincing at the pain but feeling relieved to see him.

"Yes, I didn't want to shout and give away our position if someone else is around," Jon said. He reached out and brushed moss and bark from her shoulder before offering his hand to help her up.

"No, I mean, I actually heard you telepathically. I've never done that before."

"Most vampires can hear others, especially when they're trying to project."

"Yes, Beth and Luciano tried to teach me. But the best I could ever catch was some emotion, never words." She placed her hands on her hips and looked at him, eyes squinted. "Do it again."

Jon to Kate, over.

Kate's eyes widened to saucers before a wide grin spread across her face. "I heard you again! Okay, now let me try." She planted her feet and squeezed both fists at her sides, squinting her eyes again in concentration. *Can you hear me?*

Loud and clear.

Kate raised both fists in victory. She felt like jumping up and down, but held it in. "Yes. Finally. Why can we hear one another so easily when I had so much difficulty with Beth and Luciano?"

She turned and began running towards the lab, motioning for Jon to come with her. They needed to hustle, and with her new abilities, talking while running wasn't taxing. She needed to grab the samples quickly and get back to Beth and Luciano. There was little more she could do to help Luciano tonight, but having the samples meant her research could continue, along with the hope that she and Beth could help both vampires and humans alike.

"Maybe we just speak on one another's frequency. Or maybe you were focused on something else, letting your mind open to mine. Who knows?" Jon said.

Kate liked the thought of them being on the same frequency. She wondered if that sudden ease with telepathy happened to others or if it could mean there was some special connection between the two of them. She much preferred the latter. "Now I'm excited to try it again with Beth. It is an odd sensation, but I think I understand now what she meant by being able to feel another vampire nearby. It's like low static way in the back of my mind."

"Well, I wanted to get your attention. You were really moving. I thought you might think someone was chasing you."

"I wasn't sure. I'm glad that it was you. I may have vampire strength now, but I have no idea how to defend myself."

"Then we need to work on that next," Jon said, a crooked, boyish grin on his lips that had Kate smiling in return. While she did like the idea of learning self-defense, the thought of Jon seeing how awkward she could truly be made her anxious.

They covered the distance to the lab in only a few short minutes, slowing just out of eyesight of the lab's entrance and taking a quick look around the building before Kate scanned her badge and entered. Once inside, she walked to the refrigerator and hurriedly began loading the samples into the cooler she had prepared beside it.

Jon, next to her at first, took a few steps toward one of the lab benches, cocked his head to the side, and breathed deeply. He stilled, his brow furrowed, and took in another deep breath.

Kate closed the cooler and turned toward her desk, freezing in place.

Her computer was gone.

Her head snapped to Jon to speak just as a look of recognition crossed his face. He turned to her. "Run!"

He headed for the back of the lab behind her desk, grabbing Kate's arm and tugging her with him. He was headed straight into the wall, and Kate hesitated. But Jon, nearly at full speed already, plowed into the wall, knocking the start of a hole in it. He backed up and made a second run at it, this time breaking through.

Kate, having no idea what was happening, could only follow, cooler in tow.

They had only taken a few steps beyond the lab wall before Kate tripped, sprawling forward. The cooler fell out of her hand, and she and it tumbled forward with the momentum. She looked up to see Jon, several yards in front of her, look back over his shoulder.

Then everything around her erupted into flames.

The sound of the explosion was deafening, and the force rolled her forward. As she was tossed along the ground, she saw Jon lifted into the air in front of her and thrown forward by the blast. The heat on her skin was unbearable, and she cried out, smoke filling her mouth and eyes. Coherent thought left her as the heat continued to build. Her head lolled, and the world went black.

Jon

Jon pushed himself up from the ground onto his arms, his ears ringing from the blast and obscuring any ambient noise. He blinked away the dust in his eyes but still squinted from the smoke. The heat was terrible. He could feel that his exposed skin was singed. He struggled to clear his thoughts, shaking his head.

The last few moments came flooding back.

Kate!

He had seen her fall just before the blast. He forced himself to his knees and then stood with wobbling legs. He turned back toward the burning lab and took several unsteady steps forward, his arm raised to shield his face from the heat. He could barely make out the shape of a body several yards in front of him through the thick smoke.

He ran to her, nearly tripping over the cooler she had been carrying, which was smashed flat beside her. Kate lay on her side, her jacket still in flames. Jon quickly tore it away, burning his hands in the process.

Kate's hair was mostly gone from one side of her head, the skin beneath nearly black from the burns, which extended down most of her left side. With his hearing still muffled from the blast, he couldn't tell if her heart was still beating, but apart from the burns, he could see no other injuries. He needed to get them out of here before whoever had set the explosives saw them and came to finish what they'd started.

He scooped her into his arms, wincing at the burnt flesh on his hands and forearms.

As he ran, he struggled to stay on course and had to go slowly, his balance still off from the force of the explosion. He glanced up at the sky, which was already growing lighter with the approaching dawn. He would try to make it to the shotgun house. Luciano was sure to have extra blood on hand that they could both use to heal.

Several painful minutes later, Jon ran into the street a block from the shotgun house only to see several men, all in black, exiting a black SUV and running toward the house.

Shit!

While they appeared to all be human, he was in no shape to challenge so many with his injuries and with no one else to help protect Kate.

He fled the Quarter and headed for the industrial park with as much speed as he could muster. He could already feel the prickling of the coming sunrise on his exposed and raw skin. He managed to find a large warehouse and, running around the back side, kicked open a door on the lower level before carrying Kate inside. He closed the door with his foot, then turned to assess the building.

The room was piled high with cardboard boxes and crates, all with a layer of dust suggesting they hadn't been moved in some time. A pile of wooden crates was in one corner of the room and covered with a large blue tarp. He walked to the tarp and laid Kate gently on the floor at his feet. Pulling back the edge of the tarp, Jon moved a couple of the boxes to make a flat surface long and wide enough to hold Kate. He then picked her up and laid her on them. He quickly searched what remained of her pockets and found no phone. It must have been in her jacket and was hopefully burned from the blast.

He removed his cell phone from his back pocket; the screen had cracked from his fall. Holding it in both hands, he crushed it. He didn't know what method the Master had used to find them, but if he or his men had Luciano or Beth, they could have Luciano's cell and, in turn, Jon's number to track. Destroying his phone would mean they would be out of contact until he could email Luciano again or meet him in Colorado, but there was no other choice. His friend had looked terrible when they had left him, and he prayed he would survive.

Either way, when Kate was able, they would hunt for Beth and Luciano to join up with them again or to mourn their loss. He'd lost brothers in battle through the years, their faces always fresh in his memory. He hoped Luciano's wouldn't be added to them.

He pulled the tarp back down to cover Kate. If anyone were to enter while he was on recon, at least they wouldn't see her.

He moved silently between the many rows of boxes, most with labels indicating different machine parts. Two other large storage rooms were at the end of the building, and both opened to large bays with closed floor-to-ceiling garage-type doors. The dust near one of the bays had been recently disturbed by tire tracks, but how recently he couldn't tell. He had to hope that today wouldn't be the day they returned. While he wouldn't hesitate to incapacitate or kill to protect Kate and himself, he didn't like the idea of harming innocent men just returning to work. Kate needed blood, but even though he had known her only briefly, he was certain she wouldn't agree to drinking from a human to get it, even if it was one of the assholes who had tried to blow them up.

On a raised cement platform inside the main storage area was an office surrounded by glass windows. Jon climbed the few steps to the office door, which was made from wood and closed only with a standard lock, no deadbolt.

He stopped for a moment to listen for any sounds, annoyed that his hearing, while better, was still not back to normal. But it would have to do.

He made a fist and hit the door just above the knob, easily dislodging the lock and making it swing inward. He entered to find a desk covered in papers on one side and a loveseat and mini fridge on the other. Another door in between the loveseat and fridge opened to a tiny bathroom. He walked to the sink, which looked as though it hadn't been cleaned in years, and turned the faucet. The water sputtered with air in the line, then rust colored sludge poured out for several seconds before running clear. If he could find some rags, he could use them to clean up both himself and Kate.

Jon glanced at his hands and arms, pleased to see the burns were already beginning to heal. His skin had blistered on the way, but that damaged skin had shed and been replaced in many places by new, pink-red skin. He had fed before arriving at the lab and was grateful for it. Another unit or two of blood, and he would be as good as new. But Kate would require much more. There was little he could do about it until the sun set. He could feel the sluggishness that came with the daylight hours and hoped that combined with her injuries would keep Kate unconscious most of the day. He had nothing to help her with the pain if she woke in the meantime.

A few short minutes later, Jon walked from the office, his wounds rinsed clean in the sink as best he could. He carried the loveseat and the box of paper towels, emptied and refilled with numerous damp towels to clean Kate's wounds. Rather than taking Kate to the office, which he assumed might be the first stop for anyone who might enter the warehouse, he decided to take the loveseat to Kate.

Returning to her side, he moved more boxes until he could place the loveseat on them and beneath the tarp. He gently lifted Kate onto it and arranged her arms at her side. Focusing on what he could do to patch her up, he used the damp towels to gingerly clean away what he could from her wounds, speaking softly to her telepathically in case she could hear him. He had searched for a bucket or other solid container to carry water, but had found nothing but cardboard and wooden boxes with holes too large to hold any liquid.

He smoothed her hair, his hand lingering at her cheek. He had assessed many a soldier's wounds, but before 1963, when he was turned, there were no women in combat in the Marine Corps. While her face was marred by the blast, he still saw the beautiful woman before him. His field training had taken over in the moment, and only now did he notice that what remained of her clothing was tattered. Her pants were intact enough to cover her, but her shirt consisted of only a few remaining strips of fabric clinging to her waist and side that had been away from the fire. He averted his eyes from her chest. She was unconscious, but he would respect her privacy as best he could.

Jon made another quick run to the office and retrieved a fleece jacket he had seen hanging from the back of the desk chair. He carefully lifted Kate, laid the jacket beneath her, and then put her on top of it. Not bothering to put her arms in the sleeves, he pulled the jacket together and zipped it. Kate was slender and of average height, but the jacket swallowed her as if she were a child.

He was surprised at how much anger began to simmer in him at whoever had injured Kate. Going after Jon himself was one thing; he was a soldier. But attempting to kill his new, beautiful, and harmless friend was quite another. He realized the thought of losing her stung more than he would have expected. It made him itch for a chance to show them they had targeted the wrong vampire, but with the sun now up and the drain from his wounds, he was in no shape to fight unless he had to.

Jon sat on the boxes next to Kate. While he had often cursed being a vampire since he had been turned, in this moment, he was thankful they both were. The blast would have killed them both otherwise. And though Kate's beautiful face was now horribly disfigured by the burns, with enough blood, she would heal.

As his hearing slowly returned, he could hear her steady heartbeat. She was strong. And even though they had only recently met, he could tell she was spirited and determined. Her actions to go back to the lab alone to retrieve the samples she needed had been foolhardy and dangerous, but brave. Her mind had been set on protecting her fellow scientists and helping Beth and Luciano. He respected that.

Having been a vampire for more than sixty years now, Jon had accepted his fate and pushed all thoughts of being mortal aside. There had been no use in torturing himself with thoughts of something that could never be. But since he had learned there was a possibility that he could lead a more normal life free of bloodlust, he found he couldn't keep his mind away from it. Even now, images of walking in the sun, Kate alongside him, flashed through his thoughts. He didn't understand the science, but he did realize how valuable the work of this woman at his side could be. It wasn't the only reason he wanted to protect her. It was also the way she made him feel like more than just some jarhead when she looked at him. Plenty of women had moved in and out of his life over the years, but none had looked at him like she did.

Jon turned his back toward the loveseat and leaned into it, resting his head on the seat next to Kate. He would love nothing more than to curl up and sleep next to her, but he would stay awake. He had learned in the Marines how to keep his mind alert and focused even after little rest, and his training would serve him well today. They would need to leave just after sunset. They couldn't risk being tracked here. And Kate would need somewhere quiet to feed and heal. Fortunately, he had several hours on his hands to come up with a plan. When Kate was well, he supposed they would start for Colorado, as was the initial plan.

He could only hope Luciano and Beth would be making that journey to meet them.

Chapter Two

Kate

KATE AWAKENED FOR THE second time in the hotel room Jon had rented for them while she was still unconscious from the blast. Her eyes opened slowly, but at least it was both of them this time. She raised her arms in front of her. The first time, her right arm had been red and blistered, but the left was nearly black, the skin charred and leathery where it remained. While her right arm was now back to normal, the left still turned her stomach. The black was gone but had been replaced by beefy red granulation tissue. It still hurt to move, but she wiggled her fingers, pleased that they responded. She could see some of the tips were missing, but little nubs of tissue grew at the bases. She gingerly returned her arms to her sides.

Jon turned to her as she moved. "Hello there."

"How long have I been out?" Her voice was harsh and raspy, and her throat felt like she hadn't had a drink in weeks.

"Well, both eyes opened and speaking aloud. You're healing faster than I expected. You've been asleep for about eight hours. The sun has just set." He went to a small mini fridge in a wooden shelving unit in front of her.

Kate's eyes wandered over his lean, muscled shoulders until she pulled them away. The fridge was beneath a TV that was tuned to a football game. She continued to look around the small and sparsely furnished room. It had a retro feel with slanted table legs and a 70s color scheme, but she was pretty sure the decor was so old it had become cool again instead of being a purposeful remodel. There was a single curtain-covered window with a small round metal table and two matching chairs in front of it where Jon had been sitting. A combination heater/air conditioner was beneath the window and made a rattling sound as it shuddered and then shut off.

"Here you go." Jon was back at her side with another unit of blood, the tubing trimmed into a short straw. The last time she had awakened, Jon had given her so much blood to drink she felt like she would make a sloshing sound if she walked, but it had helped her immensely. He held another in his hand now and settled onto the bed with his feet propped up next to Kate, taking a long drink. Kate thought about how strange her life had become for this not to seem odd. Things had changed so drastically since she had met Beth and Luciano. Creating a vampire monkey had not been just a normal day's work, but the reality of it all hadn't entirely hit home until she'd met them in person and they'd become close friends.

With that thought, she startled, turning toward Jon and then regretting the sudden movement as pain erupted in protest from her burns.

"Have you heard from Beth or Luciano? Are they okay? Did the v2 virus work?" She couldn't get the words out quickly enough.

The gentle smile that had turned the edges of Jon's lips vanished, and his forehead creased. "I don't know. I had to smash my cell phone to be sure we weren't traced, and I haven't had access to a computer to try to email Luciano." He dropped his head and stared at the blood bag in his hand, the other hand clenching into a fist before filling Kate in on what had happened since the night of the explosion.

Kate took this in, tears welling in her eyes. Beth and Luciano had escaped the Master once, but with Luciano in such a weakened state, there was no way they would have been able to resist. And Beth would not have left Luciano's side to save herself. Kate had no question that the Master would kill them as soon as he was able.

Seeing her distress, Jon nestled in closer to her side. Feeling him near her was comforting, and she leaned into him, her arm tingling where it touched his.

"We have to believe they made it. As soon as you're able, we will stick to the plan and head for Luciano's place in Colorado."

Kate tried to reassure herself that he was right. She was typically quite confident in her capabilities as a virologist. But the Vampyre virus was like nothing she had studied before. Examining it and mapping it was in her wheelhouse, but creating a new viral vector along with RNA to fill it was not. It was gene therapy at the extreme, and she still questioned if the final changes in v2 would be enough. She wasn't a medical doctor like Beth and had no idea how the change in Luciano's weakened state would affect him.

The only way to know if Beth and Luciano had survived was to get out of this motel and on the road.

She quickly drained the blood bag and, hoping he would return to sit next to her, asked Jon for another. He was back and nestled beside her in seconds.

I could get used to this.

Kate was careful to keep the thought to herself. Perhaps he was just trying to comfort her, but she hoped it was more.

She sipped the blood as she mulled over their options. Nothing had really changed. She needed a new lab to continue the research. And more than that, she needed Beth.

Kate sucked down the rest of the unit and then moved to the edge of the bed, wincing at the pain.

"Hey, take it easy," Jon said. "I'll get whatever you need."

"We need to get to Colorado. I have to know if our friends survived before I can make a plan for where to go from here." Moving was agonizing, even speaking hurt, but she was determined. If they had survived, Beth and Luciano might need her help. And, if the two assumed she and Jon were dead and left Colorado before they could meet them, it could take months to locate them. "I'm healing quickly, just like you said. The sooner we're on our way, the better."

"You're not ready. Can you even walk?"

Kate closed her eyes, sitting on the bed, legs dangling off the side. She placed her hands at her sides, but it was too painful to put weight on her left arm. She used the right and pushed with all her might to raise herself onto her feet. The room swam, and she half sat, half fell back onto the bed.

Jon was immediately at her side, his hand at her back to keep her upright.

"How about a couple of more bags of blood before you try that again?" he asked.

Kate nodded with her eyes still closed. Almost instantly, another unit was in her hands. She drained several units, one after another, until the sloshing feeling returned and she felt her body knitting itself back together.

After a bit she tried again to stand, Jon quickly at her side to steady her. This time, she made it to her feet. It was taxing and painful, but she was standing. When she felt steady, she took a few short steps toward the bathroom. "Keep them coming, please."

Kate looked down at her body, only now realizing she was dressed in an enormous white t-shirt that hung to her knees. With the extent of her burns, her clothing must have been burned away and Jon had dressed her in what he could. She pushed aside the thoughts of him seeing her naked; not ready to deal with the embarrassment.

Jon's eyes followed hers. "I bought you some new clothes, when you're ready for them."

"I'm ready," she said, but wasn't sure she was. The thought of dressing herself with all of the exposed flesh and the pain of movement was daunting, but the thought of sitting here and waiting felt even more unbearable.

Jon handed her a shopping bag and helped her to the bathroom. She turned to face him, doorknob in hand.

"Thank you," she said and meant it, holding his gaze. He didn't have to save her, but he did. He didn't have to stay with her and try to heal her wounds, but he did. He was a good man. The thought warmed her and made her ache at the same time. Maybe she had found her knight in shining armor. He had stuck with her this far; hopefully, he would stay a little longer.

As she closed the door, she said, "We'll leave as soon as I'm dressed."

Kate looked at her face in the bathroom mirror and sighed. Her cheek and scalp were blotchy red and pink, and her left eye was still a bit cloudy and a lot bloodshot. Her hair had begun to grow in a fine peach fuzz. The muscle had returned to her arm, and large patches of skin had begun to grow, although some areas were still just granulation tissue.

She wrapped her arm gingerly with gauze that Jon had included in the bag with the clothes, both to protect it and so that she didn't have to see it. The burns over her back and side had been less severe than those on her arm, neck, and face, and baby-soft skin had begun to fill in where the blisters had once been. Looking in the mirror was like watching an episode of *Fright Night*, but she tried to look on the bright side. She would heal. And if the baby-soft skin at her side also extended to her face, it would be like a chemical peel for free.

Regardless of how she looked, she felt better, stronger every time she drank more blood, her rate of regeneration increasing as her body recovered from the shock of the injuries. Luciano had mentioned that each vampire was a little different when they had discussed their appetites, but overall, older vampires required less blood to sustain themselves and regenerate. It might take her a bit more blood, but she thought she should look presentable, if not normal, in a couple of days. She had never thought herself particularly attractive, but she wouldn't be taking her looks for granted for a long while after this. Until she was more like herself, they could travel off the main roads so no one would see her.

Kate pulled on the new blue jeans and pastel pink long-sleeved cotton T-shirt Jon had bought for her. She was fond of pink and had been wearing the color the first night they'd met. Kate wasn't sure if he remembered that or not, but thinking he may have chosen the color intentionally made her smile.

She brushed the hair that remained on the right side of her head with her fingers and avoided a final look in the mirror. She knew her image would still be ghastly, and it wasn't something she wanted to remember. It was better not to look. She cringed at the thought of Jon having to see her this way, but there was little she could do about it.

She opened the door, her head lowered, and turned as she tried to keep the best side toward him. With her head at an odd angle, she bumped her hip on the corner of the TV stand. "Buggar."

Jon looked up at her from his seat near the window, ignoring her clumsiness, and beamed at her, rising from his chair to meet her. "You look more like yourself every minute."

"The reflection in the mirror is still frightening to me, but knowing it will all heal soon is reassuring. I've never really considered how burn victims feel looking in the mirror, expecting to see their own face and seeing something far different. I'm very fortunate to be able to regenerate. Beth is right, we have to figure out a way to get this to the humans who so desperately need it."

"The two of you are trying to make something good out of all this. I admire that."

His praise made Kate blush, although given the state of her face, she doubted he would be able to tell.

"I'll get a car for us if you're still set on going tonight," Jon said.

"I am, but where are you going to rent a car at this time of night?"

Jon walked to the door and opened it. "Not so much renting; more like borrowing," he said, a mischievous grin on his face as he closed the door behind him. He was back in minutes with a late-model black sedan. He loaded the car with the remaining blood in a cooler, and they were on their way.

Kate felt a tinge of guilt at the "borrowing" but was committed to leaving the car unharmed for the owner as soon as she was able to make her way on foot.

As they began the long drive from Louisiana to Colorado, Kate thought about how often good things came from bad. Perhaps her being injured and stuck in a car with Jon for hours was to allow her to get to know this handsome man who she could feel herself becoming more and more attracted to. She tried to think of something to start a conversation and remembered Jon's kind words about her desire to help others with her research before they left the motel.

"You give me too much credit, you know. I should come clean. When I first received the information from Beth, it was my curiosity and not my will to help others that made me begin experimenting. It was a mystery I had to solve." Kate turned sideways in her seat to face Jon as she spoke, grimacing at the pain the movement caused as the seatbelt pressed against her chest, but she wanted to see his reactions to her words. "It wasn't until after Beth and Luciano joined me and I saw the regenerative abilities of the monkeys we were studying that I began to think of how it could be harnessed for good."

"It makes sense. You're a scientist. Curiosity is part of who you are."

Kate nodded in agreement, thankful he saw it that way. "So what is your nature?"

Jon chuckled. "Fighting, I guess. They put me on suspension the first time in fifth grade for starting a fight in the cafeteria." A crooked smile crossed his lips.

"What on earth could have made you start a fight at that age?"

"Jake, the school bully, was picking on a girl I liked. He grabbed one of her braids and pulled so hard she fell off the cafeteria bench and hit her head on the floor. I was pissed. Even though he was a year older, I was at least a foot taller. I helped her up and then bloodied Jake's nose. He started bawling louder than the girl who had hit her head and screamed at his buddies to 'get him'," Jon said, holding both hands out from the wheel, eyes wide and scrunching his shoulders forward, pretending to be scared.

Kate stifled a laugh.

"I didn't want to wait for them to hit first, so I tucked my head and ran at them with both arms out, knocking them all on their asses before setting in on the biggest and punching while another one of them jumped on my back. The principal pulled us apart, but we had knocked a bunch of trays of food off the nearby tables and were covered in it, mixed with a little blood from the noses of the kids I had punched." Jon chuckled at the memory, shaking his head. "I remember it well because one of the other kids' parents called my mom and made her cry. So it was also the first time my dad really laid into me with his belt. I couldn't sit down for a week."

Jon screwed his face into a grimace and glanced out of the corner of his eye at Kate.

"So you got into the fight defending someone else." Kate thought that Jon might well like to fight, but so far, he seemed more like the type to be pulled into a fight than to start one.

"Yeah, I guess so, but the principal didn't see it that way and suspended me. It was worth it, though. The girl passed a note to one of my friends at school, who brought it home to me while I was on suspension. We went steady for at least a month." His grin was so engaging that Kate had to return it and laughed.

"Ouch! Don't make me laugh. My face still hurts." But she laughed anyway. He was like a knight in a romance novel she had read once. The knight had been forced to flee the kingdom for killing the son of one of the king's generals, who was abusive to his wife. He was noble, just like Jon, and the image of Jon in chain mail with a sword and shield made Kate feel a little too warm.

Once their laughter calmed, Kate said, "We've talked about a lot of things, but you've never mentioned how you were turned."

The laughter left Jon's eyes, and Kate immediately wished she hadn't asked. "I'm so sorry. I didn't mean to invade your privacy."

"Nah, it's okay. It's just not a good memory, or at least not all of it." Jon focused on the highway in front of him, gripping the wheel with both hands.

Kate tried to lighten the mood. "It has to be better than my story. I was bitten by a vampire monkey I was experimenting on when he broke out of his cage."

This revelation seemed to pull Jon from his memories for a moment as he glanced over. "Really?"

"Yes, really. I was stupid enough to try to crawl under a lab bench with a syringe of tranquilizer to inject him. He bit my hand, and I swung him around the room, shaking my hand like a cat with tape on its paw until I turned a UV lamp on him and burned him to a crisp."

With that, Jon's eyes lit up, and he bent over with a belly laugh.

"Beth and Luciano watched the whole thing on video cameras. I kid you not."

While the story was a little embarrassing, it at least had put Jon more at ease. She really liked seeing him smile. It was one of those grins that took her breath away.

"Stop. I'm going to puke." Jon laughed more, tears forming in his eyes before he finally calmed. After a few minutes of gaining his composure, his face grew more serious, and after a quick glance at Kate, he returned his eyes to the road.

"My story isn't nearly as funny, I'm afraid."

Jon shared his story of the bar fight that ended in his death, at times becoming emotional. Kate could tell by his anger at being called a traitor that Jon was proud to serve his country and was honorable. The images of chain mail and armor returned, and Kate felt her cheeks flush.

But when Jon described lying on the cement, dying, after being stabbed on the pavement outside the bar, Kate sucked in her breath. The feelings of helplessness as she had watched Luciano aging returned, and her heart went out to Jon. The choking anguish of losing both her parents had been horrible, but she hadn't been forced to watch them die as Jon had his friend. She fought back the tears that welled in her eyes.

As he told his story, he placed his right hand on the seat between them, and Kate reached out to place her hand on his. When he finished, explaining how his maker had fed him his blood and left him to turn alone, she said, "It wasn't your fault. You couldn't have known what they would do, and you didn't ask for their taunts. You fought to defend your honor."

"It doesn't change how it turned out. And now, when people ask me about my name, the anger and guilt come right back. I guess I should have changed my name, but that felt like giving in and letting them win."

"I can understand that. It's who you are. You shouldn't have to change it." She paused for a few moments to let Jon settle his thoughts. "Your fighting skills clearly make Luciano, Beth, and me safer. I'm not capable of defending myself. But beyond that, I am thankful I have had a chance to get to know you, Jon Wilks." Her hand was still on his, and she squeezed it gently before releasing it and returning her own hand to her lap.

Jon looked at his hand before returning her gaze. Perhaps she had overstepped her bounds by touching him in that way, but his gaze didn't look annoyed or relieved; his gaze looked more like...longing.

"You know, I could help with that," he said, a mischievous grin on his lips.

"With what?"

"I could teach you how to fight." It was the second time Jon had mentioned teaching her to fight, and she could tell by the look on his face that he meant it.

"Oh, you have no idea what you would be getting yourself into." Kate was mortified. Hadn't he seen her trip over her own feet exiting the lab? "I am hopelessly clumsy. Me with a weapon is a horrible idea."

Jon laughed again. "Oh, come on, it can't be that bad."

Chapter Three

Kate

Jon drove their third "borrowed" car as the radio blared Madonna's "Like a Virgin." It was Kate's thirty minutes to choose the radio station. They had been trading off for the last two days as they made their way to Colorado.

"I was never a big Madonna fan," Jon said. "Sure, she was a looker, but I just wasn't into her music."

Kate could not for the life of her imagine why someone would not like Madonna. Beyond her music, she had been a voice for women during Kate's younger years. She had been bold and her music in your face. Her music had made Kate feel like she could be bold, too.

"Well, on your turns, we've listened to Elvis, Little Richard, Chuck Berry, Aerosmith, VanHalen, AC/DC, Kid Rock, and more 80s hair bands than I can remember the names of." She counted them off an her fingers as she spoke. "You like all of those different voices and styles, and you don't like Madonna? Do you just not like female vocalists?" As she thought about it, he hadn't sought out even one female-led band.

"That's not it. There are a lot of female vocalists I like. Joan Jett, Janis Joplin, Billie Holliday...oh, and Celine Dion. That woman can sing."

Kate nearly laughed out loud. "Celine Dion? Really? What's your favorite Celine song?" She crossed her arms, not believing he was really a Celine fan after the parade of rock and electric guitars he had chosen on their trip so far.

Jon cleared his throat and then sang the chorus for the theme from *The Titanic* completely off-key.

Kate looked at him with her mouth open, speechless. Not so much because of the horrible singing, but because he got every word right.

Jon looked at her and said, "What? It was a great movie."

Kate shook her head. "You've seen the Titanic movie?"

"Of course."

Kate sat back in her seat and thought for a moment. Could it be Jon was a hopeless romantic just like her? "What was your favorite scene?" If it was the one at the end when they came together, or the one where she jumped off the lifeboat to come to him, or maybe even the one in the car when she told him to put his hands on her...

"The sketch scene. That was hot."

Kate sighed. *At least it wasn't when the iceberg hit.*

"Slug bug, no hit backs," Kate said and playfully punched Jon in the arm.

"Are you sure? I didn't even see that one," he said, chuckling.

They had traveled six hours the first night until Kate's wounds were uncomfortable enough that they got a hotel room and stayed the day. They made it eight hours the second night, stopping just before dawn, and were almost four hours in tonight. Over the course of their journey, they had played every travel game Kate could think of. They had also talked about their favorite movies; Jon's was *Saving Private Ryan*, which Kate had never seen but thought sounded horribly sad. He hadn't seen her favorite either, *The Notebook*, but they had both agreed to rent the movies one day and watch both of them together.

They had covered all of the usual topics for first dates and then some, and Kate found she liked him more with each new discovery, even the sketch scene. But they were getting close to Breckenridge, and Kate was excited to reunite with Beth and Luc. She couldn't wait to tell Beth all about him. They just *had* to have made it out of New Orleans alive.

"What time is it?" Kate asked. She didn't wear a watch and had lost her phone in the explosion.

Jon glanced at his arm. "Nearly 23:00."

"I think we should leave the car and take the last two hours on foot. If anyone does track our progress, they won't know where we've gone from here," Kate said.

"Do you feel up to it?"

"Absolutely. I'm nearly my old self." And she was. When she had showered and dressed this evening before they left, the old Kate stared back at her in the mirror, and was she ever thankful. While some humans would believe her to be a monster since she was a vampire, she didn't want to look like one.

"Okay, I'll find a gas station and fill 'er up." She and Jon had left each "borrowed" car in a public spot where it would be easily discovered with a full tank of gas and a note apologizing for borrowing it without permission. It was the least they could do for the disruption they had caused the owners.

Several minutes later, they had drained the remaining blood bags in the cooler, disposed of them, and were moving at a comfortable jog toward the Rocky Mountains. The sky was cloudless, and with her night vision, Kate could just make the mountains out in the distance.

Jon whistled, his gaze upward. "Will you look at that?"

Kate followed his eyes up to the clear sky, lit with more stars than Kate had been able to see in her lifetime before the gift of her vampire vision. "I hope I can still see all of this after we're cured." She tripped but caught herself and kept going. "Buggar."

"I thought the new shot only took away the bloodlust and sun sensitivity," Jon said, ignoring her stumble.

"It's supposed to, but as with all experimental things, you never know for sure."

Jon nodded at her words, his lips tight and his eyebrows furrowed as he thought. "After having your new abilities for such a short time, would you give them all up to be human again?"

Kate thought about it. She was capable of so much more now. It would be hard to go back. She hated not being able to be in the sun, and she really did miss eating, but it would be a lot to give up.

"Well, thankfully, v2 should allow us to keep our abilities. But if I had to choose between the two today, I don't think I would. We can get access to blood without harming anyone now. Before that was available, I would probably have chosen differently. I couldn't stand killing to save my own life."

Kate saw Jon grimace, but only for a fraction of a second. She wished she had kept her big mouth shut. She thought plasma centers had come into being in the 1960s, but they hadn't been nearly as widespread. She didn't know what Jon had been forced to do for blood at the time he was turned and felt like slapping her palm to her forehead. Instead, she said, "What about you?"

"I hated being a vampire at first, since I didn't choose it. But over time, I got over it. Now that I can easily get the rejected blood units to eat, no, I don't think I would. I never imagined that I would get a chance to be in the sun and eat human food again, though."

Kate understood. She wanted ice cream in a bad way.

The time passed quickly as they ran and talked. Not getting winded was another wonderful benefit of being a vampire. They wandered from topic to topic easily, and as much as Kate wanted to see her friends and be certain they were okay, she couldn't squelch the little wash of disappointment that they were about to reach the end of their journey.

Luciano's cabin was adorable, like a hobbit house hidden back among the pine trees. It radiated charm, built with enormous logs and a single red brick chimney. The A-frame roof was decorated with freshly fallen snow that glinted in the moonlight. Kate imagined it would be a fantastic romantic hideaway, maybe for newlyweds on their honeymoon. She picture the young couple snuggled up together in front of a blazing fire.

As she admired the house, Jon made a wide circle, looking for signs of Luciano and Beth.

"The snow is dampening the scent. If they're here, I can't smell them, but I can't smell any humans either. Let's head back a little way to find somewhere to shelter in the daylight if we have to. Then we'll stay in the woods nearby and wait. I don't want to risk going inside. If the Master and his men have found this place, I don't want to give them a chance to attack or blow it up while we're inside."

Kate nodded and followed. She wanted nothing to do with another explosion. Beth would need to be inside before dawn, too, so they would know in a few short hours if their friends were still alive.

CHAPTER FOUR

PETER

PETER USED HIS KEY in the door lock and entered his Kansas City apartment, feeling as though he could finally exhale. The day had stretched on well after his interest in it had passed. Since he'd returned from New Orleans, he had barely been home long enough to sleep. Between his duties at the morgue and errands for the Master, he'd had little time to think, let alone look at the material he had stolen from the shotgun house and hidden from the Master. But the rest of today would finally be his own.

The Master had been as puzzled by his report of the old man with Dr. Ramsey, Dr. Giffard, and the third vampire as he was. Neither could explain why they would be protecting an aging human or Luciano's absence from the group. Peter thought perhaps Luciano had grown tired of Beth and left, or more likely, that Beth had seen him for the inferior mate he would be and had left him behind to work with Dr. Giffard. Regardless of the reason, it seemed they may have parted ways. From his short glimpse of Beth, she was even more beautiful as a vampire.

Peter walked to his bedroom, pulled his duffel from the top shelf of his closet, and opened it on his king-sized bed. He grabbed the external hard drives he had pocketed from the satchel at the shotgun house and headed for his computer, curious if they would hold any information about what Beth and Dr. Giffard had been working on. He wasn't entirely sure what he hoped to find. He wanted to become a vampire, not be cured from the affliction as was Beth's pursuit. But if the Master thought her research could be dangerous, he wanted to know why. He would no longer follow blindly; he needed answers.

The second surprise for the trip had been that Dr. Giffard had been made a vampire. Peter wondered if Beth had turned her. It irritated Peter. He had waited for years, dutifully serving the Master with the promise of being turned "when he was ready." Yet, here was Dr. Giffard, who probably had no knowledge of vampires before Beth shared her research, already turned and enjoying the benefits. It wasn't fair. But at least he had settled the issue. Dr. Giffard was dead, along with whoever the tall male vampire with her had been.

Peter had described the male vampire to the Master, but he was an unknown. He had initially thought, with Luciano gone, that Beth had found a new vampire lover or perhaps turned him herself. But he had returned to the lab at Dr. Giffard's side. Maybe the two were a pair, and Beth was still up for grabs.

Peter hadn't been close enough to get a clear photograph of the man, but there wouldn't have been time anyway. He had left men to seek out any other vampires in the area to see what they might know, but for now, the man's identity would remain a mystery.

Peter sat at his desk and kicked off his shoes, lining them up neatly next to the desk. It was another thing he appreciated about his own space: order.

After booting his computer, he plugged in the first of the two external hard drives. A prompt opened asking how he would like to handle the drive, and he chose to open the files automatically. A second dialogue box then opened, asking for a password. He had expected as much, but had hoped access would be easier. He considered his options. He didn't know who the drive belonged to and couldn't begin to guess at a password. If the drives contained information on their research, and Beth had known anything about what was on them, he knew she wouldn't have made it something easy.

Peter hadn't told the Master about the hard drives, knowing he would have ordered them destroyed. But Peter needed to know what Beth and the others were up to and if they had made any progress toward a cure for vampirism or toward harnessing the regenerative abilities all vampires shared. He supposed they hadn't been entirely successful, as Beth and Dr. Giffard were clearly still vampires. Unless, of course, Beth's desire to be human had gone since enjoying the benefits of being a vampire.

Peter leaned back in his desk chair with his fingers laced behind his head. He believed his hacker, Alex, was loyal. He had never spoken to the Master directly, only provided information through Peter, at least as far as he was aware. Alex was used to doing jobs that weren't exactly legal. Should he reach out to him, pretending to be on a mission for the Master, or ask him for a private job? Alex had continued to work on locating the remaining scientists, so having him on the Master's payroll shouldn't raise any concerns.

He dug his cell phone out of his front pocket, found his contact information, and called.

A sleepy voice answered after the fourth ring. "Hello?"

"Alex, I have a job for you. On an outing for the Master, I retrieved two external hard drives. They are encrypted and password-protected. Can you hack the security so I can access the files?"

"It's two a.m.," Alex said, groggy and clearly annoyed, the latter a feeling Peter shared.

"I'm aware."

Alex sighed loudly, and Peter could hear the rustling of blankets followed by the sound of wheels rolling, and seconds later, the chime of a computer waking. Peter waited, listening to Alex type.

"Okay, I'm online."

Peter waited, and after a few more seconds saw his pointer begin to move across his computer screen. Alex had already taken control of his machine, and he made a mental note to work on the files only after disabling his wi-fi. It would likely be of little help. If the Master did get wind of this, he had no doubt Alex would know how to glean any information he touched from his computer, but at least it was something.

Peter saw the password dialogue box open again on his screen. "This must be the drive?" Alex asked.

"Yes, the first of two."

The screen flashed, and then another window opened. Code flew by faster than Peter could follow, and as it did, asterisks began to fill the password field. After a few moments and fourteen asterisks, the password window closed, and the drive opened. Several file folders filled the screen. The first, labeled "RNA mapping", and the second, "VRV_v1". Before reading more, Peter took control of the mouse and minimized the window, not wanting Alex to see any more than necessary.

"I'm attaching the second drive now," Peter said.

"Got it," Alex said. Then the process repeated until the drive opened. The first folder read "Rhesus notes." Beth and Dr. Giffard must have been doing animal testing. Again, he minimized the window.

"Are the passwords now removed?"

"Yes, you can add your own password protection to the drives now," Alex answered. "Is that all?"

"Yes, but bill me directly for this one." Peter didn't know how closely the Master monitored his payments to Alex, but he wasn't taking any chances. He was already taking a risk in using him, but Alex was the best he had ever worked with and so far had shown he could keep his mouth shut. But if push came to shove, Alex feared the Master far more than him; everyone did and would until he was turned.

"Got it. Then I'll head back to—"

But Peter had already removed the phone from his ear and ended the call.

He opened the drive, which appeared to contain the experiment notes first. There were multiple files with the word "non-viable" added to the end of the folder name. These appeared to be failed experiments, mostly with rats and guineas. The interesting ones were in the Rhesus notes file, particularly those labeled Rhesus one through three and a single file named "Vampire test subject." That one certainly caught his attention.

The file contained what appeared to be a summary of the subject's DNA mapping findings, with a note to refer to details and the raw data on the other external drive, noting several segments of DNA that appeared to be of particular interest. Some of the information was well beyond Peter's wheelhouse, but he got the big picture. They were narrowing down the segments in the subject's DNA that provided for their special abilities and weaknesses.

They were close. If they could map and sequence the virus, could they create a cure they could use on vampires against their will to level the playing field? That could certainly ruin his plans. Was she planning to use it on the Master? It raised so many questions.

But the second file, a simple Word document labeled "Experiment notes," was what drove it all home. The Word file was a scientific journal of daily and sometimes hourly observations of the test subject. And that subject had a name. Luciano Verde.

CHAPTER FIVE

BETH

BETH AND LUCIANO SAT in the back of the Breckenridge Brewhaus, Beth's phone between them. Beth's mouth hung open, eyes wide.

"Hello, are you still there? I said this is Dr. Henri, and I could use some more samples." His voice sounded both nervous and agitated, and Beth was afraid he would hang up. But he had caught her so off guard that it took her a moment to clear her head.

"Yes, I'm here. Are you still working out of your Chicago lab?" Beth had never heard Dr. Henri's voice and had no way of knowing if it was really him or one of the Master's men, attempting to obtain more information on their whereabouts. She wasn't going to give him anything. They would be leaving Colorado soon and would dump this phone if need be so they couldn't be tracked any further.

"No, someone broke into my lab there. You had warned of those who would kill me for what I now know, so I left and found...other means of studying the virus. Not to be rude, but who are you?"

She glanced at Luc, who gave a slight nod. Dr. Henri was just as hesitant about giving away too much information as she was. Perhaps it really was Dr. Henri, but she needed to be certain. "This is Dr. Ramsey." She paused to let it sink in. Like Kate, he probably assumed she was dead.

"That's not possible. Dr. Ramsey is dead."

"I was very nearly killed, but I managed to escape along with my...test subject." Beth glanced at Luc, who raised one eyebrow but said nothing. Again, the less Dr. Henri knew at this point, the better.

"How do I know you're not with the people who came after me?"

Beth decided to take a line from Kate. "Do you remember the chromosomal studies I sent you?"

"Yes."

"Only one of the chromosomes showed no visible abnormalities. Which one was it?" There was a slim chance that the Master had actually studied the information she gave him, but most would read the long list of abnormalities and go cross-eyed. Nowhere had she specifically mentioned one chromosome with no abnormalities. However, a geneticist would have easily gleaned the information in their study.

"Chromosome 10."

Luc gave her an anxious grin, remembering the answer from their first meeting with Kate.

"Correct." It wasn't much, but the fact that he knew this bit of information, along with having the address she had sent, made her fairly certain he was, in fact, Dr. Henri. But Beth had a lot of questions and needed time to process it all. "Dr. Henri, as you understand, I must continue to be careful to keep my location hidden. I'm willing to travel to meet you and provide additional samples. But I am also in need of a lab. Would you be willing to consider a partner in your research?"

Dr. Henri paused for a moment, and Beth glanced anxiously at Luc before he spoke again. "I think I may be able to arrange that. I'm in a private, secure lab, working with an investor. An extra set of hands could speed the process, and I think he may be open to that. Do you still have access to your test subject?"

"Yes." Dr. Henri didn't need to know she was now a vampire and a better source for the original virus than Luc was. When they met and could assess the situation more fully, she would decide how much to share.

"What state are you working in?" Even though Dr. Henri would need to discuss the plan with his investor, she could at least make plans for travel.

"Florida. We could meet in Tampa. Let me speak with my investor tomorrow. Should I call this number when the plans are set?"

"No, I won't have access to this number." It wasn't a lie. She was going to ditch the phone after their discussion, just in case. "I'll call you back tomorrow at 9 p.m. Eastern. Will that work for you?"

"Yes. Perfect. I will look forward to your call." And with that, Dr. Henri hung up. Beth memorized the number, dropped her hand with the phone into her lap, crushed it, and looked at Luc, exhaling deeply.

Her emotions were warring back and forth between excitement and anxiety. This could be her chance to finish her work, for both she and Luc to be on even ground. And if they made enough progress, perhaps she could begin the journey back to her old life.

"This could be our chance, Luc. I know we need to be cautious, but I believe it is really him."

"Is it common for a geneticist to find a new job so quickly? And what do you make of his comments about a private investor?"

She was certain he was concerned, but it hadn't dampened his appetite. He had devoured four scones and one of the two cups of coffee he had brought back to the table. Beth raised her tea and took a long sniff of the rich aroma, pretending to drink.

"No, it's not. I'm not sure what to make of that. My first thoughts were government and military. He will eventually have to share more information about his investor so we can make a decision. The last thing we need is the military trying to make a vampire army."

Luc nodded and looked at his empty plate as though he was surprised the food was already gone. In the eight days they had been in Colorado, they had managed to get a better handle on Luc's caloric needs. He had lost a few pounds in the first three days after the change, but it seemed now that a well-balanced intake of 4,000 calories a day was enough to keep his weight and energy levels stable. But it seemed he ate nearly constantly. His growling stomach had become a regular alert for them to seek food. Beth was pleased that it was the only downside to his change from the version two VR virus.

"Let's leave for Florida tomorrow night, if Dr. Henri gives us the green light with his investor. Perhaps we can get enough information to find his lab and watch him before we meet," Beth said. "That will give us time to gather anything we might need and for me to process all the thoughts swirling in my head."

Beth took a deep breath and tried to slow it all down to focus on what was most important. At the top of the list was security. Every move they made was a risk, but she would assess the situation as best she could before moving forward, even if that meant stalking Dr. Henri. They had already lost two friends to the Master and placed Dr. Henri in enough danger that he had fled. Their safety had to be priority one.

She was chewing on her bottom lip, staring at the table and beginning to weigh priority two when Luc interrupted her thoughts.

"That means we only have this evening in Colorado together. We should probably avoid town tomorrow night as we leave, just in case the call was traced, but the house is far enough from Breckenridge that we should be safe there. Fresh snow is falling to help cover our scent, and we can take a long route back. So, after I have a little more to eat, I'm taking you ice skating." Luc beamed at her like a teenager who had just gotten the keys to his first car. Already, he knew her well. If they went back now, she would stew over every possibility for hours. The distraction would keep her mind occupied and dissipate the anxiety, so she would be able to approach the problem with a clear head.

"I've never been ice skating," Beth said.

"Then you are in for a treat, because I am an excellent skater." He winked at her and leaned forward to place a gentle kiss on her lips. "Be right back."

Beth watched him as he walked back to the counter to order another round of food. She let her eyes travel over his wide shoulders and muscled back, lingering on his butt for a long second before traveling down his muscled legs. This was a body built for blue jeans.

But he would look even better naked. Beth had dreaded the conversation about sex after he was healed. She knew he would think it was finally time for them to be intimate. But the fact was, not much had changed; their roles were simply reversed. She couldn't hurt him physically; he would regenerate. But Reese, the first successful vampire rhesus monkey, had died following being re-exposed to the original Vampyre virus after he had received version one of their cure. Whether it was because he was so weak before the change or because of the exposure to the virus, she didn't know. If the original virus didn't kill Luc with exposure, she didn't know if he would be infected by it, thus returning him to his original vampire state. She currently had no lab, no supplies, and, she swallowed hard, no Kate to help them if he became ill again. As much as she wanted to take their relationship toward the logical next step, she wouldn't risk his life to do it.

Luc smiled at her from the counter when he caught her staring at him. Busted.

He returned to the table to wait for his order. Beth asked, "So what does it say about us that we can consider ice skating at a time like this?"

He chuckled. "I suppose it says that we are tired of letting the Master control our actions."

Beth nodded, a wry smile on her face. "I think it's because losing Kate and Jon, and very nearly you as well, has made me realize that this life is unpredictable. Even with what should be long lives, we don't know how long we will have together. I'm not willing to let the Master or anyone else take away the joy of being with you."

Luc leaned in close and kissed her gently on the forehead.

Tomorrow they would be off on the next leg of their journey, but for tonight, she would just let herself live in the moment.

———————

Luc had not been lying about being a good skater. Beth was agile from her years of running and thought her vampire strength would help keep her legs from slipping out from under her, but Luc had skated laps around her. When Etta James' "At Last" began playing over the PA system at the rink, Luc had come up behind her and pressed her back to his chest, one arm around her waist. She had followed his lead and moved when he moved. The feel of him so close against her, his chin over her shoulder as they glided over the ice, had been exhilarating. They skated until the rink closed and laughed as they ran the long way home, Luc poking fun at her lack of ice skating prowess.

As they closed in on the final mile before reaching Luc's house, Luc stopped perfectly still, his arm out to stop Beth at his side. Beth listened intently and heard footsteps far in the distance.

Two, I think, Luc said.

Beth agreed, turning her head in the direction of the noise and focusing on blocking her thoughts from all but Luc. They moved behind a large blue spruce tree to remain out of sight. The footsteps abruptly stopped. Luc closed his eyes and breathed in deeply before a broad smile nearly split his cheeks, his eyes glinting with excess water. Beth breathed deeply also and her heart nearly leaped out of her chest.

The two bolted out from behind the tree to meet Jon and Kate, both pairs once again running at top speed toward one another. In her hurry, Kate tripped and rolled forward, but quickly regained her feet. "Buggar," she said, shaking the snow from her hair.

Beth gripped her friend tightly, nearly knocking her over, unable to form words, and let the tears fall. Kate returned her hug just as fiercely as the two men also embraced, patting one another on the back. Beth struggled to regain her composure.

Beth released Kate from her bear hug to look at her face. "I... I..." she began, but couldn't finish.

Kate also spoke through low sobs. "I know. You had to have thought we were dead. And I was so worried the two of you hadn't made it. We were injured, but Jon kept us safe."

Beth's hands still trembled, but she wiped at her eyes and then dried her hands on her jeans before turning to hug Jon. "Thank you for keeping my friend safe. I will always be grateful and in your debt."

Jon gave her one of his rogish grins and slung his arm over Kate's shoulder. Beth didn't miss Kate's grin at the contact and couldn't suppress hers. Luc wrapped Beth in his arm, pulling her close to his side, and Beth reached out to take Kate's hand and squeeze it.

Kate looked toward Luc, shaking her head in disbelief. "You look so much better, like your old self. I am so thankful v2 worked."

"It worked perfectly, and I feel like my old self again. Growing old was far more painful than I had imagined. Beth tells me I eat like my stomach is a bottomless pit, but that's the only downside. Though with as much as I enjoy it, I'm not sure it really is a downside," Luc said.

"We have so much to discuss. I want to hear all that has happened since we separated, but first let's go to the house so you can get comfortable," Beth said. And they walked the last mile, arm in arm and hand in hand.

Beth realized the weight of the burden of grief she had been carrying and let it go, feeling the tension bleed from her shoulders and neck, replaced by a wave of thankfulness and joy at once again having her friend at her side.

When they had settled into the house with a fire blazing in the fireplace and seen to it that both Jon and Kate were fed after their long journey, the two ladies sat on the couch. They curled their legs beneath them while the men relaxed in oversized leather chairs to enjoy the warmth and aroma of the fire.

"So, how did the two of you escape the blast?" Luc asked.

Kate nodded for Jon to start and sat quietly while he shared their story until he reached the part about running through the back wall of the lab.

Jon explained, "Kate was right behind me and then..." He glanced at Kate and then continued, "She must have fallen—"

"It's okay, Jon, they know me," Kate said and then turned toward Beth. "I tripped."

While Kate's clumsiness was often comical, especially for someone so brilliant, the seriousness of what had happened made it difficult for

Beth to find any humor in it. Memories of her despair while watching the lab burn returned to take her voice.

Jon explained their path from the lab to Colorado and their careful, yet slow progress, given Kate's injuries.

"Jon was burned, too, trying to help me. He left that part out." Kate shared a look with Jon, and Beth smiled inside for her friend. It seemed Kate might have more to tell her later when they were alone.

"Before we headed here, we made a detour by the shotgun house. Kate figured the Master would have taken the hard drives she left there, but she wanted to check, if it looked safe. When we got there, though, it had all been torched. There's not much left but the foundation."

Beth looked at Luc and then back at Jon, sadness filling her. "We saw it on our way out of town."

"When this is all over, you and I will build another," Luc said. "But it is a shame to have lost my first saxophone."

Beth made a mental note to surprise him with a new one as soon as she had the chance.

"How did the two of you escape the Master? Luciano couldn't have changed that quickly," Kate said.

"No. An hour or so after the two of you left, I was beyond worried. I had injected Luc with the v2 virus, and as weak as he was, I couldn't leave him alone. So, I called his friend Lilly."

Kate's eyebrows nearly hit the ceiling. She clearly remembered Lilly from Luc's show at Preservation Hall.

"I know, I was desperate," Beth said. Beth glanced at Luc, who was shaking his head, a crooked grin on his face. He clearly did not see Lilly's behavior in the same light she did. She gave him a mostly playful evil eye in return.

"Lilly stayed with Luc while I ran to the lab to look for you and saw it all in flames." She choked up again, pain flashing from the feelings of loss. She paused for a moment, cleared her throat, and continued. She recounted the rest of the night's actions, answering Kate's questions about the changes in Luc as she went along. "It was a very long twelve hours or so, but Luc woke the next evening, starving for real food, but otherwise in perfect health. He's been stable since." Beth beamed at Kate. "We really did it."

"Of course we did," Kate said, reaching over to squeeze Beth's hand. "Now we just have to find a lab to make more, and we will all be walking in the sun again." Kate glanced in Jon's direction and gave him a small nod.

"About that," Beth began and shifted forward to lean on her knees and look at Kate more directly. "We received a message from Dr. Henri at the fake address I created."

"He's alive?" Kate asked, eyebrows raised.

"Who's Dr. Henri?" Jon asked.

"He is a geneticist from Chicago. The Master killed a virologist there, and Dr. Henri disappeared. We thought he was dead," Kate explained to Jon before returning her attention to Beth.

"He figured out someone was after him and left town. He's somewhere around Tampa, Florida. He wouldn't say exactly where. It seems he has a private investor providing him with a lab. He didn't share details. Luc and I were planning to leave for Florida tomorrow to see if we could track him down and watch him. He doesn't trust me entirely, as he shouldn't. The feeling is mutual. We're supposed to call him again tomorrow night. He is going to discuss our working together with his investor. If it all looks clear, I plan to meet with him." Beth sat back and waited for Kate and Jon to have time to process that.

"I agree we need to know more about his setup, but this could be our chance to finish this thing," Kate said. "We would have the geneticist that we kept saying we needed to fill in the gaps in our research. We need to be cautious, but I am *so* in."

Beth let out a sigh of relief. She wouldn't have blamed Kate for bowing out after all she had been through, but now that she knew she was alive, she couldn't imagine doing the research without her.

"Well, you're not leaving without me. This is the most fun I've had in years," Jon said, his eyes twinkling as he shared another glance with Kate.

"Are you feeling up for traveling on foot now, Kate?" Luc asked. Beth was pleased he was so considerate, worrying about their friend's health before continuing on with their plans for the trip. It was one of the things she loved about him.

"I'm back in fighting shape as far as I can tell," Kate said. "I'm ready when you are."

"Then I think we should stick with our plans to leave as soon as the sun sets. We'll stop for food, of course, and can grab whatever supplies you need," Luc said.

Beth thought about how little she seemed to need or want of late. There were a few things she missed among her possessions back in Kansas City, but surprisingly few. She hoped Kate would feel the same since she couldn't return to her home either. Kate was always well dressed in comparison to Beth's t-shirts and blue jeans, but clothing could be replaced. It was things like family pictures that Beth wished she could have retrieved for her friend. She hoped some of those things would still be there if they were ever able to return.

"If the call tomorrow night goes well, I can arrange a meeting with Dr. Henri somewhere in Tampa," Beth said.

"We should set it up somewhere public where I can make sure no one can join the party without us seeing them coming," Jon added.

Beth nodded. His military training could be very useful to keep them out of trouble.

"I'll meet with him alone. That way, the three of you can keep watch." Beth turned to Jon and continued. "Do you think you can track him afterward so we can figure out where his lab is and what we might be getting into?"

"Not a problem," Jon said, smiling and seeming pleased he was able to help. "We should find out what we can about this investor he has, too. It sounds a little shady to me."

"We were worried about the same," Luc said. "We will check it all out, and if it looks too risky, we can call it all off before going any further."

Kate stretched her arms and settled further back into the sofa. "The sun's up, and it has been quite a night. I think we could all use a good day's rest before we leave."

Kate was right. Beth could feel the weight of the sunrise as well.

As she stood, preparing to show them to the bedrooms, she wondered if they would want one or two. She could tell something was up between the two, but until she could get Kate alone, she didn't know how much. She had decided to just show them the three extra bedrooms and let them choose when Jon spoke. "I remember where the bedrooms are. I'll show Kate, so the two of you can turn in."

And with that, Kate stood to follow him, waving goodnight as they went.

Beth looked to Luc to find him already watching her, eyebrows raised in question. She shrugged her shoulders, smiled, and headed toward their room.

CHAPTER SIX

BETH

BETH SAT AT A table for two near the front of the coffee shop they had chosen at the outskirts of Tampa. She had arrived early along with Luc, Kate, and Jon, who all waited in various places within view of the shop. She gazed out the window, as if people-watching, but let her eyes wander over Luc, who stood leaning against a street light. He looked at his phone, pretending to read, glancing up through his lashes periodically.

Mr. Verde, you are without a doubt the most handsome man I have ever seen. Even in the dim evening light, her vision was excellent, and she saw Luc's lips curve into a gentle grin, which made him even more handsome.

Dr. Ramsey, you are embarrassing me.

So I shouldn't comment on your butt?

Beth was sure she could see him fighting back a laugh even from her vantage point. She leaned forward with her elbows on the table and cradled her chin in her hands.

It was amazing to Beth how close they had become. And now that they were hopefully on the last leg of their journey, she had begun to dream of their future together. She had even flipped through a bridal magazine when no one was looking, the last time they had stopped for food for Luc. Kate's influence was rubbing off on her. Her thoughts had turned from just her to "us." It was uncharted ground for Beth, who had all but given up on finding someone to share her life with. From what Luc had said, he had felt the same, believing he would never be so fortunate as to find love twice, even in his long life.

Her daydreaming was cut short by Jon's voice in her head. *Coming in from the north. He looks to be alone.* He was standing watch at that end of the block, Kate to the south. They hoped to pick up on anyone following him with enough time for Beth to flee. But Beth, after her second conversation last evening, had been quite convinced that he was who he said he was and not working with the Master. It didn't mean his intentions were pure, but at least they weren't tainted by their nemesis.

She raised her hand to Dr. Henri as he walked past the coffee shop window. *I see him.* He looked exactly as he had when she and Luc had last seen him on the Chicago lab's video feed. He walked confidently, his chin slightly lifted beneath his round glasses. His partially balding head reflected the glow from the streetlights between the strands of what was to become a comb-over. He wore a wrinkled white dress shirt with a crooked striped tie. He entered, and the bell above the door chimed, then strode to her table.

She stood and extended her hand. "Dr. Henri, it is good to meet you in person."

His eyes swept over her body, which she ignored, as he stretched out his hand.

Luc did not ignore it, she realized as a wave of irritation flooded over her before she could block it.

"I am so pleased we could make this happen," Dr. Henri said.

"Would you like something to drink before we talk?" Beth said.

"Yes, let me grab a coffee. Would you like anything else?" He asked, gesturing toward the cup of tea in front of her.

"No, thank you."

He was back in a few short moments with a large cup, clearly coffee, as Beth could tell from the stench. She lifted her cup of Earl Grey and pretended to drink while breathing in the comforting aroma. One day soon, she would taste it again. "We spoke in broad strokes last time. What details have you and your investor— What is his name, by the way? I can't continue to call him 'the investor.'"

Dr. Henri chuckled. "His name is Kenneth Rice. He is a very wealthy man who wishes to use all his available resources to help his daughter. When she was ten, she and her mother were hit by a drunk driver. His wife was killed. His daughter survived but was paralyzed from the waist down. She's now fourteen, and despite all of the available technology, there is still nothing to help her walk again. He has been a major investor in robotics, particularly rehabilitation robotics and brain-spine interfaces. But, as I said, none have been able to help his daughter. As you likely know, since you chose to send me your research, a pet project of mine has been repair proteins, primarily as inherited genetic defects. But I recently learned of Mr. Rice and reached out to him. When my lab was invaded, I left town and contacted him, sharing the details of my...our research on a very high level. He was happy to provide me with a secure place to work in exchange for the opportunity to use the fruits of our labors to heal his daughter."

Beth made a note of the name. She would want to research this fellow as best she could. "How did he accumulate his wealth?"

"He has had various business investments, many in tech, that have served him well."

Beth felt a twinge of nervousness at his answer and felt he may well be hiding something. *I'm not sure he's being honest with me about the*

investor's income streams, but his name is Kenneth Rice. We will need to
dig up what we can.

"You can understand my concerns, of course. While this could be
a huge step forward for the medical field, it could also be a horrible
weapon in the wrong hands." Beth looked Dr. Henri in the eye and felt
what she thought was another twinge of unease. "When will I have an
opportunity to meet Mr. Rice?"

"He is out of the country on business this week, but made
arrangements to meet with you on a video call. He assumed you would
have some questions."

No go on tracking Mr. Rice, he's out of the country and will meet us by
video call. It's going to be harder to get a read on him that way.

Beth spun the cup of tea in her hands and then lifted it again.
Pretending to drink while she considered the next question. Dr. Henri
took the opportunity to take several large gulps of his own coffee. Beth
noticed a brown spot on his tie and wondered momentarily if it was
new or if it had been there when he arrived. "What arrangement is he
proposing?"

"Mr. Rice is happy to provide you with living quarters, a private lab,
and any and all equipment and supplies you may require."

"That sounds wonderful, but I won't be needing the living
quarters."

"I understand, but that is one stipulation of his agreement. The
facility is under high security, knowing what kind of men might be
looking for both of us and the information, as well as the nature of our
research. He wishes for you to leave the facility only when absolutely
necessary to minimize risk and limit possible exposure."

Mr. Rice wishes for me to stay on-site to minimize exposure. I'm going
to mention the rest of our team.

I hope he agrees to house the rest of us because I'm not staying outside without you.

Beth could hear the protective tone in Luc's thoughts. She was glad he had said he wasn't staying without her, instead of that she couldn't go without him. It was a small difference, but it left the choice to her rather than making it for her.

Mr. Rice's request made sense to Beth, and the security would be appreciated, but it did make the next part of the conversation difficult. She pretended to take another drink, and Dr. Henri's eyes followed her closely.

"Dr. Henri, in my initial communications with you, you will remember that I said I would be reaching out to several researchers in the field. One of those researchers has been working with me, a virologist. I would like to continue our work with her assistance."

Dr. Henri was quiet for a few moments, and Beth couldn't get a read on his thoughts or emotions.

"Is she trustworthy?"

"Completely. I would stake my life on it. And she has made incredible progress."

The last sentence had Dr. Henri sitting forward in his chair with an eager smile. "Having a virologist on the team would move us forward more quickly. It is the one specialty I have regretted not having access to. I'm sure Mr. Rice would agree to it; we have plenty of room. And what of your test subject? Does he have a name, and will he be joining you?"

His excitement at the thought was palpable. Beth thought he might salivate. *You're in, Kate, and he wants "the test subject."* Beth thought with a hint of sarcasm in her last two words.

Saving the best for last? It was Luc this time, and Beth rubbed her lip in pretend consideration to hide the grin that threatened. He was joking, but she could feel the concern in his thoughts.

Getting there, she thought back.

"His name is Jon, and yes, he will be joining me. And if I am to be confined to the site, I would wish to bring my significant other, Luciano." She wasn't sure how this would go over, and was very glad Luc couldn't hear her using such an indifferent term for him.

She noted the rise in Dr. Henri's brows with the mention of a significant other. It sounded cold and distant, but what else could she call him? "Boyfriend" sounded like a high school crush.

"Jon, such a simple name for such a miraculous creature," Dr. Henri mused. "I will discuss the others with Mr. Rice. Assuming he accepts, which I believe he will, what are Jon's dietary needs? Does he require..." Dr. Henri leaned forward and lowered his voice, "live donors?"

"No, bagged blood is sufficient. He will require four to five units of either whole blood or packed red cells daily. Whole blood is preferred." Beth wondered what Dr. Henri's response would be if live donors had been required. Perhaps she didn't want to know. He was well aware that a virus was the cause of their afflictions, but he may not be aware of its infectivity, given his lack of virology expertise.

"And what of your dietary requirements?" He paused and met her gaze. "You requested a meeting after sunset, and while you have pretended to drink your beverage, the fluid level is the same as when I arrived. Either you don't like sunlight or your drink, or perhaps you have been exposed to the virus you have studied."

He was more observant than she thought. *He knows I'm a vampire,* Beth thought to her friends.

If we have to stay there, there's no hiding it. He may as well know now,

Kate thought.

Did he agree to my joining you? It was Luc again.

He has to discuss everything with Mr. Rice first. Don't worry, if he says no, so will I. She felt a brief wave of satisfaction from Luc.

"Yes, my needs are similar to Jon's. And you will find Dr. Giffard, the virologist I spoke of, has similar needs."

Dr. Henri could scarcely contain his excitement. He wrung his hands before clasping them tightly together, his foot tapping incessantly beneath the table. Beth supposed she understood his giddiness, but it was a little unnerving.

"Most intriguing. I should like to hear those particular stories. And what of your last companion? Luciano, you called him."

"He is human but prefers a high-calorie, high-protein diet to maintain his body type."

Dr. Henri's brows furrowed at her comment, but he said nothing more about it.

"Splendid. I will discuss this with my investor. How should I contact you?"

Beth removed a piece of paper from her back pocket and passed it to him. The number of her new burner phone they had picked up on their trip to Tampa was jotted on it.

"You can contact me at that number when the two of you have arrived at a decision. I hope we will have a chance to continue the work together." With that, she stood and once again offered Dr. Henri her hand. He and Mr. Rice had their decisions to make, but much of Beth and her friends' decision would rely on what they uncovered about them both after tailing Dr. Henri tonight.

He's on his way out.

Ready, Jon thought back.

"I will contact you soon," he said with a nod.

He exited quickly, and Beth followed several steps behind. She was nervous about this relationship, but their lack of other options made her push the feelings aside. They had to trust someone. The only remaining scientists were overseas, and the thought of making that trip and navigating an unfamiliar country was daunting.

He's already on his cell. I'm on him. It was Jon. While he tailed Dr. Henri, the remaining three of them walked two blocks east before gathering in a pizza shop Luc had chosen earlier. Beth sat and filled them in on any details they had missed, including passing Jon off as the test subject and Luc as a human, as they had discussed. Keeping Luc's identity and physiology a secret gave them an advantage. Dr. Henri and Mr. Rice wouldn't expect his speed, strength, or regeneration, or that he had been genetically altered. While they hoped his abilities wouldn't be needed, having someone who would be perceived as no threat could only help them in a pinch. But it all depended on Jon not finding any red flags.

They sat at a table near the back and ordered drinks as well as a couple of pizzas and a salad while they waited for Jon.

"I can understand the secrecy, given what they are working on," Kate said. "And being on-site would make it easier to keep the progress moving forward and allow us to work during daylight hours without worrying about going back and forth." Kate was excited, talking with her hands and leaning forward as she spoke. Beth knew how anxious she was to move on with the research, but didn't want her to get caught up in her eagerness and lose sight of the details or the risk.

"I do agree with that and don't have a problem staying at the facility. The security might give us some heads-up if the Master's men come snooping around. But I want to know more about the ground rules.

They must have a policy for leave that Mr. Rice or Dr. Henri could share with us."

"If they are open to it, we could tour the facility, speak with Mr. Rice, and then make a decision about moving forward when we have a better idea of what we are getting into," Luc said. "Or maybe we could discuss just giving them some samples and the two of you providing direction and reviewing data from outside of the facility." He took another bite of his pizza.

Beth and Kate shook their heads at Luc in unison. Beth knew Luc's primary focus was on their safety, but if she was going to be involved, she needed to be there to be certain the knowledge wasn't used for nefarious purposes.

She turned to fully face Luc to make her point. "It won't work, Luc. You and I both know the dangers here. We have to be careful to control the process. If I'm not on-site, I can't monitor how the information is being used or who they might try to use it on." Beth could see Kate nodding vigorously out of the corner of her eye. "They are out of samples and can't proceed unless we give them more. It puts us in the driver's seat. I don't completely trust Dr. Henri, and none of us know anything about Mr. Rice. We can't just give them more virus and let them run with it."

"I get it," Luc said. "But like you said, we don't know these people, and we need to be cautious."

They had been involved in their discussion for about an hour when Jon joined the group.

"The place is massive with tight security. There are guards posted on both sides of the fence and numerous cameras. The fence walls are chain link and about twelve feet high," he said, raising one hand above the table to emphasize the height before crossing his arms in front of him and resting his elbows on the table. "The strange part is that they've got razor wire on top facing in both directions, like it's as much to keep people in as it is out."

It was a little unnerving and made Beth wonder if they were just overly cautious or what they might have inside the facility that they didn't want to escape.

"Dr. Henri said they were sticklers for security," Kate said.

"If they had other vampires, Dr. Henri wouldn't require additional samples," Beth said, more thinking aloud than as a discussion. "Did the fencing look new?" she said, looking at Jon.

"No, not really, why?" Jon said, one eyebrow raised.

"I was just wondering if it could have been put up for us," Beth said. "We haven't found any ties between Dr. Henri and the Master to suggest this is an attempt to capture us, but we have no information on Mr. Rice. Could you see anything inside?"

"No, the buildings are all at least a hundred yards from the fencing. There are windows, but they're way up on the walls, so you wouldn't be able to see inside without a ladder anyway." Jon said.

Beth wasn't sure what she hoped he would see. Mostly, she just hoped for something more to make the decision easier, but it didn't seem they would get it without stepping inside the building.

Luc had finished all of the food and was listening intently while sipping a soda. Looking at Kate and Beth, he said, "I know you two want to move forward, but we need more information on Mr. Rice before we make a decision."

"I'll stop by a library and borrow a computer to see what I can dig up on Mr. Rice on our way back to the hotel," Jon said. His searches on Dr. Henri had revealed that he had changed universities several times in his career, but there were no red flags.

"I'll go with him and fill him in on what you've shared about your talk with Dr. Henri," Kate said, gesturing toward Beth. "We should travel in pairs whenever we can," Kate added, giving Jon her warmest smile, and he returned it, holding her gaze.

The look wasn't lost on Beth, and she suspected there was more motivation than safety behind her words. She and Kate hadn't had a moment alone since regrouping in Colorado, and Beth was eager to hear her thoughts on the matter. She was a hopeless romantic, and if she was falling for Jon, Beth hoped he was interested too, for Kate's sake. He had come to help Luc when she had called and had stuck with Kate to help her heal after her burns. It showed Beth what kind of man he was.

"So, assuming we find nothing substantial on Mr. Rice, are we moving forward and going to the lab?" Kate asked, her tone hopeful.

"It's not perfect, but considering our other top options are overseas, if there are no red flags, I think we move forward with caution." She looked to Luc. "We go to the lab and meet Mr. Rice, as you suggested, and then make the final decision as to whether or not we stay." Beth wanted Luc to know she was listening and trying to be reasonable, not just rushing forward, caution be damned. "Jon, Luc, are you on board with that? It's all of us or none of us."

Jon raised his brows and looked at Luc, letting him speak first. Kate leaned forward, her hands clasped beneath her chin, eyes darting back and forth between the two.

Luc exhaled, tightening his lips before speaking. "Okay, if there are no red flags."

"Then I'm in, too. There could be a fight, and I don't want to miss it," Jon said, eyes squinting above his smile.

"Not helping," Luc said to Jon.

"When you get back, Kate, you can read over my notes, if you like. I'm sure there are gaps compared to the ones lost in the fire, but maybe they could jog your memory to add notes of your own as well as add to my questions for Dr. Henri," Beth said. "We can take our new notes along, but I plan to stash my original notes in a lock box at the bank before we join Dr. Henri."

"Good plan. I'm not sure how much of our progress we should share. I don't want him figuring out that Luciano and Jon aren't what we've made them out to be," Kate said.

Beth sat forward, elbows on the table, and wrapped her hands around her glass of ice water, rubbing at the condensation on the outside of the glass absentmindedly. "I think we tell him as little as possible. He can know that we had started to narrow down the active regions of the viral genome. Surely he's come that far. And we can tell him we were beginning work to get rid of the negative effects of the virus and starting animal trials when the Master found us. That should leave the door open for him to share his progress."

"We have to find a way to continue our work under the radar, at least until we're certain we can trust him and Mr. Rice with it," Kate said. "He's human and likely works days. Perhaps we can convince him to work with us in the evenings after dark, continuing his work by day with us trying to make further progress overnight. With someone working nearly around the clock, we could move forward more quickly and buy ourselves time alone to work on a cure."

"It's a plan, then," Beth said. "Luc and I will gather what supplies we think may be helpful and meet you at the hotel to hear what you've found. Let me know if you need us to pick up anything in particular for you." She pushed back from the table, and the others followed suit.

Beth glanced at each of them. Until a few short months ago, she had spent her life in relative solitude, and now here she was, surrounded by friends, not just acquaintances. Well, one best friend, one man well on the way to being a great friend, and the love of her life.

The world had a funny way of changing. She hoped the next changes would be as sweet as these.

CHAPTER SEVEN

MASTER

THE MASTER SAT AT his desk, his chair turned toward the fire. It wasn't a particularly cold night, and he wouldn't feel the cold if it was, but the fire was peaceful, which was exactly what he needed. While Peter had been successful in locating Dr. Giffard and disposing of her, there were many other loose ends and unanswered questions. Dr. Ramsey still lived, and he didn't know who the elderly gentleman and the younger male vampire were. *Perhaps Beth has an elderly friend or relative that my detectives missed, someone I can use as leverage to lure her back. Who has she joined forces with, and how was Dr. Giffard turned? If Beth thinks she can create her own vampire army to defeat me and then cure them all, she is sadly mistaken.*

His thoughts were interrupted by a knock on his door. One of his drudges poked his head in cautiously. "Mr. Anubis is here to see you, Master—" He was interrupted by an arm shoving him aside.

A man, almost exactly the Master's size, entered the room. It had been some years since the Master had seen him. He wore a similar finely tailored tan suit with a blue tie, which he had worn the last time they had met. It had been too long, and seeing his old friend grounded him. He knew this man, above all others, understood him and where he came from. He was perhaps the only man on Earth who could. But his presence also stirred feelings of longing and loss from so long ago.

It was a bittersweet meeting every time they saw each other.

"Sabef, I have been eager to see you," the man said as he pushed his way through the Master's door.

"Neheb, it has been far too long," the Master said, calling him by his real name and not the moniker he had adopted. He met the man in the center of the room with a rough hug.

"Life has been dull since the last time we shared space. I'm looking forward to serving you once again. I see you still surround yourself with humans," Neheb said with a disapproving look on his face.

"They are useful for more than just a food source with the proper motivation."

Neheb chuckled. "I suppose, given our long lives, a moment's pleasure is a reason to endure them."

"Some are indeed a treat, but still others are a nuisance. It is because of one of these I have called you," the Master said. "Please come and have a seat by the fire."

Neheb followed him, and they both settled into the comfortable furniture arranged in front of the fireplace.

"Do you remember Luciano Verde?" the Master asked.

"Yes, the vampire you made in Venice that has haunted you for what is it now, three hundred, four hundred years?"

"Yes, the very same. Peter attempted to kill him but failed. He was healed by a doctor who was then turned into a vampire. She was investigating our origins through our blood, which, of course, I couldn't allow to happen," the Master said.

"I agree. The knowledge is far too dangerous, and the Vampyre deserve to be lost to history except for being the namesake of the evil creatures they created," Neheb said.

"Mr. Verde and the doctor, Dr. Ramsey, have escaped and are

continuing to attempt to research our origins. They wish to create a 'cure' for vampirism." The Master said the word "cure" with so much distaste that even Neheb cringed. "Dr. Ramsey also wishes to harness our attributes to help advance and heal the human race."

"How can I be of assistance? You know my sword is pledged only to you and for as long as my heart still beats."

"My loyal friend. You are a salve to my soul," the Master said, turning to give Neheb a warm glance. "Dr. Ramsey was last seen in New Orleans working with a Dr. Kathryn Giffard. We have taken care of her, but Dr. Ramsey escaped once again. Mr. Verde was not seen in the area, but I believe he cares for her. He must have been close to her. I have deployed my men to the area to track Dr. Ramsey's movements, to find a lead and information on where they both may have run. I have no confidence in my humans to complete the task"

"And you wish for me to continue the search?"

"Yes. I received a call only moments ago that my men have tracked Dr. Ramsey to the West Hotel in New Orleans, Louisiana. Since she has eluded me for a second time, I wish for you to go to New Orleans and meet with the owner of the hotel in an attempt to gain information to continue to track her and Mr. Verde. One of my men will be waiting for you when you arrive to assist as needed and fill you in on the investigation as it now stands."

"Very well, I will leave at once. Do you need this owner, Dr. Ramsey, or Mr. Verde alive if I find them?"

"No, you have my permission to do whatever is necessary to rid me of them once and for all."

"Splendid. You know I prefer it when I don't have to be concerned with my mark's survival." Neheb smiled, a small, closed-lipped expression that didn't meet his cold black eyes.

"I have arranged for a private jet," the Master said.

"Then I will leave as soon as it is ready. And do not worry, my old friend. Dr. Ramsey and Mr. Verde are as good as dead."

With that, the two rose and embraced again. "When you have finished, we will celebrate our victory together," the Master said.

"Until then," Neheb said and let himself out.

The Master turned to look out his window once again, feeling a sense of calm he had not enjoyed since Dr. Ramsey and Luciano had escaped. Neheb was relentless and merciless, a man after his own heart. Knowing he was now in pursuit lifted his spirits. It was only a matter of time before he was free of the annoying pair.

Chapter Eight

LILLY

She could feel the tingle of another vampire reaching out and listening, and immediately clamped down on her thoughts. She scanned the room and what she could see of the lobby from her position behind the bar, trying to look nonchalant. She smiled at the customer at the bar, a regular who was there nearly every night. While he asked her out at least once a week, Lilly had no interest in a human.

She poured the man another bourbon as her eyes landed on two men in the lobby. The first was clearly human, heavily muscled, and at least six feet tall. He was neatly dressed in chinos and a collared polo. He may have been attempting to blend in, but the clothing stood out amongst the shorts and tees of the vacationers as they barhopped or those in more formal evening wear headed out to dinner at some of the finer establishments in town. He was alert and clearly scanning the room while keeping an easy two feet between him and his companion, flinching when the gentleman next to him moved. She could feel his fear from here.

The man next to him was dressed in a three-piece, fitted, and professionally tailored suit in a light tan. His blue tie was perfectly tied at his neck, and he stood with his hands clasped behind his back. His features were Egyptian by her account, his dark hair smartly cut to suggest a successful businessman. His dark, cold, and calculating eyes scanned the room.

Lilly quickly dropped her gaze. This was the vampire attempting to read her thoughts, and she had never seen him before. With Luciano and Beth having left just last night, his presence could not be a coincidence.

"Excuse me for a moment," she said to her customer and motioned for the bartender to cover. She walked slowly to the end of the bar and pushed through the hinged gate before turning toward the back entrance to the hotel. The private stairs were just to the right of the exit, and she debated running, but she was fairly certain the vampire already knew she was here. Running would only tip her hand, letting them know she was involved.

As she walked, she felt the vampire and his human following her. She could smell the vampire and his age. He was ancient. She had never met the Master and wondered if this could be him.

Shit. There's no use in putting this off.

Lilly turned to see that the two had closed the distance to join her in the hallway leading out the back. She pasted on her best salesgirl smile, placing a hand on her hip and bending one knee. "Is there something I can do for you two gentlemen?" She swallowed her nerves and looked the vampire in the eye.

He extended his hand, and she took it. His grip was firm, overly so, and as they shook, he never dropped his eyes.

"Anubis," he said, releasing her hand. Lilly wondered if the Egyptian god of death was his given name or a moniker he had acquired through his many years. She wasn't yet sure if she should be thankful it wasn't the Master or not.

"Lilly West." She turned to the human, but he remained silent, still keeping his distance from Anubis and seeming even more uncomfortable in the presence of two vampires. *Smart human.*

"Are you an employee?" Anubis asked. His implication that, despite her last name, she could not be the owner because she was female was clear. He intended it to sting and insult her.

While internally she wanted to rip him apart, she buried it and continued politely. "I am the owner. What can I help you with?"

"A female vampire visited your establishment yesterday, possibly in the company of an elderly male. Her name was Dr. Elizabeth Ramsey. As there are few vampires in the area, perhaps one visiting the hotel may have caught your attention."

His cold eyes watched her closely for any hint of reaction to his words, and Lilly once again felt the pressure of his attempt to scan her thoughts. An outright lie was sure to be felt by an ancient. It was likely he could already sense her nerves, even with her thoughts masked. But she had become quite good at telling half-truths over the years and decided that was the best approach for this situation as well.

"I don't typically give out information about our guests. Why is it you wish to know?" She would share the information if pressed. But if he was looking for Luciano and Beth, he was most certainly doing the Master's bidding, and she wouldn't willingly help him with that.

"My employer has business with her and has tasked me with locating her to deliver a message."

The sinister innuendo was clear, and considering that this vampire already gave her the creeps, it wouldn't be hard to play the weak female in fear for her life. So Lilly nodded and cowered, pretending to consider whether or not she should speak. She couldn't care less if the Master were to get his hands on Beth, but since Luciano was with her and had no doubt been the "old man" one of his spies had seen, she would give them nothing that could help.

"Well, I suppose to help another vampire..." Lilly said, lowering her head submissively to make her lame excuse seem like surrender. "Yes, a female vampire did stay with us, but only for one night. I don't recall her name. If she had an elderly gentleman with her, he wasn't with her at check-in."

Anubis continued to hold her gaze, and she met it with her face soft and submissive, not wanting him to think she had anything to hide. Her years as a prostitute, becoming whatever the clients wanted her to be, served her well.

"Did she happen to mention what brought her to town or where she might be headed?"

"I overheard her talking to a gentleman at the bar, and she mentioned she was in town for business, but didn't say what kind. I don't make a habit of eavesdropping, mind you, but since it's a bit unusual to have other vampires in town, I listened to be sure she wasn't intending to cause trouble. I don't put up with that here. And no, we didn't discuss where she was headed next."

That was true, actually. Beth and Luciano had left before Lilly had returned to her rooms and didn't share their plans, only a promise to contact her if the cure was completed. She had, however, overheard Beth talking with Luciano about a house in Colorado while he was unconscious. Lilly had pretended to sleep for a time to avoid further conversation with Beth.

"I would very much like to stay tonight in the room she occupied. My employer will be happy to cover any charges."

Shit! Any room she might supply would not carry the scent of a vampire. And since Beth and Luciano had stayed in her rooms overnight, she certainly was not going to allow this man and human in there.

"I'm afraid that room is occupied. A lovely couple here on their honeymoon checked in this afternoon and have rented it for the week. I could certainly offer you another room, perhaps on the same floor."

Anubis gave her a hard stare. She wouldn't have thought his stare could have become more intense. But as he studied her face, his features became harsher, his jaw tightened ever so slightly before he relaxed it to give her a smile that made gooseflesh break out over her arms.

"That won't be necessary. Did she perhaps list an address?"

"I'm sure she did. We require one even when the guest pays in cash, which she did, along with a two hundred-dollar deposit, which we refunded at checkout when no additional charges or damages were incurred. Follow me to the front desk, and I'll look for that address." She stepped past the two and slowly walked to the lobby and behind the counter. She typed her password into the computer and pretended to check the files. She would give them the address to Luciano's shotgun house since the Master had already located it.

"That's odd," she said. "Her scanned paperwork shows she listed 934 Barracks Street here in the Quarter. Why would she need a hotel room with a house here in town?" She put on her best puzzled look and met Anubis' gaze, pretending to wait for an answer.

"Quite odd, I would agree. I suppose we have taken up enough of your time, Ms. West. I hope you don't mind if we stop by again if any other questions arise."

While his forced smile made her cringe, Lilly offered her widest grin in return. "Of course, I would be pleased to help. Although I'm not sure what else I could possibly share."

"You might be surprised what one can remember when properly motivated," he said.

Lilly felt her gooseflesh return, and her smile faltered for only a moment. The threat was clear. Either he knew she was hiding something, or he wanted to be sure she was frightened enough to tell him anything she might hear in the future. Either way, it shook her. She could only respond with a nod and watch them walk toward the front doors.

She needed to leave and soon, but how would she locate Luciano to warn him?

Chapter Nine

Dr. Liam Henri

Liam stretched out on the low-backed sofa, his arms draped over the back on each side of him, feet crossed on the glass coffee table before him. He waited patiently for the screen on the wall in front of him to flicker with the start of the video call.

He glanced around the room he had become familiar with; its modern decor was the same as what was throughout the halls of the facility. Light gray walls surrounded sill-less windows mounted high in the wall to provide light but no view. A dark wood cabinet filled the wall below them and housed a refrigerator and microwave behind closed doors. The only items on the counter were a single-serving coffee maker and a set of small drawers that held every coffee brand and flavor anyone could ever want, plus hot chocolate and tea for the crazy non-coffee drinkers.

He had made himself a cup of what appeared to be the most expensive brand, which sat steaming on the coffee table beside his feet, along with a few drips of coffee that had sloshed over the edge when he'd set it down.

Liam was eager to talk with Mr. Rice about Dr. Ramsey and her entourage, and eager to see what else they knew about the virus. He'd been elated that Dr. Ramsey had seemed willing to join him along with her test subject, Jon. Having a virologist too was just icing on the proverbial cake. The sooner they could create both a cure for Mr. Rice's daughter and a small army of soldiers for his other pursuits, the sooner the money would begin rolling in. Liam would collect what had been promised and spend the rest of his life in luxury.

Liam leaned over, reaching for his coffee cup without lowering his legs and sloshing a few more drops onto the glass table in the process. He attempted a sip but winced at the heat and returned it to the table. Money had a way of drawing women. He was a nice-looking fellow, but a scientist was not something women on the dating sites clamored for, at least not the beauties he was interested in. They didn't need to be smart; he was smart enough for all of them. They just needed to be gorgeous and good in bed.

A lewd grin crossed his face at the thought, but as the screen began to flicker, he lowered his feet and sat upright, snapping from his daydreaming.

"Dr. Henri, I trust your meeting with Dr. Ramsey last evening went well. When will she and her test subject be joining us?"

Liam smoothed his shirt. Mr. Rice was always impeccably dressed in a tailored suit and tie. Today he appeared on the video screen wearing a deep chocolate brown suit with a paisley peach tie. His full head of brown hair was something Liam envied as his own hair thinned. Even on a video, Mr. Rice's deep brown eyes were riveting and watchful. Liam was certain nothing ever got by him. While he wasn't a doctor, this man was highly intelligent and one of the few people who made Liam feel like he may not be the smartest man in the room.

"Yes, even better than I expected. She has agreed to join us here but had a few additional requests," Liam said.

"And what might those be?" Mr. Rice said with narrowed eyes. He shifted in his seat and linked his fingers in front of him.

"It seems she has been working with a virologist, a Dr. Kathryn Giffard, associated with Trelane at a New Orleans lab. The lab was recently destroyed by whoever has been chasing her and Dr. Ramsey. Dr. Ramsey would like to bring Dr. Giffard along as well. I believe, as I have mentioned before, that a virologist would be extremely helpful to our efforts."

"Yes, I agree. Invite her to join our team."

"Dr. Ramsey also requested that she be allowed to bring what seems to be her human lover, since they will be required to remain on campus. I believe she must fear for his safety during her absence."

"Interesting. I see no harm in it since none of them will be leaving anyway. If that's what it takes to assure she joins us, then agree to it. If she or Dr. Giffard become difficult during their time here, we may be able to use him as leverage to improve their performance."

Liam wasn't surprised at this comment. He had seen Mr. Rice do something similar with others during his time at the lab. While he had no intention of getting on Mr. Rice's bad side, he supposed it was good that he had no one who could be used as leverage

"Those were my thoughts exactly. I am hopeful that when Dr. Giffard and Dr. Ramsey see the fulfillment of our goals, they will willingly join us in further pursuits. Being welcoming can only help us in those efforts."

"As we have discussed, if they choose not to continue their work here, they will be quietly disposed of," Mr. Rice said, staring intently at the camera and making Liam shift a bit in his seat.

"There is one other item of information that may make things more difficult," Dr. Henri said.

"Yes, continue."

"It would seem that both Dr. Ramsey and Dr. Giffard are also infected with the virus."

Mr. Rice sat forward in his chair, his eyes darting back and forth as he considered this information.

This would certainly make the research easier with a fresh supply of virus and subjects to observe from the start. Dr. Henri felt a passing twinge of guilt knowing that this would make them not merely expendable resources, but Mr. Rice's new prized specimens and a permanent part of his collection.

"Fascinating. I'll discuss the issue with security. We will need to be certain they can be contained appropriately when the need arises. Have you assessed their dietary needs?"

"Yes; no live donors are required, but they will need a constant supply of whole blood units."

"I will have it arranged. Is there anything else before we move on to the progress of your experiments?" Mr. Rice asked.

"No, I will make the necessary arrangements and notify Dr. Ramsey."

"Very well," Mr. Rice said.

Liam slipped his finger in the collar of his shirt to loosen it and readjusted himself on the couch. "Progress, as you know, has been slow. I easily mapped the viral genome. Some of the segments I have identified are similar to those in the normal human genome, so I have at least postulated what they may control. However, it would be a huge step forward if I could map the DNA of the original affected host to confirm my suspicions of where they are inserted. We have attempted to infect mice, rats, and guineas, but all have died. As a result, we have no remaining sample and no infected host from which to draw additional samples. So, effectively, until Dr. Ramsey arrives, we are at a standstill." The timing of Dr. Ramsey's arrival could not be more perfect. While he doubted they could have progressed further than he had with the same limited samples, they had the benefit of an unlimited supply. So he was eager to hear details of their research.

"And on our second project?"

"We have gathered ten individuals so far. Six have required detox to make them adequate candidates for infection. The remaining four are healthy but psychologically impaired. They should be good candidates for infection, but will likely be more difficult to control and less helpful in providing verbal feedback on the process." Liam found the whole process distasteful. He didn't care that they were collecting these societal rejects. It was probably the only chance they would ever have to contribute something positive to the world. But he refused to work with them until they had been cleaned.

"And where were they obtained?"

"Various areas around downtown Tampa, living on the streets. Your colleague, Mr. Smith, has been most helpful."

"Direct him to gather the next group from farther away so as not to draw attention. The last thing we want is for the police to become suspicious of missing persons."

It was Dr. Henri's only real concern. If someone in the scientific world discovered his involvement, they would bring him up on ethics charges, and his research would be discredited.

"I will, although I doubt there is anyone looking for vagrants."

"We will take no unnecessary chances here, Dr. Henri. Contact my assistant when Dr. Ramsey and her team have arrived, and she will arrange for a video call to welcome them. Until then..." Mr. Rice nodded, and the screen went blank.

Liam hated it when Mr. Rice was so dismissive, but he had all the money. So, Liam bit his tongue and took it. He would prepare a lab for

Dr. Ramsey and Dr. Giffard to share, separate from his own. There was no need to risk them discovering his side project with Mr. Rice until they had completed their research and healed Mr. Rice's daughter.

With the viral vector he assumed they would build containing the test subject's gene for regeneration, and a sequence of his genome, it wouldn't be too much of a leap to repackage the segments that encoded for strength and agility along with it for his human trials. By then, he would have a much better feel for Dr. Ramsey and Dr. Giffard and how amenable they would be to his side project. It may seem more appealing when they realized their choices were to assist or die, but they would discuss those options when the time came.

For now, he would just enjoy his morning coffee.

CHAPTER TEN

LILLY

"MISS WEST! MISS WEST!"

Lilly heard her name from behind her just as she was about to open the door to the stairs that led to her apartment. She turned to see Ian round the corner out of the office. He was walking quickly and waving his arms, making quite the spectacle.

"Shit! What is it, Ian? You're disturbing the entire lobby," she said, stopping in front of him and crossing her arms.

"I'm sorry, Miss West, but you have an urgent call in the office from a Mr. Green."

Her thank you was nearly lost as she hurried past him, down the hall and into the office, closing the door behind her. She put the receiver from the old landline she just couldn't get rid of to her ear. She shared the number only with those close to her, used an old phone with a plug-in cord so radio scanners wouldn't work on it, and kept it unlisted for just this purpose. Nothing was entirely secure, but this was as close as they could get.

"Hank?" she said, worry clear in her voice.

"Yes, Lilly, it's me," Luciano said. "And before you ask, I'm fine. We made it to our destination and have moved on."

Lilly let out a sigh with her eyes closed. It had been a stressful day, and Luciano in danger was not something she needed to add to her plate right now.

"We didn't get to talk much before we left, but I've been thinking about the Master tracking us to you," he said. "It might be best if you leave town for a while."

"Yeah, well, you're a little late."

"Are you alright?"

"For now. Some short but scary as hell vampire came here tonight with some muscle-bound human in tow. The vampire, who said his name was Anubis, if that wasn't enough to scare the bejesus out of me, was asking for information about your Dr. Ramsey, fishing to see what I knew. It sounded like they had seen you when you were sick and thought she was traveling with an elderly man." Lilly chuckled at that one. "Even though it was unintended, it worked well as a cover. As far as they can tell, you aren't here. I'm guessing they tracked us from the shotgun house. If so, and they get anything to scent me, they will know I helped. Anyway, I don't know the guy. I gave them the shotgun house as Dr. Ramsey's listed address. I figured that place is already blown, so there would be no harm."

"You did well. And you're right about the house; they burned it down after ransacking it. There shouldn't have been anything left to lead them to us, but Dr. Giffard did leave notes behind. I'm hoping they burned with the house, but I am not sure. You need to leave until things blow over. If they find out you helped us, the Master will not hesitate to kill you. Do you have somewhere to go?"

"Of course. I was just headed upstairs to pack. How can I reach you if I need to?" Lilly asked.

"I left my contact info where you would expect to find it," Luciano said.

Lilly smiled, knowing exactly where he had left it. Back in the day, they left each other messages hidden in the decorative woodwork around the altar in an old church in the town where Lilly was born. It had been made a historical site some fifty years ago for the part it played in the Underground Railroad. The place held good memories for Lilly, not because of her childhood there, but because of the time there with Luciano.

"You have my cell, but you can leave a message here if you need to," she said. "Keep it brief and watered down just in case the Master's men infiltrate while I'm gone. Where are you headed?"

"It's probably best you don't know. We've put you in enough danger already. Just steer clear of your hotel until the Master's men move on. And, Lilly, take care of yourself."

Lilly's lips curled into a seductive smile. He was concerned about her safety. He cared, and it made her little black heart flutter.

"Got it. I'll let you know when I'm clear. Watch your back."

She ended the call and re-entered the hallway to find Ian. He had provided management assistance on her past "business" trips, and she needed to tell him she would be in New York for a few weeks, looking at a new business venture.

It was about fifteen minutes past midnight, and Lilly had just finished packing. She had a single bag and a briefcase. The briefcase held nothing but a legal pad and pens. She had changed into a comfortable pantsuit and flats that would be acceptable for travel. In her duffel, however, was another change of clothes and athletic shoes. She would have a long run ahead of her, and while she could just as easily run in dress shoes and clothes, the outfit wouldn't hold up to the wear like the sneakers, leggings, and fitted t-shirt would.

She had thrown in a small cooler with a couple of units of blood in case she needed them. Unlike Luciano, she still occasionally fed on humans but didn't share his guilt over it. There was always a hateful ass that deserved a more painful death than she delivered if she looked for them. Her early life had sometimes taken her through society's underbelly, and she could sniff it out no matter what city she was in. But she did know the value of keeping her vampirism a secret and had learned to drink donated blood to keep her and her kind off the radar.

She closed the bag and slung the duffel over her shoulder, her briefcase in the opposite hand, and headed for the door.

Anubis...that name still made her skin crawl...either believed the information she shared with him and would possibly have a human or two watching the hotel, or didn't believe her and may be waiting for her to leave himself. If Anubis was waiting, her chances at escape were slim. One-on-one, she was no match for an ancient. She would have to do whatever she could to get free of him, clear the city on foot, and keep going. Once she ran, she had the skills to be sure she was nearly impossible to track. But the longer she waited, the more time they had to check her story and gather more of the Master's goons. She hadn't survived this long waiting for her enemies to strike first. Whatever waited for her, it was time to face it head-on.

She closed the blinds, shut out the lights, and headed down the stairs to the back of the hotel.

Lilly stepped from the back door and crossed the pool of light from the security pole toward the back of the parking lot. She would wait until she was clear of the area to break into a run, hoping to get a short distance away before changing clothes.

She stepped into the shadows and had almost crossed the lot when several figures stepped from the darkness. There were five in all, and they looked like clones, all within a couple of inches of each other in height and hovering around six feet tall. They were all muscle-bound and dressed in various colors of what looked like the same polo shirt and chinos. Had she not been so worried about what might happen next, it would have been comical.

"Where are you off to?" It was the man who had been with Anubis a few hours earlier. *He speaks.*

"I have business to attend to. Why does my work concern you?" She would play it cool until it wasn't.

"Our employer would like you to stay where you are in case your assistance is needed."

"Well, I can't imagine what else I could help with. I've already told you everything I know. I have a business to run, gentlemen. My staff knows how to reach me should you have further questions." She dismissed them and continued on her original path, planning to walk between two of the large men. She held her head high and her shoulders back, making her intentions clear and suggesting the matter was settled. One of the men held his arm in front of her, and she turned to glare at him with her most wilting stare, allowing her fangs to extend just beyond the lower edge of her lip.

He flinched but held his ground.

"You don't want to do that," Lilly said, her voice venomous.

"But yet, he must."

Lilly didn't need to turn around to recognize the voice; the arrogant tone dripped over her like oil, slimy and cool. Anubis.

This was not going to go well. She had two choices. She could easily run through the line of humans and evade them; they were of little consequence. But she didn't know if she could outrun Anubis. If he was an ancient, then with those years often came enhanced abilities unlike humans, who grew more fragile with each passing year. Her second choice was to stand her ground, negotiating or fighting for her freedom, depending on how it played out.

She decided to continue to play her part. She had spent years pretending to be submissive and whatever her clients wanted her to be, both standing upright and on her back. If anyone could play the game, it would be her. She pivoted on her heel to see Anubis standing, hands clasped in front of him, between her and her hotel.

"Anubis. While it is a pleasure to see you again, I thought our business was finished." She offered him her most placating grin, which he did not return.

"I had hoped so, but I've been in this line of work for some time. I've learned to listen to my gut, and it tells me you know more than you are sharing."

Lilly refused to cower and looked him in the eye. "I know nothing more. I have cooperated with your requests as best I could as a favor, one vampire to another. But I have nothing else to share. I would very much appreciate it if you would release me to continue my business. I will only be gone a couple of days. Surely I could assist you with whatever you need when I return." She held his gaze, knowing that looking away would make her look guilty and, worse, weak.

Had she looked away, she may very well have missed the small nod Anubis gave to the human who had visited her earlier this evening at his side.

She saw the muscles of the man to her right clench as he prepared to rush toward her. She turned and delivered a blow to the center of his chest with the flat of her hand, hearing bone crunch. He had been only a fraction of a second faster than the rest to respond, but Lilly was ready. Spinning in a circle before the first man even hit the ground, she sliced out with her nails and slashed the throats of two more before grabbing the outstretched arms of the fourth and flipping him feet over head into the fifth.

Humans. She considered for a fraction of a second if Anubis would really believe they could stop her or if they were merely a distraction to slow her down.

The answer came swiftly.

Lilly found her legs dangling above the ground, Anubis' hand at her throat, arm stretched nearly straight above him to overcome the height difference. Her eyes were slits, and she hissed at him, fangs fully exposed now as she grabbed at his wrist and squirmed, her left shoe flying from her foot and into the shadows in the process.

A grin that sent shivers down her spine looked back at her. "You're a vicious little thing, aren't you? I admire the spunk. But you will tell me what you know, voluntarily or by force. It's your choice." But then he cocked his head to the side. "Actually, it's not. You had your chance. Over the millennia, I have become quite efficient at extracting information. I find the process cathartic."

"But I don't know anything else," Lilly rasped as his grip tightened, refusing to give in to fear. Keeping her head would be her only way out of this.

"No matter. I will enjoy the process just the same."

Two things happened in rapid succession. A car drove into the lot with its brights on, momentarily blinding Anubis, and Lilly brought her knee up to meet Anubis' chin with all the force she could muster. It caused his grip to loosen, and she dropped to the ground on her feet. Giving him no time to recover, she kicked him squarely in the chest, launching him into the radiator of the car. Before the sound of the impact cleared, she was running at top speed in the opposite direction of her original path, not taking time to remove her remaining shoe. She didn't look back, knowing that even with the force of the blow combined with the momentum from the car, he wouldn't be down long.

Lilly knew the streets well and wove in and out of them, jumping fences and crossing courtyards until she reached the river, where she dodged the trees along the bank at top speed before taking a hard left through the countryside. Her heart hammered in her chest, fearing Anubis followed, but she heard no footsteps. She reached out with her mind, and still nothing. After several more miles, she paused briefly to remove her remaining shoe and then continued on her run, crossing as many streams as she could. Surely she had come too far for Anubis or dogs to track her.

And then she heard it, a train in the distance. While she could run faster, she would still leave a scent trail. Riding the train, even for a only few miles, would cover her trail.

She ran until she approached the train and matched its speed, leaping easily to grab a ladder on one side and climb to the top. She searched the landscape behind her but saw no one.

It would be dawn in just under two hours. She would ride the train for an hour and then find a place to spend the day.

She slumped back onto the roof of the train car and looked at the stars, trying to calm herself. She hadn't felt that sort of fear since before she became a vampire. Lilly had fought to make her way in life after fear of starvation and death had driven her to prostitution. Over the years, she had learned to turn the fear into anger and a will to fight, fueling her drive to move forward and take control over her future. The Master and Anubis were interfering with that future and expected her to cower in submission, but she wasn't that kind of vampire.

She was pissed.

CHAPTER ELEVEN

PETER

PETER HAD SPENT MOST of his waking hours away from work, studying Dr. Ramsey and Dr. Giffard's research. It was fascinating. Having reviewed the last bit of information on the external hard drives, he sat back in his desk chair and steepled his fingers, elbows on the armrests. He had come to realize, by references within the data on the drives, that they had belonged to Dr. Giffard. While he was no virologist, her personal notes were very clear. They had created a treatment to halt the undesirable effects of the Vampyre virus, but the notes ended before there was any real follow-up to know with certainty that it worked, and there was no mention of whether or not Mr. Verde survived.

Peter rose from his desk to walk to the small bar table in the corner of the room. He poured himself a glass of bourbon and stared out the window. The old man they had seen the night they had blown up the lab must have been Mr. Verde. Dr. Ramsey, who wore honor like a badge, would not have left his side. Peter had received a report that the dogs had tracked Dr. Ramsey's scent to the West Hotel, which meant that somehow they had gone there together. But whether Mr. Verde had recovered or not was unknown.

He took a sip of the bourbon, wincing slightly at the sting.

The notes on Mr. Verde after the VR v1 virus were remarkable.

He had lost his sensitivity to sunlight and was free of his need for blood. If the two doctors had gotten it right with the v2 virus, Luciano would retain all of the gifts of vampirism without the drawbacks. He would be able to easily pass as human. Peter knew the Master had done everything he could to stop Dr. Ramsey's research on the VR virus, even tracking down and killing scientists who had received the information but might not have been continuing her research. If the Master could have all the benefits without the negatives, why wouldn't he embrace it? It made no sense to Peter.

He had been sorely tempted to inject himself with the sample he had stolen from Dr. Giffard's lab, but now he was reconsidering. If he could track down Dr. Ramsey and obtain some of the new virus, he would be every bit as powerful as the Master but have the advantage over him of being free from the blood requirements and conducting business, including attacks, during the daylight hours.

Dr. Ramsey was naive and a dreamer. She would want to share this virus and its possibilities with the world, but imagine what it could be worth if its distribution were controlled. How much would other vampires pay for this? And what about the military or other private armies? It could be worth billions.

Peter could recruit his own scientific team to work with the sample he had, but it was a small amount, and they couldn't rely on it alone. Where would they get more, unless they found another vampire to get more viral samples from, or made a vampire of their own? But that would take money and time while risking the Master discovering that Peter knew about their current research, that he had withheld a sample from him, and that he would be going behind the Master's back to investigate something the Master clearly did not want studied.

It was a big risk, and he still needed to locate Dr. Ramsey and

Mr. Verde to see if v2 worked. If the Master found out about the information he had already withheld, he was a dead man. He was already concerned that the Master was watching him. If the Master became more suspicious and questioned the people Peter interacted with, he could put it together. Men had been with him when he found the satchel at the shotgun house and may have seen him take the drives. Alex had hacked the drives on his dime, which would also be a red flag. But Peter had chosen his path, and there was no turning back now.

He returned to his desk and packed up the hard drives, placing them in a fireproof pouch. Then he walked to his bedroom to access his safe, which was hidden behind a painting consisting of a black line and a red circle in broad brush strokes on a white canvas. He typed in a lengthy password and opened the safe before placing the drives inside, locking it, and sliding the painting back in place.

He turned on his heel to go to the closet, unbuckling his trousers and pulling his shirt off to prepare for a shower as he walked. Beth was clever, more clever than he had thought. He needed to find a way to track her down to see what more she had discovered before the Master had her killed. But she had once again vanished into thin air. Their one lead, Lilly West, was now in the hands of the only vampire the Master truly trusted, Anubis.

Just the thought of the vampire sent chills through Peter. He had seen him on only two previous occasions, both when the Master wanted a matter resolved with no survivors and no loose ends. If the Master had called him in to find Beth, Peter's chances to get to her first and find out what she knew had become much, much lower.

CHAPTER TWELVE

BETH

THEY ALL GATHERED OUT of sight of the main gate of New Dimension Analytics about an hour after sunset. The security Jon had described made Beth more nervous now that she was seeing it for herself.

The searches on Mr. Rice had flagged his pharmaceutical company, but he seemed to have popped onto the radar out of nowhere at about age thirty, when he had married and purchased New Dimension Analytics. He was incredibly wealthy. Some articles alluded to his "humble beginnings" but didn't elaborate, nor did they elaborate on how he began to amass his fortune. But there were no clear red flags.

"I guess this is it. Either we all go together, or we all turn and leave together. If anyone has reservations, now is the time to speak up," Beth said.

"I have concerns, sure, but to me it's worth the risk. I don't know when we'll get a better chance at it," Kate said and glanced at Jon. "Plus, we're an excellent team. If things go south, we will figure it out together."

Jon returned her glance with a mischievous smile and nodded, leaning his shoulder into hers.

"Luc?" Beth asked.

"Let's do it."

And with that, they turned toward the main gate and walked toward the gatekeeper.

When he saw them coming, he exited the guard station, assault rifle in hand.

Jon raised his arms, palms forward. "No need for alarm. We were invited by Dr. Henri."

Beth stepped forward. The guard's manner and uniform were military, but he wore no emblems she recognized.

"I'm Dr. Ramsey, and this is Dr. Giffard, Jon Wilks, and Luciano Verde." She gestured toward each in turn.

The guard relaxed, seeming to recognize the names. "Dr. Henri is expecting you. Give me a moment, and I'll escort you to the entrance." The guard returned to the station, where they could see him talking with a second guard through the large glass window on the front of the small building. He spoke into a two-way radio and then returned, this time without his rifle, and said, "Please follow me."

Beth glanced at her friends once more, giving them a chance to turn or speak before falling in line behind him. The walk to the entrance took several minutes at human speed. The outside of the building had a distinctly institutional appearance. It was modern in design, covered in glass and chrome. To Beth, it felt stark and cold.

As they passed through the entryway doors into a two-story lobby, the modern design continued with sparse furnishings and more security; only the guard in the lobby wore a black suit and tie rather than military dress. He stood as Dr. Henri approached the impeccably clean and blindingly white marble desk.

"Dr. Ramsey, Dr. Giffard, welcome." Dr. Henri paused to give Kate a lingering once-over before extending his hand to greet them both.

"Dr. Henri, this is Jon Wilks and Luciano Verde."

Dr. Henri's eyes widened as he extended his hand once again and stretched his neck to look up at Jon, who towered over him.

"Mr. Wilks, I am most pleased to meet you," Dr. Henri said then turned to Luc. "Mr. Verde." They shook his hand in turn before he said, "Please follow me."

He led them through two additional security doors, badging through each before leading them through a maze of corridors and locked doors, and finally entering what looked like a combination of a conference room and break room. A low-back sofa sat across from a video screen with a glass table in front of it. Two additional chairs were placed at right angles to the sofa at each end. Dr. Henri had seated himself on the sofa, nearly in the middle, and sat with his arms outstretched over the back, one knee crossed over the other. He offered them each refreshments when they entered, including units of blood kept in a refrigerator behind a cabinet door.

Beth refused. She preferred not to eat in front of a stranger. Feeding from a blood bag still made her self-conscious. It was like a big red sign saying she was no longer human like she wished to be. She assumed it must be the same for Kate and Jon since they, too, declined the offer. Luc, however, had a steaming cup of coffee and a plate of finger sandwiches. They settled into the chairs on either side of the sofa.

"I'm sure Mr. Rice will be initiating the call shortly," Dr. Henri said.

"Does he visit the facility frequently?" Beth asked, curious about Mr. Rice's schedule and hoping to meet him in person at a later date.

"Mr. Rice is a very busy man. He checks in frequently by video from his private jet, but he is rarely on the ground long enough for an in-person meeting."

Beth remembered Jon's research and that Mr. Rice had properties in multiple countries, including Yemen and Syria. While it seemed a bit odd, both countries did have active pharmaceutical companies, and Beth assumed he had business dealings with them that required him to be overseas frequently.

It sounds like a safety measure to me. Who could he be avoiding? Luc thought.

I agree. He'd be very tough to track, Jon thought back. *I wouldn't think peddling legal drugs would be as dangerous as the illegal ones.*

At that moment, the screen flickered, and the virtual meeting software connected. A fifty-something man dressed in a slim-cut and well-tailored navy blue suit filled the screen. With so much time on the run and in the lab, Beth had become accustomed to jeans and t-shirts and felt a bit underdressed. The man, with his brown hair in what looked to be an expensive cut, steepled his fingers in front of him and donned a broad smile around very white teeth. His eyes were intelligent, and Beth couldn't help but feel as though he was sizing her up even before she had spoken. But then, she was doing the same with him and decided she should be more concerned if he hadn't. Surely Dr. Henri had told him she was a vampire. If he had dismissed her, it would suggest he didn't see her condition and this virus as the threat it could be.

"Dr. Henri, I see our guests have arrived safely," he said.

"Yes, Mr. Rice, this is Dr. Elizabeth Ramsey and Dr. Kathryn Giffard." He gestured to each of the ladies in turn. "This is Mr. Jon Wilks, who is the individual who so kindly provided samples for study and started this investigation of ours. And last, Mr. Luciano Verde, Dr. Ramsey's...companion." Dr. Henri's gaze passed quickly over Luc and then darted back to Jon. He clearly did not see Luc as anything special, believing him just another human, and Beth was pleased that their ruse held. She felt irritation from Luc with the word "companion," but he didn't show it.

"I'm pleased to meet you, Mr. Rice," Beth said. "Dr. Giffard and I are eager to continue our research and appreciate the opportunity you have so generously provided."

"I am pleased to have you join Dr. Henri in our pursuits. As Dr. Henri may have told you, my daughter was paralyzed some four years ago now. While I have scoured the world and poured millions into investigating a cure for her, my efforts have failed. I had begun to believe the task was impossible. However, with the discovery—your discovery—of the vampire virus, I am once again hopeful that my daughter will be able to walk and enjoy a normal life," Mr. Rice said.

It rang true to Beth, and his eyes showed the sadness of a father who had watched a child suffer. She had read the article about the accident as well as his support of spinal cord research. It all fit.

"We would like nothing more than to find a treatment to heal your daughter and so many more who could benefit from the regenerative effects of the virus. If we are able to produce a safe virus for injection, how do you intend to share it with the rest of the world?" Beth asked.

"I own a large pharmaceutical company, Biovitalis. You may have heard of it. We do not currently work in the area of gene therapy, but it would seem a simple addition to our current processes, assuming a suitable viral vector could be created and grown."

"I am sure you are aware of the other facets of our affliction. Will you be investigating those as well?" Kate asked, ticking off one of the questions on the list the four of them had made for this meeting.

"We hope to study all aspects of the virus and harness whatever we can to improve the human condition," Mr. Rice said.

Beth wished he were here in person so she might catch a hint of his emotional reaction to her questions.

"I'm sure you are aware that some aspects of this virus could be weaponized. How is it you plan to guard against that?" Beth asked. It was a direct question, and she watched Mr. Rice's face closely for any clues of his intent.

He sat back in his chair, a serious expression replacing his smile. Beth would have been able to feel the tension in the room even without her vampire senses.

"I am quite aware of the possibilities, but New Dimension Analytics is private and secure. No one but the five of you and I will know of our experiments here. The world will never need to know of the other aspects of our research unless we choose to share them," Mr. Rice said.

"It is a great responsibility, protecting the rest of the world against what would make such a powerful weapon," Beth said, not feeling particularly reassured by his response and how he had dodged her primary concern.

Mr. Rice nodded his response. Then he said, "If it is not too personal a question, might I ask how you and Dr. Giffard have become infected with the virus?" He glanced at Jon. Perhaps he was concerned that Jon attacked and turned them.

They had anticipated the question, so she was prepared with her response.

"My change was required to escape those who wish to prevent further research on the virus," Beth said.

"And mine was a result of a lab accident," Kate said. "The study of this virus and those infected with it, human and animal alike, comes with significant risks. It makes Dr. Ramsey and me uniquely qualified to continue it."

"Yes, I suppose it does. You will find we have strict protocols in place to prevent any risks we can anticipate and hopefully to help with those we can't," Mr. Rice said and turned his gaze to Jon. "Mr. Wilks, I would be lying if I said my curiosity about you and your very long life was not piqued. I would enjoy hearing your story when time permits."

"I'm sure it is far less interesting than you imagine," Jon said.

From what little she knew of Jon's story, Beth doubted that very much.

Mr. Rice shared a smile with Jon, curiosity glinting in his eyes before he returned his gaze to the group.

"Speaking of protocols," Beth said, "I know you wish for us to remain on campus as much as possible, but what is your policy on leave?"

Mr. Rice shifted in his chair, leaning toward the camera. "Just let Dr. Henri know what you require, and we will make any necessary arrangements." He sat back and once again laid his hands flat on top of the desk as if ready to push away and stand, not missing a beat as he continued. "I have given Dr. Henri leeway to provide for whatever needs you may have for your work, but please reach out to me again if you lack anything. Dr. Henri will show you to your living quarters and give you a tour of the facility as well as the areas in which you will be working. Welcome."

"Thank you," they said, nearly in unison, and the screen turned black.

He had answered Beth's question, but a small niggle of unease washed over her at it. She glanced at the others, who seemed unbothered, decided she was being overly critical, and let it go to follow Dr. Henri on his tour.

"We have prepared a room for each of you," Dr. Henri said, leading them down another long hallway. They had already toured the common areas of the facility, including the cafeteria for Luc. "There are two here and another two at the opposite end of the hall."

Beth thought she had been clear with her comments that she and Luc were romantically involved, but perhaps Dr. Henri wasn't taking any chances.

I'm glad our rooms are close together, Kate thought.

Luc and I only need one. Kate, perhaps you and Jon should have rooms beside one another, unless you would feel safer sharing. Beth said the last part with a question in her voice. She didn't want to make either of them uncomfortable if they chose to sleep together, but didn't want to suggest they were more than friends unless they had decided it themselves already.

Side by side will be just fine, Kate said, her cheeks flushed.

So, not that close yet, then, Beth thought, but kept it to herself.

"Thank you," she nodded to Dr. Henri, being certain her face remained neutral.

"It is quite late. Perhaps you would prefer to settle in until morning," Dr. Henri said, yawning.

"We would like to drop our things, but our condition confines us to the nighttime hours." Beth didn't think he needed to know they could still function adequately during the day, just in a more weakened state. "Dr. Giffard and I are accustomed to working from sunset until dawn. We would be happy to work with you in the evening hours to collaborate and then continue with our tasks overnight. That would allow for you to have some privacy for your work during the daylight hours before we join you again in the evening."

Dr. Henri nodded. "That would work nicely. Come then, and I will show you to your lab so you can get the lay of the land, so to speak, before you begin work. You can assess what's there and what else may be needed. Leave me a list of anything you might need for the morning." With that, he turned to reenter the hallway. "I'll show you to the other two rooms and then meet you in the commons when you've placed your things."

While they didn't anticipate trouble, the groups of rooms were far enough apart that they may or may not be able to hear one another if they shouted. Their telepathy worked just fine, though, which put them all at ease. They would do their best to keep that little tidbit of information from Dr. Henri and Mr. Rice.

Each room was identical, but the adjacent rooms were mirror images of one another. There was a queen-sized bed in the center with a low, dark wood headboard. The walls were a light gray, similar to those in the common areas. It felt clean to Beth, but sterile. The bed linens were white and neatly tucked under the mattresses at the edges. Two bedside tables, each with a single small drawer, were on either side of the bed and made of the same dark wood. There was a small closet complete with bathrobes and slippers, and a sleek modern desk with no drawers and a single rolling desk chair across from the foot of the bed. A dorm-sized refrigerator with a single-cup coffee maker on top sat next to the desk. On one side wall was an open door to a spacious bathroom with a tub shower and a large vanity. None of the rooms had windows. Beth supposed this was intended to keep the sunlight out, given their sensitivity, but it did make the rooms feel more claustrophobic, despite their size.

It only took seconds to store their few belongings, and they all made their way back to the commons. Dr. Henri seemed surprised to see them, and Beth thought perhaps it was their speed until he spoke. "I assumed only the two of you would be interested in viewing the lab space," he said, looking from Kate to Beth and back again, shifting his weight.

"We often work as a team. Jon and Luc will frequently join us in the lab," Beth said.

"Yes, yes, of course. It's this way," he said, and continued to the opposite side of the facility from their living quarters. After a few minutes' walk and several security doors, Dr. Henri stopped in front of a lab at the corner of two intersecting hallways. It was surrounded on two sides by glass. He scanned his badge at the doorway and held the door open for them all to enter. "This will be your space. My laboratory is in the next section over. I will give you a brief tour tomorrow evening if that is all right. I would like to get some rest before an early morning meeting."

"Certainly, thank you. Do you have access cards for us to make the trip here and back on our own?" Beth asked.

"Oh, yes, yes, forgive me." He reached into the pocket of his lab coat and produced two key cards with Kate and Beth's names printed on them. When Beth paused and glanced at Luc and Jon, Dr. Henri said, "I'm sorry, I didn't anticipate them requiring individual access to the laboratory. I didn't know they would be assisting you with your work outside of providing occasional samples. I'll request additional cards in the morning. Our IT department handles those requests, but only during the day."

"Not a problem. I hope you rest well, and we will see you after sunset tomorrow," Beth said.

Dr. Henri nodded awkwardly before turning to exit the lab, scurrying back in the direction of the living quarters.

Jon and Luc scanned the room as casually as possible, but Beth knew they were taking in the details.

Jon was the first to share his thoughts. *I don't see any cameras in here, but there are two in the hallway, one across from the door and the other halfway down the hall. I would assume there is another similarly placed in the second hallway, but I'll have to check when we leave. Do you see anything else, Luciano?*

No. There's no manual door lock, only the electronic one, Luc thought back.

So, no holing up in the lab if trouble comes, got it, Kate said. She and Beth had begun to walk around the laboratory, opening cabinet doors and assessing the available instrumentation. The lab was even better appointed than Kate's. The back of the lab was a clean room with independent ventilation enclosed by another pane of glass. Freezers with digital indicators showed temperature readings well below zero and adequate for the prolonged storage of viral cultures. On the remaining solid wall of the laboratory were two work stations complete with computers. Each had a small tent card in front of it with a login and temporary password, along with instructions to change the password.

Kate began assessing the supplies and reagents in the refrigerators while Beth continued through the cabinets, making mental notes of any additional items that seemed to be missing.

With the computing power and supplies we have here, we will be able to continue our own research while working on whatever we need to collaborate with Dr. Henri, Kate said.

Kate sounded like a kid in a candy store, and Beth shot her a grin. She shared her friend's joy. It was more than they had hoped for.

I'm betting they didn't put us in the room with all the glass by accident, Jon thought. *It'll make Beth and Kate easier to monitor.*

It seems a little paranoid, but I guess we'll get in the habit of turning our backs to the cameras with anything important, Kate thought back.

That's my girl, Jon thought, and then immediately backpedaled. *So to speak. Er, you know what I mean.*

Three smiling faces turned to look at him, but said nothing aloud.

"Kate, I'll log on to the computers and have you enter your password when I get to the right screen while you start on the instruments," Beth said, already sitting in front of the first screen and starting it up.

"I'll do the same on the analyzers" Kate said.

"I think we're good, gentlemen. You can head out if you like. Luc is probably hungry," Beth said.

"Again," Kate said. "He's a bottomless pit."

"You're just jealous that I can eat my weight and still keep this girlish figure," Luc taunted.

"Just don't torture me with ice cream, okay?" Kate said.

Luc chuckled in return. "Seriously, though, ladies, I would rather not leave you here alone on our first night. Let's settle in first."

Jon nodded his agreement.

"Okay, we won't be much longer. Once we're into the networked computers and I send Dr. Henri a list of supplies, we can go feed Luc," Beth said.

Luc's stomach growled loudly right on cue, causing another round of head shaking and laughter.

Beth glanced at each of them before continuing her login. She completed her entries and found the internal email setup that the card had mentioned. Since she was on the computer already, she looked over the available programs. Most had shortcuts already linked on the desktop, but there was no internet access. She searched the available programs and again found nothing. She pulled up the internet access window and saw that the New Dimension Analytics network was active, but was intranet only.

"That's odd," Beth said aloud.

"What's odd?" Kate stopped typing and looked at Beth.

"We don't have internet access."

"Did you check for a network? Maybe it just isn't connected."

"I did. There are only two, both password-protected, of course. The one this machine is logged into is intranet only."

"I'm sure it's just an oversight. We'll have to mention it to Dr. Henri tomorrow," Kate said.

Beth nodded. Kate was probably right, but it would be an easy way to keep them isolated. She pulled her phone from her pocket and looked at the signal; no bars. It was a huge facility with tons of concrete, far from the city. The signal was probably just weak, but she felt uneasy just the same.

CHAPTER THIRTEEN

BETH

As promised, the next day Dr. Henri met them at their lab just after sunset. The additional supplies they had requested were already in place in the laboratory, including two additional access cards for Luc and Jon. Still concerned about their safety, and with nothing else particularly interesting to do, both had joined Beth and Kate on their way to the lab. The two ladies greeted Dr. Henri at the lab door and entered, donning their lab coats as they went.

"Good evening," Dr. Henri greeted them, starting to give Kate an all-over inspection but then glancing at Luc and Jon before completing his appraisal. "I thought we could begin by catching each other up on our research to date so we know best how to continue."

Beth spoke quickly, not wanting to give Dr. Henri the chance to ask for their information first. "That sounds wonderful. Kate and I have been eager to hear what you have accomplished so far. During our work, we frequently mentioned how much a geneticist would be of help."

Beth knew it was blatantly stroking his ego, but it worked. A knowing smile spread across his face, and he jutted his chin forward a bit. Beth thought that if he had feathers, he would look like a rooster preparing to crow. He strutted to the end of the lab before turning to face them all. Kate settled into a desk chair, and Beth leaned against the edge of a lab bench, ankles crossed. Luc and Jon stood, arms crossed in front of their chests.

You two look like bodyguards. Relax. The message and Beth's grin prompted them both to find seats atop the lab benches across from Beth and Kate.

Dr. Henri clasped his hands behind his back and began, pacing slowly as he spoke. "I succeeded fairly quickly in mapping the viral RNA. There are several proteins similar to what we see in the normal human body, but they are, of course, altered. Because of their similarities, I believe I may have located one that could be causing the effects on muscle strength, and perhaps the one related to sun sensitivity. However, I have not been successful in creating a viable host for study. Injections into mice, rats, and guinea pigs have been uniformly fatal. My attempts at viral culture have also failed, thus prompting my request for additional samples. With those, I plan to attempt to inject rhesus monkeys. I postulate that the virus must require a host more similar to a human for complete incorporation into the host DNA."

I didn't think there could be bigger science nerds than the two of you, but I'm pretty sure we found one.

Kate muffled a laugh at Jon's thoughts and pretended to cough to cover it.

He didn't get nearly as far as we did, Kate thought, and Beth could feel pride rolling off of her.

"We encountered similar difficulties. We did find that the viral cultures require incubation in human or primate blood. We used human out of concerns that the sample could be contaminated by primate DNA and induce unwanted mutations," Beth said. Dr. Henri listened intently, raising his eyebrows and nodding vigorously at the latter statement. "We were able to successfully inoculate rhesus monkeys, although not all survived the change. The mapping of the viral RNA showed several segments that appeared to code for individual proteins, as you have discovered. We were also able to map the rhesus monkeys' DNA. We could locate the proteins and where they had been inserted, but lacked the genetic knowledge to easily identify what particular normal human genes were being affected."

Beth paused there to let Dr. Henri or Kate comment.

"I would be most pleased to review that data. I'm sure I could shed some light on the locations and possible effects of the viral proteins," Dr. Henri said.

Beth shifted to place her hands on the desktop at her sides. "And we would be most pleased to share that with you, but the records were destroyed along with Kate's lab," she said.

Kate nodded and then continued with the information they had agreed to share. "We were able to separate the unique segments, injecting rats with the individual segments and later short combinations of the segments. We were able to identify those needed for enhanced strength, sun sensitivity, bloodlust, and regeneration. We will remember the segments we identified when we are able to replicate them again, but there were additional segments that produced no identifiable effect in an infected host."

Beth knew that some of these had to code for their telepathic abilities, but that was a topic they had agreed not to discuss.

"And what vector did you use?" Dr. Henri asked.

"Adeno-associated virus," Kate answered.

"Adeno-associated virus, yes, yes," Dr. Henri mumbled to himself, continuing to slowly pace and rub his chin, excitement flashing in his eyes.

They had agreed not to provide additional information from there. The Adeno-associated virus had been enough to infect the mice, holding only the smaller segments. To infect Luc or a monkey already infected with the original Vampyre virus, however, they had to use the shell of the original Vampyre retrovirus as the vector, both to handle the size of the RNA and to get past the immune system. They had no way of knowing if it would be needed to infect a normal human host and would insist on considerably more testing before even suggesting such a trial.

When Dr. Henri had processed the information, he turned to face them again.

"Then our next steps should be to culture additional virus for study and inoculation of rhesus monkey hosts," Dr. Henri said.

Beth was pleased he was following the path they had intended. So far, their plan was working.

"We agree," she said. "Then we can repeat the mapping to get your insight on the insertion sites of the viral segments, as well as separating the segments to use individually. With your help, perhaps we can target the segments for insertion either in the same locations as the original virus or in other stable locations where they won't disrupt other critical genes."

"Dr. Henri, I must warn you about the strength of an infected rhesus," Kate said. "Underestimating the monkey's capabilities after infection is what resulted in my own infection Unless you intend to become a vampire, we need to take proper precautions, including a cage strong enough to hold a monkey twenty times its usual strength."

"I will have the keepers gather cages meeting your requirements."

"It would probably be best to place the rats in extremely durable cages as well. While we think we have narrowed down the segments responsible for the resulting strength of infected hosts, if we are wrong, we don't want to have vampiric rats running loose and infecting other animals and humans like the plague," Beth added.

Dr. Henri nodded in agreement. "It is a unique situation. I will have to see what cages the keepers have available to serve our needs. If we do not have adequate cages, we may have to limit our injections until I can round some up." With this, Dr. Henri clapped his hands together. "Splendid. We have a plan." He then turned to Jon. "Mr. Wilks, I hate to impose, but would it be at all possible for you to show me your abilities? I have read Dr. Ramsey's accounts, but it would be helpful for me to see them for myself."

"Certainly," Jon replied, rising from his seat on the table before running in a blur around the lab and appearing directly in front of Dr. Henri, who took a stumbling step backward.

Dr. Henri swallowed hard. Beth remembered the first time she saw Luc move as quickly in her own home and saw the same awe she had felt in Dr. Henri's face.

"And your strength?" he said, his voice cracking like a teenager.

Jon walked to the lab bench where Luc sat and lifted it with one hand, balancing Luc in the center before gently setting it back on the ground. "You don't have anything particularly heavy in here to lift."

Show off, Kate thought.

"No, I...I suppose we don't," Dr. Henri said after closing his gaping mouth.

"As for the regeneration..." Jon said, pretending to hesitate.

"Let me help with that," Beth said, just as they had planned. She held her hand out to Jon, who pulled a pocket knife from his jeans and handed it to her. She winced as she ran the blade over her palm and then held it up in front of Dr. Henri as blood dripped to the floor.

Sure, she would heal, but the cut still stung.

Dr. Henri's eyes widened even further than Beth would have thought possible as he watched the wound close and heal. He stepped forward and reached out to touch the now-pink line where the wound had been.

"Incredible," Dr. Henri said, dropping his hand and shaking his head slowly back and forth.

"I would prefer not to demonstrate the sun sensitivity," Jon said. "I will heal from a brief exposure, but it is quite painful." With that, Jon returned to his seat on the lab table, long legs stretched out in front of him.

"No, that won't be necessary. Thank you." It took Dr. Henri a few moments to recover from the display. Beth remembered how she'd felt when she first witnessed Luc's abilities and gave him time. It was a lot to take in.

"Dr. Henri, I will have Kate draw my blood and begin the cultures," Beth said.

"Yes, of course... Your blood? I thought we would be drawing Jon's blood for study as the source subject," Dr. Henri said.

Beth had anticipated this issue as well. If he had mapped the Vampyre virus from the original sample, he would compare it with a new sample from Jon. Beth and Kate had agreed that it was very possible that Jon's viral strain would be slightly different from Luc's. If they used Jon's blood now and Dr. Henri mapped it, the variations would be obvious to him as a geneticist. They couldn't risk his discovering that Luc was the real source subject. Beth had drawn Luc's blood as well as Jon's before coming to the facility so they could investigate this, but had hidden the samples.

"Jon is not particularly fond of needles, I'm afraid," she said. Jon gave Dr. Henri a convincing, chagrined look. "He will, of course, provide samples if necessary, but I was infected with the original source virus, so my blood will yield the same result, and I have no aversion to donating. Kate, would you mind?"

"Not at all," Kate said, going to a nearby cabinet and collecting the needed supplies. After the sample was collected with additional tubes for their research, the group followed Dr. Henri to the area where the animals were housed. Beth was pleased to see that they were in large, clean cages and appeared well-fed.

"Dr. Ramsey and Dr. Giffard, your keycards will allow you access here as well for whatever you may need," Dr. Henri added before continuing through another segment of the facility to his own lab. While they had passed a few other all-glass spaces, Dr. Henri's lab had a single narrow vertical window in the outside door, but the remaining walls were solid. Beth again suspected that they weren't entirely trusted.

Dr. Henri opened the door and held it for Kate and Beth.

Oh...my...God... Beth thought to Kate. The place was an absolute disaster. Beth couldn't imagine someone actually working in there. It wasn't just piles of papers and journals, but trash and food, even on surfaces that weren't suitable for food.

Beth tried to conceal her disgust, but Kate's face said it all. Her eyes darted from one surface to the next, wide. She had moved to the center of the room as she placed her hands in the pockets of her lab coat, as if to keep her body as far from the mess as possible.

Beth looked to Jon and Luc, who quickly schooled their expressions, but not before Beth saw their shock.

How can he work in this mess? Kate thought.

I have no idea. It looks like we will be doing any shared projects in our lab. And did you notice the lack of windows?

Yes, they want to keep an eye on us, don't they?

Beth knew that in addition to keeping their backs to the cameras, they would have to work on their private projects at vampire speed. Though she supposed it may be possible to slow down a recording enough that their actions could still be monitored.

Dr. Henri noticed Kate's expression. "I like to spread out a bit when I work."

Kate nodded but continued to take it all in as Dr. Henri placed the newly collected samples of Beth's blood in his refrigerator.

"If you don't mind, Kate and I would like to get comfortable in our space. We could inoculate the cultures there and split them between our two labs for incubation. The virus replicates quickly, so we should have adequate material to begin testing tomorrow evening," Beth said.

"That is fast," Dr. Henri said, his face brightening. "Very well. We'll work in your lab this evening."

On the walk back to their lab, Kate asked Dr. Henri for more information on his insights into the virus and what made him believe the particles functioned as they did. He was absorbed in the conversation, eager to share his thoughts, which allowed Beth and the men to focus on their surroundings.

The layout of this wing appears to mirror our own, with a main corridor connecting the two. I think the animal research labs are in the center of what essentially is a wide H or an I shape. Each end has four short hallways extending off the base, which appear to be lined by other labs, although we haven't been able to enter any of them, Beth thought.

I agree, Jon thought. *Dr. Henri's lab lies at the base of the second hallway from the left, the second lab down on the right. I see cameras midway in each of the hallways, as well as one at the corner of each joining hallway. The main corridor has a camera every forty feet or so. I didn't see any exits in the animal holding area or hallways. There is a keycard pad at each end of the main corridor as well as at each of the four hallways. But these keycard doors don't look like the one to your lab.*

No, instead of being all glass, they are more like Dr. Henri's, solid with a narrow vertical window, but these have the little wires running inside the glass, Luc thought.

Those are tough to punch through, but I can usually pull it off with a little effort, Jon commented.

When they had returned to the lab, they began setting up the cultures using Beth's blood. Kate assisted Dr. Henri with the first, and then both women moved at vampire speed to continue the process. Dr. Henri tried to focus on their movements at first, but then shook his head and focused on his own work. In just under an hour, all cultures had been set, properly labeled, and the supplies neatly returned to their shelves. Half of the samples were placed in the incubators in Kate and Beth's lab, and Dr. Henri rose with the second half in hand to return to his lab.

"That was impressive. With your help, we will have results for Mr. Rice and his daughter in no time," Dr. Henri said, beaming.

Beth returned his smile and said, "We certainly hope so. We'll see you tomorrow evening, Dr. Henri."

"Liam, please," he said.

"Liam," Beth said and nodded, eager to be free of him. She held the door for him as he left, hurrying down the hall to his lab.

Jon and Luc had been quiet throughout the process, but as soon as the door closed, Jon spoke up. "That is by far the weirdest dude I have ever met." His comment brought chuckles from the group.

"He is odd *and* messy," Beth said, cleaning up Dr. Henri's

workspace. "But from what I can tell so far, he is a good geneticist." *While Kate and I believe we can remember the setup we used for the v2 virus, his insight on the locations for insertion could help us understand why it worked and make me feel more confident replicating it.*

I agree, Kate answered.

The men settled into their own conversation, primarily focused on their favorite historical battles, several of which, it seemed, Luc had been involved in.

"I think we should start mapping my DNA," Beth said to Kate, walking to the refrigerator to retrieve her sample at vampire speed while pulling Jon's blood sample from her pocket. *We need the information to share with Dr. Henri, and it will be good cover for also mapping Jon's to see if there are differences. Let's set up a series of changing passwords on the laptops we brought along for the data. It won't slow down a good computer geek, but it would thwart Henri for a while if he goes snooping. We can say it's to protect the data as a failsafe if he questions it. Nothing we do should be without a password, shared with Henri over the network or not, so he won't suspect anything from the inconsistency.*

"I'll load the sample and enter the data into the instrument," Kate said, also beginning to move at vampire speed so that it would be difficult to tell what sample she was loading. She shifted her back to the hallway camera whenever possible, but not all the time, so as not to appear suspicious.

Beth sat at her computer and began building secure files for the data, only entering notes for the information they had shared with Dr. Henri into the network computer. She would type her notes for Jon's sample when results were available and save them to a flash drive she had brought with her, deleting the files from the hard drive as she went.

Again, it wouldn't be a perfect failsafe; a crafty hacker could retrieve almost anything, but if they didn't arouse any suspicions, there would be no reason for someone to look at their private laptops.

"These DNA sequencers are top of the line. I've never had my hands on this level of computing power," Kate said, sounding almost giddy. "We should have results in about five hours."

"It's 11:30 p.m. now, so roughly 4:30 a.m. We have time to kill," Beth said.

"I'm starving," Luc said.

Jon snorted. "What's new?"

"Why don't you two head to the cafeteria, and Kate and I can stay here and catch up. We haven't really had a chance to talk since we all got back together," Beth said.

"Girl time, got it," Jon responded as he rose from the table and winked at Kate, who immediately blushed. "Be back when we manage to fill the bottomless pit."

Luc shook his head as he rose, then walked to Beth, kissing her on the forehead. *Be safe.* Then the two left, laughing as they walked down the hall.

"Even a relationship idiot like me can see how you're looking at Jon. You're taken with him, aren't you?"

Kate's blush deepened. "You should have seen how gentle he was with me when I was healing. I guess I didn't expect a military guy to have a soft side. I thought at some point he might ask me out on an actual date, but obviously that's not happening anytime soon."

"It would be difficult here, but not impossible. You might just have to get a little creative."

"I'm not sure he shares my feelings, though. He was amazing when I was injured, but what if he just has a big heart and was helping a friend of Luciano's?"

"Luc knows him best, I could ask what he—"

"No!" Kate said, a half grin beneath her wide eyes as she waved her hands back and forth in front of her. "I would be mortified. Let's just let it play out and see what happens."

Beth chuckled, "Okay, okay, mum's the word. I saw him teaching you some self-defense moves when we arrived in Tampa."

"Yes, it's actually been very helpful. He told me that we all should learn how to better defend ourselves. He agrees with Luciano that, sooner or later, we'll have to face the Master and his supporters."

"He's probably right. I trained all my adult life for a career in medicine to help people. I never thought I would have to take a life. I hope it doesn't come to that, but defending myself against an attack is something I could do. Perhaps Jon *should* teach all of us."

"I'm sure he would. Fighting is kind of his thing."

"So I've heard," Beth said, remembering Luc's story from the night Jon was turned.

They chatted as they worked, settling into their usual banter. They filled each other in on the time they had been apart, including the continued blocks to Luc and Beth's relationship until they saw Luc and Jon approaching, talking in earnest as they strode down the hall.

"Aren't they cute?" Kate said.

"Yes, they are," Beth said, shooting a sideways glance toward Kate. "I've missed our talks."

Kate leaned over and bumped Beth's shoulder with her own. "Me too."

Chapter Fourteen

Liam

LIAM WAS NOT A morning person, but he was up at 7:00 a.m. and on his way to his lab with coffee in hand at 7:30 a.m. He'd had a hard time getting to sleep, and his eyes had popped open, ready for the day, much easier than usual. He was excited to see the progress of the cultures. If the ladies were right, and the blood stabilized the culture, they should have workable amounts of virus in a day or two.

He hurried to his lab door and patted down his pockets with his free hand, looking for his key card. He was forever misplacing it. He knew he should always put it in the same pocket when he left for the evening, but his thoughts were usually elsewhere.

He located it and scanned it for entry, hurrying toward the incubator and absentmindedly placing both the coffee and his badge on the open edge of a lab table.

Pulling on gloves, he removed the blood-filled flasks from the incubator and looked them over, not expecting to be able to see anything, although the blood did appear thinner. The ladies had told him the virus grew rapidly, but he didn't believe adequate amounts for sequencing could be obtained overnight. Still, his curiosity got the better of him. He returned all but one culture flask to the incubator and placed the remaining flask under a fume hood. This virus was only transmitted through direct blood exposure or saliva contamination of a wound, from what they knew, not airborne or by droplet, but being cautious wouldn't hurt anything.

He used a syringe to extract a portion of the sample and injected it into a closed filtration system to process, then returned the flask to the incubator.

While he waited, he booted up his computer and logged in. He had an email from Dr. Ramsey with a link to a shared drive. The drive required a password, which she had texted him early this morning before he woke. She was quite a stickler when it came to security. He supposed he couldn't blame her, given that she had run for her life to escape her enemies at least twice now.

He navigated to the drive and entered the password to view the file.

It was Dr. Ramsey's DNA, the entire genome already sequenced. Having these two around was going to be like the old folk tales of cobblers' elves that worked overnight to leave you finished gifts in the morning. He hoped they would agree to join him for his special project when Mr. Rice's daughter was cured. He could get used to this sort of teamwork. While Dr. Ramsey had seemed concerned about the weaponization of the virus during their video call with Mr. Rice, Liam hoped she could be persuaded. As with all new breakthroughs, it was a matter of time before someone used the virus for their own selfish endeavors. They may as well capitalize on it first.

He reviewed the data, comparing it to what he'd sequenced in the original samples Dr. Ramsey had provided. He ran a computer program he had tweaked himself to compare the similar regions between the two samples. Remarkably, there was an identical match in numerous regions. It clearly represented the same virus that had been incorporated into the same regions of each host's DNA. Jon had clearly been the one to infect Dr. Ramsey, as she had suggested.

Liam, grinning like a fool, set to examining the locations of the identical segments and the identifiable genes on either side of the insertion sites. If they could understand where the virus was having its effect, the altered genes could tell them what each segment did. He would love to examine the DNA of a human test subject before and after infection, but that would have to wait until later.

The sun had finally set, and Liam was waiting expectantly outside the ladies' lab. He was most pleased to see them walking toward him without their male companions several minutes later. While he was confident he was a far superior choice, it was much easier to put his plans in action without the two men watching.

He hurried forward to greet them in the hallway, unable to wait until they crossed the distance. He had seen pictures of the two on the internet from before they were turned, but they didn't hold a candle to the beauty he saw before him now. He didn't know if it was just seeing them in person or the effects of the virus, but they were positively stunning.

"Good morning, ladies. I received the genome sequencing file you completed last night. Excellent work. Dr. Ramsey, the virus in your blood is identical to that of Jon and is inserted in the same locations. But, I suppose you likely knew that already."

"We did, but having confirmation by a geneticist is reassuring," Dr. Ramsey said, following Dr. Giffard to the lab door and smiling warmly at him as she waited for entry. Her eyes were a brilliant blue and seemed to be constantly vigilant in scanning her surroundings. This woman was no buxom idiot like he usually dated, but he liked a challenge. She was already involved with a human. He could easily compete. "Kate and I have been eager to see which genes you may have been able to identify surrounding the insertion sites," she added.

Liam followed the women into the lab and seated himself at a workbench, placing his coffee cup on a small, neat stack of papers. Coffee sloshed from the mug, staining the papers immediately. He flicked the liquid from the table to the floor with his hand before wiping his fingers on his pants. The housekeeping staff would clean it up. It was their job, after all.

Liam spread the contents of his folder haphazardly over the bench, shuffling through until he found what he was after. Dr. Ramsey and Dr. Giffard pulled over chairs to sit beside him. "You see this first segment here?" he said, pointing to a particular region on the printed DNA map. "This is adjacent to regions that have been localized for skeletal muscle diseases. And the segment here," he pointed to another nearby region, "this area has been shown to be upregulated in professional athletes. We think it has something to do with increased oxygen affinity. So I think it is likely that this region is what allows for Jon's...and your increased speed and stamina."

Liam imagined that increased stamina would also make them excellent in bed. He had planned from the start to harness the abilities of this virus for himself. This bonus would be better for him than Viagra.

"Now," he said, shuffling papers again as Dr. Ramsey and Dr. Giffard looked on intently, waiting until he found the next pertinent document in his pile, "this segment is inserted near an area we know codes for a repair protein. I am guessing, an educated guess, mind you, that this segment may modify this protein, perhaps increasing its effect or increasing the production of the gene. I think this is the segment that allows for your regenerative abilities. This is the segment we should focus on first for aiding Mr. Rice's daughter." And the sooner they solved that little problem, the sooner he could move on to the real money-maker.

"My notes were destroyed," Kate said, "but I believe those match with what we saw in the rats we injected with the individual and combined segments. Is that region also associated with abnormalities seen in patients with rapid aging, like the disease progeria?"

Liam wondered what had caused her to consider injecting the limited segments into the rats after the intact virus had failed. She was indeed clever.

"Yes, very astute, Dr. Giffard. That region is here, just after the inserted viral segment."

Liam looked up to see Dr. Ramsey and Dr. Giffard exchanging a glance, but then both quickly returned their gazes to the paper in front of him. The ladies seemed very attuned to one another, and he wondered if that was a trait of all vampires or just because they had worked together for some time.

"What about the sun sensitivity or need for blood?" Dr. Ramsey asked, bringing him out of his thoughts.

"Well, that's another segment. Let me find it," Liam said, once again digging through his stack of papers. "Ah, here it is. This segment here is inserted in the middle of a gene that we know to be altered in patients with some forms of xeroderma pigmentosa, a disease associated with extreme sun sensitivity. It is possible this codes for some other protein and was inserted in the wrong location, disrupting the gene and resulting in your severe reactions to UV light. I think it would be quite interesting to inject this segment alone with attached nucleic acids to insert it in an innocuous area to see what changes in the infected host."

He saw both women nodding at his assertion. Liam was thrilled with the finding; it was possible he would unlock hidden abilities and even more lucrative applications for this virus.

"As for the need for blood, there is another segment...here, that is inserted in a region that codes for heme biosynthesis. Disruptions in the activity of this gene have been seen in patients with porphyria who cannot properly synthesize red blood cells. Damage to the base protein by this insertion may be the cause of your requirements for blood, but it doesn't explain the rapid metabolism of it for a food source."

Liam, as yet, had not seen any of them drink blood. While he didn't doubt that they did, he wondered why they ingested it in secret. Perhaps they had other physical changes to the ingestion, like in the movies, that they found unsettling. Glowing red eyes or distorted features would be disconcerting. He made a mental note to ask about this once they were more comfortable with one another.

"This makes so much sense. I am very curious to see what those regions were intended to code for," Kate said.

"Intended to code for? Yes, your thoughts and mine have taken us down a similar path, I believe. These proteins appear far too complex, even though the location insertions are errant, for me to assume this was a natural phenomenon. I believe this virus was created with the express intent for genetic manipulation. It would appear that some of the targets just missed their mark. Can you shed some light on this?"

Liam peered through the glasses on his nose and looked back and forth at the women. Their clever conclusion surprised him. He had been waiting to share these thoughts when they had finished discussing all the segments the viral RNA had coded for. Perhaps the good doctors knew more than they were sharing.

Dr. Giffard and Dr. Ramsey shared a glance before Dr. Ramsey spoke. "We have been told of a vampire legend, but we have no proof. The legend suggest an ancient but advanced civilization created this virus in an attempt to modify the genomes of villagers loyal to them, but with catastrophic results."

"Fascinating. How could that be possible? An alien race? No past civilization on record, even the Egyptians and Romans, had capabilities near this realm of sophistication. How could it be that we have no knowledge of them?"

"We don't have an answer to that, but if the legend is true, these segments were meant for something else but erroneously located in the test subject DNA," Kate said.

"How old are the oldest vampires?" Liam asked, rubbing his chin in thought.

"We are told millennia, but we don't really know," Dr. Ramsey answered. "The same vampires who fight to discourage our research seem to want to bury vampire history as well."

It was quite possible that the vampire race was purposefully created. Liam thought that perhaps long ago, an alien race had attempted to create superhuman soldiers as he and Mr. Rice hoped to. There must be a reason vampires didn't want this secret in the history books.

"Do you have any other insights?" Dr. Giffard asked.

"There is another segment in a region that codes for some neural transmitters, but we don't really understand their function as yet. Do you have an increased capacity for learning or any other abilities this could code for?"

Dr. Giffard glanced at Dr. Ramsey as if waiting for her to speak. While they worked as a team, Liam had noticed that Dr. Giffard had deferred to her on several occasions. They worked seamlessly together, but Dr. Ramsey was clearly the leader of the group. That meant that if he had any hope of bringing them into his other research, he would have to convince her first.

"No other abilities, per se," Dr. Ramsey responded, "but we are able to read with considerable speed and more quickly absorb and retain information."

"Perhaps that's it then," Liam said, wondering what he would be capable of with his already brilliant mind working overtime. He could be a god amongst men. They were able to live their lives on fast-forward compared to the rest of the world. The advantages of that alone were mind-boggling. After they completed testing and had safe mechanisms for delivery and placement, he would find out just how that felt.

"Well, I think that's all I have for now. There are additional short segments that are in regions of the human genome for which we as yet have little information. Until we can test them all, we won't know if they are significant or just additional DNA fragments mistakenly picked up as the virus has been transferred or mutated over the years. We often see drift in the makeup of a virus, as I'm sure you know. There has been quite a lot of information in this regard with SARS-CoV-2 and the recent COVID-19 pandemic."

"That is very possible," Kate added. "Some viruses are less than particular about their replication with 'sticky fingers' so to speak."

Liam appreciated Dr. Giffard's humor and her intelligence. He was eager to pick her brain about how she had so quickly created an AAV vector to insert only her chosen fragments into her rat hosts.

"I was amazed at the speed of viral replication in the blood cultures," Liam said. "There was already sufficient virus for me to begin amplification and mapping early this afternoon. You will find those results in the shared drive. Since we've located the individual fragments as they are incorporated into your DNA, I suggest we start synthesizing the individual fragments to begin animal experiments as soon as possible."

"I agree," Dr. Ramsey said. "It will be our task for tonight and tomorrow night, with hopes of replicating adequate amounts of at least the first two segments we discussed to be able to begin inoculating rats the following evening. We'll let you know how far we have progressed before we leave in the morning."

"Well, then, for my part, I will begin synthesis of another two fragments and hopefully we will have enough of at least four segments to inject rats the evening after next."

He couldn't hide his excitement as he left the lab. With the ladies here, he would be several steps ahead of where he was on his own in only two days. He would be on his way to more women than he could handle, and more wealth than he could hope to spend, in no time.

He made one final glance over his shoulder to look at Dr. Ramsey and Dr. Giffard. These two would be quite the prize.

CHAPTER FIFTEEN

LIAM

"LIAM, GOOD AFTERNOON. I'M hoping you have good news to report," Mr. Rice said from the wall-mounted monitor.

While Mr. Rice was cordial, Liam knew what was expected of him, and today, he was pleased to deliver.

"Excellent news, in fact," Liam said from his usual seat on the couch. "With the assistance of the good doctors, I have four segments of the viral DNA synthesized and ready for injection into rats this evening when the ladies wake." Liam shared his summary of their research so far, elaborating on his insights into the location of the DNA segments and their likely effects.

"Our findings so far lead me to the second discovery." Liam paused for effect.

"Yes, go on," Mr. Rice said impatiently.

"The actions and complexity of the viral RNA are far too extensive to be a natural occurrence. The virus was engineered."

As Liam expected, Mr. Rice sat back in his chair and blew out a breath.

"Engineered by who?"

"That was exactly my question." Liam shared the legend with Mr. Rice, who shook his head.

"Unbelievable. So we are dealing with a virus engineered millennia ago. All this time it has been right beneath our noses, and we didn't even know it existed."

Liam understood his disbelief. Had he not seen it with his own eyes, he wouldn't have believed it either.

"It is why the doctors refer to it as the Vampyre virus with a 'y' rather than an 'I', pronounced vam-peer-aye. It appears that was one of the first English spellings and pronunciations for the ancient tribe, which has been morphed into the current spelling through the years."

"This is all excellent news. Bringing the doctors in-house was a good call. You have made significant progress in only three days. I will expect an update on the infected rats as soon as you have results," Mr. Rice said.

Liam sat taller in his chair. It was about time Mr. Rice recognized the value of his work.

"I have never seen a creature undergo infection with the original virus. I believe injecting one with the full Vampyre virus would be beneficial for the study. I will attempt it this evening now that we have an unlimited supply of the original virus." He knew Dr. Giffard and Dr. Ramsey had already accomplished this in their research, but this was his lab, and he needed to see the process from beginning to end for himself, especially before attempting human trials.

"I agree that would be beneficial. I have reviewed the security footage of the women in action while working. Their speed is amazing. Even slowing the speed of the recording, they're blurred," Mr. Rice said.

"You should see it in person. It is quite unnerving but extremely helpful. We can accomplish the more laborious tasks in record time with all three of us working together." Liam wanted to be sure that Mr. Rice understood he was integral to the process. He was directing their progress and utilizing their talents like a maestro and his mini-orchestra.

"And your impression of the doctors?"

"In a nutshell, idealistic and philanthropic."

"Yes, that was my initial impression. It is disappointing, and I hold out little hope that they will willingly join us in our pursuits after my daughter is healed."

"While I agree, I will do everything I can to persuade them. There could be discoveries in the misplaced segments still to come. If I can convince them that the undiscovered benefits are substantial and a boon to human health, they may relent." While these discoveries were fine and good, Liam knew they were in addition to the monetary benefits, which would be significant. Every discovery could take him one step closer to his dreams, whether the ladies came along for the ride in the end or not.

"I appreciate your optimism, Liam, but my experience with this personality type tells me that chances are slim," Mr. Rice said. "It is possible, however, that with proper leverage we could make them useful for a time. What have you learned about their test subject and the human companion?"

"Not much, I'm afraid. The two did not accompany the doctors to their lab last evening, and the first evening, they were nearly silent unless answering direct questions," Liam said.

"I will ask the housekeeping staff to keep an eye on them during the day to see what they might be doing to occupy themselves, and have the footage from the hallway cameras reviewed. Try to assess the relationships there. If they're close enough, holding the men apart from them may be enough to keep them working for as long as we find them useful."

While it could be effective, Liam wasn't thrilled about the idea of forcing the doctors to work with him after their initial tasks were complete. These were highly intelligent women, and manipulating them would not be easy.

Dr. Ramsey had brought her human companion, but Dr. Giffard hadn't made a similar request. Perhaps his efforts toward her would be more effective. If he could gain her affections or at least her friendship, it should make her more likely to consider his proposal later. It certainly couldn't hurt, and he wouldn't mind getting closer to her in the least. Dr. Ramsey was clearly open to a relationship with a human; perhaps Dr. Giffard would be too.

"Studying Jon would certainly provide insight into his capabilities and what we may be able to instill in the soldiers you wish to create." Jon had mentioned his sensitivity to sunlight, which was the only aspect of their affliction Liam had not witnessed for himself. If it came to it, Liam would use their separation to study this further, along with their blood requirements to not only maintain their abilities but also to survive.

Liam heard a repeated beeping in the background and knew it was Mr. Rice's secretary vying for his attention.

"It seems our time is up. I will expect to hear from you soon," Mr. Rice said, and then the screen went black.

CHAPTER SIXTEEN

KATE

KATE RAISED HER ARMS above her and stretched, releasing a big yawn. She lifted the romance novel she had been reading before falling asleep from her chest, where it had fallen, and placed it on the nightstand. She wondered if Jon was waking up next door. She hesitated for a moment, not wanting to be too forward, and then decided to go for it.

Good evening, she thought to Jon and waited.

Good evening, Kate. I hope you slept well.

The reply from Jon had her sporting an ear-splitting grin. She was pleased both with his response and the fact that she heard nothing from Beth or Luciano, meaning she had focused her thoughts appropriately. The process was becoming easier and easier.

I did, thank you. Would you like to join me for breakfast in about fifteen minutes? With her vampire speed, showering and dressing took a fraction of the time it once did. Her shower time was only limited by the water pressure and the time it took to have enough water flow to finish the task.

Absolutely.

Jon's response had her up and moving in a fraction of a second. She made her bed at breakneck speed, stashing her romance novels in the closet. As she showered, she imagined him doing the same on the other side of the wall. Her body flushed with heat, and she turned down the water temperature. When she had brushed her teeth, dressed, and run a comb through her wet hair, she heard a knock at the door and tripped running to answer, sprawling in the center of the floor. She stood and brushed herself off, straightened her shirt, and walked at a more normal speed to the door. Knowing how sensitive a vampire's hearing was, she suppressed the "buggar" that she wanted to say and hoped she had muffled it in her thoughts.

Kate put on her sweetest smile and opened the door. Jon returned her smile, and if he had heard her fall, he didn't let on.

"Good morning," he said, his playful grin making her heart speed.

"Please, come in," Kate said, moving aside and sweeping her arm in toward the room. It made her think of the old vampire films where the owner of a place had to welcome a vampire before they could cross the threshold. They had so very many things wrong.

Kate walked to the refrigerator and opened the door. "Would you like O positive or A positive this morning?"

"Two A positive would be wonderful."

"You've got it," Kate said, retrieving the units and holding them out to Jon along with a pair of scissors for cutting the tubing.

"The breakfast of champions," Jon said, and lifted the units as if to toast her.

Kate grabbed a unit of O positive and settled on the corner of her bed, motioning for Jon to take the desk chair. "I'm pretty sure the makers of the cereal never imagined this."

Jon chuckled in response and began to drink from his unit. "I don't remember what food tasted like. I remember a few things that I liked or didn't by name, but the flavors that went with them are long gone. Steak, for example. I used to love a good steak. It's amazing how fast those memories faded." He shook his head and sighed.

"I agree. I still remember ice cream and long for it, but I find many of the foods I ate fairly regularly are starting to fade. Oh, but not chocolate. That one I still crave," Kate said as she looked, disappointed, at her bag of blood.

"When we are both free of our need for blood, I'll take you out for dinner and chocolate ice cream wherever you choose, just to celebrate."

"It's a date. Well, I mean not a date-date, but you know what I mean." Kate could feel the heat in her cheeks. She wouldn't mind it being a date, but didn't want to make Jon uncomfortable.

He laughed loudly. "I won't bring flowers," he said, ribbing her a little more. He was so easygoing. It made the awkwardness of the moment pass quickly, and in no time, they had each had their fill of blood. "I'll walk with you to the lab."

"What are you and Luciano planning to do for the night? I hate that you're both stuck here." Kate locked the door behind her as they left her room. Luciano and Beth weren't twenty feet away, coming toward them down the hall. Luciano greeted them, and Beth shot Kate a sly smile. Kate widened her eyes at Beth, trying to keep her from saying anything.

"I forgot to tell you. The night housekeeping manager gave me a job," Luciano said. *It could give us a better idea of security and the layout of the rest of the facility.* "It will be a good way to get to know a few people for our stay here and to keep myself busy." *And it couldn't hurt to have some friends here if things don't go as well as we hope.*

"I'm going to see if I can chat up one of the guards. Maybe there's something I can help with there. It's the only thing I'm really trained for," Jon said.

"How is your research progressing?" Luciano asked.

"More quickly than we had hoped," Beth answered. *We were able to map Jon's DNA last night while we worked. He has some minor differences in the incorporated viral DNA areas, but they look minimal. We are hopeful the differences are not significant enough to cause him not to respond to the v2.2 virus we will be making.* She linked her arm in Luciano's as they walked.

"We've synthesized segments for animal testing to begin tonight," Kate said. *We know the v2.1 virus was effective against our strain of the Vampyre virus, so we will be repeating what we know has worked first and then attempting to modify the process, making subtle changes to suit what we see in Jon's DNA.*

Kate paused to scan her key card, and Jon held the door for all of them to pass through. As they turned the last corner before the lab, they could see Dr. Henri there, reviewing something on the laptop he carried.

"Good evening," Dr. Henri said. He looked at Jon and Luciano. "Will you be joining us tonight?"

"No, we were just spending a few extra moments together before going our separate ways for the night," Luciano said.

Kate could clearly see the relief in Dr. Henri's face. He seemed intimidated by the two men. She could understand him being wary of Jon since he was a vampire. And she supposed that Luciano's strong build did make Dr. Henri look slight in comparison. Dr. Henri seemed to be a brilliant geneticist, but physically he wasn't impressive. Perhaps that was all it was.

"Ladies, we will leave you to your work," Luciano said, turning to Beth and placing a gentle kiss on her cheek before nodding toward Kate.

"Have a great day," Jon said as he turned. *And call if you need us.*

Beth badged into the lab and shrugged into her lab coat. Dr. Henri hurriedly dropped his things onto a lab bench, grabbed Kate's lab coat, and helped her into it, his hand lingering on the lapel as he made a show of straightening it for her.

"Did you have any success with the additional fragments today?" Beth asked.

"Yes, yes, they are ready for injection after packing in the AAV shell," Dr. Henri responded. "I was thinking that in addition to the individual segments, we should inject a rhesus with the full Vampyre virus. I haven't had an opportunity to study an infected subject and, while I have reviewed and appreciate your observations, Dr. Ramsey, I would like to make observations of my own."

Kate could understand that. She, too, had read all of Dr. Ramsey's notes that were submitted with the original blood and tissue samples from Luciano, but seeing and studying an infected monkey was something entirely different. It hadn't really hit home and made it all real until then. Although Dr. Henri had the opportunity to see Jon, Beth, and her in action, she hadn't had that opportunity until after infecting the little rhesus they had nicknamed Reed.

"With the rapid growth of the virus in our recent cultures, we have more than enough to spare," Beth said. "Let's prepare the samples." Then the work began again in earnest with all the doctors working at top speed, Beth and Kate clearly visible only to one another as they finished their tasks. In just over an hour, they had a completed rack of samples for injection, along with enough prepared syringes for dosing ten rats with each segment, forty in all, and a syringe of the original Vampyre virus.

"Dr. Henri—" Kate began.

"Liam, please," Dr. Henri interrupted, giving her a smile she found unsettling.

Boy, is he laying it on thick, she thought to Beth, who turned her back toward her as a sly grin began on her lips. Kate wanted to roll her eyes, but remembered the old bees and honey adage and decided to play along.

They gathered their supplies and headed to the housing area for the lab animals in the center of the research wing, Dr. Henri walking a little too close for Kate's comfort.

The keepers for the animals were surprisingly well prepared, and their injections proceeded uneventfully. The rhesus was also injected. Clearly, the monkey had not received the degree of interaction those in Kate's lab were used to, as he recoiled from them as they approached. The cage he was in was large enough for a human. If they had the cage already on hand, it made Kate wonder what animal they could possibly have used it for. Since the monkey easily evaded them in the large space, Dr. Henri asked for one of the handlers to assist in accomplishing the injection.

Kate went to the side of the cage afterward, cooing to the monkey and giving him small bites of fruit to calm him. "He reminds me of Reese when he first came to my lab," Kate said to Beth.

"He does look a bit like him." *Before the gray developed in his coat.*

Kate noticed Dr. Henri watching them, his brow furrowed.

"Reese was the second monkey injected in my lab. I was fond of him," she explained to Dr. Henri, who raised an eyebrow but said nothing.

"I have never observed the change, and there was limited information in your notes. What can I expect?" Dr. Henri asked, looking first at Beth and then at Kate.

"The reaction to the individual segments can be more unpredictable. Some of the rats will likely not survive. But the overall process is like infection with a flu-like illness followed by a period of unconsciousness, which usually lifts with complete transformation at sunset on the day after injection." Kate remembered watching Luciano's transformation after the v1 virus, and the feeling of waking up from her own as herself, but not quite. It had been unsettling. And to be more human, or at least free of the bloodlust and light sensitivity, she would have to go through it once again.

"I will arrange for cameras to be placed on the animals overnight just in case there are changes I would otherwise miss," Dr. Henri said.

"Kate and I will trade off monitoring them through the night, along with synthesizing additional fragments for injection the evening after tomorrow," Beth said. *That will be the last round we will have where we are certain of the outcome, since we've done it before.*

So we should enjoy the calm while it lasts, Kate thought back.

"I'll take over in the morning with a handler here assisting me. Please leave me notes on what segments might remain for synthesis, and I will begin working on those as well," Dr. Henri said and looked at the two doctors for agreement. "Very well, then. Kate, Elizabeth—" he began looking at them both in turn.

"I would prefer Dr. Ramsey, if you don't mind. No one refers to me as Elizabeth," Beth said.

Dr. Henri nodded, his eyes squinting at Beth before flashing a smile at Kate. "Until tomorrow," he said before he turned and left the lab.

Why do I feel like a juicy steak when he's around?

Kate's thought had Beth chuckling and hiding her face in the bend of her arm, pretending to stifle a cough.

I was going to say I felt like I needed a shower, but yours is better, Beth thought. *How can you stand for him to call you Kate? He hardly knows you.* The two ladies exited the animal lab and began their walk back to their lab.

He's a little creepy, but I've known worse. I thought it would be a good idea to play along and earn his trust. So he flirts a little and uses my first name, it's not that big of a deal to me, Kate thought.

Maybe, but I can't do it. I want to be certain he knows I am not in the least bit interested in anything more than a working relationship. I'm terrible at flirting anyway.

Kate smiled. She and her friend were much alike, but when it came to interacting with the opposite sex, Kate knew she had the upper hand. She wasn't a socialite by any means, but the interactions were obviously easier for her. *Well, if he goes too far, I'll shut him down. But until then, I don't see any harm in playing nice.*

Beth shrugged and continued down the hall alongside Kate. "I'll get what I need from our lab and then come back to start charts for each animal so you can begin work on the remaining segments. Having so many will help us to get a better idea of the survival rate for each segment as well as the response." *And with no one's life on the line this round, the research will be far more enjoyable.*

Kate nodded to both statements. "I'll come take over in a couple of hours." Beth was right, the research would be far less stressful without worrying about Luciano this time around. She was comfortably back in her wheelhouse with a geneticist for backup, working side by side with her best friend, and getting to know a man she may just be falling for. It seemed all of the pieces might finally be fitting together.

CHAPTER SEVENTEEN

LUC

LUC MOPPED THE LONG hallway that led to the holding area, part of the new duties for which he had volunteered. He hadn't been allowed to actually go into the holding area until tonight. They were shorthanded, and Mack, the overworked nighttime shift manager, had decided he was harmless enough.

He finished the hallway just as Mack came back down the hall to check his progress. He was a big man, dressed in the standard navy cargo pants and light blue, short-sleeved, button-up work shirt of the facility. It was a little snug over his belly. It protruded over his belt, which seemed to be losing its battle to hold up his pants. Mack's cheeks were red as he puffed up and down the hallways. He wasn't a great conversationalist, but he seemed fair and polite. His badge hung from his pocket on a cord that allowed him to scan it and let go for it to retract back to him. The picture on the badge from a few years earlier showed a man with more mouse brown hair above the same small, dark eyes.

"Good, good," he said. "I'll badge ya into the next hall. Mop it and clean the rooms that ain't locked like I showed ya. I'll be back in an hour or so to check in."

"Will do, Mack," Luc said as the door to the hallway opened. Luc wheeled his cart inside. "See you in an hour." He heard Mack's slow footsteps and puffing breath as he continued back down the hallway to badge out into the main corridor.

Luc looked at the hallway in front of him. It was lined by ten or so identical closed doors, a mirror image of the sleeping quarters wing he was assigned to. But beyond those were doors with vertical bars, much like cage doors.

Luc stood for a moment, listening carefully, and could hear both a steady heartbeat and breathing from one of the cells. It was too slow to be a vampire but faster than a human's usual rate.

He breathed in deeply. *No, not a vampire.* The scent of the person was musky and earthy. Whatever it was didn't smell like a human either. Luc had never encountered a supernatural creature apart from vampires and assumed there were no others. Perhaps he was wrong, or Mr. Rice was experimenting in more ways than they were aware of.

Not wanting to arouse suspicions if someone was watching, Luc began at the nearest door. He twisted the handle and found it open. The room was a carbon copy of his own and looked like it had been recently used, the bed linens rumpled. He straightened the bed and moved to the bathroom, giving it a quick cleaning and emptying the trash can into the bag on his cart. He continued on down the hall, finding all but three of the regular doors locked.

Whomever the heartbeat belonged to was in one of the cells on his left. The first two cells were empty and unlocked but appeared unused. He dusted them and swept, which was all they required. The contents of these rooms were similar to those in the regular rooms, but without the refrigerators or coffee makers, and the beds had no headboards or nightstands. Instead of a rolling desk chair, simple wooden chairs sat at each desk.

Luc approached the next cell on his right first, wanting to give whoever was in the cell on his left a chance to see him before he approached, hoping they would be calmer. He was already considering a number of reasons a person would be kept here in a cage and hoped the prisoner would be willing to talk.

The cell on the right was also empty, and Luc made quick work of the cleaning, being careful to remain at a normal human speed both for the prisoner behind him and any watching cameras. When he finished and turned to the cell behind him, he saw a lean, wiry man looking back at him. He wore light blue scrubs, his hair long and wavy to his shoulders, hanging loose. It looked clean but shaggy, like it had once been a more tailored cut that had grown out. It was nearly black and matched his thick beard, which also appeared a bit unkempt but clean. His eyes locked on Luc's, the color similar to his own brown, though the man's were sad and curious and followed him as he moved. His hands held the bars in front of him.

"Good evening," Luc said. "I'm sorry if I disturbed you. I was trying to be quiet in case anyone on the wing was sleeping." He rolled his cart back into the hallway and paused, hoping for an answer.

"You're new," the man said.

"Yes, I've only been here a few days. My name is Luciano."

Luc thought the man wasn't going to respond. He reached out mentally to see if he could get a read on him, but couldn't gather anything more than a vague sense of curiosity.

After a long pause, the man quietly said, "Ben."

"It's nice to meet you, Ben. I assume your door is locked, so I can't enter, but I would be happy to take your trash or anything else you would like to get rid of. Do you need any towels or toiletries?"

The man dropped his hands to his sides but maintained Luc's gaze. "The regular guy never asks me that; never speaks. He just skips my

cell and lets the handlers take care of it when they force themselves in."
With this, his gaze fell.

Luc's heart clenched at the word "handlers" and what it implied.

"If you would prefer I didn't bother you, I'll just—" Luc began,
hoping to draw him out.

"No, it's nice to speak with someone," he said.

Luc moved slowly and cautiously toward the door of his cell and
could see past him into his room. The walls were shredded in many
areas with long marks that were slightly curved in groups of four, each
spaced about an inch or an inch and a half apart. Similar marks were
on the desk. The bed was rumpled but looked otherwise intact. Either
the sheets had been changed, or whatever happened to the walls hadn't
affected the bed.

Ben followed Luc's gaze to the walls, but he didn't offer an
explanation. Luc felt sadness and longing before the man spoke again.

"I'll get you the trash. I don't have much. They don't give me much
of anything except food." With this, he walked to the bathroom.

Luc could see angry-looking red scars on the backs of Ben's arms
as he walked barefoot across the room, a smooth and lithe gait that
reminded Luc of a dancer he had known long ago.

He returned with the trash bag from the bathroom can, along with
a couple of towels slung over his shoulder, and handed them back
through the bars to Luc.

"Thank you," Luc said, taking the trash and handing Ben a couple
of fresh towels. "Let me get you a new bag, too." He rummaged in his
cart for a moment and then returned the bag to Ben. "Is there anything
else you need?"

A faint flicker of a smile played on Ben's lips. "No, you've been
kinder than anyone I have seen in a long time."

The words tugged at Luc's heart. What was Mr. Rice up to that entailed keeping men prisoner, and what could this man have done to be held and treated like this?

"Well, it's nice to meet you. I don't know if they will have me in your hallway tomorrow night. If they do, I'll be sure to say hello."

Ben nodded and then turned slowly from the cell door, retreating into his room. Luc cleaned the remaining cells and mopped the hallway. As he passed Ben's door on the way back, his hour nearly up, he heard a soft "Goodnight" from Ben's cell.

"Goodnight," Luc said just as quietly in return. He could hear Mack already puffing toward the hallway door and didn't want him to know about their conversation.

"Everything go okay?" Mack asked.

"Yes, easy enough," Luc said. He didn't know Mack well enough to risk asking about the prisoner, so unless Mack asked specifics, he wasn't going to mention him. Ben said the others just ignored him and kept working. Perhaps Mack would assume he would do the same. The policy here seemed to be to keep your head down and your mouth closed. He could do that.

"Good, good. You're faster than the regular guy. I might assign you here tomorrow night," Mack said.

"Sounds good. I like the quiet," Luc said. He wanted the duty but didn't want to sound too eager and raise suspicions. He wasn't sure what Ben was or why he was imprisoned, but he wanted a chance to find out. If Mr. Rice was collecting or experimenting on supernatural beings, they were all at risk.

"There's another hall just like this one on the other side. I'll take you there next."

Luc followed silently, happy to be alone with his thoughts. He couldn't wait to discuss this with Jon and get his take. The fact that Mr. Rice was keeping prisoners was something they all needed to know. Luc couldn't think of a scenario in which holding someone against their will could be anything but nefarious.

CHAPTER EIGHTEEN

JON

THE NIGHTTIME HOURS WITHOUT his friends dragged on, and Jon wandered the halls he had access to, trying to think of something to do. It was amazing how quickly Jon had become accustomed to having his friends around, especially Kate. He hadn't met anyone quite like her before. She was brilliant and just as gorgeous, but humble and kind. She and Beth were much alike, and he understood their friendship. But where Beth was stoic and on the quiet side, Kate was bubbly and quick to laugh. She was always stepping in with a quick-witted response to make him smile, and returning it with one just as warm that lit up the room. She was newly turned and had been through a lot, but there was no hint of bitterness; her thoughts were fixed on a bright future. He admired her determination to make her life and the world better while making the best of what she had. His early days as a vampire had been filled with anger at what had been taken from him, and he realized being with Kate had taken a little sting out of the old wounds.

Luciano had set off on his newly acquired housekeeping duties, but Jon, who had cleaned enough for a lifetime in the military, had no interest in it. He needed to find something that made use of his strengths. He checked in on Kate and Beth from time to time. He was concerned for their safety, and it gave him a good reason to be around, but he had to admit to himself that, more and more, it was just to have another chance to see Kate's smile.

His current path led him near the front of the building, where two guards were approaching the inner checkpoint doors. Seeing Jon, they paused and cautiously turned toward him.

"Evenin', no need to worry about me," he said. "I'm just wandering and trying to find something useful to do. The name's Jon." He held out his hand.

While one of the guards eyed him suspiciously, the other, younger with a carrot top red buzz cut and freckles, stretched out his hand. "Eric, pleased to meet you. What skills are you looking to offer?" he said as he shook Jon's hand firmly.

"Well, I'm a retired Marine, Precision Weapons Repairer, so helping with security and repairs would be right up my alley." His actual designation had been twenty-two foxtrot, Hercules Electronics Mechanic. But those missiles had been deactivated in the early 1970s, and the Military Occupational Specialty codes had all been changed. But twenty-one twelve in the new system was as close as he could get.

"That would require approval by Mr. Fields, head of security. They are very particular about the team here," the second guard said, looking at Jon through squinted eyes, his chin slightly raised. Considering Mr. Fields likely knew that Jon was a vampire in addition to an ex-Marine, he doubted he would pass muster.

"I kinda figured as much. I am pretty handy with repairs, weapons of course, but small engines and equipment as well as some appliances," Jon said, raising his hands palms up in a shrug.

"Got any experience with two-way radios?" Eric asked, getting an exasperated look from the second unnamed guard. "Well, you haven't been able to fix it," Eric said to him.

"Actually, yeah. How can I help?" Jon said.

"Well, the damn thing sounds like the drive-through speaker at McDonald's. I can't understand a word," Eric said.

"Common problem. I've worked on almost every military grade model made since the late 50s. I can't promise I can fix it, but I'd say there's a damn good chance."

"If I can't fix it, he can't fix it," guard number two said.

"So, how about a bet, Tom? He fixes it, you owe me twenty bucks. If not, same to you," Eric said, a goofy, wide grin on his face.

Tom, not about to back down, stuck out his hand. "Deal," he said.

Jon's face lit up. He was excited to have something to keep him busy and to have a chance to get to know one of the guards.

"C'mon, I'll show you the equipment room," Eric said, heading down one of the halls Jon didn't have access to and badging them through. As they entered the hallway, another guard exited a room to his left, pausing in the doorway to let them pass. Jon nodded a hello and glanced over the guard's shoulder to see an arsenal of weaponry. Tiered storage, just within his line of sight, held enough ordnance to supply a small army.

There was no way that kind of firepower would be needed to secure a lab, no matter what they had in it.

They continued down the corridor to the equipment room, where Jon began to work.

"You have got to be shittin' me," Tom said, sitting back from the table and crossing his arms in front of him, a sour look on his face. It had been just under fifteen minutes since Jon sat down with the broken two-way in hand, and he had purposefully moved slowly.

Eric laughed like it was the funniest thing he'd heard in ages and slapped his knee. He brought his own two-way radio to his mouth and said, "You owe me twenty bucks," which came through crystal clear on the one in Jon's hand.

Jon, trying hard not to humiliate Tom any further, stifled his chuckle behind his hand. Eric held out a fist, which Jon bumped in return.

"I'm going back to the guard station," Tom muttered after unceremoniously dropping a twenty-dollar bill on the parts-covered table in front of Eric.

"I'm going to see what else Jon can fix that you couldn't," Eric said.

"I feel kinda bad for the guy," Jon said after the door closed behind Tom.

"Don't. He would be rubbing it in our faces if you hadn't been able to fix that thing. He's always bragging how good he is at fixin' stuff, but look at all the broken crap in here," Eric said, waving his hand at the shelves on two sides of the windowless room. They were stacked with boxes of used parts and disorganized tools, with small pieces of equipment scattered in between. "So, I do have to get back, but if you're lookin' for more to do, how about I leave you here and you fix whatever you feel like working on? Maybe I can get Tom to agree to another twenty for everything you fix. I'll split it with you."

Jon laughed. "Thanks, man. I was starting to get a little stir crazy."

"Not a problem. I'll come back in a couple of hours and badge you out."

Jon didn't know if there was anything in that room that would be useful to his group if they had to make a break for it, but if nothing else, it would keep him sane until they could leave. And making nice with a guard could only be a positive. They were the ones who had access to everything, including the weapons, and they would have the best handle on everyone's comings and goings. While he hoped not to need it, learning as much as he could about the strengths and weaknesses of the facility's defenses was the best way he could help to cover all their asses. But the first order of business was organizing a few things so he could actually find what he needed in this room.

He set to work, happily whistling off-key.

CHAPTER NINETEEN

BETH

KATE AND BETH ENTERED the lab animal holding area to the deafening sound of shrieking. The handler was on duty and trying her best to calm the animals that were housed around the edges of the room, avoiding getting too close to those they had injected the night before. Beth glanced around at the animal cages and saw that much of the screaming was coming from the cage of the rhesus and a subset of the injected rats.

The handler followed Beth's gaze, a look of terror in her eyes. "Those animals are...not okay."

Beth understood. To the woman's human eyes, the rhesus and a few of the rats were likely a blur. "Where is Dr. Henri?" Beth shouted over the din. Kate was already headed to the cages, pouring blood into feeders for the affected animals who clawed at the feeders and then drank greedily. Beth crossed the room to be closer to the handler, making a point of moving slowly so she wouldn't scare her any further.

"He went to his lab a couple of hours ago and said not to do anything with the animals injected last night until he returned."

Beth nodded. "We'll take care of them. You worry about the rest." She offered her what she hoped was a reassuring smile. Beth wasn't sure if it was her actions or the fact that the shrieking continued to lessen as the animals fed, but the handler appeared calmer, if still shaken.

"What is she feeding them?" the handler asked.

Beth's forehead creased. There was no use in hiding the truth. No doubt if she chose to continue to work here after tonight, she would be required to feed them. "Blood. Their physiology has been changed by the experiments we're running, making their bodies require blood to survive."

To this, the woman only nodded, turned, and walked out of the room, probably to rewrite her resume.

Beth sighed. She hadn't considered the reactions of the animal keepers if the animals woke before they returned. Lesson learned.

Both Kate and Beth turned toward the door of the lab area as they heard it open. Dr. Henri hurried into the lab and looked up in surprise to see them. "Time got away from me. I didn't realize the sun had set until moments ago. How are our test subjects?"

"They awakened ravenous and agitated. I've offered them all blood, and those that have survived are feeding. They should return to their normal behavior when their thirst is slaked," Kate said.

Beth made her way around the cages, observing all of the animals involved in the experiment. "It seems we lost five rats in total, four from the probable speed and strength segment group and one from the probable regeneration group. We should save those animals for necropsy."

"I'm afraid I won't be of much help in that regard. Animal dissection is not one of my skills," Dr. Henri said, walking to the rhesus monkey's cage and staring wide-eyed as the monkey ran and jumped at vampire speed.

"Not a problem. I am quite familiar with rat anatomy," Beth said. "I am curious to see if the findings will match those of our original study."

"So, let's begin our observations," Kate said. "Dr. Henri, I suggest that since you have not been infected with any portion of the virus, you leave the handling of the animals to us."

"Of course," Dr. Henri said.

For the next two hours, they examined the rats and the rhesus methodically, recording their vitals, avidity for blood, strength and speed, regeneration after sustaining a small wound, and their reaction to UV light, with Kate and Beth being careful to be certain they controlled the light. While their experiments in Kate and Beth's lab had let them know what the segments coded for in regards to strength and regeneration, with Dr. Henri's input, they now better understood why. It was the same with the segments that coded for regeneration. All ten of the animals that they had injected with the segment they suspected was inserted incorrectly, resulting in their need for blood, did indeed require blood for food, refusing all else. So if the segment was not intended for this purpose, the fragment had been inserted in the wrong location and would need to be fixed. That bit would be next on the list after the first round of experiments was complete.

"These results are very similar to our own but with larger numbers," Kate said, withdrawing her hand from the clipboard she had been giving to Dr. Henri. Beth watched as his hand brushed hers and lingered longer than necessary before accepting it. She felt Kate's disgust and exchanged a glance with her when Dr. Henri had turned away. Kate was still playing nice. Beth didn't understand how she could put up with it, but she was a grown woman. She would have to choose when enough was enough for herself.

"It is fascinating!" Dr. Henri said. "Things are coming together much more quickly than I expected. I think our next step should be to map the DNA of the survivors and confirm the insertion sites. We could also try inoculating rats that have had a limb or tail amputated to see if the regeneration allows for regrowth, even if the infection does not occur before the injury. We need to look at the DNA of the rats that died to see if we can find anything that may have gone wrong on the genetic level."

Beth shared his excitement. They were finally going to start honing in on the regeneration aspect of the virus that had started her down this path to begin with. They would be one step closer to her goal.

"We have blood samples from each animal," Beth said. "We should check a titer on the samples of both living and dead rats to see if the ones that didn't survive had a viral load that was in some way different from the survivors. I would also be curious to see their baseline viral loads now that they have completed the transformation. As opposed to the original Vampyre virus, the AAV virus used to transfer the segments we chose should have cleared after the DNA was incorporated into the host cells. We don't want future treated patients to continue producing live virus that could be passed to others with potentially fatal results."

"Those are excellent suggestions. Let's split the samples and begin mapping," Dr. Henri said.

"Beth and I can run the titers on the blood samples tonight. It won't take us long," Kate said.

"Splendid. I'm going to retire for the evening unless you need me for something else." He paused with his suggestion, looking pointedly at Kate. Then he said, "I'll get your data from the shared drive and combine it with what I obtain tomorrow so we can review it together tomorrow evening."

"Dr. Henri—" Beth began.

"Liam," Dr. Henri insisted. And Beth attempted a friendly smile in return.

"I believe you should have a discussion with the handler as to which animals will require normal foodstuffs in normal or increased amounts, as well as those that require blood, unless you would rather we take care of those requiring blood. The handler was caught by surprise when the animals awoke," Beth said. She assumed the increased nutritional requirements would make sense to Dr. Henri since the animals would be expending more energy with rapid movement and regeneration. She just hoped he wouldn't begin to question Luc's voracious appetite because of it. Since Dr. Henri believed Luc was human, his dietary habits might not be on his radar.

Dr. Henri's forehead creased as he processed the information. "I suppose she was. Yes, I will handle it. Perhaps it would be best for her safety if the two of you managed those with blood requirements," he said. With that, he headed toward the back room.

Beth hoped the woman was still there. She hadn't seen her make an appearance in the main room since they had spoken.

That went well, Beth thought.

Except for the creepy touching, yes.

I noticed that. Perhaps you could arrange for Jon to kiss you when he's around, Beth suggested and couldn't help a small grin at Kate's blush, followed quickly by a look of exasperation.

Dr. Henri hurried back into the room on his way to the main door. He talked over his shoulder as he left, "It seems Ms. Morati will not be continuing with us. I'll make the appropriate arrangements. Goodnight."

"Goodnight," Beth and Kate said in unison.

"No surprise there," Beth said, and Kate chuckled.

"Poor girl."

"I suppose I'll begin the necropsies," Beth said.

"And I'll start on the sequencing samples and titers unless you need help," Kate said.

"Nope, this is right up my alley."

Since we're working with the data tomorrow and not sharing samples, should I begin synthesizing more of the v2 virus? The remaining segment samples from two days ago are finished, Kate thought.

Let me check all of the samples first, if you don't mind. Nothing had been moved for the last two days when I checked. I marked everything specifically so I could tell. If I don't see anything amiss today, then I think we should continue.

I think we should hold off on injecting ourselves for as long as possible. When we inject ourselves, Henri will see us changed, and they will most certainly start looking more closely at Luciano, Kate thought.

I agree. But we should have it at the ready. Hopefully, we will have time to make modifications for Jon, if needed, before we have to use it. I also hope that Dr. Henri and Mr. Rice are on the up and up. Maybe it's just me being overly suspicious, since we're all just beginning to get to know one another, but I can't help feeling both are holding something back.

Chapter Twenty

Liam

LIAM WAS EAGER FOR his weekly video call with Mr. Rice. He began speaking animatedly as soon as the call began, not even waiting for the usual niceties of a greeting. "The experiments with the rats have been going swimmingly. Our initial fears about the regeneration only working if a limb had been amputated or an injury sustained *after* receiving the virus proved unfounded. The viral segment seems to not only allow for regeneration of a recently injured area but can somehow read the amputee's DNA and regenerate anything that is missing."

A genuine smile, so unusual for Mr. Rice, spread across his face, urging Liam on.

"You've seen from the videos I sent that we watched as paralyzed rats regained use of their limbs. But not only that, digits as well as whole extremities regrew. The regeneration is sped along by feeding. A nutrient, protein, and calorie-dense diet lets the transformation occur at record speed. It has taken a few trials to find the right mix, but now we have it, and we're moving on to trials in larger mammals. We had some animal losses early on, but found in those animals what we think to be either subtle metabolic defects or a nutritional deficiency. Modifying the rats' diets prior to receiving the virus has solved the latter problem, but it is likely we will need to screen for common metabolic defects in humans to see if they would be candidates for therapy."

He excitedly rushed on to the next subject, Mr. Rice watching intently.

"The study of strength and speed is another matter entirely. A good number of the infected rats die. Those that survive require similar intense dietary changes, but on a sustained level, with additional nutrients needed after bursts of activity. The details regarding the non-viable specimens are still unclear. Perhaps the stress of the change is too much. Perhaps they would benefit from the injection of the regenerative genes first. We will attempt trials on that shortly. It could also be the viral material itself. It may be dissimilar enough from rat DNA that some cannot incorporate it. We have seen evidence in the mapping that some of the non-viable subjects had only partial incorporation of the material. Perhaps that proves lethal, or perhaps it is something we haven't yet considered."

"Let's return to the first topic for a moment," Mr. Rice said. "When will you be ready for human trials? We need to send our acquisition team to gather them."

"We're not ready for that yet. We need to attempt the transformation in larger mammals first to see what other adjustments might be needed. The dietary changes in a monkey may look much different from a rat, and there may be other pitfalls we haven't even encountered in the smaller mammals."

"How long do you estimate then?"

"We have plenty of the viral material and vector. We do need more rhesus, but I expect to have them tomorrow. If we don't run into anything unforeseen and our experiments go perfectly, we could have it in a week. But you realize even with our successes now, we can't predict the long-term effects until we have had months, if not years, of follow-up—"

"I'm not willing to wait that long. My daughter suffers every day. Take your week to find whatever kinks exist and then begin human trials. How many test subjects do you have waiting?" Mr. Rice said.

Liam had assumed this would be his reaction, but he wanted him to know the risks, which he would remind him of again and again, even if they were successful with the initial human trials. He did not want to be blamed for a failure, especially with Mr. Rice's daughter. Mr. Rice was not someone he would want as an enemy.

"We have five candidates for regeneration presently. I would like to test many more before we consider injecting your daughter. We could attempt to establish a phase one trial to legally gather consenting test subjects," Liam said, not hopeful Mr. Rice would consent, but trying nonetheless. He knew Dr. Giffard and Dr. Ramsey would be far more amenable to this path.

"That will take too long. After my daughter is whole again, we will follow the proper channels to bring this to market. Tell the acquisition team to retrieve whatever additional subjects you need for the study. The cities with VA hospitals in Florida, as well as the surrounding states, would be a good place to begin. The homeless populations there should provide what you require."

The call ended as abruptly as it had begun, leaving Liam alone with his thoughts. Using test subjects who had not consented made Liam nervous. If anyone found out about it, not only would he likely be prosecuted, but he would never be considered credible in the scientific community again. So, this had to work. If it did, he would never need to worry about working again anyway. He would be the bigwig calling the shots with others scurrying around to do his bidding and wondering if their performance was good enough. The thought brought a smile to his face.

Mr. Rice hadn't allowed him time to tell him of the rest of their work. But since their attempts at combining and placing the other fragments in areas that did not interfere with other genes had not yet provided usable results, he supposed it could wait.

He grabbed a fresh cup of coffee and headed for his lab.

Chapter Twenty-One

Beth

"OH MY GOD," BETH said, raising her hand to cover her mouth. "Do you see that?"

Kate nodded her head so vigorously that her loose ponytail whipped and bobbed from side to side. Dr. Henri stared wide-eyed and pushed his glasses further up his nose.

"It worked. It actually worked," Kate finally spoke as they all stood staring into the little rhesus monkey's cage.

"I wish Jon and Luc were here to see this," Beth said. The monkey lay on the side of the cage, still unconscious, having recovered from infection with the viral segment for regeneration in the wee hours of the morning, but not yet awake after the change. Beth and Kate had remained in the lab even though it was daylight to watch just for this purpose.

"This is the moment we will be remembered for. Our mark on the world," Dr. Henri said as they watched the end of the monkey's amputated arm start to elongate from the stump with a red-pink nub, which slowly continued to grow. It made it perhaps an inch and a half before it slowed, then stopped. "Well, perhaps not."

"He needs nourishment to continue, I would bet. Just like a vampire requires blood to consistently heal, I think this little monkey needs food," Beth said, and tapped her upper lip with her index finger, thinking. "I know we didn't give this monkey bloodlust, but I wonder if a blood transfusion would do any good. I mean, it shouldn't because the AAV virus we are using to infect them doesn't lyse the red blood cells like the Vampyre virus does, right?"

"No, I don't think it will be helpful, but we could try a little whole blood just to be sure," Kate said, leaving their side and returning in a flash with an aliquot of blood in a syringe. She opened the cage and felt for a vein, and then slowly injected the blood. For a monkey his size, it would equal about a unit of blood for a human. Then they watched and waited.

After a few moments, Beth spoke. "No, but it was worth a try."

"I suppose we'll have to wait until he wakes," Kate said. "I'll prepare the food he needs and leave it in the refrigerator so that when he does, it will be ready. Beth and I will be back just before sunset to watch for changes."

Beth rose a half an hour before sunset to shower and woke Luc with a gentle pat. "Luc, it's time to get up."

He rolled over and looked at his phone. "It's not time for sunset yet," he said.

"I know, but you will want to be up for this. Remember the rhesus we injected with the regeneration segment? Well, even though he remained unconscious this morning, his amputated arm began to regrow. It stopped after an inch or so, but we believe that as soon as we feed him, it will begin again. Kate and I want you and Jon to see it with us."

With that, Luc sat up quickly and headed for the bathroom. "Be out in five."

Kate, who had also roused Jon early, joined Beth and Luc in the hallway a few moments later, all of them arriving at the animal lab about ten minutes before sunset. Dr. Henri quickly joined them. With the food placed in the animal's cage ready for him when he woke and the camera rolling, the five stood around the cage watching. The red nub, Beth noted, hadn't changed since she had left that morning.

As they stood, waiting, Beth noticed Jon's eyes scanning the room, no doubt assessing the layout. Then she heard his voice in her head. *That handler is pretty lax with her keycard.*

Waiting for a few seconds so that her change in attention wouldn't be noticeable, Beth glanced to the area where the handler had been working. Her jacket with her keycard attached had been tossed over an empty cage near the edge of the room as she worked nearby. *I think she's a manager and might have higher clearance than the rest of us. I'll keep an eye out and see if it's a pattern,* Beth thought.

Have you been in the back room to see if there are additional exits? Jon thought, glancing toward the only other door in the area apart from the entrance.

Not in it, but by the entrance when the door was open. There's nothing else back there, Kate answered. They still only knew of one entrance, the main one that they had used to enter the facility. It would be heavily guarded. If they could find a less fortified exit, their chances at escape would improve, if ever needed.

Their attention was drawn back to the monkey as the sun set. The little animal began to wake and sat up, a little groggy at first, scratching himself and sniffing the air. His eyes zeroed in on the food, which he ran to and ate ravenously. When most of the food was gone, he finally noticed the five humans staring at him and began screeching loudly.

Kate cooed to the little monkey, and he began to settle, still making quiet, nervous vocalizations. He became calmer as they stood there watching.

Nothing happened for twenty minutes, then thirty. Dr. Henri had been fidgeting for the last fifteen minutes when the little monkey began gently rubbing his amputation site, then licking it.

Beth leaned in a little closer, and the nub of fresh tissue began to expand again, elongating slowly at first and then more rapidly until the red nub was only a couple of inches shorter than the intact arm, a bend in the middle which Beth assumed would be his elbow when his regeneration was complete. The monkey paced nervously, continuing to rub and lick the arm, but settled as the growth once again stopped.

Luc wrapped his arm around Beth's shoulder and hugged her. "You three did it. You really did it." Jon fist-bumped Kate, and Dr. Henri beamed at the group. The little monkey, who seemed exhausted, curled up in a corner of the cage and was quickly asleep.

Kate checked his vitals, during which he didn't even budge, and declared them normal. "The regeneration must be incredibly taxing. I'll prepare more food for when he wakes."

The monkey continued to sleep and wake about every four hours, ravenous, eating copious amounts of food and then collapsing again, exhausted. Not wanting to miss anything, Kate and Beth stayed through the daylight hours. After nearly twenty-four hours following this pattern and consuming an incredible number of calories, the rhesus had a hand, perfectly formed and identical to the non-amputated hand except for a lack of hair, which appeared to be growing in last. The little monkey seemed fascinated with the new hand and used it to climb around the cage as though he was testing it out. While they would need a longer observation period and additional testing to compare strength in the two limbs, it looked like a complete success.

She and Kate shared a glance and then a big hug. "Congratulations, my friend," Beth said. "Even if there are complications, this is a huge step forward."

"Congratulations. I'm overwhelmed thinking of what a difference this will make in so many lives." Kate's eyes began to fill with tears. "I wish my parents could have seen this."

Kate's words reminded Beth of her father, and she felt tears threaten as well. She hugged her friend again, patting her gently on the back until she pulled away, wiping her eyes. "I know your parents and my father would all be proud of us."

They stood, arm in arm, watching the little monkey play for a bit, relishing in the moment.

CHAPTER TWENTY-TWO

JON

THE EQUIPMENT ROOM HAD become a comfortable place for Jon. All of the tools were now organized, along with the spare parts, so he had been able to focus on the pieces of broken equipment one by one. He had amassed quite a stack of repaired items that were ready to return to service. While Tom hadn't fallen for the bet, Eric kept track of how much they would have made if he had.

Jon now sat at the work table in the center of the room, working on a spotlight that kept flickering on and off when used. It was just a matter of some loose connections, but it kept his hands busy and his mind occupied, while also allowing him to think.

He'd had another breakfast with Kate this evening. It was becoming routine and his favorite part of the day. Conversation was easy with her. One question would seem to start them talking, and they would comfortably wander from one topic to the next. He had never felt so at ease with a woman, but the ease turned to a welcome excitement whenever her hand or shoulder brushed his. He just wasn't sure she felt it, too.

It had been at least thirty years since he had asked anyone out. He had kept himself busy with security jobs and some detective work here and there, but was completely out of touch with the dating scene. He'd had a few flings with other vampires along the way, but none he was really interested in. He couldn't bring himself to consider human women. They were too fragile to risk a relationship with while mortal, and he wasn't about to try to turn any of them. For one, he wouldn't push this curse on another. He knew how that felt. And two, if he did turn one, he would feel bound to them. The thought of spending the rest of what could be an incredibly long, immortal life with one woman was terrifying. At least it had been until now.

Jon heard footsteps in the hall, followed by the turn of the knob, before Eric, a broad smile already on his face, opened the door. He walked over to Jon, a bottle of soda in hand, and sat down opposite him. The soda hissed as he popped open the top and took a big gulp. "How goes it?"

"Very well. That pile there is ready for action," Jon said and tilted his head to indicate several items at the end of the table.

"That looks like about a hundred bucks to split to me," Eric said, grinning again at their inside joke.

Jon chuckled and then said, "How did you end up here, working for Mr. Rice?"

That wiped the smile off of Eric's face, and he leaned forward with his forearms on the table. "That's a long story."

Jon gave him a minute, not wanting to be nosy but curious about his story. "Well, all I've got right now is time. I am all ears," Jon said.

Eric sighed deeply and drummed his fingers on the table, seeming to consider what to say before speaking. "I was a dumb kid, nineteen, and caught up with some drug and gun runners working across the Mexican border. I was high myself half the time. I had some close calls, and they were becoming more frequent as the jobs got bigger. One night, my boss was doing a deal with Rice that went sideways. Rice got pinned down, and I saw a chance to make a change. I helped him get out alive, and when we met up with his crew, I stayed with them. He kept me on, and when he opened this place, he offered me a job here. It paid the bills."

Jon nodded but continued to work, hoping it would better encourage Eric's sharing if he wasn't staring at him. "It sounds like a good career change."

"Yeah, I guess so." Eric tapped his fingers on the table. Jon could feel the vibrations from his leg shaking under the table, too. He was nervous. Jon thought a change of subject might help.

"I heard Tom ribbing you about a hot date last night. You got a girl?"

That brought a grin to Eric's face, and he relaxed a bit. "About a year ago, I met this cute researcher and started taking her out. She's a great lady, way too good for me. I never thought I would want to settle down, but she's got me thinking." The grin faded a little, and his brow furrowed.

Jon could tell there was more he was holding back. They had talked about a lot of things over the last couple of days, and he had never once felt like Eric was dodging a question.

"How 'bout you?" Eric asked.

Jon chuckled. "Too soon to tell. I met a researcher, too, and followed her here. The more I get to know her, the more I like her. I'm a little rusty on the dating scene, but I'm hoping when she's done with her work here, I'll get a chance."

Eric fidgeted in his chair. Jon could tell he wanted to say something. "What's up, man? You're like a cat on a hot tin roof."

Eric leaned forward and said in a near whisper, "Mr. Rice, he seems on the up and up. He's got some big and legit companies now, but he hasn't stopped funding them with the other shit he was into before. Just do what you've gotta do and get you and your girl outta here while you can still leave."

"What do you mean, while I can still leave? Rice said he didn't want us to come and go, not that we couldn't. Is he keeping you here?" The image of the fences with razor wire on both sides flitted through Jon's mind. Had they all walked into a trap?

"No, not me."

"Then who? What did we step in?" Jon was done with pussyfooting around. He needed answers.

Eric ran his hand through his hair and exhaled roughly. "My girl Nancy had dreams of using her work to really help people. She saw what Mr. Rice had to offer and jumped at the chance to work here. Only she didn't know what other stuff he was into. When she saw that he wanted to use her research for some bad shit, she confronted him." He took another swig of his soda, licked his lips, and then caught them between his teeth before leaning closer. Jon watched him now, holding his gaze so he knew he was listening. "Nance made me believe that there could be more for us. We're trying to find a way to make that happen...somewhere else." He cut off as they both heard footsteps outside the door before Tom walked in.

"Well, Mr. Fix It, so nice of you to join us," Eric said, sitting back and taking another drink of his soda.

"Hilarious, Eric. Did you come up with that nickname all by yourself?" Tom said.

"All joking aside. Thank you both for letting me work in here. It has made the nighttime hours a lot easier to pass," Jon said.

"As much time as Eric has been spending in here with you, you'd think you two were dating," Tom said.

"Are you jealous?" Eric asked.

"He's not my type," Jon said. He could tell Eric was still nervous despite his joking. He would play along and hope to get more answers the next time they were alone.

"Yeah, you have better taste. I've seen those two doctors you and the housekeeper guy hang out with, a couple of hotties. Which one is yours?" Tom asked.

"Neither. They're friends of mine, but Dr. Ramsey, the brunette, is spoken for," Jon said.

"So, do you have dibs on the blonde?" Tom asked.

Jon smiled. "Not yet, but I wouldn't mind it. She's as smart as she is beautiful."

"So I guess that means she's out of your league," Eric said with a mischievous grin.

"You're probably right," Jon said, wrinkling his brow and sighing.

"No, I'm kidding, man. If you like her, go for it. I felt the same about Nancy, but I'm sure glad I didn't let it keep me from asking her out," Eric said.

"Once we're done here, I'll make a move, but not until I can take her on a real date outside," Jon said, sharing a glance with Eric.

"I hear you," Eric said, and his forehead creased as he nodded.

"Where do you and Nancy like to go around here?" Jon asked. Eric bit his lip again and made a sideways glance at Tom. Jon could feel a wave of anxiety rolling off of him.

"We just hang out around here...she needs to be close to her work," Eric said, not meeting his gaze, and Jon saw Tom eying him. There was more to it than he was comfortable sharing in front of Tom. He would have to ask him the next time they were alone. Mr. Rice had asked that he and his friends not leave the facility while they were working here to keep the facility safe from discovery. Maybe Nancy was here with the same request. Or maybe it was more of a demand.

Luciano had shared with them his discovery of a prisoner named Ben while doing his janitorial work. It had them all wondering what he could have done to end up that way and what Mr. Rice was up to here besides vampire research. But they had agreed it wasn't time yet to ask questions and draw attention. Now it sounded like this Nancy was being kept here, too. Eric had said they should do what they needed to do and leave while they still could. Maybe leaving wasn't going to be as easy as they had hoped.

He needed to talk to Luciano.

Chapter Twenty-Three

Beth

THEY HAD ALL RETURNED to their rooms before dawn, having decided that it would be the safest way to have a discussion and not worry about looking oddly still for the cameras. Beth and Luc lay on the bed, Beth curling close into his side and taking his hand in hers.

You all know about me meeting the prisoner, Ben, and you know about the weapons Jon saw, but Jon also had a disturbing conversation with one of the guards tonight. Jon, will you share? Luc thought to the group.

I was talking with Eric. He's the young redheaded guard I told you about. He met Rice during a gun deal that went south and followed him here, Jon thought. *He says Rice is still in on it all, but now has the legit companies to cover. Eric's girl, Nancy, is one of the docs here. She came here for research and got on Rice's shit list. Now, it sounds like he won't let her leave. Eric said to finish what we have to and get out while we can. He's decent. I don't think he's lying.*

Beth's grip on Luc's hand tightened as she absorbed Jon's thoughts.

Do you think Dr. Henri knows? Luc thought.

Beth was wondering the same thing. While she didn't entirely trust him, he hadn't done anything suspicious. And if he didn't know about Mr. Rice's questionable dealings, he may be in the same danger that they were.

I don't know. We haven't talked about other employees, and he hasn't mentioned any other experiments. He's a scientist and focused on the research like we are. Surely he wouldn't knowingly be a part of holding prisoners, Kate thought.

Dr. Henri and Mr. Rice both mentioned not leaving unless it was necessary; maybe Nancy is just under the impression that she can't leave. Dr. Henri came out to meet us, and Mr. Rice said we could request leave, Beth added. They didn't know this woman. She could be completely unreliable and overreacting. Or perhaps she just wanted Eric's sympathy and made the story up. How would they know?

Have any of you met a Nancy? Jon asked.

No, they all thought in unison.

If Eric's on tomorrow night, do you think he would let us leave? Luc thought.

The guards don't work alone, so it wouldn't be just Eric. And it could put him in the middle of a shit storm after we left, Jon said.

And we haven't finished what we came here for. We need to at least finish making more v2. We are so close to perfecting the injection for regeneration, Kate said. She was right about that. While Beth wanted the regeneration research, too, the cure for the three of them was a must. And they needed to consider all they would leave behind.

Beth chimed in quickly so that Luc wouldn't stop her before she got it out. *If they are up to illegal research here, we need to know. We've given them the virus. If we just walk away, who will stop them from doing whatever they want to with it? And who will help Dr. Henri leave if he isn't in on it?* Beth had gotten him into this, too. She didn't want to leave him behind if he was innocent.

It was Luc's turn to squeeze her hand as he turned to look at her, propping himself up on one arm. *Beth, I understand that you would feel responsible, but if you are trapped here or worse, dead, you won't be helping anyone.*

I'm just saying we need more information before we turn and run, Beth thought. *See what other people you can get information from while you're working, Luc. And Jon can try to get a clearer picture from Eric. Maybe he knows if others come and go freely or if Dr. Henri has been involved in anything else. Meanwhile, Kate and I can look around and ask about Nancy and try to get a better feel for what Dr. Henri knows.*

What if we ask for leave? Jon thought. *Rice said we could.*

We're getting close on the regeneration vector. We'll know a lot more in a few days. And when we finish that, it will be a good time to ask for a break. We can say we want to celebrate with a little R & R, Kate offered.

Beth looked at Luc and raised her eyebrows in question.

How about we see what we can find, and if it takes until you finish your work, then we ask for leave even if we haven't found anything, Jon thought. *R & R sounds good.*

Beth thought it was reasonable. If they found something awful, they could reconsider, but at least it gave them time to hunt.

Deal, Beth thought.

Works for me, Kate said.

Beth could see in Luc's eyes that he wasn't happy about it, but he pulled her in close, nestling his chin in her hair and thought, *Deal.*

CHAPTER TWENTY-FOUR

BETH

BETH LOOKED AT THE four vials of v2.2 they had created, hidden amongst their other vials in the lab fridge, but not moved in their absence. They had started work well before sunset, eager to finish the last details before meeting with Dr. Henri. After all the work and discussions with him, they were certain it would work on them and now understood why their first efforts had failed. Correct placement of the genetic material was everything to avoid triggering a malfunction somewhere else.

After inspecting all the samples, Beth stood and closed the door to walk over to her computer. With their constant work on the regenerative animal experiments, they had not yet been able to begin synthesizing a new injection specific to Jon. But, with their recent insights, they didn't believe it was necessary for the injection to work. Both viruses seemed to have a single original source in their similarity, but Jon had clearly not been infected by the Master. His strain had been passed down a few times, gathering bits and pieces before being passed to him. They likely already had what they needed to remove the undesirable side effects from the Vampyre virus from the three of them, and they were making quick work of the process for regeneration.

True to their discussion a few nights back, Beth and Kate had asked the names of any of the staff they encountered, hoping Nancy would be among them, but they had no luck. They did learn that the handlers were on a rotating schedule and allowed to leave each weekend when they weren't assigned to the lab. Neither Beth nor Kate could think of a way to question Dr. Henri without tipping him off to what they knew, but hadn't seen anything suspicious in his recent behavior. Luc had been assigned to the same nightly janitorial rotation and had found nothing more. Jon had spoken with Eric, and he was adamant that Nancy was no longer allowed to leave the facility because she had questioned Mr. Rice's methods. So here they were, nearing the end of the animal phase of their regenerative research and ready to ask for leave.

Beth typed the last of her notes into the computer's shared drive and hit save. Over the last several days, they had perfected the delivery of the regeneration viral segments for the rhesus monkeys and four large pigs with no hiccups. They had even tweaked the nutritional support to make it a smoother process for the host. They had maximized their nutrition and supplements prior to injection, and then continued to support them through the change until the regeneration was complete. They had used TPN, a sort of intravenous feeding that allowed their regeneration to continue without them eating while they slept. The process still took up to twenty-four hours to complete, but the growth was steady and appeared less taxing.

Beth pushed back from her computer and turned to Kate, who was loading yet another round of samples. "How could we accrue patients for a phase one trial without drawing the attention of the Master? If the word gets out that we have a cure for amputees and spinal cord injuries, it will blow up in minutes."

"I agree," Kate said. "And even if we could stay under the radar, it would probably take months to get FDA approval, and how much could we hide about where it came from? Do you think Dr. Henri and Mr. Rice have discussed that?" *It would be so much easier if we knew we could trust Dr. Henri and come clean about our work for a cure. With his help, we could start producing a truly universal injection. He would have a better handle on what differences between segments are important versus just baggage along for the ride.*

Let's start by asking for leave and see if there are any red flags. Maybe it will give us an opening to ask more questions, Beth thought.

Beth was prepared with her thoughts, and Kate was on board, when Dr. Henri arrived. Excitement crackled all around him. He carried his open laptop and set it on a lab bench near them.

"Good evening," he said. "I have something you are going to want to see." With this, he turned the video screen toward them, which showed a man in a beaten-up wheelchair and dirty clothes. He was talking to himself and waving his arms, clearly not mentally sound, as Dr. Henri performed an examination showing that he had no movement or sensation in his legs. The video cut to the man lying on a small cot with an IV in place. Dr. Henri announced the details of the TPN he was infusing, as well as that he was injecting the patient with the AAV virus containing the segments for regeneration, to the camera.

Beth was immediately appalled. This man was clearly not able to provide legal consent, and beyond that, Dr. Henri was experimenting on a human subject. She saw the same emotions reflected on Kate's face as she stared at the screen.

The camera moved to fast forward as the fluids infused and the time lapsed at the bottom of the screen. At about ten hours from injection, the man's lower extremities began to twitch, at first small movements and then more pronounced. When he finally woke at nearly twenty-four hours from the injection, he was moving his legs voluntarily and thrashing about the bed, clearly confused. He sat up and then tried to stand, but while his legs moved under his control, they were not yet strong enough to carry his weight, and he collapsed to the floor.

Dr. Henri stopped the video feed and looked at the women, beaming, seeming oblivious to their scornful looks.

"What have you done? We don't have approval for human trials. You could have killed him," Beth said.

"And that man was clearly not capable of consent. How did you even find him?" Kate added, both women closing in on Dr. Henri and backing him up until he bumped into a lab bench, grabbing it with both hands.

"Ladies, you are getting caught in the details. Look at the success. We have created something that allowed a paralyzed man to walk again. I have a second video showing the regrowth of another man's leg. We have it," Dr. Henri said, his cheeks now red. He moved his hands to his hips, looking defensive.

"We wanted to discuss the possibilities and risks of applying for a phase one trial, but we need mountains of research yet before we would get approval. If word gets out that you've cured these men, the whole process will be put at risk for rejection or worse, imprisonment. You have broken nearly every ethical code we live by," Beth fired back, her voice a bit louder than she'd intended, her index finger poking him in the chest. He winced as she applied more pressure than she realized.

"These are vagrants, homeless men that no one has missed or will miss. Our secrets will be safe," Dr. Henri said, pushing Beth's hand aside only to be lifted from the ground by Kate, hands twisted in his lab coat and shirt as his feet dangled.

Beth couldn't believe what he was saying. *Could he possibly have believed that showing us his success would make us look past all of that?*

"How could they possibly be safe? Someone is going to notice even homeless men who regrow limbs. Someone has to have seen them before they—" Kate's eyes grew wide with the realization of what he truly meant. "You have no intentions of ever letting them leave to be discovered, do you?"

Beth had never seen her friend angry, but it was written in every cell of her body, her squinted eyes, her clenched fists as she shook Dr. Henri, every muscle of her body rigid, including her jaw as she glared at him with a look that could boil water. Beth knew her body mirrored Kate's. She was furious and wanted nothing more than to join Kate in her assault. The man they had worked with to bring this dream to fruition was about to throw it all away, or perhaps already had, harming and experimenting on innocent people in the process.

"We need to speak with Mr. Rice immediately," Beth said and turned to leave the lab. Surely, with his pharmaceutical holdings, he wouldn't allow this black mark on his company.

"Who do you think ordered the experiments?" Dr. Henri shot back, stopping Beth in her tracks as Kate's hand moved to his throat. "You are very naive," he choked out, holding on to Kate's outstretched arm.

Beth turned on her heel to face him, her hands balled into fists. *Careful, Beth,* she thought to herself. *With your strength, you could kill him with a single punch, and you would be no better than him.*

You need to let him go before you hurt him, Kate, Beth thought to her.

Kate held on for a moment longer before dropping Dr. Henri unceremoniously onto his ass. He rubbed his neck and scrambled to his feet as Kate stepped back. Beth could feel her struggling to keep her temper in check.

"You will regret that," he hissed at Kate. Beth hoped it was a hollow threat, but given what he'd revealed, she didn't think so.

"You need to stop this immediately. I won't be a part of it," Beth said, the rage barely contained in her voice.

"Oh, I think you will. It's a shame you can't see the opportunities here. But Mr. Rice has set measures in place to assure you will have time to consider your limited options," Dr. Henri threatened with squinted eyes. Spit sprayed from his lips as he spoke and backed toward the door to the lab.

"And what measures might those be?" Kate asked through clenched teeth, arms now crossed in front of her chest, hands squeezing her upper arms, as if to hold herself on the spot. "You can't possibly think there is anything that would make us stay here after this."

A sinking feeling began in the pit of Beth's stomach, thinking of the only reasons she could be persuaded to stay. She tried to reach out to Jon and Luc, shouting in her head, *We need to leave, now.* But there was no response.

Kate's eyes snapped to her, following her train of thought, and Beth could feel her fear matching her own. The smug look on Dr. Henri's face made her worry grow.

What if they have Jon and Luc?

Chapter Twenty-Five

Beth

BETH AND KATE FLEW out the door of the lab and down the corridors toward the residential wing, only to find their entry into their usual side of the wing blocked. They tried both badges, and when they didn't work, looked at one another as they reached out to Jon and Luc.

Jon, Luc, where are you? Beth thought.

Being lazy and lounging in bed until sunset, Jon thought. *What do you need?*

I'm in our room just down the hall. I didn't expect you back until sunrise, Luc replied.

Beth lowered her face into her hands, pretending to cry for the cameras that were undoubtedly watching them, so they wouldn't question her silence as she reached out to Jon and Luc again. Kate placed her hand on her shoulder as if to comfort her. They hadn't found cameras in their rooms, but they needed to be cautious.

Listen to me, but don't react yet. We need to get out of here. The door to our hallway in the residential wing is locked, and our keycards won't work. We just discovered Dr. Henri is conducting experiments on human subjects, and Mr. Rice is aware. He basically said he could make us stay here, and we thought of the two of you. Kate and I are going to try to get through this door.

But after several moments of punching, kicking, and tearing at the door, they discovered bars within the battered door still held.

Anyone could hear the two of you. I'm getting up to try my door, Jon thought. *Shit! It's locked too.*

Same here, Luc said.

No go on our end either, even with two of us, Beth thought, holding the rising panic at bay.

Son of a bitch! Jon said. *I'm going to bust through.*

Me too, Luc thought.

Luc, no, keep pretending to be human. If we're stuck here, their underestimating your abilities may work in our favor.

But we might be able to break this door down with all four of us, Kate thought.

Let Jon try first. If he can break free, then we'll have you do the same and join us, Luc. Don't reveal yourself just yet, Beth replied. She could feel Luc's fear and frustration, but he didn't argue.

It wouldn't have taken vampire senses to hear Jon demolishing his room in the next corridor. Beth and Kate waited, Beth pacing, until Jon thought back, *There are fucking bars in the walls, thick steel bars.* They continued to hear the sounds of demolition. *They're in all four walls. I can't budge them, not alone.*

Then there's no use in Luc trying and giving himself away, Beth thought.

Unless they still believe I am human and didn't put me in a barred room, Luc replied.

But we've been sharing that room, Luc. And they didn't know which ones we would choose when we got here. They will all be barred like Jon's.

The two ladies looked at one another, and Kate said, "What now?"

"Until we have a way out, we're stuck here," Beth both said aloud and through her thoughts to Jon and Luc, and then flinched at the expletives that followed from them both, but they knew they needed to regroup and figure it all out before making a move. For now, they were at the mercy of Dr. Henri and Mr. Rice.

Beth looked at Kate, thinking, her eyes just out of focus, and thought only to her, *We need to inject v2.2. Henri needs us; he as much as said so, and they have no intention of releasing us. We need to inject v2.2 before they take it from us.*

As much as it killed her to walk away knowing Luc was so close but out of reach, the two turned and went slowly back to the lab. Beth was fighting back the rage that filled her. If they wanted to force them to stay, fine, they would stay until they found the way out. And they *would* find a way out. Mr. Rice and Dr. Henri were overly confident, believing they were always the smartest people in the room, and people like that always made mistakes, with the biggest one usually being underestimating those they thought were beneath them.

As the two approached their lab, Dr. Henri met them in the hallway. Beth had no doubt he had been watching them on the video cameras. *Play along, Kate.*

"I'm pleased to see you've decided to return to the lab," Dr. Henri said, fidgeting when neither Kate nor Beth responded, keeping his distance but following them into the lab. "I know the circumstances are not ideal, but together we can still fulfill our goal of bringing the gift of regeneration to those who need it. And your involvement is the best way to assure it is done humanely and safely."

"The last part is likely true. But I'm not lifting a finger until you release Jon and Luc," Beth said, crossing her arms and cocking her hip. She had to stay, but she didn't have to help.

"Oh, I think you will. Your vampire and human are safe and comfortable right now, but that can change."

It took all of Beth's willpower to stop herself from killing him on the spot. Her body shook with the rage that filled her, amplified by the same emotions rolling off of Kate. She clenched her fists and closed her eyes until she had enough control to speak again. She had no choice but to cooperate...for now.

"What else have you not shared with us?" Beth said, trying to keep her voice calm. Dr. Henri's smug expression didn't do a thing to diminish her anger.

"Nothing regarding the regeneration experiments. I will be continuing human trials and would appreciate your *help* in tweaking the required supplements as well as the injection to make the process both faster and seamless. Mr. Rice would like to treat his daughter at the end of the month."

"I assume you have discussed the risks of injecting her so early in this process? Not to mention she is still a child," Beth said.

"We have no guarantees that the process won't have lasting effects on her future growth and development. We can't compare the changes in chronically ill or homeless men with those of a young girl," Kate added through clenched teeth.

"Yes, yes, I have informed him that it is a risky endeavor and have managed to talk him into waiting for three more weeks, but he is insistent. It seems her birthday is the last Friday of the month, and he wants nothing more than to give her back the use of her legs. I plan to go over the risks with him again and will stress the lack of information for such a young person with no long-term follow-up available, but I am doubtful it will dissuade him."

Beth wasn't satisfied with his response. There was absolutely no way she would be the one to inoculate a child at this stage, but she knew if Mr. Rice insisted, Dr. Henri would. Everything about these experiments rubbed her the wrong way, but Dr. Henri was right on one thing. Their involvement *would* be the best chance for all of the human subjects they intended to experiment on to be safe. Perhaps with their involvement they could somehow sabotage and slow the process. But how could they cause concerning outcomes without harming anyone? She and Kate would need to discuss it without Henri present.

"You said, 'in regard to the regeneration experiments.' What else have you been working on?" Beth asked.

"Mr. Rice has another pet project that we could use your help on," Dr. Henri said, and the glint in his eyes made Beth's skin crawl.

"Which is?" Kate asked when Dr. Henri didn't continue. She crossed her arms in front of her chest, mirroring Beth, irritation and anger rolling off of her.

"I will give you more details shortly. But for now, we continue our focus on the regeneration project," he said. "The time from injection to infection in the human subjects was nearly three days compared to eight hours in the rhesus. We need to shorten that. Patients will be anxious enough without waiting that long."

"Did you give them the same injection we gave the rhesus?" Kate asked.

"Yes," Dr. Henri said.

Kate looked to Beth for a nod before speaking, breathing out a deep sigh.

"The time difference is likely an effect of dosing. A rhesus weighs less than a tenth of the average man. We gave them small doses so as not to overwhelm their immune systems and kill them. We can up the dose, but we need to be cautious as we do. I would recommend no more than five times the rhesus dose to begin with to make sure a human's body can take the more rapid infection," Kate said.

"Kate and I can work on that tonight, keeping the volume to a minimum if possible," Beth added, turning her back on Dr. Henri and walking toward the nearest lab bench.

"Very well. I will expect test doses to be available in the morning, then. Just leave them on the designated shelf in your refrigerator, and I will retrieve them."

Neither Kate nor Beth responded, Beth ignoring him completely and Kate openly glaring at him. Dr. Henri let out an irritated "humph" and turned to walk away.

We need to check our samples and make sure nothing has been touched, Beth thought to Kate. She walked over to check the fridge. Everything was still as they had left it. Clearly, Dr. Henri didn't consider that they would be doing anything other than exactly what he demanded of them. *Pompous ass.*

We have about seven hours until sunrise, when we would typically return to our rooms for the day, Beth thought. *The v2.1 dose we gave Luc kicked in about two or three hours after I gave it to him. I think we should inject ourselves about an hour before sunrise to make sure we will be safely back in our room, after gathering some human food from the cafeteria on our way. We will be starving when we wake tomorrow evening, and we won't be able to hide our change in dietary needs. Dr. Henri will be alerted that we've worked on something else and may watch us even more closely. What can we do with the third dose for Jon until we can get to him?* Beth couldn't use her go-to under the trash can hiding space. The specimen had to be frozen since they had no way of knowing how soon they could get it to Jon.

Beth closed the door to the refrigerator after taking longer than usual to gather some reagents for their night's work. She was consumed with her thoughts, working through scenario after scenario as Kate began booting their instruments. They had to keep moving. Sitting and looking at one another but not talking was certain to raise suspicions.

Ice cream, Kate thought. It took a few seconds for Beth to realize she was suggesting a hiding place. *We hollow out part of a pint of ice cream and keep it in the refrigerator freezer in our room. Unless they really dig through what we're eating, they'll look right past it.*

I like it. Now we just have to decide how to slow down Henri.

CHAPTER TWENTY-SIX

BETH

As soon as they had left the lab and gathered food for the morning, Kate and Beth tried to return to their wing as usual, only to be met by the same battered but still locked door to their corridor. After each had attempted to use their badges, a male voice came over the speaker next to the keycard panel.

"Dr. Ramsey and Dr. Giffard, you have been reassigned to the main corridor on the opposite side of this wing. Dr. Giffard's belongings have been relocated, and your things will be brought over as soon as possible, Dr. Ramsey. You will find the doors to your new rooms open when you badge through the door behind you."

Beth and Kate exchanged a look before turning. Neither was surprised. They had assumed they would be moved and separated from the men.

They reached the end of the new corridor before Beth spoke. "Maybe we should stay in the same room. If we're together, they won't be able to separate the two of us without force." And while Beth wouldn't say it aloud, she didn't want to be alone. She also didn't want to risk Kate being harmed if they were apart. The two of them together was a more intimidating threat.

When they had settled in the new room and searched it for cameras, they sat to fill Jon and Luc in on what had happened.

We've been assigned to the same wing, but in the opposite corridor from the two of you, Beth thought.

We're going to share a room to prevent them from separating us, Kate added.

I can't wait to sink my teeth into Henri, Jon thought. *He and Rice need to pay for this.*

For now, we are all at risk. We need to keep ourselves in check until we have an escape plan, Luc thought, but Beth could feel Jon's temper continue to simmer. She hated to add fuel to that fire, but they needed to talk about v2.2.

We need to put ourselves in the best position to leave that we can, Beth thought. *That's why Kate and I have decided to inject ourselves with v2.2 now.*

Hell, no! Jon thought. *You'll be sitting ducks with neither of us there with you.*

Luc remained quiet, and Beth could feel his anxiety. She knew he was trying to let her explain before he countered. *If we have to escape during the day, we need to be ready. Figuring out how to get v2.2 to Jon to do the same will be our next order of business.*

So go one at a time, at least. That way, one of you can protect the other, Jon replied.

Beth looked at Kate before speaking again. *We discussed that. But the change will take all day. If we show up tomorrow with one of us eating and the other only drinking blood, they might lock us down and prevent the other from changing. They expect us to sleep through the day as usual. Doing it together tonight is our best chance.*

Another round of expletives erupted from Jon before Luc spoke. *I understand your reasoning, but I still don't like it.*

Neither was pleased, but they couldn't disagree with their logic.

Kate and Beth injected one another and prepared to sleep for the day. About an hour after sunset, they were already feeling the effects of the v2.2 virus with chills and fever. Beth couldn't remember much of her first change, pretty much nothing before she woke up, but she had watched Kate change and Luc change with v2.1. She was thankful in some way that she would likely be unconscious when Kate made the change. Watching her a second time and worrying would be painful, even though they knew now that their chances of success were high. Going through it herself would be easier.

"I feel like I've been hit by a truck," Kate said.

"The same one got me, too," Beth said. "Ugh. I think I'll be thankful when I pass out."

Kate bobbed her head slowly, looking like she might fall down before making it to the bed, but she didn't and crawled in next to Beth.

Luc, I don't think it will be long now. I love you, and I will let you know as soon as I'm awake. Beth could tell Kate was already unconscious at her side, breathing deeply.

I love you too. As soon as we get out of this place, I'll buy you a pizza, M&M's, a Diet Coke, and a hot tea.

You do know the way to my heart, Beth thought. She could tell he was trying to relieve his worry by joking.

I wish I could hold you through this like you did for me.

I know. I do too. But we'll be together again soon. And we will finally be the same. And it was true. The last barrier between them would be gone. They just had to fight their way out of Alcatraz to get on with their lives together. And for just a moment, Beth wondered if this was it. If they did break free of this place, maybe they should just keep running. Maybe they should just find a place at the edge of the world somewhere to be together and forget all of this. Maybe it was time to let it all go. She wanted to help the world, but at every turn, it risked the lives of those she cared about. Sending out samples of the virus had set this wheel in motion. Maybe thinking that she could stop it now or prevent someone from using it for evil was naive. But could she live with herself if she just let it go?

Sleep well. Beth heard Luc's thought, but unconsciousness took her before she could return the wish.

Beth woke before Kate, and for the first time in months, she couldn't tell what time it was or if it was day or night. She sat up enough to see the clock on the desk. It was 7:00 p.m. and just a few minutes before sunset. She lay back down and stretched her limbs. She didn't feel any different, but she did feel well. She rose slowly from the bed, trying not to disturb Kate.

Luc, I'm up.

Oh, thank God! Beth could feel the relief in his thoughts. *How do you feel?*

The same, actually, except...

Except what?

A broad smile spread across Beth's lips. *I'm starving.* She stifled a laugh as her stomach growled. She never thought she would be so thrilled to be hungry. She ran to the coffee maker at vampire speed, pleased to see her ability was still intact, and started a cup for Kate. She would make herself a cup of hot water and treat herself to a cup of Earl Grey afterward.

Opening the fridge, she nearly inhaled a breakfast sandwich, not bothering to heat it up. She moaned; the taste was so exquisite.

My goodness, what are you doing over there? It was Luc, probably feeling her excitement.

Oh my, I had forgotten how good food tastes. She continued to eat with fruit, milk, and cold cereal. It was three times what she would have eaten before she was turned, but she didn't feel stuffed. She held her newly made cup of tea under her nose and inhaled deeply before taking a sip. Her eyes closed in pure bliss. She had really missed this.

How is Kate? It was Luc again.

Beth had been so caught up in eating that she had forgotten for a moment that Kate hadn't yet awakened and felt more than a little guilty.

She's still asleep. Beth put down her cup of tea and was immediately at her bedside.

"Kate, can you hear me?" Beth said. "Kate?" She gently touched her shoulder and shook her. *She's not waking up, Luc.*

I'm sure it is just taking her a little longer. Don't worry.

Beth ran to grab Kate's coffee and returned to the bedside, sitting on the bed next to her. She knew Luc had to be right, but a small niggle of panic began to creep up her spine. *What if she doesn't wake up? What if I really lose her this time and have to go on without her?* She kept these thoughts to herself, trying to hold it together. She sat silently and listened to Kate's heart. It beat fast but steadily. It reassured her, and she tried to remain calm.

She needed to move. Moving always made her feel better, so she stood and began to pace, leaving Kate's coffee on her bedside table.

We both took the exact same dose. It worked for me, and we share the same strain of the virus. I just need to—

"Oh my God, did you make me coffee?" Kate said, sitting up slowly and reaching for the cup. She took the smell in deeply and then took a tentative drink. "Oh...yes." Tears began to well up in her eyes, and one escaped down her cheek.

"Kate, thank God you're awake," Beth said, but then saw her tears. "What's wrong?"

"I have never been so happy to have a cup of coffee in all my life."

Beth couldn't hold back the laughter, and Kate, who looked confused at first, then smiled and joined her.

She's okay, Luc. She's awake and drinking some repulsive smelling coffee.

It's about time. Jon's thoughts joined theirs. *I was starting to get nervous.*

You're next, Jon, just as soon as we can get to you, Kate thought. *We've hidden a dose of v2.2 for you.*

Thank you, ladies.

Kate must have been as ravenous as Beth because she devoured the remaining food items in the fridge, including a few bites from the pint of ice cream they had hollowed out for Jon's dose of the v2.2. A series of small moans escaped Kate's lips as she licked the ice cream from the spoon.

Should we give you a few moments alone with that ice cream? Beth thought to the group and could feel their amusement.

Yes, please, Kate thought back and smiled, a small drip of chocolate on her chin.

Alright, I'll hit the shower, and then we should head to the lab. We'll run a few tests to check our regenerative abilities and UV sensitivity when we can. But we need to get moving before someone comes looking for us, Beth thought.

Agreed. Just one more bite, Kate said.

You have no idea how much I would like to join you for that shower,

Luc said.

Beth felt her cheeks heat, wishing the same. *Soon. Very soon.*

LIAM

Just after sunset, Liam watched the monitors in the guards' office as Dr. Ramsey and Dr. Giffard left their room. Dr. Giffard sipped from a mug, which he assumed to contain coffee or tea by the color of the liquid, while Dr. Ramsey carried a bottle of water.

He scratched his chin as he watched. The guards had alerted him to their change in behavior when he woke this morning. Since they had been instructed to notify him of any unusual activity, they flagged the footage for him to review, which had shown the two retrieving food and drink from the cafeteria before retiring, something they had never done before. After a few moments of thought, he gestured to the guard beside him.

"Come with me. I would like to speak with the human prisoner."

Dr. Henri waited until Dr. Giffard and Dr. Ramsey had entered their lab to work before continuing on to Mr. Verde's room with the guard. When they arrived, the guard badged the door open to find Mr. Verde sitting in the desk chair, his elbows resting on the armrests. Liam grudgingly admitted that he was a handsome man with his lean muscles and dark features.

Liam stretched himself to his full height as he stood beside the guard and eyed Mr. Verde through the bottom of his glasses.

"Mr. Verde, I have a few questions for you," Liam said.

"I would feel more cooperative if my friends and I were not separated and confined," Mr. Verde replied.

"Answer my questions and perhaps we can work on that," Liam said. He had no intentions of releasing any of the vampires, but if Mr. Verde's responses were acceptable, they might be able to continue to allow him to work. Housekeeping was always short, and the supervisor had assured him his work was adequate. Mr. Rice would never allow him to leave the facility, but he could remain alive if he earned his keep.

"I assume you are quite familiar with the vampire diet?"

"Yes, of course. They only eat blood," Luciano said.

"I understand they require it to sustain themselves, but can they eat other foodstuffs if they want to?"

"No, only blood. Eating regular food makes them sick. They can't digest it."

Liam watched Luciano's face closely. He held his gaze with no indication that he was lying. If they truly could only drink blood, then the two doctors had been working on more than their shared projects. He knew Dr. Ramsey was searching for a cure for their bloodlust and sun sensitivity; that intention had been clear in her initial notes. If they had cured themselves of the bloodlust, what else had they changed? Surely they wouldn't give up all their abilities to be human again. Creating a new virus that would remove the unwanted viral particles would be nearly impossible, but halting the expression of certain proteins would be within reach. He didn't particularly care about them removing these weaknesses in themselves, although it might make them more difficult to dispose of when the time came. What he really wanted to know was if they had already attempted to make a Vampyre virus with those bits removed. It would be perfect for creating the enhanced soldiers Mr. Rice wanted.

But if they had created a new Vampyre virus, why had she not used it on Luciano?

Dr. Henri nodded slowly and rubbed his chin as he considered his next question. Dr. Ramsey had wanted Luciano here; she clearly cared for him in some way. Perhaps she didn't find him worthy of this gift, or wasn't fond of him enough to consider spending her long life with him. "Why has Dr. Ramsey not turned you?"

Luciano's face twitched in a fleeting grimace before he responded, which suggested to Liam that this might be a sore spot in their relationship. His suspicions may be right.

"She wants to help cure the vampires from their bloodlust and sun sensitivity, not make new ones. She is happy with me as a human." With this, Luciano crossed his arms in front of him and lowered his eyes. Luciano wasn't pleased about this decision. This was interesting and possibly something he could use to drive a wedge between them if he chose to.

"That's all for now," Liam said and turned to leave. He would have their lab and rooms searched for any signs of additional projects. If they were hiding more, he would find it.

"May I at least speak with my friends by phone if I can't see them?" Luciano asked, halting Laim's departure.

"I'm afraid that's not possible. But I assure you, as long as you remain cooperative, they won't be harmed." Liam nodded for the guard to close and lock the door behind him. As they continued down the hall, he spoke again. "Send one of the guards to collect Mr. Verde and escort him to his housekeeping shift, but be certain he doesn't encounter his friends along the way."

BETH

Dr. Henri entered their lab looking even more smug than usual. He eyed their drinks before he spoke.

Here it comes, Beth thought.

"Coffee and water today, along with more food and ice cream before you retired this morning. And you didn't collect your usual allotment of blood. I've never seen you eat or drink anything before, and Jon has consumed only blood since you arrived. You've been working on more than just our shared project," Dr. Henri said, watching them both intently as though he was trying to see what other things about them may have changed.

Beth and Kate had decided that hiding their nutritional needs with cameras all around would be impossible. They were right. Clearly, Dr. Henri had watched or been told of the footage from before their injections this morning.

"So have you," Beth threw back at him and then changed the subject, refusing to give him anything more. "I assume you found the new injections satisfactory?"

Dr. Henri paused, staring at Beth for several long seconds, which she returned. Kate, who stood watching them initially, turned, miscalculating where the edge of the lab bench was and hitting it hard with her hip.

"Buggar," she muttered.

Continuing to hold Beth's gaze, Dr. Henri continued. "I injected our next round of test subjects this afternoon after making the adjustments to their nutritional supplementation as you suggested in your notes. They are being continuously monitored, but there is no change as of yet."

Beth had expected a royal inquisition, and yet he was allowing her to redirect. *That was easier than I expected. Too easy.*

He must have something more important to him right now and doesn't want to start a fight, but I doubt he will let it go for long. He has to realize it means he can have it all minus the bad stuff. He's evil, but not stupid, Kate thought.

"We may need to up the dosage again, but these are humans; we need to be cautious," Kate said. "We can work on another round, bringing the dose up another twenty or twenty-five percent." If they could continue to pacify him with tiny dosage increases, it would slow the process and cause less harm.

"I presume you will want us to monitor the patients tonight so we can make any adjustments to their supplementation in real time?" Beth asked, thinking that when they were lucid, she might be able to get information from them about how they got here or how they were brought in as a possible means of escape.

"I have given you video access. You can monitor them remotely, and direct whatever changes need to be made or samples collected through the technicians caring for them. Just dial 341 if you need to speak with them. They have your number."

Beth's heart sank, but she didn't show it, wanting Dr. Henri to think it didn't matter to her either way. She gave a small nod and went to the computer to pull up the feed.

"Our continued work on the other segments has yielded additional fruit," Dr. Henri said. "The segment we suspected allowed for your extreme resistance to infection proved correct. We have tried infecting the treated rats with everything bacterial and viral, including rabies and tetanus, and their enhanced immunity has cleared them all. I would like for the two of you to begin creating an AAV virus with the genes for regeneration, strength, speed, and enhanced immunity combined right away."

"And the purpose of this virus?" Beth said.

"For use at Mr. Rice's discretion," Dr. Henri said.

"Is he planning to inject himself?" Beth asked. Though she believed it was far more likely he intended to create his own team of super soldiers, either to defend the facility and protect him, or worse, as an army for hire or sale.

"His plans are his own." Dr. Henri's look was smug, his nose raised even more than usual in arrogance. He knew something she didn't, and he was behaving like a child with a secret, taunting her.

It lit a fire in Beth's chest, and her hands went to her hips as she glared at him. "And you just do what he wants. Do you even pause to think about what you're doing anymore, or did you give up your morality when you took the job?" Beth bit back.

Her comments met with an irritated huff from Dr. Henri.

"I'm smart enough to know where my fortune lies. You can't be so naive as to have expected no one would try to take advantage of this. If it is going to happen anyway, wouldn't you rather be on this side of it?"

Beth agreed with him on the first part. She had thought about it often enough after her discussion with the Master many months ago. But the same could be said about nearly anything of substance. You develop computers, some users evolve into hackers to use them to steal or worse, kill. Guns used for hunting were also weapons of war. Someone was always willing to take something good and twist it into something horrible for some perceived or real advantage. If Mr. Rice was determined to turn this into a weapon, then Beth needed to be sure she harnessed the same for good. What was once an altruistic and idealistic endeavor was now a necessity. And now both the Master and Mr. Rice would want her and her friends dead for opposite reasons, but the same outcome.

"Oh, I was certainly naive. I trusted you," Beth said, seething at him while taking a step forward and pointing her finger at him. She had never been so close to striking another person in her entire life.

"We'll start working on it," Kate broke in, no doubt feeling Beth's rising anger, even if it hadn't been written all over her face. She stepped between them and repeated herself. "We'll start working on it."

"Thank you, Dr. Giffard," Dr. Henri said, sarcasm heavy in his voice. "We'll embark on the next round of injections with your virus as soon as it is complete."

"Wait, next round? What do you mean, 'next round'?" Beth demanded.

Dr. Henri pursed his lips, and his cheeks became flushed. He stood with his hand on the door to the lab. "I attempted to engineer and inject the segments for regeneration, speed, and strength unsuccessfully. But now we will move on—"

"What does 'unsuccessfully' mean? They didn't turn, or you killed people by carelessly exposing them to something you hadn't tested first?" Beth said.

"The subjects were non-viable," Dr. Henri said through clenched teeth, his eyes narrowed at Beth.

Beth knew she had to stop. She didn't want to know more and was painfully near losing her temper. Knowing would change nothing. She turned and walked toward the back of the lab, beginning to pull out reagents and samples to work. There was nothing else she could do. Even killing Dr. Henri wouldn't stop this. Mr. Rice would just find someone else as amoral and vile as this man to do his bidding.

Dr. Henri, seeing the discussion was over, turned and stomped out of the lab.

Kate moved to retrieve the materials they would need to begin more cultures. *There is no stopping him without killing him, Beth. We can only hope to slow him down and keep the people as safe as possible through the transition until we can get out of here.*

He has failed on his own, Beth replied. *We could refuse to help him synthesize the new virus. We're helping with the regeneration component. That was the deal.*

It may slow him down, but he's already threatened to harm Jon and Luc. And even if Mr. Rice has us all killed for resisting, he'll find someone else. He knows Dr. Henri needs the help of a virologist now. He's seen what's possible, and we have no way of getting to him.

Beth paused and slammed both palms flat against the counter in front of her, hanging her head. Kate stopped to watch her. Beth hated that Mr. Rice and Dr. Henri were forcing her participation in their horrible plans. They needed to do something unexpected, something that could give them the upper hand to get out of this mess.

She closed her eyes. *We have to complete our own version of this virus before allowing his experiments to be successful. When we leave, it goes with us, along with the injection for regeneration. I had hoped we could prevent someone from weaponizing the virus, but it has gone too far to pull back now. Even if we destroy this lab, how do we know the same isn't going on in Australia or Italy? And the government will no doubt get ahold of it eventually. All we can hope to do here is destroy what we can.*

She never wanted to make these choices. The fate of the world was on her shoulders, and she felt it.

After a prolonged exhale, Beth continued her thoughts to Kate.

When we get out of here, we send the regeneration injection to every pharmaceutical company we can. If we destroy what we can here, it will at least set Dr. Henri and Mr. Rice back until they can produce more. If all the pharmaceutical companies have the new virus, at least Mr. Rice can't monopolize it. There has to be someone amongst them who will use it for good. Then we decide what to do with the revamped full virus.

Beth raised her head to look at Kate, her friend returning her gaze with a weak smile.

"Let's get started," Kate said.

Chapter Twenty-Seven

Luc

THE NIGHTS HAD BECOME long. He and Beth spoke through their shared thoughts each night before dawn when she and Kate returned from the lab, but it wasn't enough. He missed seeing her face, kissing her, and holding her as they slept. They had all demanded to speak to one another in person, by phone or video, even written correspondence, but had been summarily refused with thinly veiled threats from Dr. Henri of what would happen if they didn't stop asking. Each was told merely that the others were safe as long as they cooperated. If it were not for the telepathy, he would surely have gone crazy with worry by now.

Luc had assumed they would keep him confined to his room as they had the first night. But, after his discussion with Dr. Henri, they apparently still believed he was a harmless human, because they had unlocked his door each night when the sun set and escorted him to the wing where he performed his duties. He had at first refused, once again demanding contact with Beth, but the guards had reminded him that her safety depended on his cooperation.

It was clear to Luc that with what he had already seen of the facility and their practices, they had no intentions of allowing him to leave alive. He was now both leverage and slave labor.

Mack made no mention of his imprisonment or that of his friends.

He was tight-lipped about anything not related to his housekeeping duties. And tonight, Mack led him to another corridor he had never been down. This door, however, was different. Rather than a barred door, it was solid and thick with what looked like heavy weather stripping on all sides.

Mack paused at the door, Luc pulling his cart close and waiting for Mack to badge him through. Mack reached into his back pocket and pulled out a pair of over-the-ear headphones. He handed them to Luc.

"You'll need to wear these the entire time you're in this section. Don't take them off. There is only one occupied cell. You can enter the cell, but don't let the occupant out of your sight, even when you are cleaning. If it should wander into the hallway, tell it to go back, or it'll get the usual," Mack said. "The other rooms probably just need to be dusted, but take a quick look and clean whatever needs cleaning."

"Okay. But, what is *it*?" Luc thought of Ben and wondered if it was some other non-human creature. He had not been handed ear protection to be near him. How many non-human creatures were out there in the world, and how many of them were being held here against their will? He had hoped to find potential allies; maybe this was another opportunity to do just that.

"I don't get that info," Mack said, "only orders about what to do if it doesn't behave."

Luc nodded. He wasn't about to try to get more information from Mack. Luc would have to see for himself.

"I'll be back to get you in thirty minutes. That should be plenty of time," Mack said.

Luc put the headphones on and continued through the door after Mack, another set of headphones covering his own ears, opened it.

Luc pushed his cart down the brightly lit hallway. He checked the rooms on his way, not seeing much of anything that needed attention. He continued down the hallway until he reached the only cell with a closed door. He peered in and saw a twenty-something woman seated on the bed. She was stunningly beautiful, slender, with coppery red hair that hung to her hips in ringlets. Her cheeks were dotted with freckles, and when she looked up at Luc, he could see riveting blue eyes the color of the summer sky. Her face was somber as she watched Luc stop at her door.

"I'm just here to clean. My name is Luciano." His words sounded oddly muffled in his head with the headphones in place. He wasn't sure if he was whispering or yelling, but she didn't flinch, so he assumed he wasn't too loud for her ears.

She mouthed something back to him. With the headphones on, he couldn't hear anything. "I'm sorry, with the headphones on, I can't hear anything. I don't know why they told me to wear them, do you?"

She nodded solemnly.

"Is it because of something you do?" Luc guessed. If she were the only person on the wing, the sound they were protecting him from either came from her or was used to detain her. But she seemed comfortable enough, making him think it was the former. And Mack had referred to her as 'it,' which meant they didn't see her as a person.

She nodded again.

"If I take these off so we can talk, will you promise not to harm me?" Luc was careful to keep his back to the camera as he spoke to her. She looked at him squarely, then dropped her eyes for a fraction of a second before returning her gaze to him. She was thinking it over, it seemed.

Luc considered his next move as she watched him. As a vampire, he was resistant to almost everything, but his hearing was very sensitive. It was possible that whatever sound this woman could make would be harmful to him. But if he wanted to gain an ally, and he did, he needed to give her the benefit of the doubt.

Pretending to adjust them, in case the cameras caught his actions, Luc reached up and slowly moved the right ear cover back so that the headphones still looked as though they covered his ear but left enough room for sound to reach him.

The woman cocked her head and held his gaze.

"I'm sorry, I couldn't hear you when you told me your name. I would like to begin again. My name is Luciano, what's yours?"

"Anteia," she said.

"Anteia, I am pleased to meet you. I'm supposed to clean your room for you." He waited for a response. "I'm going to open the door now, okay?" Still nothing, although he thought he saw her eyes narrow.

He turned the handle on the cell and began to open the door. An ear-splitting thrumming filled his head, making him lose his balance for a second before he righted himself. He paused for a moment, blinked, and then continued forward. The thrumming grew louder, and his head swam again, but only for a second before he regained his balance and moved forward.

Anteia's mouth was open, and her eyes were wide. Clearly, she expected a different effect.

"I'm just here to clean. I won't disturb you." Having acclimated to the sound, he continued into her room and headed for the bathroom. As he reached it, he looked back at her, fear now etched in her features, so he froze where he stood. "I'm not going to harm you. I don't know what they have done to you here, but I am captive just like you." The sound, which was beginning to make his head throb, stopped abruptly.

"What are you?" she said, her brows furrowed.

"If I tell you, can you keep it a secret?" Luc asked.

"No one here hears anything I say. They all wear the headphones because they're afraid of me."

It wasn't a yes, but from what he had seen, she was right, so he decided to come clean to gain her trust. "I am a vampire. But the staff here doesn't know that."

Her eyes grew wide like saucers and then returned to normal. "Vampires aren't real."

Luc chuckled. "Yeah, that's what most people think."

She looked at him curiously, then a very timid grin crossed her face before she looked away. There was something about her features that was off, but Luc couldn't quite put his finger on it. She was a beautiful young woman, but as she turned her head to look away from him, he thought he saw faint lines behind her ear, but couldn't tell what they were. She quickly pulled her hair forward to cover her neck. Perhaps she had scars that she didn't want seen. He could understand not wanting people to stare.

"I know you aren't human because my power didn't work on you."

"I heard it. What does it do to humans?"

"It makes them unconscious."

Luc smiled. "That could come in very handy," he said, and she grinned wider this time.

"So, what are you if you are not human?" Luc asked.

Her face immediately went blank, as though she was blocking all emotion from her features. She raised her chin, as if in defiance, but said nothing. Perhaps she thought he was trying to trick her.

He decided to let it go. His goal was to form alliances. She was clearly not human, but he wouldn't press for now. "It's okay if you don't want to share." He continued cleaning her room. He cleaned the bathroom shower and sink, but when he tried to rinse the cleaner away, he found that the shower and sink had no drain covers, and only a small trickle of water came from each. The toilet operated on some kind of vacuum system with no tank on the back to hold water for flushing. It was very odd.

"Does your bathroom normally have more water pressure?"

Anteia lowered her head and shook it slowly.

Luc didn't know what to make of it. Was it some kind of punishment? "Well, it is clean, at least. Is there anything else you need? Towels, maybe?" he offered.

"Why are you being nice to me?" she asked, meeting his gaze.

"Because I have no reason not to. Everyone deserves respect and decency."

She watched him carefully as he returned the trash and cleaning supplies to his cart.

As he placed his hands on the cart handle and prepared to leave, he heard her whisper, "Eanai." Luc looked at her and cocked his head slightly. "I am Eanai," Anteia repeated. He had no idea what that meant, but clearly it wasn't something she shared lightly.

"You're secret is safe with me, Anteia," he said. He offered her a smile as he closed the door to her cell, which she returned before he continued back down the hallway.

Chapter Twenty-Eight

Kate

That's two non-human prisoners now. We can't leave them here. Do you think there are more? Kate thought. She sat on the edge of the bed and stuffed a boiled egg into her mouth. They had all awakened in time to talk before continuing their work for the night. Luciano had told them about Anteia the morning before, and now that Kate had time to sleep on it, she felt strongly that their escape plan had to include freeing them.

I don't know. I've only seen about a fourth of the facility, Luc thought.

It would be great if we could spring everyone who wants to leave, but we have to focus on getting ourselves out first. If we try to do too much and get killed, it won't help anyone, Jon said.

Kate looked at Beth and could tell by her expression that she wasn't thrilled with his comments either. He was being practical, and Kate knew it. They had given it their all and couldn't even open a single door.

What if Luciano steals the night manager's keycard and lets Jon and us out? Kate thought. *All four of us together would surely be able to bust down a door.*

It's a risk. He would only get one shot, and then they would lock him down. And if the guards are watching the cameras, they would be on to him long before he could reach Jon's door and lock out the card. Even at vampire speed, he would have to stop at each door. The locks take a few seconds to kick over, Beth thought as she sat in the desk chair and took a sip of her English breakfast tea. *If he didn't make it, they would all know he was a vampire, too.*

He could hypnotize Mack into bringing him here to let me out, Jon thought.

They would see them letting you loose and lock it all down. And even if Luciano did get you out, they wouldn't let him get far enough to let us out. It would be the two of you beating on a door like we did, just from the other side. And they would never let Luciano out again, Kate thought.

It was so frustrating. She'd been running scenarios through her mind since they had been locked down, but nothing worked. She was a scientist, not an escape artist. She wished she'd spent less time reading romances and more time reading thrillers.

The two of us are one door away from the main corridor. If we took Dr. Henri's keycard and got through it, we could get close enough to the main entrance that they would send guards. Against two vampires, they are surely going to bring some of the guns Jon saw. The two of us are fast. We could get the guns away from them and use them to shoot through the door, Kate thought.

And risk the two of you being shot? Luciano said. *While most bullets won't kill you, they could if they have weapons large enough to obliterate your heart. Or they could hit you with enough bullets to bring you down while you regenerate and leave you vulnerable for whatever else they have that might kill you. A knife or sword to the neck to remove your head, and it's over. With only the two of you, untrained, against who knows how many guards, it is too dangerous. And even if you were successful, there are few weapons that would go through the steel beams in the doors and walls. You could kill them all and end up right back in the same situation.*

Kate knew he wasn't trying to be condescending, but she couldn't help feeling chastised. At least she was trying to come up with ideas. If he knew more, why wasn't he offering up a plan?

Beth had set her tea down on the desk beside her and was staring intently, taking it all in. But now she turned her gaze to Kate. *If Mr. Rice is keeping one employee here against their will, there may be others. I don't want anyone to be killed when we leave.*

I don't see that happening, Jon thought. *If it comes to them or us, and I think it will, some of them are going to die.*

Then we need a better plan...and help, Beth thought. *Eric's a guard, and he confided in Jon. He might have access to the security system. If he could unlock the doors long enough for us to get together, we would have a chance. Maybe Ben and Anteia could get out, too, if they knew when to be ready. If we can find a way to get to Eric, do you think he would help us?*

Only one way to find out, Jon said.

Kate and Beth were meticulous in the organization of their lab. It was one of the many reasons they worked so well together, being equally obsessive about the details and order of their supplies and samples. That's why it was so easy for Kate to tell, as she opened the lab refrigerator, that someone had rummaged through their lab while they'd slept. She wasn't terribly surprised; in fact, she was more surprised they hadn't done it before now. The samples they had both collected and created were all in the same order, but turned slightly from where they had left them. To any casual onlooker, it likely would look the same.

She and Beth had developed the system for just this purpose. But they had another system as well. A code was applied to each sample with numbers for the type of specimen, the species from which it was collected or intended for, and what it contained as to the viral type and DNA. This had allowed them to label the tubes with whatever they wanted to make them appear as one thing, while the vial contained something else entirely. It was why the samples that used the shell of the original Vampyre retrovirus were still there. They were labeled as drawn blood samples from the rhesus, but in fact contained blood merely as a support media for the virus that grew within them.

Everything is still here, but they've gone through them all.

I'm not surprised since they went through our room last night. I wonder where Dr. Henri is, though. I figured he would be here, irritated that his test subjects haven't changed yet. Beth flipped through the footage from the test subject cams from today on the computer to see what may be keeping him.

Dr. Henri was a hopelessly annoying man, but him being absent did make Kate nervous that something had gone wrong. She and Beth had loaded up the AAV virus, knowing it wouldn't work. The amount of DNA the AAV had to hold to incorporate all of the segments needed for regeneration, as well as strength and speed, was much too large for the little virus to handle. It quickly became unstable and wouldn't infect the host. Kate had worked with the AAV virus many times and knew this, but Dr. Henri didn't. It was a simple way to buy them more time. They would feign ignorance and pretend to evaluate it to solve the issue.

The segments would need to be packed into a retrovirus shell. She and Beth had grown and created one for their own infection, but that was another thing Dr. Henri didn't need to know.

I don't see anything amiss here, Beth thought. *The test subjects he injected are on a live feed, but well, as we expected.*

I do love it when a plan comes together. Maybe Henri is just running late. Oh, good, here he comes now. Kate couldn't keep the thick sarcasm from her thoughts.

Dr. Henri badged into the lab, his laptop under one arm and a rack of samples in the other. "What did you do to it?" he said.

Kate had expected his irritation and was ready for it, feigning surprise.

"Do to what?" Beth asked, revealing nothing in her expression.

"The new AAV virus, of course. None of the subjects has shown evidence of infection. I drew blood samples from each and examined a sample of one of the prepared viruses. There is no viable virus in the blood of the subjects, and the viral counts in the prepared vials for injection are incredibly low."

"Let me prepare a sample for the electron microscope, and we'll have a look when it's ready. Are those samples from the patients after injection?" Kate said.

"Yes, four hours afterward," Dr. Henri spat at her.

"So let's run a titer with our instruments to see what the viral load is and double-check your initial results, as well as a CBC to take a look at their white count over serial samples. If the AAV began to infect them, I would expect some kind of elevation in their white count and differential."

Dr. Henri's glare remained accusatory, but he didn't interfere. Kate hoped he was buying their reactions.

"I'll get the CBCs going," Beth said, rising from her chair, and they set to work. Dr. Henri constantly peered over their shoulders. After a couple of hours, they had their results.

"The CBCs don't suggest any evidence of recent infection, and the titers are all below the lower limits of the machine's ability to detect," Beth said, handing the paperwork to Dr. Henri.

"And here are the images on the electron microscope. I rushed the fixation a bit, so it may not be perfect. I have another sample brewing to get a better look later," Kate said while the image of the sample she had loaded slowly moved on the large monitor as they watched. After scanning for a few minutes, Kate ran across a cluster of AAV fragments, but they were broken, the capsids shattered, and their genetic material spilled. It was as she expected, but Dr. Henri didn't seem to have caught on.

"What would have caused them to destabilize and break that way?" Dr. Henri asked.

"Well, since this is from the sample we prepared for injection, it can't be the host immune system. And the process we used to synthesize it was exactly the same as for the smaller fragments," Kate said. Beth sat on one of the nearby lab benches, her arms crossed in front of her chest, watching them both intently. "We can try again tonight. Maybe we missed something."

Dr. Henri's eyes narrowed, clearly assessing Kate, probably trying to judge if she was telling him the truth or not.

Kate didn't budge, pleased to let him stew over it for as long as it took. They had bought themselves a day with this ruse, and she hoped it was much longer before he figured it out.

After a moment, though, he looked away as if thinking before he spoke. "The individual segments for regeneration alone were quite small, and the AAV virus performed perfectly. I injected additional subjects with it again last night. The segments for strength and speed are much larger and, combined with those for regeneration, make it even bigger. The original Vampyre virus is a retrovirus. Is it larger than the AAV?"

Damn, that didn't take as long as I had hoped, Kate said to Beth, her disappointment clear. "Yes, the AAV is considerably smaller."

"Perhaps it is too much. Maybe we need to package and give them separately. At some point, though, I would also like to give them the segment for immunity. Too many steps and injections increase the risk of something going wrong. We can start there, but we need a larger vector. How difficult would it be to use the original retrovirus?" Dr. Henri asked.

"Difficult," Kate said. As irritating as he was, he was quick. She would have to try to think of any way possible to make the process slow and painful without being obvious.

"But can it be done?" Dr. Henri asked.

"Yes, it can," Kate said. *Well, we won't have to worry about explaining the cultures we already set yesterday anymore.*

"Well, then, you have your work for the evening. Begin synthesizing the retrovirus to hold all three components, as well as creating human concentrations of the individual segments in an AAV shell."

Kate kept her face blank, but irritation bloomed within her. She was used to her own lab, her own rules, and creating her own plans. He was ordering them around like slaves. If it weren't for Jon and Luciano, she would happily tell him what he could do with the retrovirus.

"We can only do so much at one time. Even with our speed, it will take at least a couple of days, assuming all goes smoothly," Beth said.

Well done, Kate thought to Beth. They could complete the task much more quickly, but Dr. Henri didn't need to know that.

"Then you should start now," Dr. Henri quipped. "But there is one more matter to discuss before I let you get on with your work."

Kate leaned back in her chair and crossed her arms in front of her chest. Inside, she rolled her eyes, not wanting to imagine what else he would order them to do. She could feel the same frustration emanating from Beth as she raised her eyebrows at him.

"Mr. Rice would like details on whatever you created to free yourselves from the need for blood. You have kept your other abilities intact, it seems, as we have observed you moving normally. I assume it explains your rather healthy appetites, similar to what we have seen in the lab animals."

The glare from Beth would have curled Kate's toes if it had been leveled at her. Beth's eyes narrowed, and her speech was forced when she spoke. "We have provided you with plenty of the original virus and taught you how to continue to grow more. We are assisting with the projects as you have *requested*. The changes we have made to make our lives easier have nothing to do with you or Mr. Rice."

"Oh, but they do. If you have created something that can remove the negative effects of the virus, it could be very useful for our future endeavors. And for now, with the two of you tainted, Jon is the only natural source we have for study until we create another vampire on our own," Dr. Henri said and stood to leave. "I'll expect your report tomorrow," he threw over his shoulder as he exited the lab.

Beth sat with her hands on her thighs, her head lowered, and stared at the ground. Kate could feel her despair. "I should never have brought us here," Beth said.

"Beth, you couldn't have known any of this would happen, and we all agreed." Yes, things had gone south, but Beth didn't need to shoulder the blame. *So they find out what we've done to ourselves. They could eventually have gotten there on their own.*

Beth took in a deep, slow breath and then exhaled. *It's not that. Dr. Henri's focus for future Vampyre virus samples is shifting to Jon. If he looks at Jon's DNA, he will know he's not the real source patient. He knows we have made ourselves able to eat food, and we need a lot of it. The changes make us better able to pass as humans...*

Kate looked up at Beth with wide eyes, her forehead creased. *They'll wonder about Luc.*

Chapter Twenty-Nine

Jon

It was not his nature to patiently wait, and it was also not his nature to back down from a fight. But against his instincts, and how much he was itching for a good brawl to blow off steam, he was doing just that.

It had been two days since he had been locked in this damned room, and it was already very old. He lay on the bed, ankles crossed with his feet hanging off the end, fingers interlaced, staring at the freaking gray ceiling. It was mind-numbingly boring, not to mention the new "observations" Dr. Henri had started, along with restricting his blood intake. He would be in no danger of losing control with his current provisions, but it would keep him with a constant nagging hunger and irritable. His abilities were still in full force, but it wouldn't take much of a drain for him to exhaust his body's resources. He wished he had restocked his refrigerator before it happened, but he had been feeding with Kate each day, and they only restocked hers. It was even more torturous knowing that blood was right next door.

He hadn't laid eyes on any of his friends since the day they'd locked him up. Of course, when they were all in the same wing for the daytime hours, they could share their thoughts, but he couldn't physically hear them. Though Kate's voice in his head was a comfort, it wasn't the same as seeing her, and he missed their shared breakfasts.

He heard the beep of a key card being scanned down the hall and then the click and swoosh of the door as the lock released and it opened. He sat up and threw his legs over the bed, waiting to see who was coming. He had completely destroyed the walls of his room and the door, revealing a cage of solid steel many inches thick. The only room he had partially left intact was the bathroom, but only after punching through the walls in various places to be certain there were no weaknesses.

He heard footsteps in the hallway, the clicking of heels. A woman then.

As she came into view, he said, "Good evening, Nancy." She was tall for a woman, but still far shorter than he was at six feet four inches. She denied being ex-military but looked the part with her dark brown hair pulled tightly back from her face. She had come each day since the lockdown and hadn't worn make-up; she didn't need it.

Her white lab coat was neatly pressed, and her dress was impeccable. Despite her severe appearance, she had warm, soft green eyes. Jon could only catch the occasional thought from her, but he got a good read on her feelings, and there was no animosity toward him. She had been assigned by Dr. Henri, most certainly to shield him from Jon's anger, but also as an uninvolved third party. Jon, taking a hint from Luciano, had tried to play nice and discovered in one of their previous conversations that this Nancy was also Eric's Nancy. It was another reason to be on his best behavior.

"Good evening, Jon. How are you doing?"

He was pretty sure those were worry lines around her eyes. She was also trapped here, and the anxiety would take its toll.

"I'd be better with more to eat and a jog around the wing. I'm going to lose all of my pleasing curves." Yes, it was flirting, and no, he didn't mean it, but perhaps it would break the ice.

Nancy held out the cooler she had brought with her the last two evenings, her lips pulled into a half frown, and she raised her shoulders. He understood. It was out of her control. She opened the cooler and slipped the unit through the bars, dropping it as Jon approached at full speed, catching it before it hit the floor.

"Thanks," he said, popping off the end of the tubing and sucking on it like a straw.

Nancy watched him for a moment before turning to gather a chair from where she had left it the night before in the hallway. She picked up the clipboard and flipped a couple of pages.

"I have more questions for you tonight," she said.

"You mean Dr. Henri has more questions for me."

Nancy didn't verbalize an answer but smiled apologetically and continued. For the third night in a row, the litany of questions were all about his abilities, how he was turned, what he knew of other vampires, and the virus that infected him.

Jon answered and continued to answer all of them, although he didn't tell her any more than he wanted her to know. He found her tell quickly, all the years of reading people paying off. She squinted her eyes ever so slightly when she questioned one of his answers. And she exhaled more loudly than usual.

After he had answered nearly an hour's worth of questions, he walked away from the front of his cell and clasped his hands behind his back, looking away from her. How much information would she share with him?

He turned to face her again and met her eyes, staring intently at him. "Nancy, why are you here?"

"To learn more about you and assess your abilities," she said.

"No, I don't mean here in front of my prison cell," he said, to which Nancy grimaced. Good, she didn't want him in here either. "I mean, here at this place? You seem like a good person, nothing like Dr. Henri or Mr. Rice. Why are you here?" Jon repeated his question, not revealing the little Eric had shared with him.

"I came here because the research Mr. Rice was funding was groundbreaking. There is nowhere else in the country where scientists could have the freedom to experiment with the latest technology and a nearly endless budget. I saw it as an opportunity to do pure research without all the hurdles of the bureaucracy and budget limitations of a government or state-funded laboratory."

She had been idealistic, and Jon could both feel and see the effects of her lost hope.

"Along the way, I saw a few things I questioned, and my questions landed me here...permanently."

She *was* a prisoner, too. She sat in her chair for a few moments, looking at her hands before taking a deep breath and straightening the front of her lab coat. "Things are what they are. I am allowed to continue research but required to take on extra assigned projects as they see fit."

"I'm sorry," Jon said, and he was sincere. She nodded and then began to rise from the chair to leave. "Wait...please. How is Eric? And my other friends, are they okay?" He genuinely wanted more information about what they were forced to do during the night hours and couldn't let on that they could share their thoughts.

"Yes, they're well. Eric is concerned for you and asks about you often. He misses your help in the equipment room."

"I do too. He's a great guy and thinks the world of you."

Nancy's face softened, and she fiddled with the cooler she had brought with her. Finally, she jerked it open and handed him a small package with her back to the camera. Jon took it and clutched it under his arms, crossing them in front of his chest.

"Dr. Henri has Dr. Ramsey and Dr. Giffard assisting with work on regeneration. He has them handle all of the direct animal experiments since they can't be infected. He's also forcing them to work on human testing, which they clearly don't approve of. Neither do I. Since Mr. Verde is human, he has been assigned to assist with housekeeping and the like, but never in proximity to Dr. Ramsey." Her responses were honest, especially since she didn't know he could share thoughts with them.

"Are they giving other humans the Vampyre virus?" Jon spat out, his voice louder than he intended.

Nancy flinched. "I don't know if he's injected them with the full virus, but I believe he's trying to create a virus to give them the abilities he wants them to have," she said. "But that's just my guess based on what I've seen and his questions for you."

"What's he going to do with them?"

"I've shared too much already," Nancy said, clutching the clipboard under her arm.

Jon paused, then nodded. "Thanks for talking with me. I'm going a little crazy here by myself."

Nancy nodded again, briefly. "I'll see you tomorrow evening."

Jon gave a weak smile in return and watched Nancy's back as she walked down the hall. She knew more than she was sharing, even though she had already shared more than he'd expected. She wanted to talk to him, and he would keep trying until he knew what they were up against.

He took his package into the restroom and opened it out of the view of the hallway camera. It was a two-way radio in numerous pieces, but

at a quick glance, it looked like all the pieces were there, along with a
few simple tools for the job. On the paper was scribbled a simple note.

To keep you sane. 147.

Chapter Thirty

PETER

PETER LEANED BACK IN his desk chair, fingers intertwined behind his head, and stared at the data on the screen. He wasn't certain what he had just found. There were only two companies that made and sold some of the high-level equipment needed for gene sequencing and viral replication. With Alex's help, he had been monitoring their sales across the country, watching for new clients purchasing just the equipment Dr. Ramsey might need after Dr. Giffard and her lab were destroyed. He doubted Beth would purchase it, knowing the Master's reach and that it wouldn't go unnoticed.

But here was a new client buying exactly the right instruments. The holding was in the name of Rice Industries and had a shipping address in Tampa, Florida. The timing was all wrong, though. The equipment had been purchased a few weeks before the lab was destroyed. Would she really have thought far enough ahead to have been preparing for a second lab when she didn't know the first had been discovered? And her involvement there hadn't really been discovered; they had only followed Dr. Giffard after identifying Dr. Riley and Dr. Henri.

Peter turned his head to the side, thinking, and slowly lowered his hands to the keyboard in front of him. Tampa rang a bell. He pulled up his files from the Chicago scientists, and there it was.

Dr. Henri had evaded them and had taken a flight to Tampa.

The Master had sent in a new PI after Handler's demise, but he hadn't turned up anything. None of the research facilities doing viral research or the universities had any record of Dr. Henri. They still monitored the region's universities in case he popped up, but he hadn't so far. Maybe this wasn't Beth after all, but Dr. Henri attempting to pick up where he had left off?

After a bit more searching, Peter found Rice Enterprises to consist of many holdings, and one in particular piqued his interest, a pharmaceutical company. But there was no mention of viral research, gene therapy, or vaccine development; it was purely drug manufacturing, and the factory was located in Michigan, not Florida. A search of the Tampa area revealed no new labs that they hadn't already accounted for. He typed in the address on the shipping document and got nothing.

Pulling his phone from his pants pocket, he once again leaned back in his chair, dialed, and waited for Alex to pick up.

"Hello?"

"I need you to run an address for me."

A deep sigh came through the phone, followed by, "Okay, what is it?"

"41658 Watercress Road, Tampa, Florida."

"Gimme a minute."

Peter stared at the ceiling and wiggled his chair back and forth while he waited for what seemed like forever. "Call me back when you have it."

"No, no, I'm almost there. I had to hack into the postal service server. Typing in the address now... There it is. The address is registered under New Dimension Analytics. And before you ask, I'm running it through the state business records now." Another few moments passed.

"Anything?"

"Yes and no. It's there and registered, but it's weird. There is no business description, no financial records that I can find. It's like it only exists on paper. Just a sec..."

Peter could hear rapid tapping sounds as Alex plunked in information on his computer.

"I hacked Starshield to get some high-resolution images. It's a mother of a building, and it's surrounded by at least two perimeter fences with what look to be guard stations around it, six of them, maybe. I'll send you the images. Whatever they're doing there, it's well protected."

"Keep looking. Also, see what you can turn up on Rice Industries. It looks like there could be a link between them. Call me when you have something." Peter ended the call and placed the phone on the desk beside him.

He went back to his search on Rice Industries and pulled up the pharmaceutical company's website. On the list of board members was a Mr. Kenneth Rice, board president and company CEO. Searching for more information on Mr. Rice, Peter found nothing prior to about five years ago, and then only mentions about him starting the new company. A newspaper article from a year later showed a photo of a car wreck with a heading that read, "Wealthy Pharmaceutical Mogul's Wife Killed in Car Crash." As he read the rest of the article, not only was Mr. Rice's wife killed, but his then ten-year-old daughter was paralyzed from the crash.

After the crash, Rice Industries provided financial support for several fundraisers for research into restoring limb function in paralyzed individuals, as well as several clinical trials for robotics research.

Peter placed his elbows on the desk in front of him, palms together, and leaned his chin into his hands. Beth had wanted to use the regenerative capabilities of the Vampyre virus to develop a way to regenerate limbs for amputees, but mending a damaged spine would be right in the same wheelhouse. What if she or Dr. Henri, or she *and* Dr. Henri, had somehow shared their research with Mr. Rice?

Peter sat back in his chair and put his hands on the chair arms. *Did I just find Beth? And should I tell the Master?*

Chapter Thirty-One

Jon

It was just before sunset. It had been two days since Jon had been visited by anyone. He knew the cameras were still on. They would occasionally turn and follow him when he moved. But what he didn't know was if someone was still watching them. He stood in the bathroom, where he knew they couldn't see him, and checked the two-way radio, which he had hidden in the drawer after he repaired it. It was still on, tuned to channel 147, and turned down so low that only his vampire hearing would pick up a transmission. But since he had repaired it, there had been nothing. He was certain he'd done it correctly, but had still checked it repeatedly. The battery had been fully charged, but there was no cord or adaptor to charge it again if it ran out.

Perhaps he had pushed Nancy too far in their last visit, and being left alone with no blood for two days was his punishment. It was uncomfortable. He was hungry but still easily in control. His strength, however, was already waning. He hadn't mentioned it to any of the others yet during their daily conversations. They had enough to worry about already.

The last two nights, he had been bored out of his mind. And tonight looked to be no different.

He returned the radio to the drawer, covered it with a washcloth, and returned to his room. Perhaps push-ups would keep his mind off things. He dropped to the floor and began. As a Marine, he had been able to do one hundred easy on a good day. Now, he could do them for hours and not tire.

Jon thought about the prisoners Luc had encountered. His description of the female and the sound she made was very odd, but so was that of the man he had encountered first. From what Luciano described, it almost sounded as though the man had tried to claw his way out through the walls. He guessed without his vampire strength, and after enough time in solitude, perhaps he would have tried clawing his way out, too.

He couldn't help but wonder what either of them had done to be caged like that. Dr. Henri and Mr. Rice believed Luciano was human, and while he was a prisoner inside the facility, he was allowed to move about and assist with housekeeping. Evidently, the man and woman had done something far worse than just being associated with vampires.

The push-ups weren't helping, and Jon gave up, rising to his feet.

Jon stretched out on his bed, placing his hands behind his head and crossing his legs at his ankles. Dr. Henri and Mr. Rice were experimenting on humans with vampire DNA. Perhaps these weren't their only experiments. But if these prisoners weren't human, what were they? Other than the myths about supernatural creatures that everyone knew, he had never met another supernatural creature besides vampires, and he hadn't known they'd existed until he became one.

What if vampires weren't the only ones? Vampires were stronger than any other creature on the planet; they were at the top of the food chain. Jon liked knowing he was strong enough to face off against almost anything. But if other supernatural creatures had powers, like the woman's strange noise, were they a threat, or could they be allies that would help them escape? If it meant a chance to get out of this room, he would work with the devil himself. He would mention his thoughts to Kate when they spoke again.

Thinking of Kate always cheered him up, even if it did make his heart ache a little. He imagined her shy but curious smile when they had first met and the way her eyes sparkled when she laughed. There hadn't been much to laugh about lately. He needed to stay focused on her smile now to get him through whatever this was shaping up to be. When he thought of her, the hunger took the back stage.

Jon heard the familiar sound of the electronic door and then the click of heels in the hallway. Nancy. But Nancy wasn't alone tonight; a second set of footsteps joined hers, these more muffled and heavier.

Jon sat up on the side of the bed, his hands resting beside him, and waited. They entered the final hallway, and Jon breathed in deeply. It was Dr. Henri.

His hands tightened on the bed linens beside him until they were balled up, his anger piqued. The familiar urge to fight was rising inside him. He made a conscious effort to beat it back down and relax his hands. He would not allow Dr. Henri the pleasure of seeing the effect he had on him.

When they stood outside Jon's door, he could see Dr. Henri, laptop in hand, along with what looked like a small spotlight with a battery pack. He was his usual mildly disheveled self, wearing a wrinkled lab coat over his pale green shirt and crooked dark green striped tie. Nancy stood behind him, her head slightly bowed, occasionally glancing at Dr. Henri out of the corner of her eye. The second thing he noticed about her was that she wasn't holding a cooler. Dr. Henri was excited about something; Jon could hear that his heart rate was elevated.

Dr. Henri spoke first. "Good evening, Jon," he said.

Jon watched him, keeping his face expressionless.

Dr. Henri shifted and placed the laptop and light on the chair Nancy had left in the hallway. "I do apologize for keeping you here and isolated from your friends, but it was the only way to ensure their cooperation with our ongoing projects."

Jon reminded himself that as far as Dr. Henri knew, he hadn't spoken with any of his friends since the night they had been separated, the night Beth and Kate had found out he was experimenting on humans. He had to be careful not to share anything that could raise suspicions about how they could be sharing information. Dr. Henri wasn't aware of their telepathy, and they needed to keep it that way.

"What projects might those be? One moment they're working with you on regeneration, and the next I'm locked in here." Jon didn't so much care about his research, but knowing details might give them ideas for weaknesses and escape.

"Yes, well, they questioned my methods and required...motivation to continue," Dr. Henri said. "They have continued to be difficult, but we are making progress."

Jon once again remained silent. There was really nothing to say to that. Whatever the projects and conflicts were, Dr. Henri would surely know that he would agree with Beth and Kate. Saying it aloud would only ruffle his feathers.

"Nancy has been kind enough to gather some initial information for me, but it is time we learned more about your physiology. I would like to run a few tests and would appreciate your cooperation."

Jon raised his eyes to level his stare at Henri, then stood and walked to the door. At six feet four inches, he towered over Henri, who took a step back as Jon grasped the bars. "For a good meal, I would consider your tests."

"I'm afraid your nutritional needs are one of the tests. You seem to be able to tolerate not feeding for some time. I know from Dr. Ramsey's initial notes that you healed rather rapidly after she supplied you with blood. We would like to know how quickly your abilities begin to wane when you do not have blood readily available."

"You want to see how long it takes for me to starve," Jon said, and noticed Nancy close her eyes tightly and bite her lip at his words. She wasn't on board with whatever Dr. Henri had planned for him. That was clear.

"No, not starve, although that would be useful information as well. We would just like to test your regenerative abilities and strength when your nutritional requirements are not met."

Jon looked from Dr. Henri to Nancy. She wouldn't meet his gaze. He turned and began to walk away. "No deal." He couldn't force them to feed him, but he could refuse to help them until they did.

He heard a click behind him and turned just as Dr. Henri trained the box he had carried on him. It was a light, a UV light, and as its beam found his bare arm, the flesh began to sizzle.

Faster than Dr. Henri could follow his movement, Jon was out of the beam and beside the door, reaching through to grab the light and smash it against the bars. The light shattered into pieces and fell to the floor.

Dr. Henri yelped and leaped back, knocking himself and Nancy to the floor.

Jon stood at the door, his hands clenched tightly into fists. Blisters had formed where the light had hit his arm, and Dr. Henri stared at him wide-eyed as the blisters slowly began to fade, replaced by healthy pink skin. He and Nancy rose to their feet, Dr. Henri making no effort to help her.

Jon was appalled. It was no way to treat a lady. His eyes narrowed as he glared at Dr. Henri. He could easily have grabbed Dr. Henri by the throat, but his fear of retaliation and what he might do to Kate held him back.

"That took all of five seconds," Dr. Henri said, straightening his lab coat and meeting Jon's glare with his own. "We'll see how long it takes in a couple of more days without blood."

Nancy's head dropped to stare at her shoes.

"Clean that up and report to my lab," Dr. Henri barked at her and turned to leave.

Nancy bent over and collected the fragments from the broken light. She never met Jon's gaze but whispered, "Three a.m.," as she hurried from the room.

Chapter Thirty-Two

Kate

KATE NEARLY CHOKED ON her toast as she felt a jolt of pain, but quickly realized it wasn't hers. She and Beth had risen just before sunset to have breakfast in their room before going to the lab for the night.

Beth sat forward in her chair, a look of concern on her face. She had clearly felt it too.

Luc? Jon? Kate heard Beth's thoughts as she reached out to them.

It's not me, Luciano thought back.

Kate was on her feet and began to chew on her fingernails, a habit she had beaten in her late teens, as she waited for Jon to respond.

I'm okay, Jon thought, and Kate sent up a quick prayer of thanks.

What happened? she thought.

That bastard Henri burned me with a UV light.

Kate could feel that Jon was still in pain, but it was nothing like the jolt she had first felt. Dr. Henri was torturing Jon, and she knew it was her fault. She had attacked Dr. Henri, and this was the payback he had threatened.

She glanced at Beth, who must have felt her unease. Beth looked up at her from across the room. *Are you okay?*

Kate nodded, but she wasn't okay, and neither was Jon. Who knew what Dr. Henri would do to him next?

Is he still there? Kate asked.

No, I broke the light, and he left, along with Nancy. But she gave me a message. I'm sure it's from Eric and about the two-way radio. She said, "3:00 a.m."

How bad is it? Do you have enough blood to heal? Kate thought. Jon had tended to her wounds and ensured she had plenty of blood to heal after the lab explosion; she would happily do whatever it took to do the same for him.

I'm fine now, but they haven't brought blood for two days, Jon admitted.

Two days? You haven't fed in two days? Kate could feel the despair and guilt taking over.

"We have to get him out," Kate said aloud to Beth, not wanting Jon to hear. "How long can he go without blood?"

"At least a few days," Beth said.

Kate, I'm fine for now. I'm sure they'll bring some soon. I'm no use to them dead, Jon thought. He was trying to placate her, but it wasn't working. Even if they didn't let him die, they could starve him until he was too weak to resist anything they might do to him in punishment for her threats.

Jon, if Nancy delivered a message from Eric, they are both taking a risk to reach out to you, Luciano thought.

They are. If Eric calls at 3:00, I'll ask if he will help us and pick his brain about the security systems. I'll let you know what I find out after your shifts.

Kate knew she should be thinking through all of this more clearly, but she just couldn't get the image of Jon being tortured by Henri out of her head.

If Nancy is passing him things from Eric, she could pass him our syringe of v2.2. It would get rid of his need for blood and prevent him from being injured by Dr. Henri's UV light. It would also prepare him to leave in the daylight if need be, just like us, Kate thought, barely able to block her swirling emotions from the group.

But it would also show our hand, Kate, Jon thought back. *They would know Nancy was helping us. It would put her in danger, and we would lose an ally. And they could still starve me. I know you want to help me, but there just isn't a way right now.*

"I'm going to the lab. I need to work," Kate said, needing to get away from Beth, needing to do something, anything but sit here in this room separated from Jon.

"I'll be right behind you," Beth said, her eyebrows scrunched together as she looked at Kate.

"I just need a moment alone," Kate said as she stood and nearly ran out of the room, blocking her thoughts from the group as she walked.

If you need me, just say the word, Beth thought as Kate left. Kate knew Beth meant it, but she wasn't going to risk Beth being harmed too.

Kate walked to their shared lab, pulled on her lab coat, and continued on to the animal lab, seeing the handlers working when she entered. She walked to one of the rhesus cages and pretended to study the chart beside it while she glanced around the room. The handler's badge and keys were dangling from the pocket of her jacket, draped over one of the empty cages, as usual. Kate knew they didn't believe they could get to Jon by stealing a badge, but they couldn't be sure. She had to try.

There were cameras in the room, but Kate knew she could block them by standing just to the right of the empty cage, and with the speed of her movements, the camera wouldn't pick up a quick grab. Kate moved slowly, examining the animals as she went until she was in position. Then, with vampire speed, she gathered the badge and dropped it into her empty pocket. It was nearly an hour after sunset, and the day crew was long gone. The halls would be quiet, the staff who could leave having headed home for the evening, and those who could not having settled into their living quarters for the night.

Kate gathered another clipboard and walked calmly and purposefully into the supply room next door, opened the blood storage refrigerator, and removed a unit from the shelf. The unit with the attached tubing wouldn't fit in her pocket without sticking up to be visible, so she placed it on top of her papers, spreading them slightly to cover it, and hugged them to her chest before leaving the animal lab.

Kate, what's wrong? I can feel your anxiety. It was Beth. She must have made it to their lab.

I'm okay. I'm going back for a few minutes. I need to talk with Jon. If Henri is looking for me, tell him I forgot something.

I'll go with you, Beth thought back.

Thank you, but I need time alone, please. Kate blocked her emotions and thoughts with as much strength as she could. Her heart hammered in her chest. She didn't want this to go badly for Beth. If she got caught, it needed to be clear that she had acted alone. She was willing to die trying to reach Jon, but she wasn't willing to sacrifice the life of her friend.

She forced herself to walk at a normal human pace, even though she wanted to run. But if anyone was watching the monitors, her running at vampire speed would arouse suspicion. She knew from their studies of the security system that there was a corner just past her lab where the cameras didn't overlap. She would make it that far and then run as fast as she could. Though they would very likely pick her up on camera as she paused to badge through the main doors.

After she rounded the final corner to the lab, she continued to the next hallway, not glancing into the lab to avoid eye contact with Beth. Rounding the blind corner, she kicked into vampire speed and crossed to the next main corridor in less than two seconds. She badged through the next door as quickly as she could, the badge reader seeming to take forever before the red light turned green. She wiggled from side to side as fast as she could in hopes that her badge hand, still before the reader, would go unnoticed. The lights in the next corridor were dimmed for the night, and she hoped it would mean the guards would be less likely to be watching it and see her on the monitors.

She was now finally running down the hallway to the last security door before Jon's room. She was so close now. *I'm coming, Jon. Hang on.* She nearly yelled her thoughts to him, letting her guard down so she could hear and feel his response.

Kate? What are you doing? Jon thought back.

Getting you out. I'm almost there.

No, go back! I don't want you hurt, goddammit!

She hovered the stolen badge over the reader and moved from foot to foot, waiting for the light to change, but nothing happened. She moved the badge aside and then scanned it again. Once again, the light stayed red. But this time, an alarm sounded, blaring loudly in her ears.

"Dammit! It has to work. I am so close." But just as the words left her mouth, she heard the sound of running footsteps in the hallway behind her. She tried one final time to scan the badge. If she could just get to the room, she could toss the unit to Jon.

When the scanner once again stayed red, Kate began kicking at the door lock, hoping to dislodge it. She knew it hadn't worked before, but she had nothing else to try. The door shook but didn't give way. Then guards were behind her. There were six in total. Kate turned with her back to the door to face them, glaring at them.

One of the guards stepped forward slowly with one hand out, the other on a taser at his side. Kate wondered if a taser would even have an effect on a vampire with their regenerative abilities. By the look in the guard's eyes, he wasn't sure either. "Dr. Giffard, please come with us back to the lab wing. We don't want to harm you."

"Let me through to my friend, and then I will do whatever you ask of me," she said.

"I'm afraid I can't do that," he said, taking another step forward.

"Then I'm afraid I can't either."

Things happened in a flurry of motion after that. Kate dropped the papers, the unit of blood, and the stolen badge onto the floor behind her and spun back around in time to see the guard pull out his taser.

Kate was faster, though, by far, slapping the taser out of his hand and shoving him backward. That launched him into the air to fly into his fellow guards behind him, knocking two of them and him to the ground. One of the remaining three guards was fast on the draw and fired his taser at her. She ducked and batted the electrodes out of the air before they could hit her. But with her attention to her right, a guard on the left was able to send his taser into her left shoulder. The darted electrodes bit into her skin, followed by the electricity. It made the muscles of her biceps twitch, but it was short-lived as she swung her other hand down across the wires, knocking them free.

She seethed at him. "That hurts."

The guards that had been knocked down scrambled to their feet, and all of them ran forward toward her at once. Kate spun, kicked, and hit as Jon had taught her in their brief time together, but she pulled her blows, wanting to get them off of her to listen, but not wanting to kill anyone. As they squabbled, the men falling back only to get up and come at her again, more guards arrived, and one of these raised a gun.

"Dr. Giffard, please stop. We need you." It was an unfamiliar female voice, and Kate spun to look at the owner, a tall woman with brown hair pulled back in a tight ponytail, breathing heavily. Kate's vampire vision allowed her to read her ID badge where it dangled from the pocket of her lab coat. NANCY. *Eric's Nancy?*

Kate paused, looking at Nancy, the men in front of her, and the guard behind them with his raised gun. Luciano had been right; there was no way they were going to let her through this door, and there was no way she could knock it down. Even if she killed them all, they could keep her trapped in this hallway until she starved or was too weak to fight back, like Jon.

She bit back the tears that threatened, knowing it was over. She had failed. She stopped fighting, and her shoulders slumped. Nancy pushed through the guards toward her, holding her palms open in front of her.

"It's okay, gentlemen. Dr. Giffard won't be any more trouble tonight." Kate could feel the fear rolling off of Nancy as she pushed forward. Reaching her, she extended her arm to Kate's shoulder. "It's going to be okay, Dr. Giffard. Let's get back to the lab wing, shall we?" she said.

Kate exhaled loudly and then took a step forward. The guards flinched, and Nancy raised her hand. "It's all over," she said.

The guards, hands still on their weapons, slowly parted to let them through.

I'm sorry, Jon. If you can hear me, I couldn't get through. But there was no answer.

The two walked slowly back to the lab, Kate sullen and choking back tears.

"We'll get him out," Nancy whispered. "I've been working on getting access to your lab to assist you with Dr. Henri's experiments."

This is *Eric's Nancy.* Kate was awash with emotions. She was on the verge of tears over her failure, and beyond frustrated, but here was Nancy in nearly the same situation, placing herself at risk to help them.

It wasn't relief Kate felt at Nancy's words, not yet, but the sadness from before was being slowly replaced by anger. She could feel it building. Before meeting Dr. Henri, it had been a very long while since she had felt truly angry. And now in a few short days, her slow fuse had burned not once but twice, and as she walked, she realized she was downright pissed. Henri had not just threatened her and her friends, he had harmed someone she cared about, and he had better be ready for the consequences.

Kate looked at Nancy to speak, but she couldn't as they turned the corner and saw two guards waiting in the hallway outside Kate's lab. They stood in front of the locked door, an obviously angry Beth on the other side, glaring at them.

"Thank you," Kate said to Nancy, who nodded. Nancy leaned over to pick up a rack of samples from the floor outside the lab and hand them to Kate before she continued on her way. She must have been headed toward them to deliver the samples when the alarms sounded.

One of the guards removed his keycard from his pocket and used it to open the lock. Beth stepped back to allow Kate access.

I'm sorry, Kate thought to Beth, expecting harsh words. But instead, Beth stepped forward and wrapped her arms around Kate's shoulders.

Kate expected to cry, to let out all the despair that had driven her to attempt to reach Jon, but she found those feelings were long gone. Only anger and determination remained.

Chapter Thirty-Three

PETER

Peter closed the door to his Porsche Taycan and strode confidently toward the entrance to the Master's quarters. He had decided that if Beth was working with Mr. Rice, he had to be the one to go there first. If the Master knew he thought Beth might be there now, he would send Anubis to finish her off, and he just couldn't let that happen. Perhaps in exchange for not revealing her location, he could persuade her to change him, minus the ill effects. He had a plan to make that happen. He just needed to be convincing. Thankfully, the Master had taught him to lie, and well.

As Peter approached the door to the Master's office, Muscles knocked on it, opened it, and announced him to the Master. Peter felt refreshed after yesterday's much-needed rest and walked with intentional confidence to the Master's desk.

The Master was turned toward the fireplace, and if he were human, Peter would have guessed he hadn't heard his approach. But this was the Master, and Peter knew that not only had he heard him enter, but he heard his breathing and his heart beating. If he hadn't acknowledged him yet, it meant he wasn't ready to speak with him. It was an irritating habit of his. Peter recognized it for what it was: arrogance and a display of power. And even more irritating was the fact that Peter knew he would, in fact, wait until the Master was ready to speak with him. He had been the Master's lap dog for far too long.

After several long moments, the Master turned to face him, stood, and walked to sit in his desk chair. As he so often did, he placed his elbows on the armrests, fingers steepled in front of him as though studying Peter.

It made him uneasy despite his planning. He would have thought he'd be used to it by now. But now, he had something to hide. He'd practiced for years to control both his emotions and his body's response to them and was quite good at it. He just hoped he was good enough to fool the Master.

"What do you have for me?" the Master asked.

"I believe I may have located Dr. Henri." Peter explained how he had tracked the instrument sales, which led to Kenneth Rice, Rice Industries, and the facility just outside of Tampa. He also shared the nature of Mr. Rice's various businesses and his apparent interest in regenerative therapies. "I can't be certain, but it appears prior to purchasing Biovitalis, he earned his fortune with illegal trade, likely arms deals."

"It would explain Dr. Henri's success in eluding us. Do you believe Dr. Ramsey may be working with him?"

Peter remained calm and cool. He had anticipated the question. "I suppose it is possible, but the timing doesn't seem to fit. Dr. Henri fled Chicago at the time Dr. Riley was killed. The purchase of the equipment was dated a week or so prior to that. Dr. Ramsey was in New Orleans working with Dr. Giffard at the time we located her. I have no reason to believe Dr. Ramsey was aware of Dr. Henri's actions, and she certainly wasn't in Tampa at the time of his exodus."

The Master's face remained unreadable, but Peter knew much could be going through his mind behind the lack of expression.

"How do you suggest you gain access?"

"I'm going to need Alex to provide me with the appropriate background and credentials. But I believe I could get access to him through Biovitalis. Dr. Ramsey had reached out to geneticists, like Dr. Henri, as well as virologists. If Dr. Henri is there, adding a virologist to the team would be an advantage. I would suggest vaguely in my request for a meeting that I have had recent success with a novel approach to regeneration using gene therapy. Mentioning using viral DNA might be too much. If he knows about the Vampyre virus, he will be interested either because he will believe I am another scientist that Dr. Ramsey contacted, or that I could be a possible competitor in the field. If he has the virus, I have no doubt that with his background, he will have plans for it outside of mainstream medicine."

Peter paused, and when the Master didn't speak, he continued. "My background could include work in a private lab for a wealthy investor who does not see the financial potential the virus holds. I could gain access as a defector of sorts, looking for a new lab and an investor that shares my vision. I may need to tempt him with my own sample of the virus." "Defector" was certainly an appropriate description for what he intended to do. He just needed the Master on board to put his plan in motion.

"And how would you suggest obtaining this sample?"

"For it to be believable, it would have to come from the same viral strain as Luciano's. It would need to be a sample of your blood or someone you know to have an identical strain." It was a bold suggestion, and Peter knew it. The Master guarded his blood and the power it held carefully.

"And your desire to become a vampire has nothing to do with this suggestion?"

Shit. Peter had hoped they wouldn't need to go down this line of thinking. He didn't need the Master questioning his motives.

"No," the Master said, "you will approach him as a scientist in my lab with an offer to join our considerable resources in pursuit of the common goal of exploiting the virus for all it is worth."

Peter steadied himself and regrouped; it could still be a useful plan. "As you wish, of course. I was concerned that mentioning the virus might show our hand too soon or put him on the defensive." The Master's plan was less elegant but would play more directly to Mr. Rice's probably devious intentions. As long as it still put Peter in Tampa looking for Beth before the Master or anyone else, he would make it work. And if Beth wasn't there, perhaps Mr. Rice's team would be more open to his personal desires. Surely if they had progressed with the development of the virus, Mr. Rice would wish to be turned along with his team. Why wouldn't they with the promise of near immortality? "I will have Alex begin work immediately."

The Master nodded and held Peter's gaze. Peter made a conscious effort to keep his feet and hands in place and not fidget, even though the Master's stare was raising the hairs on the back of his neck. He fought for control and felt a few beads of sweat begin on his back. He was thankful he had worn a jacket so they wouldn't be visible, but it was likely the Master could smell his unease.

"Is there anything else?" the Master asked.

"Not for now," Peter said, and it was Peter who broke eye contact as he turned and made a conscious effort not to hurry from the room. The sooner he could get to Tampa, the better.

Chapter Thirty-Four

Beth

BETH AND KATE BOTH flew out of bed to the sound of banging on their door. They pulled on clothing at vampire speed and opened it to see a thirty-something woman in a lab coat with flushed cheeks. She was agitated, and some of her light brown hair had worked its way out of the bun high on her head to fall on the side of her face. Her eyes were wide and insistent. "Come with me. Dr. Henri's in trouble."

Beth was only a little ashamed that the thought of just leaving him in trouble crossed her mind. But she knew it wasn't the right thing to do. Selfish, manipulative, money-hungry ass that he was, she couldn't turn her back on a request for help. Evidently, Kate agreed because she followed Beth and the woman as they ran down the hall.

This is Nancy, Eric's Nancy, Kate thought to Beth as they followed. Beth looked to Kate and nodded. She was glad she hadn't argued about coming with her. She would happily repay her for the help she had given Kate.

"We can get there faster if you tell us where to go," Beth said.

"He's in the treatment wing, you can't get through," Nancy said. So they followed her as quickly as she could run since she was already winded from the trip to retrieve them.

As they were badged through the last door to the treatment wing, they could hear a male voice yelling incoherently, a second demanding, "kill it," and an occasional woman's scream. The hallway door was made of open bars, and several people dressed in scrubs and lab coats stood peering through it, along with several guards, all blocking their view. One woman had both fists jammed against her mouth so hard that Beth was certain there would be teeth marks on her knuckles. She was the source of the screams, and she let one rip as Beth heard a loud bang from the hallway in front of them.

"The bars are metal. If we shoot, it could ricochet and hit Dr. Henri," one guard said. "Who has the UV light?"

"Please move aside, move aside," Nancy said, pushing the gawkers out of the way. "I brought help."

A young guard looked at her and said, "These two?"

"Just give them a chance. If they can't get him under control, then you can kill him."

"What happened?" Beth asked now that Nancy had slowed and could catch a breath here and there to speak. She listened as they pushed their way through to the front, the guards sending questioning looks. Those who hadn't yet drawn their weapons before they arrived were now holding them in hand.

Nancy blurted out the story in between gasps for air. "Dr. Henri injected a test subject with the original Vampyre virus. He went into the room, thinking he still had time before the man woke from the change, but he woke up early and tried to bite Dr. Henri. He ran out of the cell, followed by the man who was moving so quickly that he slid past him. Dr. Henri ran back into the cell and closed it before the man could get to him. Now he's trapped in the cell, and the man is loose in the hallway."

"Unbelievable," Beth said under her breath. Dr. Henri was pathologically stupid. He'd been experimenting on men and women who were homeless, most with mental illness or deficits from years of drug abuse. Even if they could get the man's attention, there was no guarantee he was capable of comprehending what was happening to him.

"Do you have any blood?" Kate asked.

She and Kate were on the same page. Their only hope at controlling the man was to feed him and at least get rid of the bloodlust.

"Yes," a young blonde man in a lab coat said and ran back down the hall. He returned in seconds with a cooler, opened it, and handed Kate a unit.

"We'll need at least three more," Beth said, and the man gave them to her. She handed one to Kate and stuck the extra under her arm.

"Let us through the door," Beth said.

"Are you crazy? He'll bite you!" Screamer said.

Beth thought they might be just that, crazy. While Beth didn't think a bite would reverse the effects of the v2.2, she didn't know with certainty. But regardless, they had to help. The man was agitated from thirst, and no one else here was capable of handling his strength and speed.

"Open it, Nancy," Kate said. She and Beth stepped through the door, which was quickly closed and locked behind them.

The man moved back and forth between two open cells near the center of the hallway at speeds the others couldn't see, pausing to yell and throw whatever he could get a hold of. He stopped off and on to reach through the bars at Dr. Henri, who cowered in the corner farthest from him, smelling rather strongly of urine.

He was caged, just like his test subjects, and a part of Beth wanted to leave him there. An even darker part wanted to let the new vampire drink him dry. Henri would harm more people before he and Mr. Rice were finished. Killing him would undoubtedly save lives. Letting him die could be justified in the eyes of many.

Beth?

It was Kate's voice in her head. She must not have shielded her thoughts. She glanced at Kate, who said nothing more but looked at her, understanding clear in her eyes. Kate gave one small shake of her head.

It was all Beth needed. Letting Henri die *could* be justified by others, but not in her own heart. As horrible as he was and as much as he needed to be stopped, killing him was not something she could live with. Beth exhaled and returned her attention to the man.

Let's try giving him the blood. I'll open one of my units first. Beth began to tear the top of the tubing off one of the units while Kate spoke softly to the man.

"It's okay," Kate said, her hand held out and open. *Damn, we should have asked his name.*

They probably don't know. As soon as Beth snapped the top from the unit, the man raised his head, scenting the air, and rushed at her. She didn't budge but held the unit out to him in front of her. The man stopped abruptly in front of her, tearing the unit from her hand and drinking sloppily, downing it in seconds, and bringing another shriek from behind the hallway door. Beth was ready with a second open unit in hand. "This will make you feel better. It's going to be okay."

Kate prepared her units, and after downing the last, the man seemed calmer but remained agitated, pacing back and forth in front of them, but slowly enough now so that Henri and the others down the hall could follow him with their eyes. He occasionally looked over at Henri and growled, showing his fangs. Beth understood the feeling.

Kate looked at Beth. *I think we're going to have to hold him. I don't know what he will do when Henri leaves the cell.*

Okay, we go on three, and we will each grab an arm. Ready? Kate nodded ever so subtly. *One... two... three.* They both leaped forward at vampire speed. The man, who was looking away from them toward Henri, didn't see it coming, and they both had an arm tightly in theirs before he knew what happened. He let out an ear-splitting yell and thrashed, but the two women together were too much for his spastic and disjointed movements. The fact that the sun had risen was also on their side, weakening him; their strength was still at full power now that v2.2 had freed them from their sun sensitivity.

"Settle down, now. Everything is all right. We don't want to hurt you; you just need to calm down and cooperate. We'll get you some more to eat, and you can rest," Kate said, trying to comfort him, and he did lessen his struggling.

Henri, seeing his chance, ran from the cell, yelling for the group to open the door. As soon as he was through, he disappeared behind the guards. Beth and Kate continued down the hallway one slow step at a time, not wanting to spook the man who was finally starting to cooperate.

Henri reappeared, pushing his way through the guards with something in his hand. He stood without opening the barred door or saying a word and raised the object.

Too late, Beth realized it was the UV light one of the guards had been carrying.

The light struck the newly made vampire, and his skin began to sizzle and burn. Confused and in pain, he tore free of Kate and Beth, who had reflexively raised their arms to protect themselves, and ran straight toward Henri and into the UV light. By the time he reached the barred door and tried to reach through to bat away the light, he was already in flames, the stench of burnt flesh filling the hallway. The man fell to the floor in front of Henri, who kept the light trained on him until he was a pile of black-gray ash.

Screams from behind the door turned to sounds of retching. Henri turned off the light and looked at Kate and Beth, who were immediately next to the pile and in front of him, both with fury etched across every line of their faces.

"What the hell were you thinking? We had him; he was settling down. There was no need to kill him. And did you stop to consider that you may have killed us as well?" Kate spat the words at him, hands clenched into fists.

"He was uncontrollable and dangerous. I did what I had to do," Henri said, his hands shaking at his sides.

"You killed a man out of your own stupidity. He should never have been turned," Beth said, her voice much louder than she intended, and she saw Nancy flinch out of the corner of her eye. The others who had been in the hallway had turned away from the smell, leaving only the four of them. She imagined what she must look like to the woman, a vampire on the verge of ripping out Dr. Henri's throat. And she was, but she wouldn't do it. While he had no conscience, she did.

She took a step back and made a point to steady her features and relax her posture. She closed her eyes and took a deep breath, regretting it immediately as the smell of the burnt body at her feet filled her nostrils.

"Let us out," Beth said sternly to Dr. Henri, who just stared at the pile of ash on the floor blankly.

"Nancy, please let us out," Beth said.

Nancy was shaking but nodded and slowly moved in front of Dr. Henri, unlocked the door, and let them through. Both carefully stepped over the burnt remains. Kate leveled a blistering glare at Dr. Henri as she walked by, but didn't speak as they headed back to their room with Nancy.

They were all silent until they were clearly out of earshot of Dr. Henri and the rest of the staff, and the hallway was clear. Then Nancy spoke. "Thank you... not for saving Dr. Henri, but for helping all of us and trying to save Dr. Henri's patient."

"You're welcome," Beth said. "And thank you for helping Kate." Beth looked sideways at Nancy. She wasn't sure what the cameras could pick up. She wanted to speak with her about Jon and their plan, but couldn't risk being overheard. She glanced at the cameras and then back to Nancy.

Nancy's eyes showed she understood. She spoke, but in a whisper. "The cameras here don't have audio, but we should still keep our voices low in case someone is nearby."

"You can speak as quietly as possible. We will still hear you easily," Beth said. Their conversation continued with all facing forward as they walked in order not to draw attention.

"Eric volunteered for training in the security control room. He started yesterday. Since I've been assigned to work on Dr. Henri's human experiments in the treatment wing, I asked to observe the rhesus in the animal lab as well for comparison. We should be able to share information with one another there," Nancy said.

"Thank you. And please thank Eric for us as well," Beth said. She was almost giddy. They were finally making progress. She couldn't wait to share the information with Jon and Luc. They all needed some good news right now. It would help them stay focused.

"Do you know of any other exits besides the main that would be less guarded?" Kate asked.

"Not that I have access to. I believe there are more on the lower level for supplies and the like, but I've never seen them. I'll ask Eric," Nancy answered.

"We have seven days until Mr. Rice and his daughter arrive. We're guessing security will be spread thin guarding them. It may be our best shot," Beth said, and got a worried glance from Kate. Beth knew she was concerned that Jon wouldn't make it that long, but they all knew they would only get one chance, including Jon. They had to take the one with the best odds.

"Eric thinks so, too. They split the details when he visits," Nancy said.

"Can you and Eric be ready by then?" Beth asked as they approached the final door to their quarters, and Nancy scanned them through.

"We'll have to be," Nancy said.

CHAPTER THIRTY-FIVE

JON

AFTER FOUR DAYS OF being starved, it was starting to become more difficult to keep his thoughts together and to avoid the UV light. He had barely dragged himself to the bed before falling face-first into the pillow. He winced as the tender flesh over his arm rubbed against the bed linens. Henri came now during the day when he was at his weakest and struggling to raise himself from bed. With no blood for six days now, his regeneration had slowed to a snail's pace. If Henri came today, he wasn't sure he would heal at all. It wouldn't be long before he was completely helpless during the daylight hours.

Now that he knew what to expect, he'd been blocking his emotions and thoughts as best he could. But the last round, he had barely had the strength to suffer the pain of the light and keep his emotions from pouring down his telepathic bond with his friends. His thoughts now wandered aimlessly, and his awareness had become unreliable as he struggled to stay awake. He feared that the next time he would not succeed.

He thought of the despair that had rolled off of Kate after her failed rescue attempt. Jon had punched at what remained of the walls between the bars that surrounded him afterward. He knew it wasn't any use. He also knew he should conserve what energy he could, but he had needed to do something to release the anger. He and Kate had grown closer through their many talks since he'd been locked up, and he had a good feeling for the amount of rage and fear it had taken for her to attempt the rescue alone.

Eric had contacted him on the two-way at 0300 just as Nancy had said and had helped get their escape plan in action. Now that Beth and Kate had access to Nancy, they and Luciano were coordinating the plan, which seemed to be lining up to give them their best chance when Mr. Rice and his daughter were at the facility. But that was nearly a week away. There was no use dwelling on that, so Jon pushed it out of his mind. He would do what he had to. Luciano was assessing how much he could trust Ben and Anteia with, but at the very least, he would tell them to be ready to run if they had a chance.

Kate was working like a woman obsessed. The woman who had awakened the day after her failed rescue attempt had been a different person from the happy-go-lucky one he had known before. This Kate was determined. Jon no longer felt despair from her but anger. And her anger was fueling his own. He was proud of her. She'd chosen not to wallow in her emotions but to use the anger to move forward. She was now completely focused on finding a way out of here, and if that meant going straight through Dr. Henri or Mr. Rice, God help them. He thought of the old adage about hell having no fury like a woman, or something like that. Thinking of Kate kicking their lying asses with her new fighting skills calmed him and brought a weak smile to his lips. He would fight to stay alive as long as he could to get to see it with his own eyes.

Even though it was after sunset, he was so tired he began to drift off, and thoughts of Kate carried him to his dreams.

CHAPTER THIRTY-SIX

LUC

IT WAS YET ANOTHER night without Beth at his side, of squelching the anger he felt over being separated from her and the fear about what might happen to her while he could do nothing to protect her. Despite all of his abilities, he felt helpless, just as he had the night the Master had engineered the death of his wife. He felt his frustration mirrored by Ben and Anteia during their every-other-night talks when his duties led him into their corridors. He had done his best to gain their trust, but hadn't pressed for details, both because he was getting a handle on where they stood, and also because he didn't know how to have the conversation without it being recorded or overheard. But Mr. Rice's visit was getting closer, and he was running out of time. He believed they were on his side and needed to warn them to be ready if they could.

"You look like you lost your best friend," Ben said as he arrived outside his cell. His frustration must have been more visible tonight.

Luc gave a sad huff. "Just missing my friends," he said under his breath, so low that it would have been lost to human hearing. But Ben responded at the same low level.

"I can understand that."

Luc looked at him, eyebrows raised, with his back to the hall cameras. He kicked himself for not having tried that nights ago. He continued their conversation at the same volume, knowing it would be nearly impossible to pick up on audio.

"I am certain that you, of all people, do know exactly how I feel."

"Is it the vampires?" Ben said the words and then dropped his eyes toward his hands. "I heard some of the staff talking about them."

Luc paused and took a deep breath. He needed to find out more about Ben, now that they could communicate without being overheard, and sharing his and his friends' story might be the best way to get him to open up about his own. He looked at the cameras and then at Ben and began sweeping the hallway to appear busy. Ben, taking his cue, turned and sat on the end of his bed to watch Luc from a distance.

"Yes, the vampires are my friends," Luc replied. "I arrived here with them."

"I didn't know they were real," Ben said. "Why did you come here?"

Luc gave Ben the recap of their arrival and the later conflict with Rice and Henri, ending with, "So, he made us all prisoners and keeps us apart. We're stuck here until we can find a way out."

Ben's face was somber. "I'm sorry."

In a normal voice, Luc asked Ben for his trash and towels, which Ben retrieved and handed to Luc, who returned to their sub-whisper conversation.

"Why are you here?" Luc asked.

Ben returned to his spot on the bed and hung his head, breathing deeply several times. He opened his mouth once to speak and closed it. Luc waited, giving him time to think, and dumped the trash and used towels into his cart.

"I'm here because of what I am. I don't know how Mr. Rice found out about us, but he came for my family. I fought back so they could get away, but I was caught and brought here. I don't even know how long it's been. My little Casey was just about to turn two when they came for us. I'm pretty sure by now I've missed her third birthday as well. They study me, torture me to see how much I can take, and see what drugs work to take me down. They take my blood regularly and feed me just enough to survive, hoping to keep me weak." Ben finished with a slow sigh, his gaze on the floor and his forehead creased. "So, are you a vampire? I've never smelled one, but you don't smell human."

Luc was caught off guard but recovered quickly. He knew humans couldn't smell the scent of a vampire, but Ben had already suggested he wasn't a typical human. If he was going to trust Ben, now was the time.

Luc wrung out his mop and began mopping the hallway. "You're right. I'm not. I was a vampire. Dr. Ramsey and Dr. Giffard were able to remove the negative aspects of what I am, so I can walk in the sun and eat normal, human food again."

Ben seemed to mull his response over for a moment before speaking. "My people could use her help."

"You didn't say who you and your people are," Luc said, hoping Ben was ready to share the details.

"We are Lycans. Movies and lore call us werewolves or shifters, but being called a werewolf is an insult. We have lived alongside humans for millennia without problems, but in the last few generations, some of those both turned and born into the bloodline have started to change. Some can't transform at will anymore or become human again, even when they die. They are feral and have to be put down. The sickness is becoming more common, and we don't know how to stop it. Our numbers are beginning to fall. Someday, I would very much like to meet your Dr. Ramsey. If she is as kind as you make her sound, perhaps she could help my people."

"She would do her best. I know her well, and she wouldn't walk away if she believed she might be able to help." Luc paused again, organizing his thoughts. "At some point, we will find a way out. When that time comes, you should leave with us. I will help you if I can, but pay attention to your door locks. If you see the security fail, be ready to run." Luc shared the layout of the wing with Ben and gave him directions to the main entrance. While it would be guarded, it was the only exit he had been allowed to see so far.

Finished with his cleaning, Luc placed the mop into the bucket on his cart and prepared to leave.

"I'll be ready. And I will fight with you if it comes to that. I hope it's soon," Ben said as Luc walked away.

"I do too." Luc thought of Jon and wondered how much time he had left.

Chapter Thirty-Seven

Beth

Beth stood next to the cage of another dead rhesus, clipboard in hand, frustration and guilt making her grip it hard enough to crack. What were they missing? They had been able to infect monkeys with the full Vampyre virus, with a death rate of roughly ten percent. Obviously, humans could be infected with the original virus as well, but with a death rate they didn't know. Luc told them the change was not always successful, but none of them had enough data to guess at a death rate.

They could alter smaller mammals and even humans with the individual segments, but more than one or two at a time was too large for the AAV virus to hold. The retrovirus was large enough, but with only the segments of interest, it didn't work. In fact, it was worse than not working; it killed the host. The virus they injected themselves with only contained code for stop codons in the areas for bloodlust and sun sensitivity, and it only got past their immune systems because it was packaged in the same retrovirus capsular structure that the original Vampyre virus was.

She sighed deeply and shook her head.

"It has to be something in the other segments, some part of the viral RNA that we don't understand," Kate said, staring at another stack of data as though she could force it to make sense. She had been working like she was possessed since they'd found out Jon was being starved and tortured. At the same time, she was consuming anything she could get her hands on related to the facility, Dr. Henri, the experiments he performed, and their own experiments. Beth even noticed her making notes on the other people in this wing and their comings and goings. She was completely obsessed with helping Jon get free.

Beth didn't blame her, and she helped with anything and everything Kate asked. She would feel the same if it were Luc.

But they also needed to complete the retrovirus before Mr. Rice and his daughter arrived. Dr. Henri would eventually be successful, and they needed to have everything he would end up with before they left. Whatever they may do to combat Henri and Rice and their use of the virus in the future, they needed to be as close to equal footing as they could be. It was also why Beth needed to talk with Nancy and was pleased when she saw her arrive.

"Without understanding the effects of the other segments, which seem to have no effect on their own, I don't know how to test for them. We could throw them all in, but that's risky too," Beth said. *We could end up providing some with telepathy, and I don't think that is the road we want to go down.*

"I'm hungry," Kate said. "It's been at least three hours since we ate last. Let's get a bite to eat and get our minds off of this for a minute."

"No argument here, I'm starving," Beth said. "But let me speak with Nancy about tomorrow's experiments before we go." *I need to give her our list.*

Beth crossed the lab to Nancy, who was reviewing the day's results. "We're no closer, I'm afraid," Beth said, handing the clipboard to Nancy with her note on top.

Nancy read the note and nodded. They had already settled on

leaving at midnight the day Mr. Rice arrived with his daughter, when staffing was at its lowest. But today's note contained a list of reagents and equipment she and Kate would need after the escape to continue producing more of the various viruses. It also asked if Eric and Nancy would be able to leave through a different exit. It would give the two of them a better chance of succeeding if the guards were focused on Beth and her friends at the main entrance since Eric and Nancy would need a vehicle to escape rather than running.

"We could use your help. Let me know if you think of anything else," Beth said aloud.

"I will. I agree with your findings," Nancy said.

"Dr. Giffard and I are going to get something to eat. We'll be back in half an hour or so if you need us." Beth smiled at her as she turned to join Kate at the door. Beth hoped they had a chance to meet again one day, away from this awful place, so she could properly thank her and Eric for all they were doing to help them.

Beth and Kate walked to the cafeteria and filled their trays with an embarrassing amount of food, Kate making sure she got a cup of cookies and cream ice cream.

"You know the one thing I really want to eat that they don't have?" Beth asked.

"No, what?"

"Plain M&Ms," Beth said as she sat down and popped the top on her can of Diet Coke. The first few sips gave her that gentle burn that she craved. To her, it tasted like heaven.

"I saw peanut ones in the vending machine," Kate said, holding her hand up in front of her mouth that was stuffed with a turkey sandwich.

"Nope, that won't do. I don't want my chocolate contaminated."

Kate shook her head in response. "I'm so hungry I would eat almost anything right now."

"Anything but those. I'm holding out for perfection," Beth said and grinned at Kate. Her friend returned it, but it didn't make it all the way to her eyes.

We'll get him out, Kate, Beth thought, resisting the urge to put her food down and place her hand on Kate's forearm in front of the watching cameras.

Yes, we will, Kate replied and looked down at her sandwich, already nearly gone. *And right now, I hope there is a little fighting involved. I know it's not right, but I really need to punch someone, preferably Henri or Rice.*

Won't they be surprised when a woman puts them on their asses? Beth thought, trying to cheer her friend.

"This turkey sandwich is as close to perfection as I need," Kate said aloud for the cameras. *We've got five more days before Mr. Rice and his daughter arrive,* she thought. *I still don't know where they'll house them while his daughter receives therapy. I'm assuming in the treatment area where Henri has been conducting his other experiments. Regardless, it's still our best chance at spreading the guards thin. We just need a break in our research so we can leave with everything we need,* Kate thought, chewing the last bite of sandwich.

Beth froze, looking down at the table, running an idea around in her head. Kate watched, rubbing her hands together over her plate.

"Okay, you're starting to freak me out," Kate said.

"I was just thinking about needing a break in our research." Beth leaned forward with her elbows on the table and looked intently at Kate. "The autopsies I performed on both the animals and the humans Dr. Henri infected that didn't take the new retrovirus showed liquification of almost all the organs, just like the initial rats in your lab and this one. It was from an overwhelming infection." Kate nodded as Beth spoke, following her train of thought. "So what if we break the virus? We've been injecting it and letting it do its thing, but in gene therapy, they often damage the viral replication mechanisms, so once they insert their code, they can't produce more virus, and it ends there."

Kate was nodding her head almost comically now, her thoughts taking off as well. *And if we only give so much virus, there can only be so much incorporation. We could limit the expression of the virus and thereby limit the strength, regeneration, and immunity of Rice's super soldiers.*

"Oh my God, Beth, that's it!" Kate stood and turned toward the door at the same time, knocking her metal chair over with a clang that echoed through the empty cafeteria. "Buggar," she said, looking sheepishly back at Beth.

As they hurried to their lab, Kate babbled at vampire speed in her thoughts and aloud. *I know exactly how to disable the replication mechanism.* "What dosage should we use? Too much and we still run the risk of killing the host."

"Well, adjusted for the weight of the average human male, using the dosage per kilogram we gave the monkey, would be about 3.5 cc," Beth said, doing the conversion in her head.

"Then let's use half that," Kate said. *They will see increased strength and speed. Maybe it will be enough that they will be satisfied with that. They have never actually measured the strength or speed of one of us or the monkeys since they never let them out for fear of being infected.*

Two hours before sunrise, Kate held up a filled syringe. "We only had time for a single dose, but it's ready." *One more piece in place.*

"I'll email Henri and share our findings." *Minus the info about limited replication, of course.*

CHAPTER THIRTY-EIGHT

JON

JON LAY ON THE bed with his eyes closed. He wasn't sure how long he'd been lying there, but he knew it was daylight. He could feel the heaviness of it on his limbs. He tried to focus on anything but the thirst, even the pain of his charred skin. He kept the radio tuned to 147 and on low in the bathroom. He didn't know how much battery remained, and he was too weak to go and check. Eric had given a message to Beth and Kate to keep it on as a way for him to alert Jon when the plan was underway, but not to use it just in case the frequency was monitored. It gave him hope, but even that was fleeting when he was so distracted by the thirst and keeping himself together. He was so focused on maintaining his control he didn't hear Nancy approach the door to his room.

"Jon," she said quietly. But Jon was lost in the agony of his thirst and pain. "Jon," she repeated louder this time. At first, he thought that he had imagined the voice, but slowly, he became aware of his surroundings. He saw her at the door, but not before his senses keyed in on the scent of her blood and the sloshing beating of her heart. It was the sweetest rhythm to his ears. The two together made his fangs elongate, and without thinking, he licked his lips.

"Jon," Nancy said a third time. And this time, he heard her at the same time he heard her badge scan on the keypad to his room. It took all his strength to speak and hold himself prone on the bed.

"Do...not...come...in." The words came out slowly and around his fangs. He had to warn her. He was certain that if she came closer, he wouldn't be able to control himself. He was weak, especially in the daylight hours, but his instinct to feed was strong and slowly taking over his conscious control of it.

Nancy heard him and paused before opening the door. He heard the door lock.

"I thought you were unconscious."

"No...just..." He thought hard for the word. "Starving."

"I'm so sorry, Jon. Dr. Henri still won't allow me to feed you."

He didn't open his eyes, battling with the thirst. The smell of her was even more torture than being alone with the thirst.

"I came to check on you." He remained silent until Nancy continued. "Dr. Giffard says she misses you."

Jon was slow to process the information. He talked with his friends every morning before dawn telepathically. They didn't need to send a message to him through Nancy, but he was sure they did it to let him know through the night that they were thinking of him and to remind him they had an ally.

He turned his face to the door in what felt like slow motion and opened his eyes. "Thank you...Nancy." He saw her bite her lip, tears welling in her eyes as she looked at him. "Please, tell Kate...tell Kate..." There was so very much he wanted to say, but telling Kate he had feelings for her through another person was not the way he wanted her to find out. "I miss our breakfasts together."

Nancy nodded and sniffed back tears. "Please don't give up," she whispered.

Jon held her gaze for only a moment and then once again closed his eyes, spent.

KATE

Kate called out to Jon as soon as she returned to her sleeping quarters. It had become her habit. Jon needed the contact, but so did she. Apart from when she was sleeping, she spoke with Jon every time he was within range. She could feel him weakening, and with each new night, she felt more desperate to free him. He was a fighter, a warrior, but he also had a gentleness about him. He had opened his mind and his heart to her. Maybe others didn't get the opportunity to see it, but she did.

Jon, are you awake?

His response was slow, as if he had been sleeping, but the need and hunger flowed freely through their thoughts. He could no longer suppress his emotions or sensations. He was just too weak. *I'm here. I've missed you, too, Kate.*

Kate smiled a sad smile and closed her eyes to hold back tears.

Don't cry. It meant a lot to me to receive your message from Nancy. His thoughts were a little disjointed and slow, but loud and clear.

Mr. Rice's daughter arrives this week.

There was a long pause from Jon, and Kate thought for a moment he had fallen asleep, but she still felt the ache of his thirst. *How many days until then?*

His words pulled at Kate's heart. He no longer knew what day it was. She didn't want to hear the doubt and despair that came to her so clearly through the bond.

Four days, Jon. We... I will get to you. I'm not about to let you go. She didn't know what else to say; she was overwhelmed by the emotions pouring off of him. His agony made her tears fall. She sat down on the edge of her bed and put her head in her hands. *Don't give up. I...I don't want to lose you. I think I'm falling in love with you.* The revelation wasn't something she had planned to share. They had known each other for such a short time. But the feelings were raw and real, and not knowing if she would ever have the chance to tell him face to face, she needed him to know.

She felt his joy, if only fleeting, through their link. *You sure know how to pick 'em.* And Kate half laughed, half cried.

Hang on, Jon, just a little bit longer.

I will. And then he was gone. Kate knew he had fallen asleep again because the intensity of his thirst had left her.

She exhaled, feeling guilty at her relief to be free of the sensation. None of them knew how long vampires could survive without blood, but she could feel he was nearing his limits. She knew the group had agreed to hold off on giving v2.2 to Jon for as long as possible, but that time had come. Even if they had to leave as soon as Jon turned and risk their plan, it was time to get v2.2 to Nancy.

Chapter Thirty-Nine

Peter

Mr. Rice had wasted no time in returning his call. Peter wasn't certain if that was because he was eager to tap additional resources or concerned about a competitor. Either way, the ruse had worked, and he was on board one of Mr. Rice's private planes headed for Tampa.

"Can I get you something to drink, Dr. Miller?"

It took a moment to shake Peter from his thoughts. He wasn't used to the alias yet. His new identity was that of Dr. James Miller, virologist at Axis Solutions. Axis Solutions was a company owned by the Master, acquired nearly fifteen years prior. Rather than a research center, however, Axis Solutions was a private security company serving many of the Master's allies, along with other unsavory associates.

"I'd like an old-fashioned, please," and he shared his most charming smile. The stewardess beamed back at him. She was blonde, tall, and curvy; not his type. He liked them athletic and lean, more like Beth if he was being honest. But he would not be dismissive. He needed to play his part. He had even picked up a couple of virology journals to thumb through on the flight. Being up to date with the recent articles would only make his story more believable.

His knowledge of virology was rather basic, although he had brushed up on things in the few days before his departure, and of course, he had nearly memorized all of Dr. Giffard's notes on her research so far. As long as they didn't test him in the laboratory, he thought he could present a plausible front, enough to convince Mr. Rice and Dr. Henri that he was another scientist whom Beth had contacted with her initial samples. If Beth were there, he would have to think on his feet to make her believe he was done with the Master. He would admit that she was right about him. It would be a first step in forming an alliance with her that would hopefully end in his being turned.

The stewardess returned with his drink as he gazed out the window. "Here you are, doctor. Please let me know if you need anything else."

He thanked her and took a sip of the strong drink. The burn in his throat was comforting.

If things went poorly today, he would either be removed from the premises or killed, considering Mr. Rice's background. But if it came to that, he would offer the Master and the reality of his identity in trade for his life. Mr. Rice would certainly be interested in the Master's true intentions. Once the Master was certain Mr. Rice was involved with Beth, he would do whatever was necessary to take care of the threat. These sorts of tasks were Anubis' specialty. He and whatever team he had would assess the risk and make his and the facility's demise look like accidents.

Peter took another sip of his drink and settled back in his seat, opening one of the journals and trying to read. But his thoughts wouldn't let him. The final scenario, with neither Dr. Henri nor Beth at the facility, would mean a quick trip back to Kansas, where he would have to deal with the Master's ongoing denial of his request to be turned. This was the result he feared the most. His more recent interactions with the Master had been strained, and Peter was concerned the Master might suspect his loyalty was faltering. As good as he was at containing his emotions, the Master had an uncanny ability to read people. And if the day came when he considered Peter either disloyal or a threat, it would no doubt be his last.

He had trusted the Master without question for so many years, but no longer. So much so that he removed all traces of Dr. Giffard's research from his home safe and computer, placing it all in a lock box at the bank near his office. He had also placed papers and other various objects in positions that would allow him to easily tell if they had been moved. If the Master suspected him enough to have his apartment searched, he would find nothing to raise further suspicions.

The life he had imagined for himself since he was fifteen and taken in by the Master was gone. He had a new vision of his future, and this was to be the first step in his plan. He centered himself with a cleansing breath and another sip of the old-fashioned, and then focused on the article in front of him.

Peter had a good understanding of all the articles in the journals by the time they landed and was back to thinking about the Master. While the Master had paid the bill for his education, he had been the one to complete the courses and residency with high marks. His high IQ made most tasks easy for him, and his ease at understanding what he had read bolstered his confidence.

Peter stood and collected his bag, thanking the stewardess and the pilot as he exited the aircraft. A burly man in a black suit and tie met him at the bottom of the staircase.

"Dr. Miller. I'm Byron Fields, head of security at New Dimension Analytics. Mr. Rice asked me to provide you with an escort."

Byron extended his hand to Peter, and he shook it firmly. Byron's hand was large enough to swallow his own, and his biceps stretched the fabric of his suit as he returned the gesture. His hair was cut in a flat top over his alert steel gray eyes. He was clean-shaven, and a glance at his feet revealed black leather shoes that had been polished to a high shine. He screamed ex-military.

He offered to take Peter's bag, which he accepted, and then led him to a waiting black sedan, opening the passenger side door for him and placing his bag in the trunk.

The ride to New Dimension Analytics was long. Byron seemed to Peter to be far more adept at lifting weights than he was at conversation. But it was fine by him; he had never been one for small talk. So after the usual niceties, they fell into silence.

The private airstrip was a few miles outside Tampa. The downtown skyscrapers he had seen as they'd come in for landing quickly faded into the distance over their trip to the facility. Peter watched the scenery, so different from his home, pass by the window, changing from scattered palm trees and live oaks to the thicker scrub and then swampland the farther northeast of Tampa they drove. He saw the occasional ibis and even a single osprey, a small fish dangling as he flew overhead.

As they approached the facility, nearly an hour and a half later, Peter noted the guard station with what appeared to be other stations in the distance. The perimeter was surrounded by tall chain-link fencing topped by two rows of razor wire. Peter had been to several research facilities and laboratories in his career, but none had been so heavily fortified, supporting his suspicions of Mr. Rice and his interests. Byron showed his badge at the main gate, and they were allowed to pass.

The parking lot outside the facility held maybe thirty cars, surprisingly few for such a large facility. But for all he knew, there were others elsewhere around the building that he couldn't see. Rather than a large sign or name on the side of the building, a rectangular sign, around only four by five feet, was all that declared the building New Dimension Analytics. There was no tagline or other information to suggest its purpose either. Merely a symbol consisting of an intersecting N, D, and A in navy blue.

The entrance to the building, however, was impressive. Tall glass doors surrounded by silver mirrored metal showed a second row of security doors inside, which opened into a large, two-story lobby. There was no seating for waiting visitors, only a single but large white marble desk occupied by another black suit, black tie man who could have been a close cousin of Byron's. He nodded to Byron as he passed.

After they cleared both rows of security doors, Byron led Peter to another set of security doors that opened into a wide corridor. After two additional checkpoints opened with Byron's security card, they continued down a pale gray corridor until they reached an open door. Byron stopped at the entry and motioned for Peter to continue inside.

Peter thanked Byron, who nodded in return before turning abruptly to leave, looking like a soldier doing an about-face in formation.

As Peter entered, Dr. Henri raised his head and peered at him through his glasses, which were positioned near the end of his nose. He rose, wiped his hands on his rumpled tan pants, and continued toward him with his hand out. "You must be Dr. Miller. I'm Dr. Liam Henri, geneticist. Pleased to meet you."

"The pleasure is mine, Dr. Henri. Thank you for having me." Peter's glance around the room showed them to be alone. "Will Mr. Rice be joining us?"

"Momentarily." Dr. Henri motioned for Peter to have a seat on a low-backed sofa positioned to face a large video screen. He chose a seat near the end and placed his elbow on the arm. "Coffee?" Dr. Henri asked.

"Yes, please. Black," Peter replied as Dr. Henri headed to a cabinet behind him before he heard the sounds of a Keurig and smelled the bitter-warm scent of a strong roast. It removed the tension of his ride to the compound, and when Dr. Henri brought him the cup, he gave a genuine, "Thank you."

Dr. Henri sat at the opposite end of the sofa, placing his coffee on the table in front of them, a bit of coffee sloshing over the rim of the overly full cup he had carried with him.

Peter schooled his face as he studied him. He had seen pictures of him from surveillance, of course, but the pictures didn't capture his personality. He was haughty and not entirely genuine in his greeting. His shirt and pants, while clean, appeared in need of ironing. His hair was salt and pepper, beginning to show his scalp, and swept to one side as if to hide it. A manila folder lay on the table beside his coffee, papers shoved inside but not straightened. It was all Peter could do not to reach out and fix it.

"Mr. Rice will be joining us by video from his jet. He rarely visits in person but checks in regularly. However, he does have an upcoming visit at the end of the month. If we are able to come to an agreement, I'm sure he would like to meet you when he is here."

Peter supposed that being in constant motion would be convenient if he wished to avoid being located or targeted. It was, after all, one of the reasons Air Force One took to the air in times of trouble to protect the president. Well, that and the fighter planes that accompanied it. Peter assumed Mr. Rice's plane would be heavily guarded as well, even without the fighters.

The screen before them changed from blue to white and was then filled with the image of a man, probably in his late forties or early fifties. He was handsome, even though Peter wasn't into men, and impeccably dressed; his demeanor screamed alpha male. Peter sat a little straighter and taller in his seat. He was used to the Master's intimidation, but also accustomed to being in control of the situation at all other times when not in his presence.

He told himself to reel it in. Peter was playing the part of a cutting-edge virologist, a scientist who wanted to work with this man, not position himself at the head of the table.

"Dr. Miller. I am delighted you were able to make the trip to our facility. I hope your travel was comfortable," Mr. Rice said.

"Extremely. I do appreciate your arrangements, and I am eager to see the rest of the facility," Peter said.

"Dr. Henri will provide you with a tour when we're finished here," Mr. Rice said. "Dr. Miller, as you know, I was very intrigued by your request to meet with me. Forgive my curiosity, but it is the nature of my business to need to know what I can about my business associates. I had my team look into your background and that of Axis Solutions. Other than details of your training and a few papers from the time of your education, you leave a minimal footprint on the internet."

"I suppose that's true," Peter said. "Mr. Amun recruited me straight out of my PhD program, and I've worked in his private lab since. The nature of some of our work requires a high level of confidentiality. That doesn't lend itself to publications or speaking engagements." He hoped that would satisfy him. He didn't wish to raise any suspicions that would cause Mr. Rice to think that James Miller was anything but his true identity.

Mr. Rice's posture remained relaxed, his arms resting comfortably on the armrests of his leather desk chair. "I can understand confidentiality. It's something we take very seriously here as well." He took a notable pause before continuing, considering his next words. "Axis Solutions appears to have a history primarily in private security. The fact that Mr. Amun requested the services of a virologist suggests to me there may be more to it." With this, he leaned forward, crossing his arms on the desk in front of him and maintaining eye contact with Peter, likely seeing if he would flinch, but Peter had assumed they would travel this path in their discussion when the Master had chosen to use Axis Solutions as his site of employment. It tied in perfectly with what they believed Mr. Rice was up to.

"Mr. Amun thinks outside the box. Providing security solutions can meet with all kinds of challenges, and in the current age, biological threats and how to defend against them must be a part of that solution."

Mr. Rice nodded. Peter glanced quickly to assess Dr. Henri's response to their discussion. He was focused on Mr. Rice but seemed unsurprised by the topic of conversation. It made Peter wonder how much Dr. Henri knew about this man and his past.

"So, you mentioned in our brief phone call that you have had some success creating enhanced regeneration with gene therapy by use of a novel virus. I'm sure you can understand my curiosity about how you happened on this previously unknown virus."

"Of course, while I can't take credit for its discovery, I can for the subsequent study of its potential use. A little over two months ago, I received a letter, along with patient records and access to blood and tissue samples from an infected individual." Peter paused to give Mr. Rice time to respond.

"Dr. Ramsey," Mr. Rice said matter-of-factly.

Peter felt pleased. He was right. Dr. Henri had come to Mr. Rice with the information. Now he needed to find out if Beth was here.

"She contacted me as well," Dr. Henri added. "How did you manage your limited sample?"

"I had nearly exhausted it, trying to culture it or infect rats and guineas with no success. But then I thought about the most basic need of a vampire...blood. So I tried adding leukocyte-reduced whole blood to the cultures with the last of my sample, and to my great delight, it worked. I synthesized enough to map the viral RNA and separate the fragments, which, using an AAV virus, were small enough to be incorporated by the lesser mammals and allow me to identify the segments coding for the enhanced regeneration. I believe that with some refinement, they could be used in humans."

Dr. Henri shifted uncomfortably in his seat and glanced from Peter to Mr. Rice, who shook his head ever so slightly. Being used to the Master's subtle movements, Peter didn't miss it. They were holding something back.

"Your employer wishes to combine our efforts and resources to bring it to market?" Mr. Rice asked.

"Yes, exactly." Peter considered his next words. "And to explore the possibilities using the remaining segments—"

"As another of Axis Solutions' pre-emptive defenses," Mr. Rice said.

"Exactly," Peter said again. Perhaps it was time to reveal more of his plan to suggest to Mr. Rice that they would be open to whatever nefarious plans they had in mind and draw him out. "As much progress as I have made, Mr. Amun would like to take the next steps. Following the more traditional means would be a lengthy process. He feels, as do I, that sometimes the end goal is important enough that typical rules of study do not apply. There are people who could benefit from our research long before the scientific community would be willing to allow its use. Exceptions...and sacrifices must be made." Peter didn't think he could suggest human trials any more strongly without saying the words.

"We are in agreement, Dr. Miller, and prepared to proceed by any means necessary." Again, he looked to Dr. Henri, but this time nodded.

Peter believed he was finally getting somewhere, only to have his hopes dashed with Mr. Rice's next words. "I would like to arrange a meeting with Mr. Amun at his earliest convenience. I do believe we may have much to offer one another. I would like to know more about his other business endeavors. Perhaps Axis Solutions would have ideas for improvement of my more difficult personal security issues."

"I will arrange a meeting right away," Peter said, masking his irritation. If Beth was here, having the Master join them was the last thing he wanted. He had to find Beth before letting that happen. "In the meantime, Mr. Amun has left it at my discretion to share the progress of my research. I would be most intrigued to see what progress Dr. Henri has made from the standpoint of a geneticist, a specialty I have been urging Mr. Amun to recruit. Do you have other virologists and geneticists here working on this project?" Peter asked.

"Dr. Henri can fill you in on all the details of his research so far and introduce you to our personnel. I think there will be one in particular that you will be very interested in meeting, along with her guest. Dr. Henri, I trust you can make the proper introductions and relay the details of the meeting with Mr. Amun to my assistant."

Mr. Rice had said 'her' and it wasn't lost on Peter. The smile he offered was almost genuine. It had to be Beth. He wasn't nearly as thrilled to see her guest, whom he could only assume must be Luciano. It was a wrinkle he hadn't expected since Mr. Verde had not been with her in New Orleans. Reasoning with him would be difficult. He needed to speak with Beth first and convince her that they could help one another.

"Certainly," Dr. Henri said, giving Mr. Rice a single bow-like nod.

The screen went blank as quickly as it had come on.

Dr. Henri turned to him, rising to his feet and taking a last sip of his coffee, which he left sitting on the table. Peter added his alongside it. "Shall we?"

Dr. Henri hurried along the corridors, all the same anemic gray and well-lit. They reminded Peter of a hospital. Every hall seemed identical, which made making a mental map of the place difficult.

Dr. Henri stopped at a door that looked like all of the rest, with a narrow rectangular window, and badged in. Peter followed him into the room, which was apparently Dr. Henri's private lab. It was an absolute mess. It wasn't just disorganized but disgusting, with empty cups of coffee and wrappers discarded wherever they landed, and coffee rings on the tables and papers. The open spaces, which were few, appeared to have been cleaned along with the floors, and Peter was immediately thankful he wasn't the housekeeping crew that had to try to navigate what was trash and what wasn't as they cleaned.

Dr. Henri prattled on about his work, showing Peter culture plates and numerous printouts of mapped genes. Peter listened, attempting to appear interested while trying not to touch anything.

"This was as far I had been able to get until I reached out to Dr. Ramsey for more samples, and she and Dr. Giffard joined me here. Dr. Ramsey was correct in believing that the combined efforts of a geneticist and a virologist would be needed to make significant gains."

For a moment, Peter wasn't certain he had heard him correctly. Dr. Giffard was dead. How could she have possibly survived the explosion? He had watched her go in. If the Master discovered he had failed again...

But Dr. Miller wouldn't know this. He wouldn't know Dr. Giffard at all. Peter squashed his emotions and returned to his role.

"Dr. Ramsey is here?" Peter asked.

"Yes, she joined us about a month ago. She is equally brilliant and naive. I have attempted to persuade her to consider what could be gained by using more than just the regenerative benefits of the virus, but she has been resistant. We have had to resort to motivations I would have preferred to avoid."

"What motivations might those be?" Peter asked. From what little he knew of Beth, the only thing that would motivate her to act on something unsavory was to save the lives of others, and even then, it was a long shot. *What could he have threatened her with?*

"Dr. Ramsey brought her initial test subject, Jon Wilks, with her, along with Dr. Giffard. The two doctors are quite fond of Mr. Wilks. To reach our goals, we had to separate them from one another, along with her human friend."

Human friend. Peter struggled to put it all together in his head. *Why would they give Luciano an alias while using their own names? Or were they trying to pass this Jon Wilks off as Luciano? Wait, if Beth succeeded with v2, then Luciano would likely appear human; her human friend. But who is Jon Wilks?*

Whatever the reasons for their deception, Peter believed it would work to his advantage. Beth was stuck here, her friends in jeopardy. Perhaps she would be willing to bargain, his assistance with her freedom for a new downside-free vampire virus. He knew he was walking a thin line, bargaining with Beth while avoiding telling the Master what he was up to. He needed to play both sides of the fence until he could see which was going to be the most beneficial for him.

"If you are unwilling to accept our arrangement—" Dr. Henri began, mistaking his pause for uncertainty.

"No, no, it's not that. I was just processing the information. This work is important. I understand you did what you had to in order to secure your access to the test subject and ample viral samples. It won't be a problem. We have to focus on the end goal," Peter said. And he meant it, just not toward the same goal as Dr. Henri.

"Splendid. Then let's go discuss our current focus with the ladies," Henri said, and Peter nodded. He considered buying time, but in the end, it wouldn't matter. Either Beth would immediately call him out on his deception or not. As Dr. Henri had mentioned, she was bright. In her predicament, he hoped that meant she would assess the entire situation before speaking. After all, Peter also knew of her lies.

This was about to become interesting.

Chapter Forty

Kate

Kate stood leaning against the wall in the corner of the treatment area and scanned the room. Since the incident with Dr. Henri and the new vampire he had attempted to create, Kate and Beth had been allowed in the treatment wing whenever experiments were being conducted. Despite saving his life, Henri's attitude toward them hadn't improved. In fact, it seemed worse, as though he resented them for making him seem weak.

Kate watched for Nancy as it neared time for her shift. While Kate could talk with Jon through the bond, Nancy was the only one who actually got to see him to report his appearance back to her. Kate looked down at the clipboard in her hands and pretended to look it over while keeping her eyes raised just enough to still see the movements of everyone in the treatment room.

This evening would include more testing of the new limited retrovirus that Beth and Kate had created. Testing of the first small batch had resulted in men with increased strength, speed, and stamina as well as incredible regenerative abilities, but they had yet to test their resistance to infection. Even though they were obviously enhanced, Beth and Kate found their abilities were significantly inferior to their own, but this was something they were keeping to themselves. While Dr. Henri was testing Jon's ability to regenerate and survive without blood, he hadn't tested Jon's other abilities fully, so he didn't know his new test subjects were inferior.

Kate had asked Henri about Jon numerous times. Before Kate's attempt to reach him, Dr. Henri had shown her a still image of Jon in his cell, taken from the hallway camera. It had shown bits of drywall hanging from the steel bars of his room, evidence of his escape attempt. But her subsequent questions had been answered with, "He is and will be fine as long as you cooperate." Knowing this was a complete and utter lie made it all the harder not to tear off his head each time he was in the room.

Kate watched Beth as she spoke with one of the nurses. She was more stoic, rarely asking about Luciano. Kate knew from their conversations that Beth felt not discussing him would cause Henri to think him less important as a mere human companion. She hoped he would continue to leave him alone, other than the forced work detail.

Kate raised her gaze as Nancy badged through the treatment center door and locked eyes with her. Jon's words to Kate this evening were the least he had said to her in a day since they had met. She had gone to the freezer, removed the syringe of v2.2, and placed it in her pocket. She knew the others might be angry, but she also knew Beth would understand.

She walked as calmly as she could over to Nancy, holding the same patient chart in her hands. She handed it to Nancy and whispered, "How is Jon?"

Nancy bit her lip and blinked slowly, but before she could answer, Kate saw Nancy's eyes dart to the treatment room door as Dr. Henri entered with a man she hadn't seen before. He was attractive but lean and wiry. He had a short, wavy crop of light brown-blonde hair and attentive but intense green eyes. As she watched, they locked onto something and held there. She followed his stare to Beth, who stood frozen, staring back. Kate could feel the tension.

Beth, what's wrong? Who is he?

Dr. Peter James. He works for the Master.

The Master? Oh, shit. So if he's here...

The Master must be close behind and working with Mr. Rice. Beth's eyes quickly scanned the room before she turned to exit the treatment room, Kate close behind her. But their retreat was halted by Dr. Henri's voice calling them back.

"Dr. Ramsey, Dr. Giffard, could you join us? I would like to introduce you to Dr. James Miller, a virologist from Axis Solutions. He is planning to join our team," Dr. Henri said.

Kate and Beth turned and walked slowly back to the two men.

I thought you said his name is Peter James?

It is. I don't know what he's up to, but it can't be good. Keep your eyes open for any other new faces. The Master could be here with him. Beth managed to keep her face blank, but Kate could feel the Herculean effort it took, her anxiety making Kate want to fidget, so she crammed her hands in her pockets.

Something had changed with Jon, but her conversation with Nancy had been cut short. It would have to wait a few more minutes. If this man was one of the Master's minions, they needed to know his plans now.

Dr. James, or whatever the hell his name was, looked at Kate before turning back to Beth. Beth stared at him, and he returned it, until it began to get uncomfortable. Kate was certain Beth was trying to read his thoughts.

"Have the two of you met?" Dr. Henri said.

After another uncomfortable pause, Beth spoke. "I'm not sure.

Have we worked at the same facility before? I'm usually good with faces, and I could swear I've seen yours before. Where did you say you've been working?"

He's nervous, Beth thought to Kate. Kate could feel it too. Whatever he was doing, he didn't want to be found out.

"Axis Solutions. Perhaps you saw my photo online. I'm sure you researched each of the virologists to whom you sent samples," Peter said. He was lying, Kate could feel it and hear the edge in his voice. He wanted Beth to play along with whatever ruse he had concocted; the question was why.

He wants to hide his identity, but I don't know why. If the Master knew we were here and what Mr. Rice was doing, he would just level the facility, not send in Peter, Beth thought.

"That must be it. But apparently, my research and my warnings were insufficient. It seems, since you are here to work with Dr. Henri and being introduced to his slave labor, that I've managed to choose two scientists unencumbered by morality or compassion."

Kate swallowed hard and shifted her weight to her other foot as Dr. Henri glared at Beth. Dr. Miller...er, Peter's eye twitched, but he didn't lose his composure. Whatever he wanted, he must want it badly to take the insult without a reaction.

"I feared you were dead from the letter you included. I'm pleased that's not the case," Dr. James said. He extended his hand toward Beth. Kate could feel Beth's unease, but she took his hand, shook it briefly, and dropped it as though he were infectious. If Dr. Henri noticed, he said nothing.

"And you then are Dr. Giffard," Dr. James said, offering his hand to her. She shook it as well and felt another spike of anxiety from Beth when she did. She couldn't wait to hear this story.

"We have made significant progress since Dr. Giffard and Dr. Ramsey joined us. I'm hopeful that with yet another virologist, we can proceed even more quickly," Dr. Henri said and received a not-so-friendly stare from them both in return.

"I'm aware that the situation here is not entirely to your liking, but I'm hopeful we can make the best of working together," Dr. James said, looking to Beth and Kate in turn. "Dr. Ramsey, I reviewed the documents from your research on the test subject. I am completely impressed with your discovery as well as your creative ideas for its use. My initial experiments were unsuccessful, with the intact virus appearing to be too much for smaller mammals. It took some time to discover that the virus could only be cultured with a constant blood source."

"Yes, it seems his research path followed yours fairly closely," Dr. Henri said, looking at both Beth and Kate.

I'll bet they did, since he likely retrieved your notes from the shotgun house, Beth thought.

Kate lost her composure for a fraction of a second and sucked in a breath, but then recovered with a forced smile.

Is he the one who blew up my lab...and me? Kate could feel the anger that she had so narrowly contained over the last few days building again. She was glad her hands were in her pockets since they were now both balled into fists.

Keep calm. We need to know what he wants. Beth's eyes followed Dr. Henri's from hers to the watch on his arm, and Beth glanced up at the wall clock. "I suppose you would like me to fill him in on our progress here? I wouldn't want you to have to work overtime."

Dr. Henri's smile was more of a grimace. "Yes, I have another matter to attend to and will return in thirty minutes to collect Dr. Miller and show him to his quarters for the night. And I should remind you that Mr. Rice is still waiting for your report."

He's going to be waiting a lot longer, too. Kate thought.

He was referring to the report on their v2.2 virus, which they had no intention of providing. "Working on it," Beth said, a tinge of sarcasm in her voice.

A faint flush in his cheeks, Dr. Henri turned to Peter. "Dr. Miller, don't hesitate to ask one of the staff to contact me should you need me to return sooner."

"I'm certain we will find plenty to discuss," Peter said, giving Dr. Henri a nod. Dr. Henri then turned on his heel and left the room.

"Why are you here? And give me one good reason why I shouldn't tell him who you really are," Beth said through clenched teeth as soon as Dr. Henri was out of earshot.

"Because I came here to help you," Peter said.

"And you expect me to believe that?"

"Okay, I came here to help us both," Peter said, holding his hands up in front of him, palms facing Beth. "You were right about the Master."

This stopped Beth's fuming. Kate watched as she narrowed her eyes and stared at Peter.

What were you right about?

That Peter was just his underling, never to be turned, and that he would be killed the very second he was no longer useful.

"Go on," Beth said to Peter.

"I tracked Dr. Henri here. With Dr. Giffard's lab gone," now it was Kate's eyes that narrowed to stare at him, "and knowing you had sent samples to Dr. Henri, I thought you may be here as well. I told the Master about Henri, but said that the timing was wrong for his actions here to have included you. He sent me to find and investigate Dr. Henri and Mr. Rice, but I came to find you."

"Apart from doing the Master's bidding, why would you want to locate me?"

"I read Dr. Giffard's research, but didn't share it with the Master. I know about v1 and v2. I want you to turn me, but without the bloodlust and sun sensitivity."

"You're assuming Luciano's transformation was successful," Kate said, knowing this was not in her notes.

"Wasn't it?" Peter turned to her, but Kate didn't answer.

"Why would I do that?" Beth asked.

Peter dropped his head. "Mr. Rice wants a meeting with the Master. I can delay that and keep your presence here from him as long as possible, as well as do whatever I can to help you escape with Luciano and Jon Wilks. Who is he anyway?"

"A friend," Kate said. "That's all you need to know."

Peter's face looked pinched. He clearly wanted to say more, but held it back and turned to Beth.

"When you leave, I want to go with you unless you have some of your v2 here. If I leave the Master, which I intend to do, I have very little chance of surviving on my own unless I'm a vampire. I can tell you everything I know about the Master and his operations. Perhaps something could help you evade him or..." Peter trailed off.

"Or what?" Beth prodded.

"Or kill him. You know he will never stop hunting any of us while he's still alive. I know you think making vampires known to the world will stop him, but it won't. He's even called in Anubis, one of his *friends,* to assist him, and I've never seen anyone survive after he's involved."

Beth thought for a moment, clearly torn. She finally inhaled, exhaled a long, slow breath, and closed her eyes, opening them just before she spoke. "The v2 virus won't work on you. It's primarily stop codons that block the undesirable effects when someone is already infected with the Vampyre virus. We think the segments that are causing the bloodlust and sun sensitivity are not because of the proteins the segments code for, but because the fragments are inserted in or adjacent to other important genes, altering their function. It looks like an error in the design of the original virus."

"In the design? You don't think this was a natural virus?" Peter asked, his eyes wide. "Vampires have been around for millennia. No one had that kind of capability."

"Evidently, someone did. We can't explain how it happened, but this virus was engineered. We don't know what the misplaced segments code for, but when injected into small mammals, they have no obvious effects. We have been working on a new version of the vampire virus with Dr. Henri with those elements removed. He has forced us into performing human trials on homeless men whom they have collected against their will," Beth said. "We've slowed the process as much as we can, but it's only a matter of time before he has his own team of super soldiers, for lack of a better name."

Do you think you should be telling him all of this? Kate asked.

If the Master learns of what Mr. Rice is doing, he will stop him. He's already after us, and that won't change either way. I don't trust Peter, but I do know that if the Master finds out he has withheld anything from him, he will kill him on the spot. He knows he's on borrowed time.

Peter paused to absorb the information. "What's next? Do you have a plan to get out of here?"

"Not yet, but until we do, we play along," Beth said.

Kate was relieved that Beth didn't reveal anything about their plan.

They needed time to see if Peter could actually be trusted. She would much rather grab him on the way out than tell him any details. "Let us show you around as Dr. Henri requested, so we don't raise any suspicions."

They proceeded with the tour of the treatment area and summarized explanations of their regeneration trials, maintaining appearances until Dr. Henri returned to collect Peter. That finally gave Kate a chance to return to her conversation with Nancy, who was waiting, having watched the exchange with Dr. James. Nervous energy had been pouring off of her since she entered the treatment room.

"I could scarcely wake him today, and even then, only for a moment," Nancy said when Kate asked again how Jon was doing.

Kate tried to mask her facial expression and stifled a quick inhale. She couldn't give away their conversation. Something had to be done, and now. Jon's life was already in danger, and with the Master now hot on their heels, she was even more convinced that what she was about to do was the right move.

"You need to get this to him as soon as you can," Kate said, placing the syringe of v2.2 into Nancy's lab coat pocket at vampire speed. Nancy slowly placed her hand inside the pocket and felt the syringe.

"I don't know if I can get it to him without Henri knowing, but I will do whatever I can. What is it?" Nancy asked.

"A cure. We need him to be able to move in the daylight in case plans change," Kate whispered, and Nancy nodded. She handed the clipboard back to Kate to make their conversation seem work-related and continued on with her duties.

Kate had just pushed the plan forward, and they all needed to be ready.

CHAPTER FORTY-ONE

MASTER

THE MASTER LOOKED AT his cell phone; it was Peter. He had been expecting the call for some time now. "Pardon me," he said to Neheb before accepting the call. "Yes," the Master said, irritation clear in his tone as he walked toward the fireplace in his office and grabbed a poker to stoke the fire.

"Henri is here," Peter said. He summarized his day and the research Dr. Henri had completed so far, ending with their plans for 'super soldiers.'

Had he not predicted as much when Dr. Ramsey stood in front of him in this very room? After so many years of keeping the vampires in check, the truth of their nature hidden and feared, the curse the Vampyre had bestowed on him kept secret from the rest of the world, one scientist had put it all in jeopardy.

"What have you learned of Mr. Rice?" the Master said, leaning against the poker and feeling the warmth of the fire on his skin.

"He seems to be either a recluse, running from something, or both—"

"Yes, yes, I know all of this. What are his weaknesses and the best way to get to him?" The Master began to tap the poker on the floor impatiently. He wanted Peter to get to the point. They needed to know how to end Mr. Rice and any traces of the Vampyre virus along with him.

"His daughter. It is the only weakness I see. He plans to use the new regeneration virus to heal her at the end of the month," Peter said.

"Have they agreed to keep you on?" The Master raised the poker and closed the wire screens in front of the now roaring fire with the tip before replacing it in the rack.

"Yes, I am to work with another virologist to—"

"Is there an easy way for Anubis and me to get inside?" He could hear irritation in Peter's voice after being interrupted twice, but the boy prattled on like an old woman, and his time was valuable.

"Mr. Rice had asked that I arrange a meeting between the two of you. I suggested you would be interested in exploring other uses of the virus and providing additional resources toward that end. He had information on Axis Solutions and understood your interests would lean toward using it in the security field. He wishes to discuss the details."

"Very well. Arrange a video call at a time convenient to him, but after sunset, and I will make myself available. He and I can negotiate an in-person visit. Anubis can take it from there." The Master turned and walked to his favorite chair in front of the fireplace, sat, and crossed his ankles, his elbow leaning on the arm. "Any word of Dr. Ramsey?"

"No. There is no sign of her here." Peter's response was quick, perhaps too quick, and his voice pitched ever so slightly higher, as though he was nervous. But why would the mention of Dr. Ramsey make him anxious? He had been acting oddly since he discovered the Master kept records on all his associates, including him. So much so that the Master had requested that Peter's apartment be searched while he was away. But that had proven his concerns unfounded, finding nothing amiss. He hoped he could still use Peter's skills in the morgue for some years to come, but perhaps he was once again having second thoughts about his intentions to turn him. He would deal with that when this little irritation was eradicated.

"Continue to gather information. Slow their progress in whatever way you can until we have a clear means to neutralize the threat."

"Yes, Master."

The Master ended the call and rubbed his chin. He turned to his right and gave Neheb a small, tired grin. "I have another job for you, old friend. I think you will enjoy this one."

Chapter Forty-Two

Beth

You did what? Beth thought, not believing what Kate had just said. She sat down hard on one of the lab benches. Her thoughts were disorganized and flying. After all their preparation...

I gave Jon's dose of v2.2 to Nancy and asked her to give it to him. We agreed we had to wait until the last possible moment. He's dying, Beth. He barely responded to any of us last night. That time is now, Kate thought.

Beth glanced at the wall clock. It was almost 7:00 a.m. She dropped her head into her hands to try to think. Kate had forced their hand. She and Kate had argued over minor things before, but she had never been angry with her until now.

Kate shifted her weight from foot to foot and chewed the nail on her index finger. *I know you're angry. I can feel it, and I don't blame you. But what if it was Luciano? Can you look me in the eye and tell me you wouldn't have done the same?*

It made Beth even angrier, but not at her words. At herself. Because she knew Kate was right. She could no more have waited patiently while Luc died than Kate could while Jon did.

Even though she didn't need to breathe, she took several long, deep breaths to clear her head and think through what must be done. It was a full two days before Mr. Rice and his daughter were due to arrive.

If Nancy had given it to Jon already, if his body was strong enough to survive the change in his weakened state, and if Dr. Henri didn't discover something was amiss when he went to torture him today, he would awaken after sunset, starving for human food.

We have to get back to our room to tell Luc to be ready. Then we have to get to Nancy. If she has given the dose to Jon, she and Eric need to be ready to leave tonight.

Both women jumped when they heard the sound of a keycard being scanned at the lab door. They had been so engrossed in their discussion that they hadn't seen anyone approach. Both watched as two technicians from the treatment wing entered, one male, one female. Beth couldn't recall their names. Her muscles tightened. She knew the reason for their presence would not be pleasant if Dr. Henri had sent them.

The male, Travis by his name tag, spoke first. "Mr. Rice and his daughter have arrived. Dr. Ramsey is needed in the treatment room." He directed his gaze to the floor, dusty brown hair falling over his black rimmed glasses. "And I am to stay here with Dr. Giffard until her treatment is complete." The second technician, a young blonde woman who appeared to be about twenty-five, looked nervously back and forth between Kate and Beth, chewing on her lip.

"I'm not staying here," Kate said, crossing her arms and leaning against the nearby table.

Shit! Shit! Shit! Beth thought and watched Travis close his eyes as if resigning himself to his fate. *Dr. Henri must want us separated while they're here.*

He's probably afraid I'll make another run for Jon, Kate thought. Beth let the comment go. Kate already felt bad enough.

"I'll be fine," Beth said aloud, deciding this may give them an advantage. *It will give you an excuse to stay here where you're close to me as well as to put the finishing touches on the new virus, but be ready. Even if I can't reach Nancy, Eric is sure to know they're here. But, if you do get a chance to go to our room, try to reach Luc. It looks like we're going to leave tonight.*

Kate nodded and relaxed her arms to grab the table top on either side of her. Beth was certain she heard it crack beneath Kate's grasp as she squeezed her hands against it. A fight now would only bring attention they didn't want. They would comply for now so the focus stayed on Mr. Rice and his daughter. If Eric was successful in disarming the security, Kate could then happily plow through anyone who stood in her way.

The female said, "Dr. Ramsey, after you," and motioned toward the door.

Beth followed the young woman whose name tag read 'Kimberly' to the treatment room and began preparing her supplies. If Kate couldn't get to Luc, he would be out of his mind with worry when they didn't arrive in their room. At least he would know something was amiss. He would be ready to leave at a moment's notice. She still needed to reach Nancy to see what state Jon would be in, but there was no way the two wouldn't know Mr. Rice had arrived. The whole facility seemed to be buzzing with the news.

It was 8 a.m. when Dr. Henri and Mr. Rice arrived, Henri nearly glued to his side. Dr. Henri ordered the staff to make Mr. Rice's daughter comfortable and asked for an IV to be started. The girl refused help to transfer from her wheelchair to the bed, showing an independent streak that would serve her well.

Beth watched the process and could see in the young girl's eyes, despite her brave front, that she was overwhelmed by it all. Her heart rate was elevated, and her respiratory rate was increased. Worry lines showed in her forehead with the mention of an IV. Mr. Rice was oblivious, walking around the room with his hands behind his back, inspecting everything and putting everyone else in the room on edge.

His daughter was small for her age with delicate features. Her heart-shaped face and porcelain skin made her look like a living doll. Her large brown eyes flitted around the room, and she flinched at the sound of a dropped pen and then stretched her arms in an attempt to make the movement look voluntary.

Beth, whose anger flared at the sight of Mr. Rice, now felt it seep away as she watched her. She remembered how it felt to be in a situation you couldn't control, none of the decisions your own, when her father had died and she had been forced into foster care. Mr. Rice's daughter didn't deserve to feel she was on her own in all this.

Beth had been reviewing the final orders for the nutritional supplementation based on her body weight, but crossed her arms around the clipboard against her chest and walked slowly to the girl's bedside. She smiled at the girl, hoping to put her at ease, and held out her hand. "I'm Dr. Ramsey. Do you mind if I have a seat?" Beth said, gesturing toward the bed.

The little girl shook her head and then took Beth's hand and shook it as well. She had a firm grip, and it made Beth's smile widen. She might be scared and overwhelmed, but she was doing all she could to not show it.

"My name is Adira."

After sitting on the edge of the bed, Beth said, "This place can look a little overwhelming, but it's really just like any other hospital. There are nurses over there," she pointed to a young woman in the corner gathering supplies for an IV, "and doctors like me. We're all here to make sure that everything goes smoothly for you. I'm guessing that you have a lot of questions, and I would be happy to answer them."

A young nurse arrived at Adira's bedside and laid down her supplies. "I'm sorry to interrupt. My name is Sarah, I'm one of the nurses, and I'm here to start your IV."

While she put on a brave face, Beth could hear Adira's heart rate jump again.

"Don't worry, I've watched Sarah start many IVs over the last several days. She's very good at it." Hoping to distract her, Beth continued. "What questions do you have for me?"

Adira dropped her gaze to her free hand as Sarah worked on the other. Adira looked as if she were ashamed of what she wanted to ask. "Is it going to hurt? The regeneration, I mean?"

"That's a good question. It's always easier to handle something when you know what to expect, isn't it? Some people don't like to know, but I'm just like you. The more I know, the better." Beth wanted to encourage her questions, and her answers seemed to help because Adira raised her head back up and met Beth's eyes. "So, before we start, we're going to give you some liquid food through your IV. The food will give your body everything it needs to make the regeneration go faster and rebuild all the cells that need to be fixed. Others who have gone through the same process have said that when the cells start to repair themselves it feels itchy but not painful. And as the nerves in your back that were injured begin to heal, your legs may wiggle and jump a bit. It won't hurt, but it might be a little startling. Then, over the course of several hours, maybe faster, you will be able to start moving them on your own again. It may take a while for them to be strong enough for you to use them as you did before, but it will come as the muscles strengthen."

"It doesn't seem real," Adira said. "The doctors at the rehab hospital said I wouldn't walk again. I had decided the wheelchair was just going to be a part of me from now on. But my dad never gave up trying to find a way for me to walk. Maybe this really is it this time."

Beth's heart went out to her. It sounded like her hopes had been raised and dashed too many times. She felt the anger toward Mr. Rice flaring again, but Adira didn't need to see it. She wanted to be honest with Adira. This process was all so new. She wished Kate were here. Her confidence in what they had done and her ability to fix what didn't work were comforting.

"Adira, every person's body is different, so I won't promise you this will work. You are younger than our other patients, but that isn't a bad thing. Younger people often heal even faster than adults. It's possible that will be the case today. But I can tell you that in older people, like me, it has worked very well."

Adira thought about this for several seconds.

"Is there a chance I'll die?" she asked.

Beth's heart ached. No one so young should ever have to ask that question and seriously be wondering about the answer.

"I am here to make absolutely certain that doesn't happen." Their plan had been to leave at midnight two days from now, but with Adira's early arrival, they needed to leave tonight. And she hoped everyone would be ready. The usual timeline for the treatment to take effect could put them beyond that, but she would do whatever she could to make sure Adira would suffer no consequences from their escape.

"Are you the one who helped Dr. Henri create this medicine?"

The word rubbed Beth the wrong way, since they'd been forced into the human trials that had brought them to this point. Even though helping Adira walk again would be wonderful, the lives harmed or lost in the process wouldn't be justified. She could never forgive Dr. Henri or Mr. Rice for that. But that wasn't Adira's doing, so she pushed the thoughts aside to give her the most reassuring answer she could.

"My good friend, Dr. Giffard, and I did. And my friend is one of the smartest people I have ever met or worked with. I wish you could meet her, too."

Adira thought quietly for a moment and then returned Beth's gaze with a curious look. "So are you a vampire? I heard my dad say a vampire was working with Dr. Henri."

Beth hadn't seen that question coming and had to chuckle. "As a matter of fact, I am. But I don't drink blood anymore, so you're safe," she said with a wide smile and wiggled her eyebrows so Adira would know she was joking with her.

Finally Adira smiled. It did more to melt away Beth's anger and anxiety than any medication ever could.

"Can you fly?" Adira asked, leaning forward, her eyes wide and expectant.

"No, sadly, I cannot. But, I can move really, really fast."

"How fast?" Adira said, biting her lip and tilting her head toward Beth.

"Do you see that counter over there with the box of gloves on it?"

Adira nodded vigorously. Beth rose and ran at vampire speed to the box. She waited the fraction of a second it took for Adira's eyes to find her, her mouth hanging open until an ear-to-ear grin slowly spread across it. Then Beth was immediately back at her side with two gloves in hand.

"That is so cool," Adira said, and Beth laughed out loud, in part from Adira's words and partly as a nervous response to her worries about their coming escape and Luc's safety.

"Well then, we are all finished here," Sarah said.

Adira raised her arm and looked at the IV already taped in place and connected to fluids hanging from her IV pole. "I didn't even feel you do it," she said and gave Sarah an appreciative smile.

"I told you she was good," Beth said. "Now, after you get some fluids, we'll start the food. It will be in a bag just like that, but it looks white instead of clear. Once that's in, we'll start the treatment. The fluids will take a few hours, though, so you should try to rest if you can."

"Dr. Ramsey, will you be here when they give me the treatment?"

A twinge of guilt washed over Beth, knowing she may have to leave before Adira recovered, but at least this was something she could do.

"I will, and I promise to make sure you know what we are doing, whatever we need to do. In return, can you promise to ask me any questions you might have along the way, no matter what they are?"

"I promise," she said. Then she took a deep breath, followed by a long exhale.

Beth rose and headed back toward the counter to finish her paperwork. Adira's heart rate had returned to normal, and as she observed the room, her expression was one of curiosity instead of fear.

As Beth reviewed her paperwork, Mr. Rice, who had been watching and listening since Beth introduced herself to Adira, walked over to her as though he were just canvassing the room. "Thank you for that," he said.

Beth looked at him squarely. There were so many things she would love to say to him, but for Adira's sake, she swallowed them and said only, "I didn't do it for you." She turned her back on him and walked away.

When the IV fluids and TPN were infused, it was time for the injection. Beth gathered the recently drawn syringe from the counter beside her and walked to Adira's bedside, where Mr. Rice and Dr. Henri waited. As she approached the bed, Beth handed the syringe to Dr. Henri.

"No," Adira spoke up and looked at her father. "I want Dr. Ramsey to give it to me."

Mr. Rice looked at his daughter's pleading face and nodded. "Very well. Dr. Ramsey, please do the honors."

Beth watched Henri's face turn a deep shade of red, his jaw clenched, before he handed the syringe back to her. Beth didn't want to be responsible for this, but also didn't want Adira to worry any more than she had to. Whether Beth agreed or not, the injection would be given. So, she rounded the bed to the side with the IV, retrieved a saline-filled syringe from the Mayo stand beside the bed, and flushed the IV hub. Then she removed the needle from the regeneration virus syringe and connected it to the IV hub.

"The treatment works more quickly when we give it through your IV rather than as a shot. It may sting just a bit as it goes in, but it won't last for more than a few seconds," Beth said, and Adira nodded, the ends of her lips curling upward ever so slightly.

"I'm ready," Adira said.

Beth slowly injected the virus, looking between it and Adira's face to be certain she was okay. Adira's face remained relaxed.

Once it was in, Beth said, "That's it. Now we wait. It should begin to work in a couple of hours. If you feel anything, including that itching we talked about, let me know. But again, try to rest. Your body is going to need all of its energy to heal."

Adira relaxed her head back into the pillow and closed her eyes.

Beth's earlier concerns about how the gene manipulation might affect someone so young ran through her mind. She hated not knowing what could go wrong later from their actions, but her father had listened again to all of her cautions and still demanded to proceed. If she couldn't prevent it from happening, at least she could be here to help Adira in any way she could.

NANCY

Nancy entered the treatment wing at noon for the beginning of her shift. She had the syringe Dr. Giffard had given her a few short hours ago in her pocket, wrapped in a cool pack. She and Dr. Giffard hadn't had a chance to discuss exactly what it did, or how long it would take, but she suspected it would change Jon, like them, to no longer require blood or be sensitive to the sun. And while Dr. Henri would no longer allow her access to blood for Jon, she could easily get to food, at least for now. Henri could later stop that, too, but it may buy Jon some time.

She supposed it wouldn't matter much since she and Dr. Henri were the only two allowed to visit Jon. However long the virus took to have its effect, Dr. Henri would immediately know who to blame. It would likely be the end of her. But she had been forced to do so much, had seen so much, she didn't care. If she and Eric could help save one person from Dr. Henri and Mr. Rice, her death would be worth it. She'd had enough.

As she entered the central treatment room, she saw Dr. Ramsey, Dr. Henri, and Mr. Rice gathered around what must be Mr. Rice's daughter's bedside. The sight made her catch her breath, but she quickly regained her composure. They were here early, which meant the guards would be spread thin. He may not have told them he was coming, which would put them in even more disarray.

They needed to leave tonight, and Jon needed to be ready to travel. Which meant she needed to get the cure to him as soon as possible, as Dr. Giffard had requested.

The young girl was small and beautiful. She was looking at Dr. Ramsey like she was the only boat in the middle of the ocean she was swimming in. Nancy didn't blame her. She was in poor company otherwise. Dr. Henri stood, hands fisted and face red, glaring with malice at Dr. Ramsey. He raised his eyes to Nancy as she entered, and the red slowly left his face, but his look still sent shivers down her spine. He leaned over and said a few short words to Mr. Rice and then began to walk toward her.

"Follow me," he said. She turned, looking back at Dr. Ramsey, who smiled at the little girl and patted her arm. She was a kind soul, and neither she nor her friends deserved what had been done to them here.

Beth looked up from the girl and locked eyes with Nancy before glancing down at the girl and back up, her gaze intense. Nancy believed she was making sure she realized Mr. Rice and his daughter had arrived. The plan needed to go forward tonight. Nancy gave a slight nod before Dr. Henri reached her side.

She followed behind him, avoiding looking at him as much as possible, feeling the bile rise in her throat every time she caught a glimpse of his weasel face. She glanced up at the cameras as she went by, knowing Eric would position himself in the security control room tonight and would be watching. He would also know by now that Mr. Rice and his daughter had arrived. He would be ready; now she had to do her part.

She assumed they were headed to check on Jon so they could make the usual daily observations, but Dr. Henri stopped at his office, telling Nancy to wait outside while he made a phone call. When he'd finished, they continued on toward Jon's room.

They were met by a guard upon their arrival, Mr. Verde at his side.

The evil bastard must be planning to continue burning Jon with the UV light while making Mr. Verde watch. Or does he plan to torture Mr. Verde, too? Nancy put her hands inside her pockets and removed the syringe from the cold pack, palming it. She didn't know if she would have a moment alone after Dr. Henri did whatever he intended to do to Jon, or if Jon would still be alive, but she would be ready if she did get the opportunity.

"Mr. Verde, as you can see, your friend is quite incapacitated, a result of the lack of cooperation from your Dr. Ramsey and Dr. Giffard." Dr. Henri had been angry in the treatment room. Since Nancy knew the two were cooperating, albeit grudgingly, it was far more likely his anger was directed at some perceived offense from Dr. Ramsey, and that this was retaliation. "He hasn't had blood in quite some time and is more than a little hungry. I thought perhaps we could see just how hungry he really is by allowing you to...visit." With that, he nodded at the guard, who began to push Mr. Verde forward.

Nancy, immediately appalled by his intentions, put herself between Mr. Verde and the door to Jon's cell. "Dr. Henri, don't. He'll kill him," she said.

"You've been wanting to feed him, haven't you? Unless you would care to join him, step aside." Dr. Henri spat his words at her, his face flushing red once again.

"It's okay. It won't help anyone if we're both dead," Mr. Verde said.

He placed his hand gently on her shoulder, and she turned to face him.

"I'm sorry, Mr. Verde," and she held out her hand to shake his. He took her hand and shook it gently, palming the syringe and lowering his hand as the guard pushed him forward.

"It will be okay," Mr. Verde said, holding her gaze. "Please tell Dr. Ramsey that I love her."

His brown eyes were calm and gentle, and for whatever reason, she felt more relaxed. She nodded and stepped aside. The guard opened the cell door, keeping an eye on Jon as he did. Mr. Verde walked inside and turned to look at them.

"Jon, dinner is served," Dr. Henri said loudly in an attempt to wake Jon. "I've never had the opportunity to watch a vampire feed from a human. This should prove most educational."

But Jon didn't move. Dr. Henri's eyes narrowed as Nancy watched him stare expectantly at Jon. After a few moments, a slow and malicious smile extended across Dr. Henri's face, and he turned toward Mr. Verde. "It is a pity I can't stay to watch, but it's only a matter of time, Mr. Verde." He turned on his heel and barked at the guard as he left, "Make sure the hallway cameras are recording. I don't want to miss a thing. Nancy, complete your usual observations and return with the guard to the treatment wing."

She had no way to speak with Mr. Verde with the guard watching them. While she had friends among the guards, this man wasn't one of them. She had no choice but to continue her duties and offer a heartfelt, "I'm sorry," before leaving him alone to his fate.

They were out of time. She needed to help them escape tonight and hoped that Jon could control his thirst long enough for all four of them to survive. She wasn't sure if their plan would work, and even if it did, they would have to fight their way free. But it was the best chance she could give them.

BETH

Beth saw Nancy return to the treatment center shortly after Dr. Henri. She looked rattled, and as she performed her duties, she glanced nervously at Beth, but with Dr. Henri in the area, Nancy wouldn't dare try to reach out. Beth could sense her anxiety. While Beth had difficulty reading human thoughts, she did catch words now and then, especially when there was a lot of emotion associated with the thoughts. She concentrated on Nancy's thoughts as she pretended to go over her notes, and one word came through clearly.

Verde.

Something was wrong with Luc.

She closed her eyes briefly and reached out toward Luc with all her might, calling to him, but heard nothing. He was too far away. She considered reaching out to Kate, but what good would it do? If she were in the lab, Kate wouldn't be able to reach him either. And if she were back in their shared room, Kate wouldn't be able to hear her.

Beth could hear every heartbeat in the treatment room, and as they beat, each felt like a ticking clock, counting the time Luc might have left. It was excruciating, and she had to will her fists open more than once for fear that her nails digging into her palms would draw blood.

Finally, nearly an hour after returning to the treatment room, Dr. Henri called Nancy to Adira's bedside and led Mr. Rice down the far corridor, no doubt to show him the results of his other experiments.

Adira lay sleeping quietly in her bed.

Nancy checked Adira's IV and the monitor above her head and then glanced at Beth, who was already on her way to the bedside. Beth pretended to lean over to peer at the IV from across the bed and whispered to Nancy, "Whisper so low you can hardly hear yourself and tell me what's wrong." To others around her, it would appear Nancy was muttering to herself as she looked down, studying the clipboard at Adira's side. But Beth, with her vampire hearing, caught every word loud and clear.

"Dr. Henri put Mr. Verde in Jon's cell."

Beth sucked in a breath, and Nancy's eyes flew to meet hers. Beth knew from her communication with Jon that his hold on reality and his thirst were tenuous at best. While Luc didn't smell entirely human now, she knew she would have been easily tempted by his blood if she were overly thirsty. Even though Jon was weak, if he lost control, he would use every ounce of remaining strength to feed from and very possibly kill Luc. The only thing in their favor was that Luc was as strong as Jon, even when Jon was fully fed. But extreme thirst was a blinding thing, and one or both of them could be severely injured if Jon attacked.

"I tried to stop him, but he wouldn't listen," Nancy said. "But I was able to pass the syringe Dr. Giffard gave me to him without Dr. Henri noticing. It was all I could do."

Beth's heart skipped a beat. Luc wouldn't know Mr. Rice was here. If Luc found a way to keep Jon at bay and gave him v2.2, by the time their plan went into effect tonight, Jon could be well into the change and so incapacitated they would have to carry him, and no amount of blood would help.

"Can you get back to Jon's room?" Perhaps Nancy could tell him not to give Jon v2.2 and would be able to see if Luc was alright.

"No. The guards won't allow me in without Dr. Henri's order. What should we do?"

Beth looked at Adira and placed her hand on her forehead as if checking for a fever, trying to think. Her heart raced in her chest. For all she knew, Luc could already be dead. It was all she could do to keep her feet planted and not race from the room to try to reach him. But she had no idea what she could do. Until Eric turned off the cameras and security locks tonight, she would never be able to get to him.

She had to stay calm. She closed her eyes for just a moment to focus. Luc had survived three hundred years, and he would not go down easily. Jon was his friend, and she had to believe that even in his current state, Jon would recognize him and remain in control, just as Luc had for her.

Beth was so lost in her thoughts that it took her several seconds to register the warmth along with the small beads of perspiration on Adira's forehead. The virus was kicking in much more quickly than she had expected. "For now, we stick to the plan. We leave at midnight."

CHAPTER FORTY-THREE

LUC

LUC WATCHED AS NANCY left, followed by the guard, with mixed emotions. He had seriously considered ripping Dr. Henri's throat out, followed by the guard. Nancy may have been appalled, but she could have still gotten them through the first corridor door. He could even have let Jon feed on Dr. Henri or the guard, but the security cameras would have picked it all up, and the doors beyond would have locked them down. They already knew that the doors could withstand the strength of two vampires. They would have been trapped once again and starved until they could be removed or killed. So, he had kept his composure.

It was only two days until their escape. He would be uncomfortable, but he believed he could make it until then without food.

He turned his back to the camera and pretended to scratch his chin so he could get a look at the syringe in his hand. They had all discussed holding off on giving Jon v2.2 so Dr. Henri would not discover that Nancy was helping them. If Beth and Kate had given it to Nancy, something must have changed that made them decide to move forward.

Jon had been without blood for over a week now, and there were still two more days before Mr. Rice arrived and their escape plan could finally get underway. The longest Luc had ever gone without blood was five days at the hand of the Master. He had been miserable, weak, and nearly incoherent. He still wondered how he had managed to resist and not drain Beth completely. He supposed it was his love for her, already growing even so early on in their relationship.

He and Jon had been friends for a long while, and he trusted him, but the thirst wasn't about trust; it was pure and unrelenting need. A weakened vampire was still a considerable threat, especially one with Jon's military training.

Luc crossed his arms, looking at Jon for a few moments, and then decided to try to wake him with his thoughts. It was daylight, which would make him groggy all by itself, but the starvation on top of it could make him impossible to rouse. He hoped to warn him before injecting him, just in case he awoke during it and came after him.

He closed his eyes briefly, praying this would go smoothly, and reached out. *Jon, it's Luc. I have the cure here to give you... Jon, wake up, it's Luc.* He paused and waited with no answer. *I have the cure to give you. Jon—*

I hear you, just give it to me and shut up so I can sleep, Jon thought to him. The words were groggy and slow.

Jon, do you understand what I am saying? I am here, in your cell. Stay still. I'm going to come closer and sit next to you on the bed. Okay? Jon?

Luc waited for what seemed like a long while, but it was probably only a few seconds.

Jon slowly opened his eyes. They seemed out of focus and then sluggishly scanned the room around him before stopping on Luc. *Are you really here? I have dreamed this before.*

Yes, it's really me. Don't breathe right now. It will only make it worse if you smell my scent. I'm going to walk over to your bed and give you the shot, okay?

Okay, Jon thought back.

Luc moved slowly toward him, being careful to telegraph every movement. The last thing he wanted was to hurt Jon, but if he couldn't keep his thirst in check, Luc would have to defend himself.

After a few slow steps, he reached the bedside and turned his back to the camera he knew was watching.

I'm going to give it to you now, Luc thought to him before removing the cap on the syringe and inserting the needle into Jon's upper arm. He quickly depressed the plunger. *Okay, all done.*

Now...what...happens? Jon thought, one word coming across their link at a time.

Now we wait, and you rest. I'm going to sit in the chair on the other side of the room. We'll talk more at sunset.

Thankful that the injection had gone off without a hitch, Luc slowly rose from the bed and walked first to the bathroom. He crushed the syringe in his hands after removing the short needle and then flushed it all down the toilet before walking to the chair and settling in. If they were still trapped when Dr. Henri discovered Jon's transformation, at least there would be no traces of v2.2 for Dr. Henri to get his hands on.

The waiting would be difficult with so many unknowns. For all he knew, they would both now starve together just for lack of regular food instead of blood. But at least they were together now, and two would always be better than one in Luc's mind.

He knew Beth and Kate were doing everything they could to prepare for the escape, just as he had. Luc needed to make sure he and Jon were ready to go when their plan was in motion. And right now, Jon wasn't even close.

Chapter Forty-Four

Beth

BETH SAT AT ADIRA'S side, checking her IV and vitals once again. The little girl had been febrile for almost an hour now. It had come on much more quickly than the other test subjects, which both encouraged and worried Beth. Children often reacted differently from adults when it came to illness and therapy. They seemed to become sicker faster but also to rebound more quickly when the appropriate treatment was given.

She hoped that would be the case today. But all of the unknowns hung heavily in the air. Along with it, the distraction of their escape, only hours away, and the inability to share the new timeline with Jon and Luc had her on edge. Thankfully, Kate was near enough in the lab for Beth to communicate with her. Kate was working on gathering and preparing all she could for what was certain to be their best chance at escape.

And then Beth saw it, the smallest movement beneath the covers over Adira's foot. She checked her watch. It had only been a few hours since the injection. It was record time, and once again, Beth hoped this was good news.

Thirty minutes later, the twitching of Adira's legs had become more regular and more pronounced. And the last twitch, pulling the covers up on the side of the bed, was enough to wake her. Adira's eyes flew open like someone waking from a fall in a dream, her gaze immediately locking on Beth's, beads of perspiration dotting her forehead.

Beth smiled as gently as she could. "How are you feeling?"

Before Adira could answer, another twitch of her legs drew her gaze. Beth reached out and took her hand, and Adira's grip on it was impressive for such a small girl.

"Is it happening?" she asked, turning her wide-eyed gaze to Beth, who smiled again and nodded. Beth's hope for Adira to walk again and her thoughts about the joy it would bring made her anxiety for Luc and Jon more bearable, even if only a little.

"This is how it begins," she said. Adira grabbed the bed linens and tossed them to the side, exposing her legs. They were still thinner than they should be from muscle wasting, but not so much as during her initial exam. As Adira watched, seeming not to dare look away, they began to quiver and twitch irregularly. Adira's other hand went to her side.

"I feel it, the itching you talked about. I feel it in my back next to my scar."

"It shouldn't be long now," Beth said, pleased Adira was awake to relay her sensations and worries so that Beth could know that she was, for now, okay.

"Where's my dad?" Adira said, glancing quickly around the room before once again staring at her exposed legs.

Beth knew he was with Dr. Henri, likely looking at the poor kidnapped people he was experimenting on, but wasn't about to say anything to Adira about it. "Sarah?" Beth called across the room, and the young woman hurried to her side. "Would you please find Mr. Rice and tell him his daughter is asking for him?"

"Absolutely," Sarah said with a warm smile for Adira, then hurried on her way.

Adira's movements became more dramatic and jerky, nearly moving her off the bed at one point, but Beth helped her back into place and reassured her until the jerking began to slow and then stop.

Beth had seen this in the other patients. It was time for Adira to test the healing.

"Why did it stop? Did it not work?"

Beth could see and feel the girl's fear, and she gently patted her hand. "This is exactly what is supposed to happen. I believe the healing is nearly complete. Now, Adira, I want you to look at one of your feet and focus on telling it to move."

Adira swallowed, her breathing shallow. She had a vice grip on Beth's fingers, but did as she asked. After a few seconds, Adira's foot twitched. Her eyes shot back to Beth. "Did I do that?"

"Try it again and let's see," she encouraged. And this time, Adira's foot flexed and then straightened, her heart thrumming in her chest and loud in Beth's ears.

"Now focus on the other one," Beth said.

And her second foot moved as well. Adira began stretching them, wiggling her toes and bending her legs at the hip and knee. A low giggle began to roll out of her, and then it became a full-on belly laugh, tears pouring down her cheeks at the same time.

And tears welled in Beth's eyes, too. This was what she had hoped for in this research. This one little girl's joy did so much to fill her heart.

Adira turned and wrapped her arms around Beth's neck, and Beth could hold back the tears no longer.

"Thank you, Dr. Ramsey. Thank you," she sobbed. Adira curled her legs to better reach her, and Beth heard a gasp from across the room. Adira had heard it as well, and they both turned their heads to see Mr.

Rice, his hand over his mouth, staring at them, his eyes round and wet.

"Daddy, it worked," Adira said, releasing Beth's neck and wiggling her legs to show her father, who ran to her side as Beth stood and stepped back, wiping the tears from her face with her sleeve. She watched the two embrace, Adira's father closing his eyes as he held her. As much as she hated this man, his love for his daughter softened her feelings toward him...but not much. She could never forgive what he had done to them all, especially Jon. And helping your own child by sacrificing others was still unforgivable.

A glance at the monitors showed Adira's vitals, except for a mildly elevated heart rate, were back at baseline. She should be in the clear, which meant Beth's work here was done.

Dr. Henri called over two of the techs, and with one on either side, they helped Adira stand, wobbly like a new foal but upright and holding her own weight. They brought her a pint-sized walker that Mr. Rice must have had prepared especially for her, and she clung to it, giggling, her father clapping and urging her on. After a few tenuous steps, she was worn out, so they half-led, half-carried her back to her bed.

Beth wished Kate, Luc, and Jon could have seen this. One beautiful moment in all they had endured, and the fear and overwhelm that came with it, was overwhelming. She walked into one of the empty side rooms and sat on the gurney, her face in her hands.

Adira can walk, Kate. It worked, and she's fine. I wish you could have seen it after all of your work.

Thank God! Are you okay?

Yes, I'm fine. It's all just a bit much. I need a moment, and then I will tell them I need some rest and try to make my way to you. It would be best if we were together and as close to Luc and Jon as we can get before it's time to leave.

See you soon, my friend. Well done.

CHAPTER FORTY-FIVE

BETH

11:50 P.M. BETH WALKED at normal human speed back to her lab. As she approached a few short minutes later, she could see Kate through the lab windows. She was placing samples into a small cooler bag with vials from their refrigerator. Travis, apparently expelled from inside the lab, was sitting on a chair just outside the door and fiddling with his cell phone. They made eye contact as she badged through the door.

She didn't stop to ask Kate what she was packing but assumed it was the vials of v2.2, the original viral cultures, and the new version 3 of the Vampyre retrovirus with the segments for bloodlust and sun sensitivity removed that she had just completed; all as they had discussed.

Beth glanced at the wall clock. 11:55 p.m.

Beth placed a tall box of reagents beside the sink to block the view from the hallway cameras. She walked to the freezer and removed the rack containing all of the viral samples it held, setting them on the opposite edge of the sink. She turned on the hot water and added bleach before removing the caps from each vial and dropping them open into the water, all at vampire speed.

Kate joined her after filling her bag and added the samples from the refrigerator to the now destroyed samples in the sink.

It's not much, but at least it will slow them down, Kate thought. *I've deleted all the files on our laptops and the instruments here. Eric will have to take care of the shared drives.*

Hopefully, Nancy has been as successful on her end and is on her way to the lower-level entrance, Beth thought back.

What should we do with Travis? Kate thought, looking through the window at the back of his head.

He can't keep up when we run.

But he could call it in. He has his cell. Should we try to knock him out?

Do you think you can do that with certainty without killing him?

No.

Beth glanced at one of the open computers. 11:59 p.m. She walked to the wall-mounted phone in the lab and tore it out of the wall, the cord severing, causing Travis to jump to his feet.

We take his phone and run. Time to go.

PETER

Peter glanced at his watch as he entered the treatment room to check on the progress of Mr. Rice's daughter at 11:52 p.m.

His head snapped up to the sound of the young girl's laughter. She sat up in her bed, legs out in front of her, wiggling her toes as her father tickled them. Peter stopped and stared, his jaw slack. Beth and Dr. Giffard had done it. He had listened as they had explained their research, but seeing this paralyzed little girl now moving with his own eyes made it all hit home. If they could do this, it wouldn't be long until he would have his wish for immortality as well.

He scanned the room for Beth, but she was nowhere to be found.

He watched as a curvy brunette nurse walked toward him, his eyes dropping to her breasts as she approached before glancing back at Dr. Henri, who was standing guard with his nose in the air and arms crossed in front of him, watching as Mr. Rice doted on his daughter.

"Dr. Miller, Dr. Ramsey left a message requesting that you meet her and Dr. Giffard in their lab at midnight."

The wall clock said 11:54 p.m. Peter nodded his response and turned to leave, curious. Beth had hovered over the girl all day. Why would she leave now when she could stay for the accolades? And why also summon him?

He pondered the question as he badged out of the treatment area and headed toward her lab. He found most women tedious and frustrating. They served their purpose, but the hoops they expected you to jump through before getting to it were ridiculous. They wanted compliments, dinner, promises for more, and commitments. Those who were happy for a one-night stand, to have their needs met before moving on, were few and far between. The younger generation seemed more open to it, but still with expectations of more.

Beth was an entirely different animal. She was stunningly attractive and brilliant with no guile. She was equally frustrating with her extreme sense of justice and morality. But she played no games. Beth had been honest with Peter. He knew that now. She had warned him of the Master's plans for him. He had believed she was taunting him, trying to make him question the Master's intentions to serve her own needs. But she had warned him to open his eyes to the truth.

As Peter turned the corner and approached the lab, he watched as Dr. Giffard and Beth exited the door, grabbed a phone from the hands of a very surprised guard sitting outside, and turned down the corridor away from him.

Before they disappeared, Beth looked him in the eye and said one word. "Run."

NANCY

Nancy glanced up at the hallway camera outside Dr. Henri's lab and heard the door lock release. Eric was watching, just as he said he would be. Dr. Ramsey had asked that one of the nurses provide Nancy with a sedative two days ago to "help her sleep." A sedative she had passed on to Eric to place in the coffee of the second control room guard at the beginning of his shift this evening. If Eric was getting her entry into Dr. Henri's lab, it must have worked, leaving him unmonitored.

She entered Dr. Henri's lab, leaving the lights off. It was still illuminated by the single security light just inside the door. She walked to the freezer and removed the plug from the wall, dropping it behind the unit where it wouldn't be seen. If all went according to plan, Eric had already disabled the alarm that would notify the control room that the unit had lost power and had cranked the room's thermostat as high as it would go.

Nancy couldn't stifle a small smile. She imagined Dr. Henri's anger when he returned to find his samples ruined. But even more than that, his embarrassment at having been bested. She hoped Mr. Rice would be as harsh with him as he had been with her.

She repeated the process with the refrigerator and then stuck a pen between each door and its seal to keep them open and exposed to room air. They shouldn't be visible from the hallway if a guard peered through the window in the door. She also unplugged and opened the incubator to ruin the cultures inside. She hoped they would go unnoticed until Dr. Henri returned to his lab sometime tomorrow, when it would be too late to save them.

There was no easy way to get to Mr. Rice, and he would have his victory tonight with the healing of his daughter. But Nancy had gathered all of the equipment and supplies Dr. Giffard and Dr. Ramsey had requested and placed them on a cart in the storage room near the animal lab. It was her next stop before continuing to the lower-level access point, where Eric would meet her and escort her out of the building. A cargo van would be waiting, ramp down, for them to roll the cart on board and get the hell out of here. If they made it out, they would leave it at a drop point they had all agreed upon.

Nancy raised her wrist to check her watch. 11:53 p.m. She peeked through a crack in the lab door and listened before exiting into the hallway and making her way to the storage room. She badged in, removed the heavily loaded cart, and began pushing it down the hall. As she made her way past Dr. Henri's lab, she heard footsteps and stopped dead in her tracks.

There was nowhere to hide. This time of night, the hallways should have been empty. Nancy's heart raced. If it was Dr. Henri, she was dead, caught moving lab equipment she had no business transporting. And, of course, it wouldn't take long for him to suspect Dr. Ramsey had put her up to it. Their plan would be ruined.

She felt panic overtaking her as Dr. Miller rounded the corner. He was focused, appearing lost in his own thoughts as he continued past her down the hall, scarcely noticing her presence.

Nancy gasped in short, quiet breaths, beads of sweat trickling down the middle of her back as she struggled to steady herself and began to push the cart forward. She glanced up at the camera overhead before checking her watch; 11:56 p.m. Eric would still be watching and preparing to meet her. She needed to keep moving and pushed ahead on wobbling legs.

***

BEN

He was lying on his bed inside his cell, arms folded beneath his head. Ben had begun to look forward to Luciano's visits, even if they were brief. It was his only break in the monotony. Days came and went with the same parade of scientists and handlers who never spoke with him, only at him, to give an order when they demanded his cooperation. But their interest seemed to have decreased since Luciano arrived. He guessed it was because they were busy studying the other vampires. While he was grateful for the decrease in experiments, which were sometimes painful, he wouldn't wish it if it meant the same torture was focused on another being.

The lights outside his cell suddenly lit, and he shielded his sensitive eyes with his forearm, blinking. He looked toward the bedside clock. 11:59 p.m. turned to 12:00 a.m. as he heard the lock on his cell door release, but there were no other sounds from the hallway.

He crawled from the bed and ran to the door, swinging it open as the lights down the rest of the hallway lit as if leading him toward the door at the end of the corridor. Ben ran to it and found it open as well. As he passed through it into the hallway outside, it branched in two directions, one lit, the other dark.

Luciano had told him that he and his friends were making plans for an escape and to be ready. If this was it, Luciano had been true to his word that he would help him if he could. Whether they succeeded or failed, Ben had nothing more to lose by trying.

He turned on bare feet and ran in the direction of the light.

ANTEIA

She rubbed the skin of her arms as she sat cross-legged at the end of the bed. Her skin was so rough and dry. Anteia couldn't remember the last time she'd had a proper bath, shower, or swim. The scientists had been denying her access to water in any significant quantity for weeks now. She glanced at her wall clock. 11:59 p.m.

Every night at midnight, she seated herself, closed her eyes, centered her mind, and reached out to any Eanai that may be within reach of her thoughts. And every night for as long as she had been here, she had failed to reach anyone. But she was determined not to give up.

She closed her eyes and began sending out her call of distress when the lights outside her cell flashed on. Anteia thought it might be Luciano coming to clean. A glance at the clock showed it had changed from 11:59 p.m. to 12:00 a.m. just as she heard the lock on her cell click open. Luciano had told her to be ready for an escape, and her heart raced, hoping tonight was it.

She rose from her bed and ran to the door, swinging it open and racing toward the end of the corridor, the lights coming on ahead of her as if urging her forward. This door was also open, and she flew through it following the lights toward the next door, which she prayed to Ea would also be open.

ERIC

Eric watched the digital readout on the monitor in front of him closely as the last hour of the day ticked away. 11:58 p.m. His control room partner, Bill, was snoring next to him, his head on the console in front of him. A small drop of drool was dangling from the corner of his mouth. The sedative Dr. Ramsey had suggested had worked like a charm.

Eric tapped his foot on the floor, chewing on the end of a pencil as he watched the wall of monitors in front of him. They displayed all the key areas of the facility, many of them changing from one camera to the next for monitoring. He had fixed some of them to remain on his areas of interest: Nancy, of course; Jon, now trapped with his friend; Dr. Ramsey and Dr. Giffard now together in their lab; the two other prisoners the group thought may be able to assist in their escape; the treatment room where Dr. Henri and Mr. Rice hovered over Mr. Rice's daughter; and the server room where the charge he had placed should be ticking down to zero in exactly two minutes.

He had been monitoring Nancy's progress and nearly choked on his pencil when Dr. Miller passed her in the hallway with her loaded cart. But she had remained calm and was on her way to their meeting point. They were so close now.

The guards had been notified of Mr. Rice's arrival only moments before he landed, but they had planned for his arrival and immediately split the teams into smaller groups to provide security for Mr. Rice and his daughter with smaller details in all the usual places around the facility. Eric had been able to meet Nancy only briefly before his shift, letting her know he was ready to put the plan in motion tonight and that he would be ready to meet her as close after midnight as he could. With other personnel around, including some of the guards hurrying him along, he hadn't been able to give her more than a quick peck on the cheek. He hoped it wasn't the last kiss he would have a chance to give her.

As the readout changed to 11:59, Eric activated the lights outside the cells of the two prisoners and watched as they each turned toward their hallways, questioning looks on their faces. Eric didn't know what they were. He knew each guard had been issued noise-cancelling headphones with mics a few days after the female arrived, with orders to wear them if anywhere close to her, but he didn't know what she was. And he had never met the male prisoner, but their guns' rounds had been replaced with silver-tipped versions shortly after his arrival.

He hadn't thought a lot about it at the time. Mr. Rice occasionally had some odd ideas. But now that he knew vampires were real, he began to wonder who or what these people were as well.

Eric removed a two-way radio from his pocket, tuned it to channel 147, and said, "Thirty seconds, get ready to run and stick to the main halls." He hoped Jon had been able to hear it.

Eric took a deep breath and ran his hand through his hair before removing the pencil from his teeth and throwing it across the room. His hand hovered over the door lock controls, and as the digital readout clicked over to 12:00 a.m., Eric disarmed the locks and cameras and left the control room to the sound of an explosion in the server room.

***

LUC

The clock on the desk said 11:57 p.m. Beth and Kate had still not returned to their room after being out all day. He hoped Nancy had been able to reach Beth and tell her where he was and that she had given him the syringe of v2.2 they had sent. He didn't like the unknowns. Not being able to speak to them or reach them was excruciating. He sat still in Jon's room. His presence there alone would be difficult for Jon if he woke. While he didn't smell entirely human, he also didn't smell vampire. Luc's scent would tickle Jon's thirst, and he didn't want to make him any more uncomfortable or risk an attack.

He could tell Jon was sleeping, and his heart rate remained steady. He didn't go to his side to see if he had a fever or any other signs of the v2.2 virus kicking in, but the normal heart rate and stillness suggested against it.

11:58. Luc breathed deeply but quietly, then exhaled, closing his eyes. If they got out of here—*when* they got out of here, he corrected himself—they would all go somewhere warm, the beach maybe, in broad daylight, together. The corners of his lips turned up at the thought of Beth in a skimpy bikini. He imagined how she would look as the sun warmed her skin, how the waves would lap at her legs as she waded into the water, rising ever higher until they met the top of her thigh and the fabric of her bikini. Yes, a beach date.

He opened his eyes before his thoughts took an erotic turn. An erection in a cell with his starving male friend was not something he would want to explain.

His eyes drifted toward the clock once again.

11:59. Midnight marked day seven for Jon without blood. It could have just as easily been him again, starving for blood in a cell. But Beth and Kate had come through with their cure, and now Jon was hopefully just hours away from joining them.

His thoughts were interrupted by a long but soft beep coming from the bathroom. Luc stood and went toward it. The beep ended, and he heard a male voice say, "Thirty seconds, get ready to run and stick to the main halls," before once again going silent.

Luc localized the sound and found a handheld radio inside a bathroom drawer, the radio Eric had given Jon. Before he could think to respond, there was a loud click from the cell door. Luc was up and across the room at vampire speed, the door giving way as he turned the handle. They were loose. He didn't take the time to consider why, only left it open, and returned to Jon's bedside. There was no time for gentleness.

"Jon, wake up," he shouted.

Jon's eyes flew open, and his head turned to Luc, fangs extending with a snarl. He tried to rise from the bed.

Luc realized he was struggling and was sadly thankful. If he was this weak, he couldn't get the better of him and attack, but it also posed a problem. They needed to run and very possibly fight their way out. Jon was in no shape for either.

Luc took a deep breath and raised his wrist to Jon.

"Drink," he ordered.

But Jon, having realized it was Luc, was pressing his mouth closed and shaking his head, despite his protruding fangs.

"The door is open, and we have to run *now*. There is no time to argue. I can't carry you and fight. Now drink." He knew Jon's fear and felt it rolling off of him along with his hunger. He was afraid he wouldn't stop. But Luc was well fed and capable of fighting him off as long as he didn't drink too much.

Jon locked his eyes with Luc's, then bit. His eyes closed as he drank long pulls from Luc's vein, the waves of need and relief hitting Luc hard. As Jon's strength began to return, he raised his hands and held Luc's arm in a vice grip as he continued to drink. Then he sat up, still drinking hungrily. When Luc began to feel his strength ebbing, he tore his wrist from Jon in one swift motion, hoping to shake him free before he would fight. At the same time, he thrust his fist at Jon's chest, knocking him to the bed, and went to the door.

The blow and Luc's retreat were enough to shake Jon out of his trance-like feeding state, and he looked to Luc, blood still on his lips. "Thank you," Jon said.

Luc nodded but wasn't sure if he had helped them or harmed them both. He had no way of knowing how his blood, which still contained the v2.1 virus, would interact with the v2.2 virus now circulating in Jon's blood, or if Jon's bite, which still contained the original Vampyre virus, would affect him. Beth feared her bite, if she slipped when they were intimate, would have turned him again. But they just didn't know, and there was no time now to continue to worry. He would address that when they were free of this place.

"Can you walk?" Luc asked Jon.

"Hell, yeah," Jon said, standing and appearing at Luc's side. They entered the hallway, but rather than turning toward the corridor door, Jon headed next door to Kate's old room. Luc followed, not knowing what he was doing, but as soon as Jon threw open the fridge and removed the blood Kate had left there before she was separated from him, he understood.

Jon had the four units open and drunk in seconds. He grinned at Luc, the blood leaving a pink tinge on his teeth. "Let's kick some ass."

They approached the first locked door in near silence and threw it open. As they approached the second door, Luc called out to Beth. *We are out of the cell and heading toward the main corridor.* The second door was also unlocked, and Jon and Luc hurried through it. *We've cleared the second door.*

Oh, Luc, thank God. Kate and I are almost there. How is Jon? Beth thought.

Thoroughly pissed and hoping for a fight, Jon answered. They all felt Kate's relief at the sound of his thoughts, strong and clear.

They rounded the last corner and met in the main corridor. Beth and Luc didn't hesitate to fall into each other's arms, clinging to one another as though they would never let go again. Kate and Jon stopped inches apart, but Kate only hesitated for a fraction of a second before rising to her tiptoes and pulling Jon into a bear hug, which he returned, tucking his face into her hair, the bag she wore draped across her body banging him in the side. The sound of running feet coming from the direction Beth and Kate had come from drew Jon and Luc's attention just before Peter, red-faced and fists pumping, rounded the corner.

They separated nearly as quickly as they had found one another and Luc turned toward Peter, fangs bared, but Beth stepped between them, her arms out. "He's with us. No time to explain." She turned her head toward Peter. "One step out of line and so help me..."

Peter nodded in response, chest still heaving.

They all turned to head toward the entrance they had used upon first entering the building. But before they could make it to the next turn, alarms began to blare overhead and emergency lights flashed red, discoloring the hallway like it had been coated in blood.

Luc could hear footfalls in the distance once again. He expected guards, but these sounded oddly like bare feet. There was no time to waste.

They rounded the final corridor and reached the last of the two doors between them and freedom, Peter trailing behind. The doors were locked, and Jon and Luc together couldn't push them down. Beth and Kate joined them, Kate dropping her bag to the ground, and all four stood side by side before running at and ramming the doors in front of them. They heard the metal groan, and on the second try, the locking mechanism gave way, and they all stumbled forward.

The footsteps were just behind them now, and Luc spun to see if it was a threat or who he hoped it would be.

He turned to see Ben standing next to Anteia. Jon turned and took a defensive pose, but now it was Luc who moved to stand in front of him. "It's okay, they're friends. No time for introductions. Let's get out of here."

By now, a large group of guards had gathered outside the remaining door, and Luc could hear more footfalls coming down the hallway behind them. Focusing back on the front door, the four vampires once again threw themselves forward until the door gave way, this one coming off its hinges. Jon scooped up the door as it fell and used it like a shield to push forward and slam into the stunned guards, all with over-the-ear ear protection and attached mics. Some were equipped with guns, some with UV lights, and some with tasers that now launched into the air like a wall of shiny darts. Some hit the vampires, but other than a small twinge when they hit, they had no effect and were wiped away. One set hit Ben, who jerked but then steadied, growled with his now elongated teeth bared, and pulled them out.

The UV lights flared around them, ineffective on all but Jon, who yelped as the beam traveled over his face and dropped to the ground in a crouch. The light momentarily blinded them, but Luc charged, reaching the guards holding them and shattering the lights against their bodies. One of the guards with a shotgun fired at Jon, hitting him in the arm. He let out a roar that would have put a lion to shame and launched himself forward toward the man, fists flying, the wound healing though visible behind the large hole that remained in his shirt sleeve, along with his blistered face.

As all four attacked, guards flew in the air, replaced by others rushing in to slow the vampires down. Peter stood in the center of the group, eyes wide and mouth open, frozen as he watched the melee around him. Anteia crouched at his side behind the door Jon had used as a shield and pulled Peter behind it.

They gained a few feet toward freedom, to be met by another wall of guards gathering behind them. Jon glanced at Luc, met his eyes, and then Luc turned to meet the threat behind them. Only to see Ben, his long hair flying about him as he twisted and swiped with claws he hadn't had before, as he singlehandedly held the rear guards at bay.

The guards he made contact with shrieked in pain as their clothing and skin were shredded in four long and deep gashes that matched what Luc had seen on the cell Ben had been held in.

Anteia, her eyes wide, looked back and forth at the fighting on all sides. She screamed to the others, "Knock off their headphones."

All four vampires rushed at the guards, dodging bullets as they flew and occasionally impacted other surrounding guards. They ripped off their headphones as they clashed. Luc turned as Beth, four guards hanging from her body, spun and threw them off of her, grabbing headphones as she could and flinging the men into their fellow guardsmen, but not killing even one. While he admired her convictions, they would do little to stop the force in front of them.

Then his eyes flew wide, and his heart leaped in his chest. He ran as he saw one guard, who had raised a handgun and leveled it at Beth, fired. The bullet caught her in the chest, spinning her around. Luc saw the grimace on her face as she went down. He was on the guard before he could fire a second shot. Luc's hand reached the man's neck a fraction of a second before the crack that sent the guard crumpling limply to the ground.

He turned to see Beth rise from the ground, rubbing her chest. *I'm okay.* She thought to him as she looked from the guard to Luc before returning to the fight.

Kate, fighting alongside Jon, kicked and punched with audible cracks as the blows landed. They were all aimed to maim but not kill, but she was doing some damage.

Luc heard Anteia scream, "Cover your ears!"

But Ben, already engaged in battle, didn't pause, nor did anyone else. That's when the thrumming sound began, Anteia's eyes squinted, and her teeth clenched along with her fists. People on both sides raised their hands to their ears, some screaming in pain before dropping them and falling unceremoniously to the ground, Ben and Peter included. The four vampires stumbled for a moment before regaining their balance and standing upright.

Seconds later, an explosion to their right knocked them all to the ground.

Luc shook his head as he rose. *Was that a grenade?* he thought to Jon. But Jon was already up and launching himself toward the guard who had thrown it. As he reached the man, he tore his throwing arm from his body, a second grenade already in hand, and tossed both toward the advancing guards. The explosion shook the ground, but they remained on their feet as several of the guards fell to the ground, writhing in pain or dead.

The guards still standing, with their ear protection in place, surged forward. Luc and Jon moved to meet them while Kate fell back to protect Anteia and Peter. Beth hauled Ben, still unconscious, over to lie beside them before joining Kate in defending them from any guards that got past Jon and Luc. Anteia continued her thrumming noise with brief pauses for breath, neutralizing any that had their ear protection knocked loose in the battle. Luc knew there would be more bodies than Beth would have liked, but he and Jon did what they needed to in order to rid them of any remaining threats.

When there were no more conscious guards to fight, Luc bent over and scooped Ben into his arms before hauling him over his shoulder. Beth looked down at Peter and shook her head before pulling his cell phone from his pocket, tossing it, and hauling him over her shoulder as well. Kate retrieved her bag from the ground where she had dropped it, pulling it quickly over her head and one shoulder.

Luc turned to Anteia. "Well done," he said, and a shy grin turned up the corners of her mouth before they all turned to run. Anteia, being much slower than the vampires, quickly fell behind, but Jon circled back for her.

"Please don't take offense, but we need to move as quickly as we can." With that, he swung her into his arms before running to catch up with the others.

As they approached the gate, shots flew at them from the checkpoint near the main road, and they began to run in zigzags, the shots missing

widely as the guards could only shoot where they had seen them last.
Not slowing at the fence, Kate burst through the chain link, sending
small scraps of wire flying forward and embedding into the trees in
front of them as they disappeared into the dense foliage.

Chapter Forty-Six

Beth

THEY HAD RUN FOR nearly thirty minutes when Peter and Ben began to stir. They stopped, setting them both gently on the ground along with Anteia, who pressed her hands down her scrubs and ran her fingers through her waist-long hair, pulling it forward over her shoulders. Beth couldn't wait to ask her more about her ability and her origins, but they needed to put as much distance between them and Mr. Rice as they possibly could.

Ben growled deep and low as his eyes opened and he struggled to regain his focus. He jumped to his feet, his nails elongating along with his teeth. His nose protruded, and hair burst from the skin of his face, chest, and exposed arms.

Luc raised his hands in front of him, palms open. "Ben, it's okay. It's just me and my friends. We made it out."

Ben looked from one to the next and began to calm, his gaze settling on Anteia as his physical changes regressed.

"What the f—" Peter began, crab crawling away from Ben into a nearby tree trunk and freezing there.

"What did you do to us?" Ben asked Anteia.

"It is called drum song. It makes humans, and evidently whatever you are, unconscious," she said.

"How did you learn it?" Ben asked, mirroring Beth's thoughts exactly.

"All of the Eanai people know this," she answered. There was no humor or guile on her face, her tone matter-of-fact.

Beth didn't know what the Eanai people were, but they didn't have time right now for a long discussion. "I would love to learn more about you both, but right now we need to keep going," she said.

"Do you have a plan?" Luc asked.

"Have you ever been to the Everglades?" Beth asked. Everyone else in the group, except for Jon, shook their heads. "I've read it's miles and miles of swampland. They have houseboats there that you can rent and travel anywhere the waterways take you. I think we should go there and regroup. Even if Mr. Rice follow us there, which I don't think he will, he would have a very difficult time tracking us on the water."

"I've been there. Beth's right about the tracking. Let's go," Jon said, his face looking oddly flushed.

Peter, mouth still hanging open, looked almost comically from one to the next as they spoke.

"This is where I part ways with all of you," Ben said and walked to Luc, extending his hand. "You saved my life. I will find you again and repay my debt. But for now, I must return to my family and be sure they are safe."

Luc extended his arm, and Ben grabbed it just beneath his elbow, Luc returning the gesture. And with a quick and curious glance back at Anteia, Ben turned and disappeared into the trees. To Beth's astonishment, he moved nearly as quickly as a vampire.

Beth stared wide-eyed for a moment at Luc. "Right, no time."

"Are you okay?" Kate asked Jon.

"I'm fine. Let's just keep moving," he said.

"I gave him the v2.2 inoculation you sent with Nancy as soon as they placed me in his cell, but when the alarms sounded, he was too weak to run, so I had to give him some of my blood as well," Luc said.

This finally brought Peter out of his stupor, and he stood, listening intently and brushing himself off.

"Oh, shit," Kate said, immediately at Jon's side and feeling his forehead. "You're burning up."

Jon gave Luc a sour look. "You could have waited."

"If you drop along the way, they need to know why," Luc said with a shrug.

"Well, time's a-wasting. Anteia, how about a piggyback ride this time?" Jon said, and Anteia nodded.

"That will work, but I think I should be the horse until we know you're okay," Luc said to Jon and turned his back to Anteia so she could hop on.

Beth turned to Peter, his eyes slowly darting from side to side. Beth could feel the emotions warring within him and wished he were still unconscious. She had been the one to agree to his offer of information, and as distasteful as she found touching him, he was now her burden.

"Same for you, Peter, hop on," Beth said, turning her back to Peter, who stepped back, waving his hands in front of him.

"No, you can't carry me," he said.

"How do you think you got this far?" Beth asked, looking over her shoulder and then turning to face him. "Look, come or don't come, that's up to you, but we're leaving now, and there is no way you can keep up."

Peter ran his shaky hand through his hair, making it nearly stand on end, and then nodded. Beth turned her back to him once again, and he jumped up and placed his hands lightly on her shoulders.

"Hold on tight," she said.

Kate shot Jon a worried look, her hand on his shoulder, and the six continued south.

While they had initially made good time, Jon had slowed over the last of the almost four-hour run. They had stopped a couple of times for Anteia and Peter to have a break, and once, about fifteen minutes in, for Peter to vomit before he got used to the speed. But to his credit, since then, he had been silent.

It was just after 5:00 a.m., and the sky was now a deep blue but getting lighter. They would need to get Jon inside somewhere quickly, and there was no way the boat rental office would be open at this hour. They would need hotel rooms for the day.

Even though Beth thought it unlikely they would be tracked so quickly, she would feel better on the water. But they were out of options.

The houseboat marina was on the edge of the Everglades and the extension of a little town with a "Welcome to Pahayokee" sign about a half a mile from the marina. The town had a motel with an old neon vacancy sign lit and flashing. Beth and Kate went to the office and paid cash for two adjoining rooms, each with double queen beds. By the time they reached the rooms, Jon was barely able to walk with Luc's help. They made it inside and laid Jon on the bed furthest from the door, closing the blackout curtains.

Kate placed her bag in the refrigerator and then was immediately at Jon's side. After feeling his forehead, she ran to the bathroom to get a cold washcloth, returning in seconds to mop at his face and neck. Jon raised his hand to her cheek and then let it fall back to the bed before closing his eyes. Kate bit her lip and looked up at Beth, the worry clear in her damp eyes.

Beth sat on the second bed facing them.

I don't know how the viruses will interact in his body, Kate said, careful to direct her thoughts only to Beth, who nodded. *The Vampyre virus he carries will fight against the v2.2, and Luciano's v2.1 still circulates in his blood. That will also compete with it. I don't know if the immunity from the Vampyre virus will fight them off with so much foreign material, or if the two new viruses fighting for control will overwhelm his system and kill him. We have no lab to monitor what's going on.*

In medicine, we sometimes see people infected with more than one strain of influenza. They are good and sick for a time, but they recover as if they had been infected with only one strain. It may be the same here. As you said, we don't know, so there is no reason to expect the worst. Jon is strong and a fighter. He just needs time and rest.

Kate nodded. *You're right, I'm worrying before there's a reason for it. I just...* She looked down at Jon and then back at Beth. *I just want a chance to tell him how I feel.*

Beth smiled back at her. *You'll get it. Soon.*

Kate glanced over at Peter, who had taken a seat at a small table near the front window, watching them intently. Beth followed her gaze to Peter, who squinted his eyes slightly and tilted his head, studying her.

Several hours had passed, and as they all waited and prayed for Jon's recovery, his fever spiked. They had no idea what his temperature was, but he and his clothes were soaked in sweat. All of them were hungry but didn't dare leave with Jon so ill.

"His heart is flying and erratic," Kate said, her voice shaky with emotion. Beth flew to her side. She could hear Jon's heart, and just as Kate had said, it was beating so quickly that she could scarcely count the beats to get a heart rate. And every few beats, it skipped or changed the pace of the rhythm.

Beth leaned over and placed the back of her hand on his dry but flushed skin. He was burning up. They had no thermometer, but she was certain he was warmer than Luc had ever been. Perhaps the warring of the multiple viruses in his system was proving too much.

"We need to cool him down," Beth said to Kate. She turned to Luc. "Fill the tub with cold water and make sure all the sunlight is blocked."

Luc was in the bathroom and working before Peter could take a step, cold water running full stream, but Beth saw Peter's attempt to move forward and was surprised he would try to help. She wouldn't have thought that he had enough compassion to even consider it. She pulled her thoughts back to Jon.

"Help me get his clothes off," Beth said to Kate. In a flash, Jon was stripped to his sports briefs and in Kate's arms as she headed for the bathroom. Luc had tucked a towel on each side of the sliding window panes and closed them, pulling it tight and blocking the sun's rays. He moved aside to stand near the door as Kate leaned over and placed Jon gently in the tub, bending his knees up so his large frame would fit inside. She used her hands to scoop water onto his chest and shoulders as the water level slowly began to rise.

Kate's chest shook as she held back a sob. *He can't die. He just can't die.* Jon's skin turned into a field of gooseflesh, and he began to tremble, but he remained unconscious. The trembling turned to shaking and the shaking into jerking movements. He was seizing.

Beth grabbed the sides of his head to prevent him from banging it on the tub, and Luc crowded in to grab his legs and prevent him from injuring himself. Kate covered her mouth with her hand, water still dripping from it down her shirt, her eyes wide, her body frozen in place.

While it seemed to go on for a long while, it was likely only seconds. His jerking slowed and then stopped, and they arranged him gently in the tub once again.

Beth placed her hand on Kate's shoulder, and Kate startled. Beth gave her a washcloth, which she used to mop Jon's face and neck, sobbing quietly but now at least moving with purpose.

While his heart rate had become even more erratic when he was first placed in the water, five minutes after he stopped seizing, the rhythm was steady, and the rate began to slow toward normal.

It's working. Listen to his heart, Beth thought to Kate.

What if it's slowing because he is dying?

No, it's become more regular.

Kate looked at Beth and nodded, her eyes wet, and went back to wetting the washcloth and wiping at Jon's head and neck with the cool water. Beth reached over her shoulder and felt Jon's cheeks and chest with the back of her hand. *He feels much cooler, Kate. Let's keep this up for another few minutes and then try to get him back to bed.*

Beth turned to walk out of the room and caught Peter's eyes, squinting, with his brow furrowed, watching them closely from just outside the door.

"Can you talk to one another telepathically?" he asked.

Beth had suspected he'd been catching on. She had assumed he knew of all the vampire abilities, but clearly that wasn't the case.

"Some of us can, yes. It's an ability that must be practiced and seems to be variably expressed."

Peter's eyes widened before he once again squinted, his face returning to that concerned and overly alert expression he so often wore.

"Can you hear my thoughts?" he asked.

"Some of them, yes, along with feeling your emotions," she said. And right now, Peter was a mix of emotions, fear, surprise, and maybe a little guilt. Perhaps she should monitor his thoughts more closely if he was so concerned about what she might hear, but she knew she would feel guilty invading his privacy. She wasn't like him or the Master.

"And I assume this ability gets stronger the longer you're a vampire," he said, looking like he might vomit again.

"Yes, it seems to. Whether it is because of aging or just more practice, I'm not sure."

"Then the Master may know more than I thought he did."

Beth now followed Peter's thinking. While he might be concerned that she could hear his thoughts, he was clearly terrified that the Master could. If he had thought he was successfully hiding things from the Master, perhaps he was now reconsidering.

"It's a good thing I left when I did. He must not be able to hear them all, or he never would have allowed me to go."

Beth felt sadness roll off of him. Had he really still held out hope that the Master cared for him or that he would indeed change him as a reward? She couldn't tell, but left him with his thoughts.

She returned to the bed Jon had been lying in and straightened the sheets, which felt damp, and decided to turn down the side that hadn't yet been used. She pulled a blanket from the closet and spread it over the damp side. Kate would want to stay next to him, and this would help her be more comfortable. After she finished, she returned to the tub where Kate was draining the water and beginning to dry Jon.

"Here, let me help," Luc said, ducking around Beth and lifting Jon by holding him under his arms so Kate could finish drying him, wrapping the towel around his midsection so his damp briefs wouldn't get the bed wet. Luc lifted Jon into his arms and carried him to the bed and stretched him out on it, his feet hanging over the end by a few inches. Kate kicked off her shoes and curled up at his side.

Beth shooed Luc and Peter into the adjoining room with her, hoping Kate might be able to rest a bit now, too.

"Where's Anteia?" Beth asked, realizing they were one person short.

"She had to leave. We can talk about it later when we know Jon is okay," Luc said.

"We need to make arrangements for the houseboats and see if Nancy and Eric were able to come through on their end," Beth said. "But I don't want to leave Kate and Jon alone."

"It's ok. I'll go rent the houseboats. But I want to wait until I know Jon is well to see if the vehicle is at the drop point," Luc said. "I don't want to be gone that long in case you or Jon need me."

"I don't know what you're working on, but I'm happy to help if I can," Peter said, surprising the heck out of Beth, who immediately became suspicious of the gesture. She couldn't sense any kind of deception from him, but it was going to take some time before she would ever be able to trust him.

"No offense, but you would slow me down. I want to take care of this as quickly as I possibly can," Luc said.

Peter nodded. In his current state, he had to know Luc was right.

Luc leaned in and pulled Beth to him with one arm around her waist, the other cupping her chin and turning her face to his. *I love you, and I cannot wait to hold you in my arms tonight. We've been apart far too long.* With that, he leaned forward and kissed her gently but deeply.

If Beth still needed to breathe, she would have been breathless from his touch. The skin beneath his fingers flamed and sent shivers down to her core. She had missed his touch even more than she had imagined, and the sheer pleasure of it brought tears to her eyes.

I love you too. Please hurry back.

Luc released her gently and left her with a beaming smile before turning and walking to the door. Beth's eyes followed him, taking in every chiseled inch. Watching him walk, even though she preferred him walking toward her and not away, would never get old. He shot her one last glance before disappearing out the door.

Peter, who had taken several steps back as Luc had embraced her, looked at her now. While he had made his face blank, Beth could feel emotion radiating from him, and it felt like jealousy.

Beth kept her face neutral, as if she hadn't felt it, and walked to the door between the adjoining rooms. She peeked through the crack to see Kate lying by Jon, her cheek resting against his upper arm. She looked small next to him, but she had proven how fierce she could be if called upon. Beth didn't know what would develop between the two of them, but they seemed a good match.

She pulled the door a little further closed and turned to sit at the foot of one of the beds opposite Peter.

"You should try to get some rest. We've all been up a long time, and there's no telling when we will have our next chance."

Peter nodded slowly, clearly thinking as he kicked off his shoes and settled back onto the bed, his head on the pillow, not bothering to pull back the covers. He laced his fingers behind his head and stared at the ceiling.

Beth stretched out on the second bed, crossing her hands over her abdomen. She wouldn't sleep while Luc was gone or in case Kate needed her, but she could lay and think awhile. She glanced over at the bedside clock; 12:35 p.m. Still another five or so hours until sunset, when, if they were at all lucky, Jon would be through this.

"What is it like?" Peter asked, shaking her from her thoughts.

"What is what like?" she answered.

"Being a vampire. I've wanted it since I met the Master when I was fifteen. What is it like?"

Beth sorted through her thoughts for a moment. She hadn't needed to explain her feelings about it before now, and she wasn't adept at sharing them anyway. But Peter seemed sincere in his question, so she decided to just speak her mind as it came to her. "The speed and strength are amazing. I loved running before, but now I can do it with so little effort. It feels like I could run forever and not tire. Until tonight, I hadn't been seriously injured, but it still hurt." Her fingers went to the hole in her shirt from the bullet she had taken earlier. "The regeneration is also painful but not nearly as much as the injury. The bloodlust was...horrible. All-consuming. When I turned, the call of blood was like nothing I had ever felt before, more than longing, more than need. It was primal. I knew I needed it, even though taking from a human or harming someone to sustain myself repulsed me. It was a constant worry. Now that I'm free of it, I feel more like my old self, but better. I want to free all the vampires from that dependence and the guilt that goes with it."

"Was it painful, the change?"

"I don't remember it. I felt weak after Luc drank from me, and I remember him running with me in his arms and feeling like I would pass out. When he fed me his blood, it was salty, metallic, like blood always tasted when I was human, but I was unconscious soon after and stayed that way until I woke at sunset the following evening, ravenous."

Peter leaned up on one elbow to look at her. "You could have left me behind at the facility. I was unconscious, so I couldn't have even protested. The Master would have killed me when he discovered what I had done, and you would have been rid of me. Why didn't you leave me?"

Beth looked at him, the vulnerability plain in his face, catching her off guard. "Because I told you I would bring you with us. You keep your side of the agreement, and so will I."

Peter looked at Beth for a long moment and then lay back on his back and closed his eyes. "Thank you," he whispered.

Beth continued to make periodic checks on Jon and Kate, who were both resting peacefully. Peter had fallen asleep quickly as well. Beth could tell by his slow, regular breathing.

She had just returned from another check on Jon when the lock on the door to their room clicked over. Beth was immediately at the door and crouched to fight until the door cracked open and Luc peered in at her, smiling.

You could have said something.

I figured you would feel me coming.

I think I'm too concerned with Kate and Jon.

Are they doing okay?

Yes, everything has been quiet since we got him cooled down. They're sleeping, and so is Peter, Beth thought, turning her head to look at Peter and opening the door wide to let Luc in.

Do you really intend to turn him?

When I agreed to it, I didn't think we would really get this far. He seems a little shaken, to be honest, not his usual overly confident and venomous self. Maybe some time away from the Master's influence will help. I don't know. I want to wait and see how he does first. If he is sincere about turning from and fighting against the Master, he could be helpful. He knows the Master will never let him live when he figures out what he's done, and yet he did it anyway. Maybe it was just to gain power and be free of him, but maybe he could be led to a new start. He sounded so lost when we talked earlier. The Master is all he's known since he was fifteen. Fifteen. Can you imagine?

No. It's no wonder he is the way he is. What a role model for a kid.

Is everything in order?

The houseboats are rented and ready. We need to get food before we go, but there is a battery, a generator, and solar power on both. Each would easily sleep five with two bedrooms and a fold-out sofa.

Now all we need is Jon.

Luc nodded. Beth noticed Luc had oddly held one hand behind him since he'd entered the room. *Are you hiding something back there?* Beth thought, nodding her head toward his hidden hand.

An ornery grin spread across his handsome face. *Oh, you mean this?* Luc thought and pulled a family-sized bag of plain M&M's from behind him, earning him a grin from Beth in return.

You remembered. She crossed her hands over her heart, and then her eyes turned sultry. *We have almost two more hours until sunset,* Beth thought and stepped toward Luc, taking the bag of M&Ms from him and placing them quietly beside the TV before running her hands up his arms to his shoulders until one rested on each side of his neck. She looked at his brown eyes, a playful smile on her lips. *Any ideas to pass the time?*

Besides eating M&Ms? he teased. *Plenty, but most will have to wait until we are alone.* Then he pulled her to him and found her mouth once again.

Sunset was nearly upon them, early, but it was November, even though the Florida temperatures didn't say so. Beth could no longer feel it, but the change in the sunlight around the edges of the curtains in their hotel room let her know it was close. She lay on her side, Luc's arms wrapped around her, with her head resting on his bicep. She was so content, wrapped in love and warmth, and she didn't want to get up. But Jon should be waking soon and may need her help. Her time with Luc would come soon, but for now, she needed to help her friends.

As she began to wiggle free, Luc's arms tightened around her, and she looked over her shoulder to meet his eyes, a playful smile on his face. *Where do you think you are going?*

I need to be there when Jon wakes up. She didn't want to worry Luc by sharing the rest of her thoughts. If Jon woke up, all would be well. But she was more concerned about being there to comfort Kate if he didn't wake up.

Luc sighed and kissed her gently before releasing her from his embrace and then rising to follow her. Beth opened the door between their rooms to find Jon and Kate still asleep. Jon hadn't moved from the spot they had laid him in, and Kate had nestled against him, wanting to stay as close to him as she possibly could.

Beth said a little prayer for them both. Kate would take it hard if Jon didn't pull through. But his heartbeat was steady as she approached the bed and gently laid her hand on Kate's shoulder.

She sat up quickly and looked at Beth, her eyebrows drawn together in worry, before looking to Jon. Her hand went to his forehead and cheeks, and then her eyes darted to the clock, which showed 5:30 p.m. in orange-red light. Beth then followed her gaze to the window where the last of the sun's light faded and back to Jon, who still lay perfectly still.

"He should be up by now," Kate said, emotion heavy in her voice.

"Give him a few minutes, Kate. His body has been through a lot. If he hasn't awakened by the time we're ready to go to the houseboats, we will carry him and let him continue to rest there."

"No one is carrying me anywhere," Jon said, his voice raspy but strong.

His words startled Kate, who jumped and then screamed an excited "Yes!" before dropping her head to his chest with a dramatic exhale. She then sat up, clasped her hands in front of her, head bowed and eyes closed in a quick prayer. Beth knew exactly how she felt.

Jon, a grin on his lips, patted Kate's back and then began to set up slowly, rubbing the back of his neck. "It feels like one of you dropped me on my head." He turned his neck from side to side and then stretched it with an audible *pop*.

"How do you feel, Jon, besides the headache?" Beth asked.

"I'm starving, but otherwise fine. The headache is actually fading quickly too." He looked at Kate, her eyes glistening as she tried to hold back her happy tears. The feelings were too strong for her to block from any of them. "From the look on your face, it must have been a little rocky."

"You could say that," Kate choked out, then hugged him. Jon turned his head into her hair and closed his eyes just like at New Dimension Analytics.

Beth couldn't help the little upturned corners of her lips. Even if her friend was still uncertain, Beth could see it. The big fellow was falling for her.

Let's get out of here and give the two of them a few minutes. I'll grab

Peter, Beth thought to Luc. "Luc needs to go see if Eric and Nancy made it to the drop point, and we all need food. I'll take Peter with me and bring something back."

"Yes, food, please," Jon said, his stomach growling as if on cue to emphasize his hunger.

Beth grinned and walked toward the adjoining room, Luc following, to gather Peter. He was awake and sitting on the side of the bed. Beth wondered why he had stayed there, rather than coming in to see Jon wake. She knew he would be curious since it involved the cure. Perhaps he actually had a conscience and had allowed them their privacy.

"Is your friend okay?" he asked, surprising Beth by actually sounding sincere.

"He is, thank you. We are headed out for food. Would you join us?"

Peter rose and followed. They were barely out the door when Luc turned to stop Peter's progress and spoke. "Why should we trust you?"

Beth was a bit surprised by his abruptness and demanding tone but supposed she couldn't blame him. Peter had led multiple attacks on both of them at the direction of the Master.

Peter stopped to gather his thoughts. "I have betrayed the Master to get to you and withheld information from him before and after arriving. I have shared his plans with Beth and Dr. Giffard, warning them he was coming, and will share any and all of the information I know about him to help you defeat him. You know as well as I do that the Master will kill me without hesitation for what I've done. I have as much to lose as you do."

I think he will betray us in a heartbeat if it would save his skin, Luc thought.

Beth couldn't disagree, but his recent actions and their previous conversation made her a little less certain than she would have been before.

"How do we know you won't leave us as soon as you are turned to join forces with the Master?" Luc asked.

"You of all people should know he won't allow competition. If I return changed, I'll be a threat. There's no way I can survive at this point without placing distance between the Master and me."

Read him, Beth thought. *Do you feel that? He's desperate. I sense nothing but truthfulness in his emotions.*

Fine. But we watch him like a hawk, and he goes at the first hint of betrayal.

Beth nodded in agreement and turned to walk toward the small combination grocery and general goods store they had seen on the way in. She glanced back once again and found Peter eyeing her and her interaction with Luc, knowing they were likely speaking telepathically.

"You should get going. I'd like to get on the boats as soon as possible," Beth said.

"I'll go as soon as we reach the store."

Beth nodded, lacing her fingers in his. "So, what happened with Anteia?" she asked.

"She said the sea calls to her and that she needed to return to the beach and let her people know she was well. She also said that we had been very kind to her and that she and her people would not forget that."

Beth wasn't sure what to make of it. She had never heard of another being like Anteia. "Do you have any idea what she is? I mean what kind of...being?"

"I don't know what she is," Luc answered. "We didn't have time to get that far."

"Ben's and her abilities were impressive. The biology behind them has got to be fascinating," Beth said. "I never imagined vampires existed, let alone others. The world is an amazing place."

"Who is Jon Wilks?" Peter asked, interrupting their conversation.

"Jon is an old friend of mine," Luc answered.

"His name... Is he related to John Wilkes Booth?" Peter asked.

"You should ask him sometime," Luc said and received a forceful nudge from Beth.

"That's not a good idea," Beth said, giving Luc a stern look, which he returned with a shrug.

Peter furrowed his brow but paused again before speaking. "Why did you pass him off as you?" Peter said to Luc.

"Because having everyone at New Dimensions believe Luc was human was to our advantage," Beth answered. "And they didn't need to know we had a means of curing vampirism until we were ready for them to know."

Peter nodded and continued walking, appearing to mull it over.

As they reached the store, Luc turned and gathered her in his arms. *I love you. I'll grab food on the way and be back soon with your supplies.*

Hurry, she thought back, planting a quick kiss on his lips, and then he was gone.

Beth turned to enter the store, but Peter stopped her with a question.

"So, the cure worked on each of you? Have you tried it and failed on anyone else?"

"Yes, the current version has worked for four of us without issues. And no, we haven't tried it on anyone else," Beth answered.

"Do you have access to more of it?" Peter asked.

"We were able to bring some with us, but not much. We also have a new form of the Vampyre virus, with the undesirable segments removed, but it hasn't been tested. If Nancy and Eric come through, we may have a chance to increase our supply of both."

"But the new virus would turn me without the bloodlust and sun sensitivity?" Peter asked, ignoring the last part of her answer.

"Theoretically," Beth answered. "But again, it isn't proven."

Peter remained quiet for the rest of the trip as she gathered food from the store along with four large pepperoni pizzas from a shop on the way back. She loaded up a plate for Jon at the motel, who inhaled every last bite, grinning like a madman the entire time.

"Oh my God, this tastes so, so good," Jon said through a moan. "Luciano was right about the pizza."

Beth chuckled, and out of the corner of her eye, she even saw a smile break across Peter's face, this one natural and sincere. It looked good there.

CHAPTER FORTY-SEVEN

LUC

BY NOW, NANCY AND Eric should have had plenty of time to get to the drop point and leave the van. Eric had chosen a secluded public kayak launch along Highway 41. It didn't seem easily visible from the road, by the look on the map. By car, it would be about an hour's drive, but Luc was traveling on foot just out of sight of the highway, and often through swampland. Even with his speed, the terrain made his progress slow. He had bought a change of clothes and shoes in town when he had gone out to register for the houseboats and planned to shower and change before driving the van back to Pahayokee to unload. That way, if he was stopped along the drive back, his dirty clothing wouldn't raise suspicions.

While often running through shallow water in the Florida humidity with wet legs and feet wasn't ideal, Luc enjoyed the natural beauty and the sounds that surrounded him. He tried to move as quietly as possible, but his splashing still disturbed the wildlife, rousing the white ibis and anhingas from their hunts along his way in the dim light that remained. He dodged the snorkels of the black mangroves that stood like periscopes around the bases of the trees, ducking under limbs, some covered with ferns and orchids. They would be stunning when the orchids bloomed in the spring, and he made a mental note to bring Beth back here when all of this was over.

He stepped over yet another mangrove onto a fallen log and felt the ground move under his foot. He jumped forward, releasing a short yelp that quieted the swamp around him and turned to see the alligator he had mistaken for a log thrash its tail and make for deeper water. While Luc was certainly faster and stronger than the alligator, it made his heart skip just the same.

Luc trudged forward as quickly as the terrain allowed, keeping the highway in sight along his way until he reached the drop point, slowing to a walk as he neared the parking lot. It was empty.

Luc felt his chest tighten. If the van wasn't here, it meant Nancy and Eric weren't able to escape and were likely dead. While Luc hadn't met either of them in person, he knew how much they had done to help them break free of Mr. Rice's security. Without them, they would likely all still be trapped there.

The joy of their restored freedom and Jon's recovery would be severely dampened by the news of the loss of their human friends. Beth and Kate would have to start from scratch on a new plan to obtain the supplies and equipment they needed, giving Dr. Henri and Mr. Rice more time to create the army they wanted.

There was no use in changing clothes to tromp back through the swamp. Luc turned and was about to re-enter through the kayak launch when he heard the sound of tires on gravel. He ran behind the small outbuilding that housed the restrooms and showers and waited as an unmarked black cargo van slowly pulled into view, jerking back and forth as it crept along the bumpy road to the parking lot, followed by an older model, dirt brown, four-door Buick.

They parked beside one another, and a red-headed male with a military style haircut and freckles exited the van to meet a tall, lean brunette woman with her hair in a ponytail at the rear of the car. It was Nancy. The two smiled and embraced before she said, "We made it. I hope we aren't too late."

Luc stepped out from behind the building and said, "Right on time," startling the two. He quickly closed the distance and extended his hand. "I'm Luciano Verde, Jon's friend. You must be Eric."

Eric strode forward first, keeping Nancy just behind his shoulder, and shook Luc's hand. "Pleased to meet you, but I was hoping to see Jon. Is he…" Eric's words trailed off, clearly not wanting to suggest he could be dead.

"He's fine," Luc said and saw the relief in both their faces. "He had a rough go with the injection I gave him, so I thought it best if I came alone until he got some more rest and food. It's quite an adjustment."

"I'm sorry it took us so long. We took every pothole-filled back road from Tampa to Miami, where we lifted the car. It was a longer trip than either of us expected, but we did our best not to leave a trail," Eric said.

"We can't thank you enough for all you have done, both of you," Luc said, turning his gaze toward Nancy.

"And we would never have made it out without all of you keeping the guards busy. I just wish we could have done more to stop Dr. Henri and Mr. Rice," Nancy said, wrapping an arm around Eric's waist. "Please tell Beth and Kate I was able to sabotage Dr. Henri's refrigerator, freezer, and incubator. It won't stop him by any means, but hopefully it will slow him down."

"I'm pretty sure Beth and Kate have plans for Henri and Rice with what's in that van. Until then, what are the two of you going to do?"

"I emptied my savings two days ago. We're gonna use cash and lay low until we figure out where to head next," Eric said. "I don't know what our future holds, but at least now we have one together." Eric looked down at Nancy and smiled. "With any luck, our paths will cross again one day in happier circumstances."

They said their final thank yous and goodbyes and headed their separate ways.

Chapter Forty-Eight

BETH

IT WAS THEIR FIRST day on the houseboats and Beth's first day in the sun in what felt like forever. They had spent it winding through the slow-moving shallow water of the Everglades, the tall sawgrass growing in clumps on either side of them, brilliant green and dense, marking their watery highway. Beth couldn't get enough of the sun as it caressed her skin.

Now, as the sun hung low in the sky, Luc steered their boat in the lead with Jon bringing up the rear, grinning like his face would split as he preened in the sun, shirt off with his pants rolled up over his knees. Luc had shed his shirt too, and while Beth had planned to unpack the equipment and supplies Nancy and Eric had left for them, she instead sat and admired the way the sunlight played on the muscles of Luc's chest and back as he steered. She fanned herself with her hand, the warmth more from imagining the night ahead of them than the sun overhead. The equipment could wait.

When they reached an opening in the sawgrass where the waterway widened and the enormous cypress trees stretched their branches over the water, dripping with Spanish moss, they anchored. The temperature was at least ten degrees cooler in the shade of the cypress branches. Luc and Jon tethered the boats together as Beth brought out food from the galley and arranged it on the deck table. It was quiet as evening fell on the water. Crickets and frogs made a constant low chorus for the hermit thrush, whose beautiful song made Beth tear up. All of this after the stresses of the last weeks and being confined inside, fearful for their lives...it was almost too much.

With her back to the group, she closed her eyes and let the sounds wash over her, the heady, earthy scents of the marsh filling her nostrils as she took a deep breath. A gentle breeze tickled her skin. She reveled in it until Luc's arms came around her, pulling her into him, her back pressed against his chest. He bent his head until his cheek touched hers, and she could feel the stubble on his chin. She leaned into him, and the last bits of tension left her. This was exactly where she belonged, in Luc's arms. It didn't matter where they were as long as she had this.

It brought a smile to her lips, and she turned to look up at him before he led her by her elbow to the group, already filling their plates with food and beginning to laugh. Even Peter smiled and shook his head at something Kate had said.

When what food remained was cleared, the sun had set. Kate looped her arm through Jon's, looked at him and Peter, and announced, "If this were one of my romance novels, the next scene would start with a tasteful fade to black. Come on, boys, let's give the lovebirds some space."

Beth blushed at the innuendo but sent her friend a heartfelt, private thank you as the three left.

Beth knew she should feel tired, mentally if not physically. The last forty-eight hours had been, well, nuts. But instead of being tired, she was full of energy. All evening, every glance, every touch, every word from Luc in her direction had felt like electricity running through her body. And the heat in his eyes as he looked at her now was enough to melt steel.

He followed her as she entered the galley. She had barely closed the door behind them when she was lifted from her feet and in his arms, his mouth on hers. She curled her fingers in his hair and returned his kiss with everything in her, his tongue claiming hers and his teeth gently pulling at her lip. He walked her to the bedroom at the back of the boat and set her feet gently on the floor, kicking off his shoes and socks, and pulling his t-shirt over his head in one fluid motion. Beth watched the muscles of his chest flex and relax, and her fingers reached for him of their own free will, splaying across his chest and tracing the contours of the muscles as she too wiggled out of her shoes and socks.

Her lips followed her fingers as she trailed gentle kisses over his heart, up to his collarbone, and to the base of his neck. She heard a gasp escape him as she ran her tongue over the trail her lips had followed. His arms wrapped around her and pulled her to him as she lifted her head to once again meet his lips.

His hands trailed fire down her back, dipping below the waistband of her jeans and tugging her shirt free to lift it over her head. His eyes admired the tops of her breasts before running his thumbs across them just above the line of the fabric, brushing her nipples beneath with his palms as he slid his hands around her sides to open the clasp at the back.

Beth lowered her arms to let him slide the straps from her shoulders and drop her bra to the floor. Luc leaned down to take each nipple gently into his mouth, running his tongue hungrily around each. Beth leaned her head back, her hands on his shoulders, and his arms around her waist, keeping her upright.

Luc pulled her into him, pressing her breasts against his bare chest, and the sensation of skin-on-skin sent shivers straight to her core. She arched into him, a moan escaping her lips between kisses.

She unfastened Luc's jeans and slid them slowly down his hips and thighs to pool at his ankles, and he stepped free, shaking them off his foot but still not releasing her. Beth ran her hands down his back to his briefs and stuck her hand beneath the band to feel his butt and pull him toward her, his erection hard against her abdomen. She ran her hand around his waistband until she felt the hair above his erection meet her hand and slipped inside, wrapping her fingers around him with a gentle squeeze.

His head leaned back, eyes closed at the movement, and then his mouth was on hers, as hungry as his hands, which moved in a blur to free her from her jeans and lift her onto the bed. He pulled himself on top of her, leaning on one hand to hold most of his weight, while one knee slid between hers. His lips again went to her breasts and then trailed down her belly, his free hand slipping into her panties. The heat inside her fanned to flame when he slipped a single finger gently inside her, moving with her rhythm as her hips rocked in response.

Beth wanted nothing more between them, even the thin fabric of her panties, and wiggled free of him just long enough to rid herself of them before helping him out of his briefs. His fingers returned to their tease.

She shuddered and reached for his manhood, moving ever more urgently. Her overly sensitive skin melted everywhere he placed a kiss: down her neck, across her shoulder, and back to her mouth. The sensation was exquisite, but she wanted more; she was ready for more. She felt him draw back and opened her eyes to meet his above her.

"I love you, Elizabeth Ramsey, and I want you more than I have ever wanted another woman. I will wait for you until you are ready, but if you want to stop, you should tell me now." His skin was flushed and radiated heat, his lids heavy, and his voice rough with desire. She could feel the heat rolling off of him as he waited for her answer.

In one movement, Beth pushed against the bed, using her vampire strength to flip him to his back and hover over him, one knee on either side of his hips and a lustful smile on her lips. She leaned forward, her hair falling forward to frame her face as she stared into his brown eyes. She had imagined this moment so many times. Beth wanted there to be no question about what she wanted or how she felt.

"I know you love me. You have shown me over and over again, even now, and I trust you with my life and my heart. I love you too, Luciano Verde, and I want to share every part of myself with you for the rest of my life."

With those words, she reached down and guided him inside her as she held his gaze, sliding down his length until he filled her completely, trembling around him with the pleasure it brought her. He worshipped her mouth and body with kisses and soft caresses as their bodies began the slow rhythm that brought them together, body and soul.

Epilogue

Lilly

"Well, it's about damn time," Lilly said into the phone. Both relief and anger flooded over her. It had been weeks since she had emailed a message to Luciano with no response. She had begun to fear the worst, and the thought of him dead hurt far more than she would like to admit.

She threw herself down on the end of the bed. The cheap hotel mattress was so hard it rattled her teeth.

"I know, and I'm sorry. We were held against our will with no access to cell phones or email. We were fortunate to escape with our lives."

"The Master let you escape him again, did he?" she taunted. The thought made her grin. It would make the Master only more intent on giving them all a violent and painful death, but to know he would be beside himself with anger at being thwarted once again made her happy. The self-appointed dictator of the vampire world and his minion, Anubis, could kiss her beautiful black ass.

"No, although he would have if we had been held any longer. It seems he is joining forces with a human, Kenneth Rice. It's a long story."

"All I need to know is that he is associated with the Master, and I'm in if you want to take him out." She had been working on just that since the last time they had spoken. "Since you've been sitting on your ass waiting for a jail break, I've been literally running all over the country meeting with every vampire I know who's not loyal to the Master and every one of your vampire buddies you've told me about. They know what your doctor has to offer and have been waiting for a reason to remove the Master's fangs. Just tell us when and where."

Lilly waited as Luciano paused. It sounded like he had covered the phone with his hand and was speaking to someone in the room, probably Beth. Thinking the name made her snarl, even if the doctor did seem to care about him. It was just a matter of time until Luciano saw where his true love lay.

"We discussed recruiting others to the fight now that we know we can't avoid it. It sounds like you have already started the ball rolling for us. It's going to take some time, but I think we have a way to get the cure for them. Being able to attack in the daylight hours will be to our advantage against the Master, but we may be up against more than we bargained for."

Lilly sat up and listened intently as Luciano told her about Mr. Rice and what he was up to at New Dimension Analytics, and that while they had temporarily slowed his progress, he was sure to continue. It sounded like the only way he could be a more formidable enemy was if he were a vampire. His ability to create these super soldiers meant their list of enemies was getting a lot longer. They needed to act sooner rather than later.

"Beth and Kate have—"

"Kate, as in her doctor buddy that got blown up? I thought she was dead," Lilly said, standing and walking to the window to look out at the moonlit cityscape of downtown Manhattan, still bustling at 3:00 a.m.

"No, she and Jon escaped the blast. But as I was saying, Beth and

Kate think they have a way to weaponize the second virus I was given as a cure that might help stop the small army Mr. Rice is sure to create. We just need a little time."

"I have a few more contacts I'd like to reach, but I can wrap it up in a couple of days and then head to you. Where are you?" Not only did she want to see Luciano again, but she also wanted the cure before anything went further south. She wanted to walk in the sun again, especially if that was where Luciano was.

"I don't want to share it over the phone now. We're on the move. But when we are ready, I'll let you know where to meet us." It was reasonable and probably for the best, considering how many close calls she'd had with Anubis on her tail, but it wasn't what she wanted to hear.

"Fine. But tell them to get their asses in gear before Anubis crawls up mine." She looked at her nails. They looked shabby. She hadn't taken the time to fix them with all of her traveling. She didn't like looking shabby and made a mental note to grab some polish and a file tonight when she went out to feed.

"Will do. Watch yourself, Lilly, and thank you."

Despite her anger at the wait, the smile was back on her lips at his concern for her welfare.

"You're welcome," she nearly purred into the phone and hung up. She ran her index finger over her lower lip as she gazed unfocused out the window.

***

MASTER

The Master strolled down the sterile hallway of New Dimension Analytics, his hands clasped behind his back and Neheb at his side. They both wore fitted Italian suits. After all, today he was a wealthy businessman with his vice president of operations, here to join forces with Mr. Rice after the recent debacle. They followed Mr. Fields, Mr. Rice's chief of security, as he led them to the control room, holding the door open for them as they entered but keeping his distance, his eyes wary. The room was filled with monitors, each displaying a different view of the hallways, rooms, labs, and what appeared to be prisoners above numerous computer workstations. Guards sat at three of the computers, switching between views.

"We've increased from two to three guards monitoring the grounds, no less than two to be actively monitoring, even at shift changes," Mr. Fields said. "Bill, pull up the footage from the incident."

The guard in the center began typing on his computer, glancing nervously out of the corner of his eye at the Master and Neheb. One of the images on the monitors in front of him changed. It was in black and white and showed a lab, the door opening before two blurry figures exited, followed by Peter, running full out.

"Slow it down," Mr. Fields ordered, and the footage replayed frame by frame. The first out the door was Dr. Ramsey, followed closely by Dr. Giffard, looking very much alive.

The Master ground his teeth together and felt his fangs threatening as he clenched his hands behind his back.

Mr. Fields shifted his weight from foot to foot, seeming to feel the Master's agitation. From there, the camera went black.

"That's where the feed was cut. We managed to get it back online as they left the building. Bring up that footage, Bill."

This clip showed numerous guards on the ground unconscious as

Luciano and another tall male vampire, whom he assumed was Jon Wilks, ran from the frame along with Dr. Giffard and Dr. Ramsey. Luciano carried an unconscious and unknown bearded man, and Dr. Ramsey carried an unconscious Peter. They were trailed by a woman with long hair extending beyond her waist, which swished and lagged behind her as she began to run.

Peter had lied to him. Peter and the men he had taken with him to destroy her lab believed Dr. Giffard dead, but Peter hadn't revealed she had survived during his most recent call when he clearly had seen her here. He had lied about Dr. Ramsey and Luciano being here as well. He had known something was up with Peter, sensed his anxiety, but the damn boy was always anxious about something. He had become complacent, believing he had control of Peter.

The anger from being deceived was nothing compared to the anger and humiliation he felt knowing Neheb would see his failure, and from trusting a human with his business, no less.

While the Master had intended to have Neheb destroy Rice and his blasphemous experiments right away, he would wait, help him build his super soldier army to hunt and kill Luciano and his group, and then destroy them all.

But Peter, he would save Peter for himself.

Can You Help?

Thank You For Reading My Book!

Did you know? Reader reviews are very important to an indie author's success? They validate our work and help others find our stories. If you enjoyed Vampyre Law, please leave a review filled with stars.

Thanks so much!

Tammy Battaglia

Don't forget your free gift! Click here or scan the QR code below to tell me where to send it.

ACKNOWLEDGEMENTS

Thank you to my family and friends who never cease to encourage and inspire me, especially my husband, Kyle, who indulges me and my crazy ideas.

To my beta readers and launch team another heart felt thank you. Your feedback has, without a doubt, made this a better book. Some of you have been with me through all three books and I appreciate it more than you could know.

Thank you to all of the SelfPublishing.com team for guiding me along my writing journey, especially my SPS coaches Ramy and Joe for the excellent advice and constant challenges to move me forward. To my editors, Zac Tighe of Copysmyths (developmental editing—www.copysmyths.com); and to Shavonne and Brit at Motif Edits (line and proofreading—www.motifedits.com); thank you for the advice and editing to take this book from rough draft to what it is today.

And finally, thank you to my readers. Without you, none of this would be possible. God bless you all.

About the Author

During the daylight hours, author Tammy Battaglia is a doctor, a pathologist to be specific, who enjoys looking at what makes all living things tick from the inside out. She grew up in Kansas, next door to Toto and Dorothy, where she raised three children (all human) with her high school sweetheart. She recently retired from twenty-plus years of mainstream medicine to explore what her imagination believes it could be.

When night falls and the moon rises, she can't help but imagine and write about the science that would make what others believe to be mythical, well...real. Just because current science can't explain them doesn't mean they can't exist. She encourages readers to indulge her inner mad scientist and look below the surface.

Dr. Battaglia is the author of the Elizabeth Ramsey, MD series, which has received both **Silver and Bronze Global Book Awards.**

Email: tammy@friendswithmonsters.com

Facebook

Newsletter

Also by Tammy Battaglia

Elizabeth Ramsey, MD Series